I0831218

The Hanson Trilogy

Book Two

The Hanson Conundrum

Vincent M. Messbarger

The Hanson Conundrum

For information email: cochetapublishing@me.com

Cocheta Publishing books may be purchased for educational, business, or sales promotional use.

For information please email: cochetapublishing@me.com

Cover and layout design by Vince Messbarger

First edition published 2014.

ISBN 978-0-9814984-5-4 (Hardback)

Dedicated to:

Little Jack Vincent
Dulcinea Grace
Baby Bee
Baby See

and

My precious little Star on earth that helped Pop believe in the unbelievable.

Acknowledgments

Unlike *The Hanson Legacy, The Hanson Conundrum* was a grueling experience in addition to being a labor of love. Hampered by time constraints and a major move to another state; starting a new medical practice and chasing a three year-old boy; the manuscript materialized very slowly. Many times, it grew a paragraph or page a day. Sometimes, it grew a page every other day or week longer. There was plenty of story to tell, just never enough time or energy to commit it to paper.

While writing *The Hanson Legacy,* I relied upon a great many people that I knew would honestly critique the manuscript. When it was finally published, a different group of colleagues gave their opinions. They included surgeons, nurses, patients, stay-at-home mothers and many other kind people too numerous to mention them all. Because of these wonderful souls, I have a solid fan club consisting of some of the brightest people I've ever known. If it wasn't for their persistent and gentle nagging, the release of this next book in the Hanson Trilogy might not have materialized for another several months! I love and miss you, guys!

Of course, there is my patient and very talented editor, Andrew McLaughlin... This busy and genuinely talented man took the time to embarrass me with countless examples of my seeming inability to master the written language of english. Even more impressive is knowing that his native tongue is 'Aussie' and that he STILL masters the english language better than I do!

And, as always, I give much of the credit for this work to my very supportive family. They endured countless hours of a semi-absent father and husband glued to an ancient Macintosh desktop computer resting on, arguably, the most cluttered desk in all the known and unknown universes. To them, I say...

"Daddy's Back!"

Vince Messbarger, 2014

"If ignorant both of your enemy and yourself, you are certain to be in peril."

Sun Tzu - Chinese Military General, Strategist and Philosopher.

Prologue

Even for a civilization possessing immensely advanced technology and a 100 light year sphere of complete dominance, planet sterilization was a monumental undertaking. Their home world, loosely translated into English as Central, orbited around a main sequence yellow star not quite 2.7 million of their solar distances from the planet to be rendered void of life. The mission required vast technologic resources, consisting of large container vessels built specifically for hauling massive amounts of water, minerals, liquefied gases and desiccated organic matter; along with enough military assets to ensure a near effortless suppression of the intelligent beings on the planet. Much of the hardware, however, needed relocation from other star systems or reactivated from a mothballed state. When complete, the operation would span more than 120 local stellar orbits. Fortunately, for the denizens of Centralia and their colonists inhabiting worlds within their sphere of influence, planet sterilization was quite rare, only occurring an average of every 50 to 60 thousand stellar orbits.

Centralia was an old world, insofar as comparing planets harboring intelligent life. The Centralian solar system formed with three gas giant planets and a scant asteroid belt. As a result, periodic mass extinctions and evolutionary bottlenecks caused by asteroid or comet impacts were far less frequent on Central than on similar planets across the galaxy. This allowed a stable environment for earlier and

more sustained development of advanced life forms. Eventually, the premier intelligent species that evolved on Central developed technologies to thwart the rare threat of collisions from the Kuiper Belt comets not swallowed by gas giants; minimize the global effects of plate tectonics, such as catastrophic volcanic eruptions and earthquakes, and genetically alter their immune systems to conquer disease. Barring self-annihilation, intelligent life on Central would flourish and evolve for almost an eternity... or so it seemed.

Many races and cultures of the same intelligent species evolved on Central, with the dominant culture capturing total control of the planet long before the achievement of interstellar space flight. While roughly the same age as the target planet, interplanetary travel developed on Central over 600,000 stellar orbits earlier, and interstellar travel followed a relatively short time later.

The dominant Centralian culture was essentially the only culture, highly evolved in structure and purpose. The life, activities and behavior of every individual regulated to a degree that would seem impossibly strict to the inhabitants of the target world. Non-conformity was not an option for Centralians, but comparing their rigid social structure to the instinctual colony behavior of certain lower life forms would be a mistake. The Centralians were intelligently unified in purpose, not driven by genetically imprinted neurons. Every objective served the primary goal: survival of their species. This made them the ultimate expression of evolution: cold and ruthless by the behavioral standards of the target civilization; highly successful and supremely advanced by Darwinian criteria. However, attaining the cultural experience necessary to achieve that level of evolutionary development came at a severe price.

Central's first encounter with an alien civilization was catastrophic, nearly ending in the extinction of its dominant species. The enemy possessed technology essentially equivalent to the Centralians and both cultures waged a brutal conflict against each other that rained planet-wide destruction on both worlds. Tactical prowess, not technology, allowed the Centralians to eventually defeat their enemy. The war was extremely costly in both lives and infrastructure. The remaining Centralians, having barely escaped extermination, viewed the vanquished enemy as a continued threat to their survival. As a result, all remaining members of the enemy species were located and eliminated; the planets, moons, and planetoids within their former sphere of dominance stripped of life and useful natural resources.

From that moment forward, the Centralians adopted a fundamental operating philosophy that called for the extermination of a potentially competitive species when they reached certain technologic milestones, chief of which was the development of nuclear fission. The target planet reached that pivotal point over 60 local stellar orbits earlier, as evidenced by a salvo of three, telltale electromagnetic pulses in fairly rapid succession, detected by an automated sensor and telemetry station positioned on their single moon. The first of several small Centralian scouting parties arrived from a remote outpost two local stellar orbits later. They initiated passive intelligence gathering and forwarded the data to Central via micro-wormhole pellet.

Assembling the armada of 31 massive vessels required to sterilize the target planet was completed dozens of stellar orbits later. The first two ships that embarked were military, beginning their mission one-half a stellar orbit before the rest. Once the force was in place, the target civilization's technology would be neutralized, the sentient beings terminated and the planet's entire biomass rendered into various powders destined for distribution to Central and her colonies. Billions of intelligent life forms would be exterminated with no more thought than a human puts into the notion that billions of tiny animals and plants perish when iodine tablets are dropped into a quart of pond water for purification. For the Centralians, taking such measures were not moral issues. There were no discussions, and never would be, on whether it was right or wrong to annihilate the entire biomass of a planet. The Centralians learned the lessons of interstellar Darwinism the hard way. Pure and simple, it was a matter of preserving their species by any means necessary.

The journey to the target planet would take two Centralian stellar orbits. Oddly enough, very little time would actually be spent in space travel. Slightly over two dozen space-time contortions were needed to traverse approximately 50 light years of empty space, each contortion lasting only several milliseconds. Yet, in that brief flash of time, vast distances would be crossed. Recharging each vessel's massive bank of capacitors using dark matter reactors required 33 Centralian day/night time cycles to complete. Even with the overwhelming majority of time spent at a standstill, the Centralian armada would achieve an effective supraluminal velocity of 25 photon speed multiples.

The target for planetary sterilization was the third orbiting body in a solar system where the Centralians mounted an identical mission some 225,000 stellar orbits before. The world they sterilized then was the fourth orbiting body in the solar system... the one the beings on the target planet referred to as 'Mars.'

Chapter 1

One could almost feel it physically, but there was no doubt the planet was shuddering under the monumental impact of a respected United States politician disclosing the hard reality of extraterrestrial visitation. It was a moment in time where every human being old enough to care about such things would remember the exact place, time and what they were doing when they saw or learned of the news that Homo sapiens was not the only technologically advanced species on earth.

For most, it was a deeply personal moment when varied and quite powerful emotions flooded the consciousness, fear and uncertainty the most common. While well over half of Americans believed in extraterrestrial life before the announcement, actually hearing that it was true had the same impact on both believer and former skeptic. What were the aliens up to? Are they here to help us or hurt us? How does this new reality affect me, my job... my family? There were also those whose first thoughts were surprisingly superficial, wondering how the news would affect Monday morning stock prices or whether it would alter travel plans. Perhaps the most superficial of them all were those that pondered the political impact of the announcement... and how to benefit from it. Every man, woman and child had a stake in whatever the aliens had in mind for earth, and that made Dr. Benjamin Harris Hanson's legacy the single most important news event of all time.

Even before Senator Chandler finished her announcement, news media editors were screaming at their staff to squeeze every source for information that might flesh out the precious few details she included in her speech. Journalists on vacation found themselves scrambling back to their respective offices to cover the 'story to end all stories.' Newsrooms around the globe hastily redirected reporters assigned to mundane projects, tasking them to seek information on various aspects of the Hanson Revelations.

The rush was on.

The goal was to find a unique angle and use the biggest headline with the catchiest phrase possible. Nature and the business of mass media abhors a vacuum. If it is big news, fill the voids left by a vacuum of hard information at any cost. Speculate if need be, just do it before the competition does.

Even local newspapers and broadcast media were burning the midnight oil, searching for exclusives to best their competitors. It was the biggest story in human history and every news outlet, big and small, were participating in the frenzy. Only there was precious little information to feed upon.

Politicians and bureaucrats around the world were also busy. Government office buildings in Washington D.C. and every state capitol became alive with hectic activity on what would have otherwise been a sleepy Sunday evening. All major thoroughfares into the District of Columbia were jammed with drivers trying to make it into their offices for emergency meetings called by nearly every government official with enough clout to order one. Even the Director of the Environmental Protection Agency called in her senior staff within a half hour of Senator Hanson's speech. Surely, extraterrestrial visitation posed some kind of potential harm to the water, soil, and air! Of all the government agencies meeting in hurried, late night conclaves, the one that seemed the most ludicrous would be the most tragically prophetic.

Other non-government, Washington-centric groups were mobilizing as well. Political parties and Action Committees, a myriad of D.C.-based activists groups, defense contractors... the list was almost endless. By 9:00 PM EST, less than an hour after the end of Senator Hanson's announcement, airline seats for flights into the nation's capitol completely sold out. Oddly, or perhaps sadly enough, few of those rushing inside the Beltway were thinking of the Hanson Revelations' monumental impact on society. Most were concerned about the political ramifications or the impact on their bureaucracy or special interest. By Monday's daybreak, each had to be ready for any political spears thrown their way... and prepared to toss a few of their own. As with everything political in Washington, there would be dividing lines. No doubt about it. Only the delineation of those lines had yet to be fully determined.

President of the United States Gregory Bertram, former Democratic Senator from Michigan, began watching the Theoretical Physicist's show while sharing a late evening meal with his wife and First Lady Sylvia. Both sat in stunned silence as Senator Chandler, whom the President and First Lady considered a political antagonist, announced to the world that her dying ex-husband worked on extraterrestrial technology. At the conclusion of the broadcast, and before the President could pick up the phone to call White House Chief of Staff Larry Osborn, the phone was already ringing.

"Bertram here," he said gruffly, the ramifications of Chandler's unauthorized announcement just beginning to sink in.

"Mr. President," the familiar voice of his trusted Chief of Staff began, "we need to convene the National Security Council as quickly as possible."

"I know; I was watching the Science and Technology Channel!" he answered angrily. "Why in Christ's sake wasn't I told about this?"

"Sir, honestly, I don't have any answers for you."

"There sure as hell better be some answers for me in the next few hours!" President Bertram growled. "I want 'em all here; every member of the Joint Chiefs of Staff. Get Bulldog and Sarah out of bed, too," referring to the National Counterterrorism Director and the Director of National Intelligence respectively.

"Yes, sir!"

"If any of 'em are out of town, light a fire under their asses! I want this meeting to convene in the Situation Room no later than ten with as many members of the Council as possible."

Bertram hung up the phone before getting an answer. He turned to his wife who sat in stunned silence.

"I cannot believe that bitch pulled such a stunt!"

"Greg, I don't care for Teresa either, but I had no idea she had gone through such horror in her life! Did you see the pain in her eyes?"

"I don't care!" he replied angrily. "She had no authority to make such an announcement! It is an outrageous breach of protocol! I should be the one determining when something like this should be released to the world, not some bumpkin from a fly over state!"

Bertram's neck veins were bulging at the thought that a political adversary, from a State he loathed, just announced the most important discovery in the history of mankind! It just wasn't fair! Since the invention of radio and television, United States Presidents were remembered by their announcements of pivotal moments in history. Roosevelt had his inaugural "...the only thing we have to fear is fear itself" and Pearl Harbor speeches; Kennedy had his Cuban embargo and space race speeches; Reagan had his Gorbachev "tear down this wall" speech. Bertram's "great historic speech" would be nothing more than an anemic follow-up to the greatest announcement ever made. If Chandler were right in front of him, he would thoroughly enjoy strangling her.

"What do you know about this alien thing?" the First Lady asked, partially out of genuine curiosity and partially to distract her husband from the building anger she could see in his eyes.

"Nothing! Not a damn thing!" he replied, his building fury unscathed.

"How can that be?"

"I don't know, but I do know that she's released highly classified information, and I'm only guessing it's highly classified because I didn't even know about it!" He paused to focus his anger. "As far as I'm concerned, she's in really big trouble. I want her head on a pole!"

"If it will make you feel better, I'll find the perfect spot for it in the Rose Garden," she said with a wry smile.

The President looked at his First Lady and smiled, feeling the anger subsiding a bit. The woman had backed him through good times and bad. The world of politics claimed countless marriages every year. The Bertrams suffered more than their share of difficulties in their relationship and both were constantly attacked by alternate news outlets for their "grossly expensive and unrealistic utopian visions." Even so, they steadfastly kept their eyes on the goal and pressed relentlessly to attain it. They managed to endure, even in spite of the fact that their relationship was far more practical than romantic.

"I'm sure you will, sweetheart," he replied with a smile. "Just try not to scare any children and the more fainthearted of our 'fence protester' pets."

"I make no promises, Greg," she said with a wink. "What are you going to do?"

"I'm going to get some answers, first," he replied with a return of his growl. "You know," he said while patting a White House table napkin to his lips, "there just might be a silver lining to all this. If we play it right, we could use this announcement to get some of our stalled legislation passed and knock Chandler and the opposition down a few pegs. Maybe this could be the start of a promising new political initiative. If these aliens really are highly advanced, then it follows they must be peaceful too, or they would have destroyed us long ago. Who knows, they might even want the same things we want."

"Maybe. But if they are not so nice... do I have to remind you that it's your job to protect me?" she replied with a wink. "You're the big, strong man after all, and I'm the frail li'l woman!"

He laughed while giving her a shoulder hug. "Frail is hardly the word I would use to describe you."

"I know you're going to be very busy for the next several hours, so if you don't mind, I'm going to tidy up a few loose ends, grab a glass of wine and do a little reading.

"Call me if you need anything," he said to her as she was leaving the room, knowing that his wife had already formulated a well-ordered, mental list of essential things that needed attention before she retired to bed. Offering his assistance was, well... the husband thing to do.

The President's attention quickly turned to the urgent matter at hand. He pondered why they... whoever 'they' were, kept such a program from the POTUS. Was it customary for the Commander-in-Chief to be clueless on the most important discovery in the history of mankind, a discovery that had 'national security' written all over it? More disturbingly, was he the first President who wasn't briefed? Gregory was serving his fourth turbulent year in the White House and throughout his presidency, he was routinely briefed on all manner of frightening matters that would make any sensible man crap himself, as he was so fond of saying in private. Why not this?

There was much more to Senator Chandler's announcement than met the ear. She almost assuredly tailored her speech for public consumption, undoubtedly to avoid mass hysteria. There were clues in her speech, and wiggle room that allowed for a slow dissemination of facts regarding the extraterrestrial neighbors. Bertram needed answers and a course of decisive action, because by eight in the morning, the press would be on him like a pack of rabid wolves. In less than two hours,

President Gregory Bertram would start getting his answers. If he didn't, he'd fire the whole lot and replace them with people who would.

Once again, the leader of the free world would not be sleeping in the Presidential bedroom. 'All-nighters' were entirely too common. Fortunately, the White House coffee was the best he'd ever tasted... and there would be plenty of it available to keep him alert.

Chapter 2

"Christmas was coming early!" Senator Harold Melana thought to himself with an almost giddy inner glee. It was entirely too good to be true. The rising star of the opposition party had just gone solo and unilaterally released highly guarded state secrets to the world... on prime-time television! The rush he was feeling was far more intense than the one he had not a half-hour earlier with Tanya, his extraordinarily helpful intern who was 'assisting' the Senator with next week's agenda... and breaking-in his new, taxpayer-funded, $8000 leather couch. The senior United States Senator from New York and Senate Majority Leader was so charged that, if there had been more time before his core staff arrived for an emergency strategy session, he would have had another go with Tanya.

He smiled as he watched the beautiful, 22 year old black-haired intern nestle her flawless breasts back into a racy white lace bra. His wife had a body like that once, but 32 years of kids and age made her altogether unappealing to him. Senator Melana wasn't certain if his wife knew of Tanya, or any of his other dalliances over three decades in public service for that matter. If she did, she kept it to herself. Mrs. Sheryl Melana had long since succumbed to the mesmerizing allure of America's ruling class, and she would stay in the marriage even if Tanya did him in front of her. In any case, he really didn't care. As far as he was concerned, sex, almost on demand and with a seemingly inexhaustible selection of attractive women primed by the pheromones of power, was part of the job. A perk, as it were.

Senator Melana was convinced he could turn Chandler's announcement into a political home run. Up until a half-hour earlier, Senator Chandler was widely regarded as a serious prospect for Vice-President on the opposition ticket. She was truly great with people, had a spotless past, never backed down from a scrap or wavered from her beliefs, appealed to nearly every faction of her party, and was breathtakingly attractive, even at the age of 63. As bulletproof as she looked before, her Science and Technology Channel debut may have turned her armor into paper mâchè.

At the very least, Melana could stymie Chandler's move up the political ladder. The best-case scenario: impeachment and her removal from the Senate. Since the Governor of Oklahoma was a member of Melana's political party, her appointed replacement in the Senate would naturally reflect that, further tipping the scales in Congress in favor of the President. Of course, the guilt-by-association rule always apply, so anything Chandler did would be used against Presidential candidates of her party. Melana's mind was swirling with all the wonderful possibilities. He would take great pleasure in personally dismantling Chandler's political career. Bolstering Bertram in the process was just icing on the cake.

The assassination of a political career required two faces. The public face needed to be one of deep concern with statesman-like dignity. The hidden face were the hacks that performed the gritty work of slander, manipulation of information and other so-called dirty tricks. As Melana saw it, the destruction of Senator Chandler would begin by openly questioning her judgment and patriotism while sending the party's hit-men to suggest more distasteful things, like censure or impeachment.

Treason came to mind, but that was an antiquated concept in Washington. Nobody committed treason anymore, even though there were numerous examples of clearly traitorous behavior in the media and on both sides of the political aisle. Since the end of World War II, the meaning of the term blurred to become the ambiguous one man's traitor is another man's 'whistle-blower.' Damaging the nation's security for personal political gain became the accepted norm in Washington. In any case, the grass root party activists would use the t-word on their own, with or without official sanction.

Melana moved in behind Tanya and put his hands around her waist. "After the meeting... care for another session?" he whispered into her ear.

"Senator," she replied, putting her hands on his, "you are totally out of control!"

She turned around and accepted his embrace and passionate kiss.

"Damn!" Melana thought with an ever-widening grin. "If this isn't turning out

to be the best night of my life!

Chapter 3

"Mr. President! Mr. President!" Viktor Vasilevich Sitnikov, assistant to the President of Russia yelled in a highly animated voice. "Uncle Alyosha! Wake up!"

Aleksei Sergeyevich Korolyov, President of the Russian Federation, slowly rolled over on his not quite overly luxurious bed to look at his digital alarm clock. It was nearly 5:30 AM.

"Vitya," the groggy President said using his nephew's pet name, "what is so important that you rob your dear uncle of 30 minutes sleep?"

"It's the Americans! Something extraordinary!"

Korolyov rolled back on his pillow, "What have they done now, Vitya?" fully expecting something far less important than his nephew's voice suggested.

"One of their politicians, a Senator, announced to the world that aliens were visiting earth and the American Government has been studying them!"

"And this is big news, Vitya?"

Sitnikov stared at his uncle, stunned and perplexed. This was a huge revelation! Why wasn't the most powerful man in Russia jumping out of his bed?

"My young assistant," he continued after a brief pause to yawn, "we have known of such things for many decades. Our great country operates fine facilities that study this very phenomenon. No, this is not news to us, Vitya. The real news is which American statesman will be served for uzhin! 'Dinner' I believe our Yankee friends call it. Divulging state secrets in America is commonplace because

so many of their leaders are self-serving and corrupt. The Americans have an election this fall. I think this Senator will be gutted by his opponents for using such a revelation to stay in power! It will be a grand spectacle to watch, nephew. You will learn much!"

"Senator Chandler made the announcement, Alyosha," Sitnikov said, still trying to understand why his uncle seemed to be completely uninterested in the aliens.

"Senator Chandler you say!" Korolyov said with much more enthusiasm in his voice. He sat up on the edge of his plush bed and massaged his scalp with all ten fingers. "This is becoming much more interesting, Vitya. This woman Senator was starting to look like an American Vice President. Very attractive for her age. Pity... I had hoped to meet her some day."

Sitnikov smiled at his uncle's admiration of the American Senator's beauty. Widowed not six years earlier, Aleksei Sergeyevich Korolyov was Russia's most eligible bachelor, even at the age of 61. Sitnikov was absolutely certain that his beloved uncle had one eye completely devoted to looking for potential female companions.

"Uncle, you must see a replay of the broadcast for yourself! The normal satellite signal for a science program was disabled and a remote broadcast of Senator Chandler substituted!" Sitnikov said with somewhat less enthusiasm. After all, he wanted to impress his uncle, not annoy him with childish enthusiasm. "Even more interesting, her former husband was a scientist working in the American facility that studies aliens!"

"Ha! Even better! We shall have great sport with our American counterparts, Vitya!"

"How will that be, uncle?"

"Young one, we are the persistent 'pebble in their shoe!'" Korolyov replied with a grin while getting out of bed. "Much of the world resents American power and wealth, so we champion the resentful by challenging most everything the Americans do. There is great power in this, nephew. Simple, is it not?"

"Yes uncle, but how will you challenge the Americans with an issue as unprecedented and global as this?"

"When you hunt bear, do you not aim at the same place, big bear or small?"

"I am not sure I understand, Alyosha."

"You are new to this political game, this 'shenanigans' the Americans call it," Korolyov replied with a sly grin. "Within the next hour, we will issue a statement condemning the American's provocative and destabilizing act of attempting to duplicate alien weapons. We will make a similar statement at the United Nations later today and demand the Security Council convene an emergency meeting."

"But, you said we have facilities that do the very same thing, do we not?"

"Yes, and the Americans will gladly show the world satellite pictures of them, perhaps the Chinese facilities, if they've found them."

"Is this not foolishness if all the nations already know what the other is doing?"

"Not so foolish, young one," Korolyov said with more than a hint of sternness. "Remember what I said not a minute ago about much of the world's resentment against the Americans. Big issue, small issue... We do not miss an opportunity to toss coal into that fire!"

"Forgive me for my impertinence, uncle. I meant nothing by it."

"Vitya! You have my baby sister's fire!" he replied with a robust belly laugh. "Come! Hot tea is waiting for us and we have much to accomplish this morning! I will make you into a Russian statesman yet!"

"But, what about the aliens? What do we do about them?"

"Harmless!" Korolyov almost bellowed. "We do nothing! Not one Russian plane damaged or a facility attacked in what? Over 60 years? No, our little friends seem to be sightseers. No more or less."

"That is a relief!" he replied with some reservations that were bubbling to the surface of his mind. Sitnikov couldn't shake a gut feeling that it seemed improbable that aliens would travel immense distances just to do a little sightseeing. Still, his uncle was one of the most powerful men on earth. If the aliens were plotting against us, he would surely know.

"If I may, one more question, Alyosha: How much technology have we recovered from the extraterrestrials? Are the Americans or Chinese ahead of us?"

"All these many years of research... almost nothing to show for it. Our scientists say the curious sightseers are many thousands of years ahead of us, Vitya.

We have many pieces of their technology... we even have a few of their comrades in formaldehyde, but our chances of duplicating their machines and weapons? Mother Russia's best minds say it is impossible."

"Why do we continue to try? It must be very expensive to operate such a project, is it not?"

"Very expensive, young one," he paused to try and remember something he heard that would add perspective. "The cowboys in Texas have a proverb, of sorts. I believe it reads 'Even a sightless squirrel can happen upon a nut.' That is why we continue the research, Vitya. If the Americans or Chinese trip over the right nut, they will dominate the world."

"That is very funny, uncle, and it makes sense. Much could be at stake if the Chinese or Americans have a significant breakthrough."

"Precisely!" Korolyov said, pleased he made Viktor Vasilevich a little wiser. "No more talk. I am famished, Vitya. Zavtrak with hot tea awaits! Eat well this morning, nephew, because obed and uzhin may be many hours away."

Chapter 4

"Thank you for coming at this late hour and on such short notice," President Bertram announced to the present members of the National Security Council using the most pleasant voice he could muster. "Now," he said, his voice taking on a more ominous tone, "would somebody please tell me what the hell is going on and why the President of the United States is the last damn person on earth to know about it?"

"Mr. President," General Nathan Talbot, Chairman of the Joint Chiefs of Staff began, "my aide is gathering detailed information for me at this time, but with the valuable help of Air Force Chief of Staff O'Neill, I have enough details on the project Senator Chandler spoke of to get us started."

"By all means, General Talbot, proceed," Bertram answered, the ire in his voice biting into each member of the Council. "I'm looking forward to the part about why I was never informed of this."

General Talbot, a genuine old school Army officer and highly decorated veteran of most every conflict after Vietnam, looked unusually uncomfortable to President Bertram. A fit, tower of a man that belied his years, General Talbot always spoke with unerring authority... but not tonight. The news obviously caught Talbot off guard and he appeared to be very close to squirming, an observation that unsettled the President even more.

"Mr. President, Senator Chandler was referring to Project Cocheta," Talbot began, the stress in his voice obvious to everyone. "The project was established in 1947 under a secret order given by President Truman. Prior to that, the inves-

tigation into extraterrestrial technology was handled by the U.S. Army Air Force. Truman wanted the military to divest itself of ET research and concentrate on the growing Soviet threat. He ordered that Project Cocheta be off-line and ultra-black, with managerial, technical and logistical support supplied by a private corporation."

"OK, OK..." Bertram interrupted, "Let me wrap my brain around this! First, you are telling me that flying saucers are real, which is a pretty damned tough pill to swallow, next thing you tell me is that a private corporation runs this Cocheta Project? I'm not sure which of the two is harder to swallow!"

"I understand, Mr. President. This is news to me, as well," Talbot replied nervously, shooting a quick, almost menacing glance at General O'Neill, who seemed to know quite a lot about Project Cocheta. "Concerning the first pill, Sir, I have been advised that we have been under constant surveillance by an alien civilization since the mid 1940s... and sporadically before that. The second pill is somewhat easier to explain. It is not unusual for private contractors to assist in many aspects of highly classified projects, from testing nuclear weapons and advanced technology, to creating realistic combat environments to train our fighter pilots. Of course, we have the ultimate say over how operations will be conducted, and naturally, we control the purse strings."

"Go on," Bertram said, a barely noticeable bit of sternness absent from his voice, "tell me more about the thought process behind turning over a project of this magnitude to civilian contractors."

Talbot nervously shuffled a few pages about on the area of desk before him. "Mr. President, as I understand it, Truman felt that Project Cocheta needed to be buried deep within the realm of black projects. That required an equally black way to fund it. Some of it was generated by funneling DoD dollars into dozens of sham projects at several small defense contractors, all owned by a single and much larger parent corporation. That generated a huge amount of money, but not enough to fully fund the project. Using an elaborate system of laundering off-budget funds through other minor Federal bureaucracies, billions of dollars were diverted to the very same corporation. They administer payroll, equipment and logistical support to Project Cocheta. To fund such an undertaking the traditional way would have drawn entirely too much scrutiny to a project where secrecy is absolutely critical."

"What is the name of this parent corporation?" the President asked, rubbing the late evening stubble on his chin.

"Humfeld, Haveman and Pietrowski Enterprises..." Talbot began.

"They must not be all that big, General Talbot," Bertram interrupted," I've never heard of them."

"That was the company name in 1947. They go by Unified Global Technologies today."

"Holy shit!" Bertram responded in near disbelief, "Corporations don't come much bigger than that! Aren't they our third or fourth largest defense contractor?"

"Second, if you count the dozen or so smaller defense contractors they control administratively," Talbot elaborated. "Overall, they have done a superb job of managing the project and supporting their needs."

"Until recently."

"Yes, Mr. President. It would seem that the last project director they appointed was... uh, seriously unbalanced."

"Murdering over a dozen people made him a serial killer, General! Doesn't seem like the type of person that should be running such a sensitive project!"

"Agreed, Mr. President," General Talbot replied, "I'm certain UGTI management is looking into the matter quite seriously. Given the sensitive and urgent nature of the project, I'm guessing they will be appointing a replacement for Mr. Hastings very quickly."

"I want to know who this replacement is the minute UGTI makes it, General Talbot. This unexpected genie has been released from the lamp and planted his fat ass square on my lap. If I am going to be blamed for every misadventure that comes from that project, I want to know who the hell is running it!"

"Yes sir, Mr. President," Talbot replied. "For whatever it is worth, we believe that UGTI will be seriously looking at Dr. Hanson's daughter to replace Hastings."

"Would that be a wise move?"

"We think so," Talbot replied confidently. "She is currently the Chief Engineer at Lockheed's Skunk Works in Palmdale's Plant 42. She is easily the most qualified aerospace engineer in America... and quite possibly, on the planet. Her managerial skills are just as impressive. I understand she's every bit as smart as her dad, perhaps significantly more so. Lockheed swears she can walk on water! In fact,

Donna Hanson's engineering contributions to the F-22 and F-35 stealth fighters are legendary in the defense industry."

"Let me rephrase the question, General: Can she be trusted? Her dad apparently had no reservations about divulging the most sensitive of state secrets."

"The biggest cat is already out of the bag, Mr. President," Talbot stated almost flippantly. "There is little more damage she could do."

"I see... now General, tell me more about the project itself. Tell me what it does and what they have accomplished."

"If I may, General Talbot?" General Oren 'Big O' O'Neill asked of the Chairman, whose reply with a nod that O'Neill interpreted as relief. "Simply put, Mr. President, Project Cocheta was commissioned to study and duplicate extraterrestrial technology, much like the Air Force's Division of Foreign Technology studies the technology of our terrestrial adversaries. We have two intact alien vehicles and literally thousands upon thousands of wreckage pieces to analyze. The project staff also screens high-profile case reports and travels to locations where physical evidence of alien activity have been found."

Bertram stared at O'Neill. "This is completely beyond belief!" he said, shaking his head. "OK... what have we duplicated so far, General O'Neill."

"Surprisingly little, sir," O'Neill said almost apologetically. "Aside from a few of the less exotic alloys we've been able to reproduce... well, essentially nothing."

"What? Over sixty years of research, billions of dollars... and all we have to show for it is a better metal for what? Golf clubs?"

"Sir, the technology is thousands of years ahead of ours, perhaps even millions," O'Neill said with discernible defensiveness that puzzled the Commander-in-Chief. "We lack a frame of reference... I mean a technological frame of reference. We look at a piece of alien technology and have nobody to tell us what it does. Even if somebody could tell us what it does, we still have nothing remotely comparable to give us a hint on how it does what it does. It's sort of like handing a computer chip to an ancient, say... Pythagoras of Samos, then telling him it is capable of helping him write down his musings or crunch his most sophisticated mathematical problems, only... we actually don't bother to tell him any of that! He is left holding technology capable of incredible computational power, yet lacks the technologic frame of reference to understand its significance, let alone duplicate it and put it to use."

Bertram instinctively understood the dilemma. Humans tend to look at technologic progress in terms of how clever the current generation is when compared to past generations. Modern aviators look at the aircraft of World War I or II and laugh at how hilarious and primitive they were. No doubt the pilot of a Sopwith Camel laughed at the backwards hot air balloons of the late 18th Century, as Montgolfier must have sneered at technology that relied upon horses for transportation. Surely, descendents two hundred years hence will marvel at how primitive early 21st Century technology was. O'Neill said "thousands, perhaps millions" of years... and dark, terrible thoughts began to enter his consciousness. Those around him were beginning to see his change in countenance. Most instinctively knew why.

"General O'Neill, what are our visitors up to?"

"That is unknown, sir," O'Neill said, sensing that the conversation was about to become much more difficult. Like most people, Bertram loathed the 'unknowns.' The last time a member of the National Security Council member said "we don't know," Bertram asked how in hell can a President make sound decisions if the experts around him do not have concrete answers, or at least well-educated guesses. "There are a few possibilities, however," the General quickly added.

"Let's hear them."

"Basically, there are only three. The first: aliens are passively studying us without hostile intent. The second: the aliens are studying us in preparation for friendly contact. The third: they are engaging in passive recon to prepare for military action."

Bertram sat silently for a few moments, digesting what he just heard while other members of the council began to mumble and whisper amongst themselves. "Since the last option is the most dire, what is the likelihood that is what they are up to?"

"Unlikely sir, given over six decades of interactions between our aircraft and theirs."

"Interactions?"

"We engaged their aircraft dozens of times during the forties, fifties, and sixties. Not once did they ever return fire."

"Good God! We shot at them?" gasped Secretary of Homeland Security Kathryn Beckman.

"They were violating our airspace with unknown intent, Secretary Beckman. Besides, the best we can tell, we never came close to hitting one, let alone shooting one down. They simply dodge everything we fire at them. We don't even try to engage them with weapons anymore. The performance characteristics of their aircraft are beyond astounding."

"Spoken like a true Air Force General," President Bertram said, "but what do the people studying them think? Dr. Alexander and Senator Chandler will pay a heavy price for shoving this information out into the public without my consent. I have the distinct impression that Senator Chandler was holding back. Does her husband have an opinion that differs from yours?"

"Dr. Hanson believes they are in the first phase of military operations against our planet, as do the majority of the Project Cocheta scientists."

That wasn't the answer Bertram wanted to hear, but the one he expected based on his gut feeling on Chandler's career-killing speech. "They have the same data that you apparently do, so why such huge separation in beliefs, General O'Neill?"

"Years ago, an anthropologist named Heischler, a professor at one of the Ivy League schools... Harvard I believe, was asked to assess the intentions of the aliens. He believed that evolution was a universal constant and that our own past could predict the behavior of species and cultures from other planets. Basically, he hypothesized that, because of evolution, the aliens visiting earth were far more likely to be aggressive than peaceful."

"That is frightening," said Vice President Victor Callison, "truly frightening!"

"Hold on, Vic," Bertram said with a steadying voice. "General O'Neill, is it safe to say a lot of smart people think we are in big trouble?"

"Sir, Heischler was not exactly stable. Shortly after he wrote his paper, he quit his prestigious academic position and literally became a hermit in Oregon. I honestly do not know why the Project Cocheta scientists place any faith in his conclusions."

"Van Gogh was crazy... In fact, quite a few geniuses are, or were, out of their minds, yet their creations speak for themselves," CIA Director Allan Brust interjected.

"I'm not sure that applies here, Allen," Bertram said. "If I recall, Van Gogh didn't go crazy after reading something frightening. General, have you read this report?"

"No sir, I haven't. I've only read a short synopsis."

"I want a copy of the full report on my desk by 6 AM," Bertram said. "In fact, I want copies made for everyone here. I want to know what everyone thinks about it when we reconvene tomorrow afternoon."

"Yes sir."

"Let's say, for a moment, Heischler was right, General O'Neill. What kind of weapons technology are we facing?"

"We have no idea, Mr. President," O'Neill said, shaking his head. "They have taken no hostile actions against our military and all of their defensive actions have been purely evasive."

"I guess what I meant to ask was: what have the Project Cocheta scientists discovered in the way of weaponry?"

"As far as I know... nothing," O'Neill replied. "That's another reason I do not believe they hold hostile intentions."

"Humor me for a moment, General O'Neill," Bertram said, rubbing his chin again, "if they do have offensive weapons we haven't discovered yet, what might they be?"

O'Neill sat quiet for a moment, organizing his thoughts. "Mr. President, the vehicles themselves require enormous amounts of energy to perform the way they do. The source of that power is completely unknown, but it must be self-contained, perhaps inside of an impossibly small reactor of some sort. Offensive weapons would likely be very destructive and quite precise. Of course, what kinds of weapons they use would be dictated by strategy. In other words, tailored to the end result they wish to attain."

It appeared to General O'Neill that President Bertram was not completely satisfied with the answer. "Mr. President," he resumed, deciding to climb out on the safest branch of the speculation tree, "we could expect some sort of laser or particle beam of unfathomable power. Given the incredible disparity between our technologies, the weapon would probably be indefensible. If they use missiles or bombs,

they would likely dwarf our most powerful fusion devices with a delivery speed that precludes interception. Finally, there could be weapons we can scarcely imagine at this point in our technological evolution."

"Let me sum it up for you, General O'Neill," Secretary Beckman interrupted, "if they attack us, we're screwed!"

"Yes, ma'am, that pretty much sums it up. But, I repeat, there is no evidence that it is ever going to happen."

"Better hope it never happens!" the Vice President said. "We're talking 'end-of-the-world' here! Do they have any weaknesses?"

"Their technology fails... on occasion," O'Neill replied. "We know that much. They sometimes crash into things or explode."

"Well, that's a start!" Secretary of the Treasury Drew Murray said. "Maybe the fallibility of their technology can be exploited."

"Perhaps, but my gut feeling is that we would be better off taking a far less confrontational approach." Bertram said. "General Talbot..."

"Yes, Mr. President?"

"Assemble a team of your best people and begin interfacing directly with the Project Cocheta scientists. Whatever the current research strategy is, I want it changed so that the focus is on finding a defense to the alien technology, not an offense. We need to stand down, to a degree, so that the aliens do not interpret our actions as hostile. I will not be responsible for starting the world's first, and probably last, interstellar war."

With the exception of the military members of the NSC, a general nodding in agreement swept across the room as another thought entered the President's mind. "There is one thing that bothers me, General O'Neill. If the military is convinced we are in no danger of being attacked by the aliens, why the herculean effort at deception? Why the cover-up?"

"Sir, the Russians obtained examples of the alien technology at about the same time we did. The old Soviet Union established two well-hidden and well-guarded research facilities in Siberia to do the exact same thing we were doing at Project Cocheta. Every American knew of the 'arms race' and 'space race' with the Soviets, but nobody knew of the far more important 'reverse engineering' race going on. Whoever wins that one will possess military invincibility. We had to maintain an incredibly high degree of secrecy, along with elaborate public disinformation campaigns, to keep the Russians from getting nervous about what we were trying to accomplish at Project Cocheta. If they thought we were close to a technologic breakthrough, the imminent and radical swing in the balance of power might provoke them to launch a preemptive nuclear strike on us."

Bertram chided himself internally for not figuring out the 'cold war' piece of the emerging picture on his own. It made perfect sense, in an old school sort of way. Publicly deny the existence of UFOs while secretly piecing together the technology. Mr. and Mrs. 'John Q. Public' busies about his and her merry way, oblivious to the earth-shattering reality of an alien presence on earth, while official indifference lulls America's enemies to sleep. Of course, that is assuming America's enemies lacked hard intel on the project. Bertram guessed the Russians probably knew of Project Cocheta right from the very start. After all, the old Soviet KGB's ability to discover American state secrets was astounding.

"What is the status of their project?" Bertram asked. "Did it survive the Soviet collapse?"

"It is still operational," O'Neill responded. "Our best intelligence assessment of their progress has them bogged-down as much as we are. There is an additional player in this game, too, Mr. President. The Chinese also have a research program. Our intel on that program is almost non-existent. We know where it is located and not much else."

The full force of the gravity and complexity of the situation presented to him was sinking in. This was far more dangerous than just the leaking of sensitive state secrets by an idealistic scientist. A hidden and very dangerous race, with vastly greater stakes than the space or nuclear arms race, was taking place. The winner of the competition would forever dominate the earth. That is, unless the aliens decided to invade. If that happened… 'Well then, everybody is just plain fucked!' he thought to himself, the first signs of what would become a vicious headache intruding into his thoughts.

"I'm assuming we have a strategy to deal with the Russians or Chinese if they make a substantive breakthrough?" Bertram asked, wincing at the growing discomfort in his head.

"Yes, Mr. President," O'Neill answered with the authority befitting his rank. "If presented with undeniable evidence that such a breakthrough has been made,

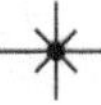

we can launch a defensive first-strike and vaporize their research facilities, ICBM sites and missile submarines."

"How can you contemplate creating such a plan if the President and the rest of us unwashed on the NSC doesn't know what in the hell is going on?" Vice-President Callison barked in anger. Animated conversations began erupting around the table.

"Hold on, Vic!" the President said loud enough to squelch the growing roar of conversation. "My guess is that General O'Neill here has been doing what has always been done. That still doesn't make it right, nor does it make it good policy. There will be no preemptive strikes or acts of war, nuclear or otherwise, without my authorization!"

Bertram's response had the intended effect of regaining control of the discussion and asserting his command over something that only a few moments ago he knew nothing about.

"Now that we are on the subject, why in God's name was I left out of the loop on this?" Bertram asked, the ire returning to his voice. "General O'Neill, you seem to be far more privileged than the President on this subject so vital to national security. Can you shed some light on this?"

O'Neill felt the sting of the President's remark hit home, but he was just the messenger! He didn't set the policy on this! That was handled at levels much higher than his.

"Sir, as you have probably already guessed, you are not the first President excluded from knowing about the extraterrestrial situation. Truman obviously knew and so did Eisenhower. Kennedy was the first President kept in the dark. Eisenhower felt JFK had certain personal... well, 'liabilities' that left him too vulnerable. Johnson didn't know, either. I'm not entirely sure about Nixon or Ford. Carter asked about it, but told there was nothing to it. Reagan was briefed, partly because of his national security stance, but more importantly, the fact his Vice President was a former CIA director who already knew. Clinton wasn't briefed but Bush junior was. No president since has been briefed.

"Should I feel lucky because I am in such good company?" Bertram said sharply. "Who in this room has been formally briefed about Project Cocheta besides General O'Neill?"

"I have, Mr. President," replied CIA Director Brust.

"Anyone else? Any other critical secrets I should know about?"

No one responded.

"Let's get one thing straight here," Bertram began firmly, "Everyone in this room is a key player in the defense of this country. Keeping the President and the statutory members of the National Security Council in the dark about this project is bullshit! O'Neill, I want everyone in this room to receive a full formal briefing at tomorrows' follow-up meeting. Larry, I want to address the Nation tomorrow at 9 PM and hold a press conference at 10:00 AM Tuesday Morning. I also want to speak to Senator Chandler and Dr. Alexander, in person, as soon as feasible."

The President paused for a moment to gauge the impact of his outburst and last statement.

"Mr. President," Nicholas Breen, Assistant to the President for National Security Affairs began, "are you sure it is a good idea to be seen with Senator Chandler? She's broken a number of laws and, in theory, should be arrested."

"I don't intend for our meeting to be public," Bertram said firmly. "I will speak with her, privately, after Dr. Hanson is dead and buried. She made a very passionate speech and there will undoubtedly be a lot of people sympathizing with her, so it doesn't make good political sense to incarcerate her. I'll let the Washington 'machine' work its magic. Maybe she'll think twice about pulling the rug out from under me again."

A nervous chuckle broke out amongst the members of the National Security Council. The 'machine' was well-oiled and always ready to gleefully chew up non-conformists and other troublemakers.

"I know the opposition party will come out tomorrow morning throwing rocks," Bertram continued. "Everything in Washington has a damn spin to it. Having the press conference tomorrow night provides time for the opposition to show their hand, and time for us to effectively nullify it. Now, why don't we take a short break before we mull over what my beloved press secretary is going to say to the pack of foaming-mouthed dogs tomorrow morning?"

The meeting adjourned about three hours later. The initial response of the Bertram administration would be that of calming, reassuring words to the public. The concerned told not to worry, that their President was on top of the situation

and that they would learn more at the 9:00 PM Presidential address. While White House Press Secretary Byron Arballo was soothing the public, the President's political advisors would be busy interpreting the chaotic Beltway political buzz. The afternoon follow-up NSC meeting would get the President's team up to speed on the facts so that a Cocheta policy could be formulated. The next meeting on the Presidential agenda would be with his top political analysts and strategists. It didn't seem odd at all to President Bertram that, in light of the new and frightening reality he was just introduced to, politics would be major part the post-disclosure dynamics. Silly or not, it would be anyway. If the President of the United States wanted to firmly attach his relevancy to this highly important discovery, he had to play the game.

President Bertram contemplated the day that plodded towards him as he prepared to steal a few hours of sleep from the remainder of the retreating night. It was going to be a restless one, of that he was sure.

The night would yield little in the way of restful sleep for Bertram... and the following day would prove to be more frustrating than he could have ever imagined.

Chapter 5

Human language, past or present, lacked a word to adequately describe Wallace William Frick. At first glance, 'predator' seemed hardly the word. Standing a frail-looking five foot eight, Frick appeared to be the precise antithesis of a cold-blooded killer. A computer geek, perhaps an accountant, but not 'professional assassin.' Yet, Wally Frick was just such a predator... and an exceptionally evil one at that.

Armed with blend-in looks and robust intellect, Frick plied his trade with the ease of a master craftsman. He lived for the kill, but not because of the rush or the money. He didn't murder his fellow man for lofty, higher purposes or to protect his country. In fact, if not lucratively 'employed' as an assassin, Frick would be content to randomly kill people on his own time and dime. Wallace Frick ended human life for one reason and one reason only: 'the look.'

So far as he could tell, all higher mammals exhibited 'the look' in the final moments of a violent death. He first noticed it when he was only five years old, living with his grandmother in New Iberia, Louisiana. A neighborhood stray tended to her batch of rambunctious kittens, when the most adventurous playfully hopped within little Wally's grasp. Eerily, and almost without conscious thought, Wallace grabbed the kitten by the throat and began squeezing. As the terrified kitten tried to escape, something primaeval fought to emerge from its repressed state in Wallace. In the final moments of the kitten's short life, a future predator of men experienced pure power for the first time. The power to take life at will. It was a taste of what he came to know as the all-empowering look, an expression of utter terror and eventual submission in the eyes of his prey.

For the next 12 years, Wally limited his killing to animals... carefully keeping his ghastly passion hidden from the world. The fear of what might happen to a frail weenie or 'juvie' in reform school was ample motivation. Unlike the vast majority of blossoming psychopaths who allowed impulsivity to render them vulnerable to discovery, Frick possessed a remarkable degree of self-control, enabling him to successfully perpetrate his brutal acts of cruelty in secret. The combination of a brilliant, if twisted, mind and an ability to delay gratification until the timing was perfect, made him a potentially formidable stalker of humans.

A month before his 18th birthday, Wallace Frick drove sixty miles to Thibodaux, Louisiana. Parking his car at a supermarket, he hiked three miles along a railroad track and a quarter mile into the woods, to a clearing he once saw while visiting his Aunt Louise... a place where small children played. He carefully chose a hiding place along a trail and patiently waited. After nearly four hours, and passing on several children that were either too old or in groups, the moment arrived. A small girl, four years old he would learn later, passed by, calling out for her brother. Frick, knowing there was nobody at the clearing, made his move. He removed the lid from a coffee can and retrieved a rag soaked in di-ethyl ether, a common engine starting fluid... and powerful inhaled anesthetic. In one quick move, he slammed the pungent cloth over her mouth and nose, then used his other arm to attenuate her struggles. She tried desperately to scream as Frick pulled her off the trail and into the deep brush, but the cloth muffled them into barely audible howls. Within a minute, she became limp, making Frick's task much easier. After carrying her a hundred yards or so, he laid her down on a small area of bare ground. He removed the ether-soaked rag and stuffed her mouth with a clean one, but only enough to keep her from screaming when she awakened.

Molesting Tiara Benning was not on Wallace Frick's pleasure list. After all, only real sickos raped little girls. What he desired from Miss Benning was just a particular 'look' that he craved to see. Years of morbid and obsessed curiosity finally brought him to the very brink of his first murder. Did humans really have the same look in their eyes that animals do when they died? Frick was determined to find out. After several minutes of waning unconsciousness, Tiara awoke to the face of Wally Frick... and the feel of hands tightening around her neck.

It was over in a few minutes, but the feeling William Wallace Frick experienced would be relived in his remorseless mind for a lifetime.

Chapter 6

It took all of about ten minutes for the press to be notified of Dr. Benjamin Harris Hanson's whereabouts. A University Medical Center phlebotomist was watching the broadcast of Senator Chandler's history making announcement to the world when he realized that the patient in the intensive care unit under armed guard must be the same Benjamin H. Hanson! Sensing there might be a buck in it, the phlebotomist grabbed the nearest phone book and called a local television station on his cell phone. In spite of the confidentiality laws pertaining to medical records and patient identity, the hospital employee divulged the location of the dying scientist in return for $200 in cash to be paid the next day.

By 4:45 PM Mountain Standard Time, most of the press around the world knew where the dying scientist was hospitalized. The local Vegas press was naturally first on the scene with their trucks, satellite uplinks and top tier reporters. It was the story of the millennia and the man responsible for it was in their own backyard! Before long, West Charleston Blvd. was packed with press vehicles, sightseers in cars and police vehicles trying to position themselves for better traffic control. South Rancho Drive was also bearing the brunt of increased traffic flow, as was Palomino Lane and South Martin Luther King Blvd. By 7 PM, the area around the University Medical Center had, for all intents and purposes, become a circus. While most were there to see history unfold, others were there to pay tribute to Dr. Hanson. At dusk, impromptu candlelight vigils began to surface around the hospital grounds, eventually coalescing into a large group occupying the southeast parking lot. Others were using the occasion to dress up like bug-eyed aliens, wookies and storm troopers. Vegas radio and television stations were both covering the news and pleading with their listeners to not join the mob already there at the

Medical Center. When it was learned that Senator Chandler would be arriving at McCarran airport a little after 9 PM, all bets were off.

The people drawn to the University Medical Center were generally benign, but the unintended consequence of such poorly controlled, spontaneous events is that people sometimes get hurt. Ambulances were having difficulty negotiating the traffic jam and some were being diverted to other hospitals. Fortunately, the only serious medical issue that didn't make it to a hospital on time was a very nervous man and his laboring wife. Delayed in the enormous sea of non-moving cars, they delivered their fourth child in the back of a small SUV... a baby girl they named Dulcinea.

At 10 minutes past 9 PM, Senator Hanson's Lear 45 taxied to the McCarran executive terminal. Having been notified a day earlier, her children and grandchildren were already waiting for her there. As suggested by her personal security detail and a Vegas security firm owned and operated by former Blackwater professionals, the Hanson family would travel to the University Medical Center in three van taxicabs rather than limousines, each taking a different, circuitous route with one armed detail in front and behind each van.

An earlier request for police escort was denied by the Mayor of Las Vegas, Dan Kincaid, stating that he could not spare the extra manpower. While superficially true, given the substantial influx of sightseers into the city, the real reason for the denial was that Kincaid had no love for her political ilk. Sadly, the information leaks from earlier that evening ensured that each van would have at least one press vehicle in tow, increasing the exposure and danger to the Senator and her family. Anyone attempting to harm them, however, would face fearsome and deadly resistance.

Well more than an hour later, each van arrived at different entrances into the University Medical center, each were potentially dangerous choke points and each had a private security expert there to hastily usher them into the facility. The press, however, had every entrance covered, even the freight docks. There was simply no way to avoid the dangerous transition from van to relative safety in the hospitals' physical plant. Fortunately, each movement of family members into the hospital was relatively fluid in spite of the throng of interested bystanders and members of the press pleading for statements and trying to shove microphones and camcorders into the faces of the terrified family. Once inside, each group of family members were quickly escorted to the second floor of the ER/ICU Building to reunite in the waiting room. It had been a very long day for the entire family and all were utterly exhausted by the ordeal.

"Senator Chandler, I'm Candace Reyes from patient relations," the plump hispanic woman announced. "Please come with me. We have prepared a temporary room for you and your family to wait in. We're having cots and chairs brought in so that you can get your rest."

"Thank you, Ms. Reyes," Teresa said. "We are all grateful for your kindness. It has been a very difficult day. When do you think I will be able to see my husband?"

"I can take you to see him after I get clearance from the charge nurse. He is in bed three of the Surgical Intensive Care Unit. Normally, we only allow one visitor at a time, but because of the extraordinary circumstances, I'm sure we will be able to allow two at a time."

"We appreciate your kindness, Ms. Reyes. Has his condition changed?"

"The last update I received, we still listed his condition as grave. I will have the attending surgeon on call, Dr. Boyer, meet with you shortly."

"Thank you," Teresa said, clearly disappointed that her husband's condition had not changed for the better. "Would it be possible for us to place him in a larger, more private room?"

"Possibly. I will look into it for you Senator Chandler."

"Please, call me Teresa, and I've taken my married name back. It's Hanson now."

Candace smiled at Teresa. She was fully expecting a self absorbed, pushy politician demanding all manner of special perks. This one was appreciative and polite, only asking for a larger room to accommodate what would likely be a death vigil for her husband. She had not seen the surprise announcement on Dr. Alexander's cable show, but within a half hour of the Senator's appearance, the entire hospital was abuzz about her extraordinary speech. When it was learned that her husband was at UMC, the hospital became electrified! To be involved with caring for the Hanson family's needs would be an honor. If she could get administration to sign off on it, she would personally handle the responsibility for the duration of their stay.

"Teresa, let me get busy making arrangements for your family. I will have the cafeteria staff prepare a late dinner and bring in pitchers of tea and water until we

can get better accommodations for you." Candace opened her aluminum clipboard and retrieved a business card with her pager and cell phone numbers. "Here is my card. Please do not hesitate to call me, day or night, for anything you might need."

"You are too kind, Candace. Thank you!"

"It is my pleasure, Teresa. I will track down Dr. Boyer and take you to see your husband as soon as possible."

Teresa looked at her exhausted family. They already endured much, and much more was coming. Tears were forming now and she couldn't stop them from flowing. After two decades, Teresa Rose Chandler was finally going to be reunited with her one and only-est. Twenty minutes later, she was stroking the grossly swollen right hand of the only man she ever loved, the only man she ever cared to be with and the father of her children. He was barely recognizable. His face was significantly swollen and his torso seemingly buried in a tangle of intravenous lines and monitoring cables. No physician was needed to determine that Ben Hanson was far more dead than alive.

Decades ago, Teresa earned her bachelor's degree in nursing, yet she never once looked at the sophisticated monitors Ben was attached to, nor did she care that he was on a respirator. She was there for him, to comfort him and to pray for him. However improbable, something inside of her seemed to know that he was reaching for her. She felt as if the more she stroked his hands and hair, the closer he seemed to be to her. She spoke softly in his ear, telling him how much she loved and missed him, and how wonderful it was that they were a couple again.

Dr. Benjamin Harris Hanson was transferred to a much larger room adjacent to the surgical intensive care unit at 1:05 AM. Teresa continued her ministering to Ben throughout the night, only leaving his side when it was absolutely necessary. She continued her nonstop vigil until she was widowed at 2:27 PM Monday afternoon.

Chapter 7

By the time Monday morning daylight arrived on the eastern seaboard of the United States, most of the civilized world had already reacted to the Hanson Revelations. Many instantly believed that the announcement was nothing more than a scam, a political ploy of some sort. Others bought into the notion that aliens were visiting earth, each having their own opinion about the level of threat, or lack of threat, they posed. The remainder did not care or were too busy trying to survive the next day.

Every major newspaper, radio, television, cable and alternate news outlet on the planet were leading with Senator Chandler's revelations. The morning network shows were recapping the news of the last nine hours, repeating the videos of Senator Chandler's short speech and the crowds surrounding University Medical Center in Las Vegas. Video clips from around the world were flooding into news outlets at an astonishing rate.

The most important of them were from world leaders. The Russian president soundly condemned the American project as 'provocative and destabilizing' and called for the United Nations to convene an emergency session of the Security Council. The Chinese president was also quick to condemn the American project as 'the short path to world domination by the United States' and also called upon the United Nations to intervene. Other world leaders chimed-in as well, each supporting their own allies in predictable fashion. What was missed by almost everyone was that Senator Chandler never mentioned the term 'reverse engineering,' yet that was precisely why those aligned with Russia and China were howling the loudest.

All across America, citizens that went to bed Sunday night unaware of the Senator Chandler's shocking announcement, awakened to face an entirely different view of the universe. That is, if the Senator was telling the truth. Many Americans were skeptical of anything coming out of Washington, even more so with the sudden and improbable announcement, by a politician no less, that aliens have been a part of the human experience since the 1940s! So why should this event be any different? It was the same old bullshit with a science fiction flair to it. Many minds began to change after watching Senator Chandler's video being aired around the world almost non-stop.

Eventually, the consensus in the objective side of the blogosphere was that she seemed very honest and sincere. If Chandler were lying, she was doing an extraordinarily good job of it. Of course, those with a political agenda were busily forging spins that were aimed at discrediting the Senator and her political allies. Was the Senator a patriot, or was she a traitor for going public with state secrets so classified that even presidents were not allowed to know of them? The answer would come in time, but never fast enough.

In a vacuum of hard data, conjecture rules... and there was plenty of that to go around. To fill-in the gaps, the press turned to both actual scientists and the metaphysicians. While all manner of pseudoscientists began to lecture audiences on the coming 'new age of enlightenment' the aliens would bring to earth, real scientists were stumbling over the smoldering wasteland of their belief systems. They had to shelve the notion that faster-than-light travel was absolutely impossible and start believing in a new and very uncomfortable paradigm. Probably the best comment came from Dr. Rodney Frost, a brilliant, Nobel Prize-winning physicist at MIT.

"Damn! Now we've got to factor everything we didn't believe in! The math is really going to suck now!"

What didn't happen was the mass hysteria that the NASA Brookings report suggested might happen. While being interviewed on a popular early morning talk show, Cornell University Sociologist Dr. Katheryn Burnett suggested that one possible explanation might be that the inhabitants of earth have been saturated with what she called a somewhat 'alien-centric' media since the late 1940's, and far more so in the last two or three decades.

"We seem to go in love-hate cycles when it comes to how we imagine aliens might behave. In movie theaters of the 50s and 60s, they were here to hurt us or warn us. In the 70s and 80s they were harmless and accepting of humans. Of late, films mostly depict aliens as decidedly malevolent. Then there are the dozens of shows on cable promoting the idea of extraterrestrial visitation. In any case, we are already conditioned to believe in them and the possibility they might actually be here."

At 7:00 AM, Eastern Time, White House Press Secretary Lola Zimmerman announced that the President met with the National Security Council late last night and would meet with them again at 5:00 PM Eastern. She also announced that the President would address the Nation at 9:00 PM Eastern. As much as the White House Press Corps loudly badgered Ms. Zimmerman after her brief announcement, she refused to answer any questions and left the pulpit rather abruptly. That left the press standing around, kicking pebbles and looking for someone... anyone, who could shed political and/or philosophical light on the new reality the inhabitants of earth would be subjected to.

Chapter 8

"OK, everyone is here," President Bertram said. "Let's get started."

The recently renovated Situation Room in the basement of the White House West Wing was, essentially, a large conference room, very much like those one might see in a corporate office building, only it was heavily fortified, bristling with high-tech, secure communications capabilities and six large monitors showing real-time video feeds from around the world. Five other satellite rooms were equipped to view video feeds ranging from the The Science and Technology Channel to real-time strike missions in impossibly remote areas of the planet. The Situation Room was manned 24/7 and instantly ready to tackle any command and control needs of the President.

"First off, I've gotta say this Heischler Report was very frightening. He was obviously a brilliant man and that frightens me even more."

"I agree, Mr. President," Secretary of State Abraham Cochran said. "I'm genuinely concerned that the aliens are biding their time."

"Wait a minute, Abe," the President said, waving his hand at the Secretary of State, "It's a frightening report, but nothing about it really fits what we are seeing."

"Mr. President," said Director of National Intelligence Sarah Whiting, quickly jumping into the discussion, "what do you believe we are supposed to be seeing right now if their intent is hostile?"

"Hostile acts, Sarah!"

"Maybe they are not ready to be hostile, Mr. President. Maybe they don't have any military assets here... yet. You know of my extensive background in science as an adviser to three presidents before you. It is an incredibly huge undertaking to travel light years of distance for... what? A handshake and a photo op? The fact that their vehicles have been buzzing around our airspace for over 60 years is terribly disturbing to me. They have plenty of information on us already and they could easily continue to monitor us from the Moon. So... why are they still here? If their friends arrive en-masse, I assure you, they will not be here for a huge, intergalactic kegger."

There were a few nervous chuckles at Sarah's pop-culture movie reference to a 'galactic kegger.' An uneasy air began to fill the room. Sarah's argument had reached nearly everyone's spine.

"You make a compelling case, Sarah," the President said to break the silence in the room, "but I'm not ready to entertain the thought that we are completely screwed just yet. I just can't believe the aliens would attack us if we make no provocative moves against them."

"Consider this, Mr. President: What is our current policy position on radical nations developing nuclear weapons?"

"To strongly discourage it."

"And, if they ignored us?"

"Discourage them by using economic sanctions and isolation."

"Let us say that doesn't work, either. Now they have enriched uranium to 95 percent. They are about to assemble their first fission device. Now what do we do?"

"We quickly take away their ability to make and deploy nuclear weapons."

"By force?"

"Yes, by force!"

"Mr. President, at what point in time would it have been easiest and most cost effective to stop the bad guys from becoming a genuine threat?"

"Oh my God!" CIA Director Brust exclaimed. "I see where you're going with this! Are you suggesting that the aliens might destroy us long before we could ever be any real threat to them?"

"In terms of efficiency, it is far safer and vastly more efficient to permanently eliminate a minimal threat than to wait for the threat to become formidable and lethal. I think you'll find that the Joint Chiefs of Staff would concur."

"That is absolutely cold and barbaric!" United States Ambassador to the UN, Elsa Sharpe protested.

"'That is nature, Ambassador Sharpe." Dr. Whiting said dispassionately. "If our visitors determine they must mount an assault on us from many dozens of light years away, at huge energy, material and societal costs, you can rest assured that they will get their money's worth. Enough to insure that they will never have to come back here again."

"I'm sorry, I just can't imagine an intelligent life form participating in planetary genocide," Secretary of the Treasury Drew Murray exclaimed. "This is not Star Wars! I think you are overstating the threat by a very wide margin."

"Maybe so, Drew. The natural world, however, is incredibly violent. If you look closely at your own backyard, you would see cruel and heartless behavior on an immense scale," she paused for a moment to lean forward in her overly comfortable office chair. "Survival of the fittest is a time-proven paradigm. Intelligent species are the ultimate expression of it. Dominant cultures remain dominant by exercising their power up to, and including, extermination. I'm sticking with Dr. Heischler's original assessment."

"Dr. Whiting, you know I genuinely respect your intellect," President Bertram said calmly, "I just can't subscribe to the notion that a highly advanced civilization would behave in such a feral fashion."

"It is not 'feral' if the goal is to preserve your species."

"Then, we agree to disagree, Sarah." Bertram said with a smile. Dr. Sarah Whiting was, arguably, the most intelligent member of the NSC and Bertram wanted her to stay there. The arguments she made were chilling... and even plausible, but Bertram simply could not convince himself that interstellar travellers might pose a genuine threat to American national security... or to the planet, for that matter.

The President then turned his attention to his military advisors. "General Talbot, now that you have been fully briefed, what is your opinion."

"Dangerous until proven otherwise, Mr. President," Talbot said sternly. "Their technological superiority makes us look like a skinny, bucktoothed nerd in a stadium full of prison bodybuilders."

Laughter erupted in the conference room. It was welcomed relief from the taxing, verbal exchange a few moments earlier. It also appeared that General Talbot was up to speed and in total command of his corner in the Situation Room.

"So, I assume you believe they are hostile, General Talbot?"

"I agree with much of what Dr. Whiting said, Mr. President. However, I won't go so far as to say we are in imminent danger. My biggest concern is how much time we will have to prepare if they do decide to attack us. My other concern is, if we are attacked, what weapons do we have that might be effective against them?"

"As I said last night, we are NOT going to provoke the aliens with a show of arms," Bertram replied firmly. "In fact, I intend to make it policy. I do not want anybody aiming anything at the aliens. I don't want them actively tracked and I damn sure don't want anybody at Project Cocheta whipping up some exotic weapon to shoot at them."

"There are some members of Congress that are going to insist that we have at least a Derringer in our pocket… just in case," Secretary of Homeland Security Beckman pointed out."

"Out of the question, Kate. If the aliens sniff a gun under the peace table, they will never trust us again. We will have lost any chance of a meaningful dialog with them."

General O'Neill leaned forward. "Mr. President, what if they have a gun under the table?"

"Again, the history of their interactions with us suggest they pose no significant threat."

"That is a bold wager with seven billion lives on the line, Mr. President."

"Stand down, General O'Neill!!!" General Talbot boomed as he quickly stood up. "That is the President of the United States you are talking to!" Everyone in the room was shocked by the fierceness of Talbot's voice.

"Hold on, General Talbot," Bertram said calmly. "It's OK. I'd rather hear a bare honest opinion than have a huge sunshine enema shoved up my ass."

"Excuse me, Mr. President," National Security Advisor Edmond Fisher interrupted, "we have a live feed from University Medical Center in Las Vegas. David, put it on screen one, please."

Almost instantly, a real-time video stream appeared on the monitor. There appeared to be a middle-aged physician in scrubs and white lab coat looking to his left as if waiting for someone to give him a sign to start talking. Though it was impossible to see it, the number of voices talking at the same time suggested several reporters and videographers were present in the room. After a few moments, the physician stepped to a UMC podium on his right and began to speak.

"Good afternoon. I'm Dr. Gary Conley, Chief of Cardiothoracic Surgery here at University Medical Center. Dr. Benjamin Harris Hanson passed away this afternoon at 2:27 PM, Pacific Time.

As many of you already know, Dr. Hanson arrived at our facility late last week, suffering from profound shock that lead to cardiopulmonary arrest. He underwent emergency surgery to stop the massive bleeding in his chest and remove a cancerous lung. He remained in a coma until 2:05 PM this afternoon. Dr. Hanson was able to briefly communicate with his family before his death.

Thank you."

The video screen flickered back to the standard, blue oval White House graphic.

"Wow, he managed to wake up just before his death," Press Secretary Arball said in a subdued tone. "My sources said he'd never regain consciousness. His brain was thought to be mush."

"The fat lady must have given him an extra chorus," CIA Director Brust said with as much reverence as he could muster. "You're only dead when you're good and dead."

"OK, OK! We'll all pitch-in and send flowers for the nice traitor and his nice traitor wife," Bertram sneered. "Let's get back on track, shall we? Abe?"

"Yes, Mr. President?" the Secretary of State answered.

"Do aliens from another planet fall within the diplomatic purview of the State Department?"

"I don't see why not."

"Good. I need you to start working on creating a State Department task force to interface with the aliens."

"Sir?"

"Let's make this a big deal, Abe," the President said enthusiastically. "America is going to extend the first human hands to our extraterrestrial visitors! Even if the aliens completely ignore us, we'll still get a lot of positive spin. Who knows? Maybe we can use it to shut the Russians and the Chinese up!"

"I think I can get something rolling fairly fast."

"Great! Add some desk space at Foggy Bottom and line up plenty of talent!" Bertram said with a grin. "I'll get you fully funded... I mean, Congress would never deny funding for the most important discovery in human history... nor will they turn down the photo ops! Larry, I'll need you to fish around the House and Senate sponsors for legislation to create a Department of Extraterrestrial Affairs or something. Miranda is already writing tonight's speech. I'll get with her on the new details as soon as we convene."

As American Presidents go, Gregory Bertram's first term would never stand out in history by virtue of his accomplishments. There simply wasn't any that could garner much more than a yawn. Bertram's oratory was predictable, pure party line and suffered from a singular inability to see reality beyond the politics. It proved to be a constant stumbling block to attacking problems with appropriate solutions. As one political observer once wrote: 'Bertram would be a masterful painter, if he ever decided to actually match the numbers with the right paint.'

In the last election, Bertram was terribly behind in every pre-election poll, even in spite of huge support by the media. He practically fell into the Oval Office because of his far more charismatic opponent's inability to explain the last-minute, October revelation of a love child he had in 1979 while married to his first wife. It was an astonishing, come-from-behind victory engineered by seasoned craftsmen that knew exactly how to exploit the new revelation. Bertram's opponent dropped 10 points in the polls almost overnight due to a brutal barrage of media spots that not only revealed his rival's indiscretion, but announced the name of the by then 33 year-old love child. Three days after the election, President-Elect Bertram and the world was informed of the tragic suicide of one Warren Foster, a seriously troubled and somewhat mentally-challenged man that never had a real father in his

life. After relentless badgering by the media, he fired a bullet into his skull. Collateral damage. The price of full-contact politics.

Only his mother and siblings shed any tears for him.

"General Talbot, I want you to personally inspect this Project Cocheta when it is feasible, and I want you to take General O'Neill with you," Bertram said in a somewhat darker tone. "I don't want any more bullshit coming out of there. Defensive research only. Non-lethal if possible. If Hanson's daughter is going to run that place, I want her on a short leash."

Both Generals, highly decorated and supremely competent American warriors at the very top of their food chains, were having difficulty keeping their teeth from shattering. Both were thinking the very same thing: 'Bertram was an ass, up to his eyeballs in his own ideological scat!' If the aliens prove to be hostile, America would be a hapless fish in a five gallon bucket. Donna Hanson? General O'Neill met with her a handful of times in Palmdale and was genuinely impressed by her engineering skills and the way she ran the Skunk Works. She earned her 'legend' status and was, without a doubt, a monumental force to be reckoned with. O'Neill briefly contemplated what a verbal, toe-to-toe Hanson/Bertram battle might be like. 'Knockout in the first round for the fierce little Hanson girl!'

"Mr. President, two things to consider," General Talbot said. "Hanson is, by an order of magnitude, the very best talent available. She may not agree to your stipulations. Second, there is often a very blurry line separating offensive and defensive weaponry."

"I'm not going to bend on this, Nathan," the President replied sternly. " No offensive weapons, period! If Hanson balks, we'll persuade her."

"Coercion won't work, Mr. President," O'Neill interjected. "I've met Dr. Hanson several times and I know her reputation. She will, politely, tell you to kiss her ass. She is already eligible for retirement and, from what I understand, she's done very well with her money."

"We'll get her onboard, Mr. President," General Talbot quickly promised. "Oren and I will pop in after she's had three or four weeks to settle in. We'll personally oversee weapons development, if there is any."

"That sounds reasonable to me."

President Bertram paused briefly to make sure he had tied all the loose knots.

"Excellent! Very productive session!" Bertram exclaimed with a smile. "Get a quick dinner. There is a lot of work to do before my address tonight."

Chapter 9

"Good evening, America." President Bertram began his historic speech to the citizens of the United States and the entire world, sitting in his executive chair amongst the familiar surroundings of the most powerful government office in the world.

"The last 24 hours have been, perhaps, one the most interesting and challenging in our nation's history. Yesterday evening, Senator Teresa Chandler made a surprise announcement that, for almost 70 years, beings from another world have been visiting our earth on a regular basis. She also revealed that our government has been operating an extremely classified facility to study the extraterrestrial technology and ascertain what their motives are for being here. This project was so secret that only a few presidents were made aware of it. Unfortunately, I was not one of them. I have, however, corrected that oversight."

With the help of certain key members of the National Security Council, I have been fully briefed on the project known as Cocheta. In short, it is a very remote research installation, built in the 1950s, that attempts to decipher extraterrestrial technology by examining wreckage left by mishaps. Senator Chandler's estranged husband, Dr. Benjamin Hanson, was the principle scientist at Project Cocheta and it appears that he was instrumental in discovering the details of 15 retired scientists murdered by project director Louis Hastings. Senator Chandler, Dr. Hanson and Dr. Tim Alexander successfully executed a complex plan to publicly expose the murders and implicate the project director's roll in them. Lastly, they informed the world of extraterrestrial interest in our planet through a rather clever bait and switch on live cable television.

Earlier this afternoon, Dr. Hanson passed away from lung cancer. The First Lady and I wish to extend our most sincere condolences to the Hanson family. May God be with them and comfort them in their time of need.

As President of the United States, I am duty-bound to enforce the laws of this great nation. Heinous crimes were committed by Cocheta Project Director Louis Hastings. I assure you, he will be prosecuted to the fullest extent of the law, as will the assassins hired by him. Other laws were broken as well. Most notable of which was the release of highly classified information to the world and our adversaries. I'm sure that we can all agree that nations must keep secret the details pertaining to their own safety. The Justice Department and the Senate will be looking very closely at the possibility that federal laws may have been broken during the unauthorized public disclosure of the classified Cocheta Project.

Project Cocheta has already created a diplomatic nightmare for the United States. Earlier today, the Russian government condemned Project Cocheta as a provocative act against their country. They have also called for an emergency session of the United Nations Security Council. The Chinese government also demanded that the United Nations address the issue. I have spoken to both leaders and asked them to voluntarily disclose their own Cocheta-like facilities to the world. Both declined my request and insisted they operate no facilities similar to Cocheta. Therefore, I will release detailed satellite photographs of the two Siberian facilities the Russians operate that are the functional equivalent of Project Cocheta. I will also release satellite photographs of the single Chinese facility. There are, to our knowledge, no other extraterrestrial research facilities in the world.

Project Cocheta was conceived during a very tense time in our nation's history. The standoff between America and the old Soviet Union was in its infancy and the specter of one country unlocking the secrets of so called 'flying saucers' before the other was the driving force behind a technology race deeply hidden by both countries. We recovered pieces from a crashed alien aircraft first. The Soviet Union recovered wreckage several months later and China, in the early 1960s. Each country began construction on well-hidden research facilities within a few years of their first recovery. In spite of nearly seven decades of intense study, very little has been duplicated by any side, though information from the Chinese facility is extremely spotty. There have been no breakthroughs that give a military edge to one country over another.

The fundamental question that we must answer is this: Why are the extraterrestrials here? Since there has been no contact between our two cultures and no

acts of aggression towards us over the last 60 years, we can only surmise that they are either friendly or indifferent. Either way, they do not appear to be a serious threat to our national security. Given this assessment, I am giving the following orders to the Defense Department: no military aircraft or missile battery will track, or fire upon, extraterrestrial aircraft. From this moment forward, Project Cocheta will refrain from developing offensive weaponry from technology gained through their research. Should the aliens decide to make diplomatic contact, Project Cocheta will immediately release all bodies in their possession to a designated envoy and all alien vehicles or hardware in our possession, intact or not, will be returned. In short, we will make all accommodations necessary to welcome our extraterrestrial neighbors.

I have directed Secretary of State Cochran to immediately establish a temporary Office of Extraterrestrial Affairs at the State Department. I will ask Congress to quickly create a permanent Department of Extraterrestrial Affairs so that we may establish a sound, mutually beneficial relationship between our worlds when the aliens decide to establish diplomatic contact. I cannot stress how important it is to be fully prepared for this eventuality.

As a country... as a planet, we must now adapt to a completely new paradigm. We are no longer alone in a very large universe. That is a sobering concept... scary and exciting at the same time! How will that affect us, our families... our planet in the long run? How will it affect our religions, our long held sacred belief systems? I believe that Americans will help define this new paradigm and lead our planet into a new age of global and interstellar enlightenment. I also believe that the human race must present itself as worthy to be considered a civilized planet. Perhaps the reason our extraterrestrial visitors have not made contact is because of the current state of our planet. Earth is plagued by violence. For as long as there have been people on earth, there has been brutality. We must make that a thing of the past if we are to become part of what I believe to be a civilized universe.

I ask Congress, the American people and the world to join hands and help abolish the evils in our culture. In the coming weeks I will be proposing a number of legislative initiatives to curb the rampant violence on our streets and in our homes, the first of which will be a ban on all privately owned firearms. I realize that this will be extremely controversial, but it is necessary to prove that we are serious about reducing the amount of murder and mayhem in our country. For our government's part in reducing violence, I will be directing the Department of Energy to have every last nuclear weapon in our stockpile dismantled. All other weapons of mass destruction in our stockpile will be decommissioned or rendered inert.

Another initiative will be to greatly reduce greenhouse gas emissions and require every citizen to drastically reduce their carbon footprint. While this will be painfully difficult and require much sacrifice from individuals, corporations and government, the end result will be a planet less toxic and more inviting to our extraterrestrial visitors. I believe one way to achieve a cleaner environment is to concentrate our population into urban centers and let nature reclaim the countryside without human presence and intervention. These urban centers will be interconnected by superhighways that avoid environmentally sensitive areas. This is, obviously, a very long-term project.

Lastly, we must make giant strides to curb the ever-growing world population. There are now seven billion people on earth. Eventually, the world's population will become so large that it imposes a much more dangerous threat to the earth's environment than it currently does now. I believe that conscientious Americans understand the dilemma we face and will lead the way in embracing measures that limit the number of children they can have. Through these measures, the population of earth will eventually reach a much more manageable 500 million individuals.

In closing, I would like to say that I believe the citizens of the United States of America are more than capable of handling the difficulties and sacrifices that lay ahead. Americans love challenges. We have always loved challenges. We thrive on challenges! We will face this one and come out of it with, what I hope to be, a strong alliance with another world."

President Bertram looked very comfortable and confident as he began his closing statement.

"God bless you, the wonderful, hard-working citizens of the United States of America... and God bless this country as she enters the exciting, uncharted waters of the future."

Chapter 10

The media response to President Bertram's speech fell right along ideological lines. Left-leaning news sources praised the president's speech as inspiring and forward thinking. They were quick to point out the boldness of his environmental and social agendas in preparing for a new age and a new understanding of our universe. They were quick to endorse the United Nations 'Agenda 21' initiative that Bertram referenced when speaking about creating 'population centers' and allowing the countryside to return to its natural state.

"I believe that President Bertram is on the right track to preparing our world for alien and human coexistence," Senator Lydia Woodward from California stated during the post-speech analysis. "Humans have damaged our planet to the point that I can understand why they haven't contacted us in the first place. We need to put all of our effort into saving the planet."

Right-leaning news sources condemned much of the speech as "radical and unconstitutional," with provisions that would drastically curtail personal freedoms, including the right to own land and firearms. Many complained that the President's suggestions were wholly premature given that the aliens have never bothered to contact any government on earth.

"Why in the world would we make these crazy and hugely expensive changes that Bertram proposes if the aliens don't seem to be interested in having even so much as a chat with us over lunch?" Florida Congressman Chet Palmer asked. "It seems like the President wants us to roll on our back in submission before we get a chance to figure out what their intentions really are!"

The majority of the rest of the world's media, however, was solidly in favor of Bertram's proposals, which did not come as a surprise to anyone. On the surface, Bertram was a cookie-cutter Democrat, faithfully towing the party's agenda. Below the surface was devout globalist with rigid political leanings rooted in early 20th century progressivism. This moment in history was his opportunity to do something no other American President had been able to do: negate certain pesky provisions of the Constitution in order to force America into a new, enviro-centric world order where resources were "shared," carbon is the bastard child of the periodic table and guns only in the hands of police and military. Of course, it would take ratified treaties to force America to give up some of her freedoms, but pounding the extraterrestrial angle would be a novel, and hopefully effective approach to demand the world, America specifically, to spiff itself up.

"Let me make this perfectly clear to President Bertram:" House Majority Leader Lanny Gaines began, speaking on a cable network, post-speech wrap-up. "There will be no appropriations bills passed by this House of Representatives that will dilute or scuttle ANY part of our precious Constitution. Not while I'm drawing a breath!"

Within a half hour, White House Press Secretary responded to Congressman Gaines, stating that the President has no intention of "...throwing the Bill of Rights away," but America must adapt to the new world we now live in."

The blogosphere was sizzling with both vicious and thoughtful posts aimed at opposing opinions. Many believed that is was time for humans to clean their act and planet up, only to be blasted by others who believed that Bertram was a naive fool for suggesting that Americans needed to be disarmed and stuffed into UN-mandated supercities. Young and old, educated and the uneducated, voiced their opinions on what would become a historic surge of worldwide internet traffic for a 24 hour period.

Chapter 11

Early Tuesday morning, Senator Majority Leader Harold Melana held a private meeting with his staff and strategists to discuss the lofty business of determining if Senator Hanson had broken any laws in exposing Project Cocheta. In reality, it was more like generals plotting the capture of enemy territory. Every proposed detail of the stratagem was weighed for political impact. The sure-fire 'good ones' would be published in talking points and repeated often by surrogates and robotic media hacks throughout the coming days. The mediocre ones would be sent up as trial balloons to see if they were worth repeating or tossed into 'File 13.'

There was, however, a tangible danger in attacking the Oklahoma Senator: She had very high approval ratings to begin with and her surprise speech, coupled with the loss of her husband, gave Senator Hanson even higher ratings. The pitfalls were so obvious that one of the strategists suggested that Melana abandon any attempt at character assassination, concentrating strictly on the law and in the end, let her off with a public hand slap.

Melana would have none of that.

"I want her taken down!" he almost yelled. "This bitch is their biggest gun right now and I want her blown out of the water. I don't care how it's done. Everyone has a trunk full of regrets and misdeeds. Find 'em!"

Looks were exchanged around the table. Some were wondering how they were going to tell their wives that he would be participating in destroying the poor lady who just lost her husband.

"Harold, we'll dig up something on her," Melana's Chief Political Advisor, Andrew Pearce promised, "and if not, we'll just get creative."

"I also want the Senate Hearings to start on Friday, Andy."

"Why so soon? Isn't that the day after her husband's funeral?"

"Yes... and why are we supposed to give a damn?"

"It could be construed as, well... insensitive and perhaps even mean. It might look as though you are intentionally adding insult to injury."

"I don't care. She's a hick from a hick state. Her very presence in the Senate is an insult and a hindrance to the America we're trying to build. We start on Friday come hell or high water."

"It's your call, boss."

"Yes it is, and time is wasting away, people," Melana said with a growl. "We're not going to get anything done sitting on our asses. Get me air time and interviews on every outlet you can. Bertram has set it up and it is our job to slam dunk it. We've got elections to win. I don't want the opposition to know what hit them!"

Chapter 12

"Dr. Cooke, as a distinguished sociologist, I'm sure our audience would be interested in your take on President Bertram's proposals to move people into mega-cities and reduce the world's population to 500 million people," began Mona Blankenship's second hour of her very popular, syndicated radio talk show, 'Blankenship On Topic.'

"Wow, Mona, where do I start?" Frederick Cooke, PhD replied through the phone-distorted connection. "President Bertram is obviously referring to the United Nations Agenda 21 'Sustainable Growth' initiative to forcibly move people into nodes of concentrated urban areas so that the newly-created, restricted access rural areas can return to their natural ecology. Reducing the world's population to 500 million is engraved on a strange, granite monument erected on a small Georgia farm called the 'Guidestone'. Some believe modern descendants of the Rosicrucian Order were behind the monument's erection. I don't think anybody really knows for sure except the people who built it. Other groups and individuals have mentioned the 500 million limit, including NASA. That means that, somehow, we must trim off 6.5 billion people from the planet and restrict millions of people from having children for decades."

"How on earth would we do that?"

"It obviously cannot be done overnight, nor can it be done voluntarily. We would need to forcefully sterilize many millions of people every year then wait decades for them to die off."

"Oh my God! That's awful! Millions and millions of couples forced to be childless and never live to see grandchildren?"

"That would be one of the terrible consequences," Cooke said. "To implement and enforce it would require forced sterilization of boys and girls before child bearing age. Putting the problem into mathematical form, it would take 140 years of zero population growth and sterilizing 100 million people per year for the first 65 years to reach 500 million."

"So, realistically, the 500 Million population cannot be achieved without extreme measures."

"That's correct. It would take a well-coordinated, single world government to implement it."

"Frightening, to say the least. I can't see Americans going along with this."

"I can't either, Mona, but that doesn't mean it won't be forced upon us."

"Let us hope not. That is not a future I want to live in!" she paused to drink from her water bottle. "Tell me about Bertram's proposed population centers."

"Well, back in the 90s, the UN crafted a global plan for the management of earth's environment and resources. They eventually nicknamed it Agenda 21. My professional interest in Agenda 21 is the population centers the UN intends to create. First, all living areas will be built as multiple family apartment complexes stacked vertically to conserve space. Second, individual dwellings will be very compact and space efficient. No game rooms, guest rooms or extra bathrooms. No second home in the mountains, either. Agenda 21 forbids the private ownership of land."

"No land ownership?"

"None at all. The UN believes that if there is even one person on earth who can't afford to own land, nobody can own land."

"There is a lot of politics in play here, but you are a sociologist. What is your angle?"

"The idea is utter foolishness," Cooke said sternly. "It would lead to more crime, homicides, rape, psychotic and neurotic behavior."

"How is that?"

"A concept known as 'behavioral sink.' The tighter you pack animals together, the more dysfunctional they become. I believe that concept also applies to humans."

"Did you come up with the idea?"

Cooke chuckled, "No, not me, an ethologist, someone who studies animal behavior, named Dr. John Calhoun. He spent decades studying the effects of population congestion on rats."

"What kind of effects are we talking about?"

"In female rats, premature birth, infant mortality as high as 96 percent, perinatal maternal death and inadequate maternal attention to her litters. In males, reclusive behavior, sexual deviance, cannibalism and hyperactivity. The rat populations, as a whole, became socially disturbed. Unprovoked acts of violence erupted and reproduction eventually stopped. Not long after that, the rat society imploded."

"So, are you are saying that people who live in places like here, in good ol' New York, are a lot more crazy than those in Gaterswamp, Louisiana?"

"Well, that is a loaded question! Let me answer you by saying this: year after year, crime in urban areas averages three to four times higher than rural areas. Murder rates? Up to 13 times higher than in rural areas. Is there a correlation between urban overcrowding and crime? Sure seems like it."

"Disturbing statistics, Dr. Cooke!" Blankenship replied. She had never come across the term 'behavioral sink,' but there was something familiar about the concept. A movie or book or something. "If I, say... spread New York City over the entire state of New York, you're saying that drivers wouldn't give me the finger as often?"

Dr. Cooke laughed out loud. "Probably, but I'm not sure that there are statistics for vulgar hand signals."

"Dr. Cooke, you believe the President's initiative will lead to increased crime and mental illness?"

"Yes, I do," Cook replied confidently. "I believe there is ample evidence to suggest that what the UN and President Bertram are proposing will only create misery, violence and eventually, societal decay and implosion. I also believe that this initiative has more to do about power and control than it does about saving the planet or welcoming aliens."

"How so?"

"The people behind it are corrupt," Cooke replied flatly. "The UN has a long history of corruption. If I were taking my son to a tour of the UN, I'd sew his pockets shut before entering the building. Agenda 21 is a Robin Hood scam. Wealth redistribution, nothing more. Misery, however, will be equally shared by all."

"You're painting a very bleak future, Dr. Cooke."

"That is my intention."

"One last thing before we close out this segment: You're an accomplished sociologist. What can we expect from the aliens?"

"Well, I might have a good answer for you if I had a PhD in exo-sociology, but I don't know of any universities on earth that offer a doctorate in that."

"That's funny!" Blankenship replied, almost snorting hot coffee out her nose. "Maybe give our audience your best earthly guess."

"OK, they are obviously intelligent and appear to be very technologically advanced. I'm somewhat concerned that they have not made contact with us. In fact, they seem to be completely indifferent. What bothers me about that is how they might view humans. If they view us as insignificant, then they may never contact us. If they somehow view us as a threat, then we could be in trouble. Who knows, they might finish what they are doing and disappear forever. To be honest, I have no idea what they are up to, but my gut feeling is that they are benign."

"Well, that's all for this segment. Thank you, Dr. Cooke, for joining us this morning."

"Thank you for having me on your show, Ms. Blankenship."

"Coming up next on Blankenship on Topic, Senator Chandler - Patriot or Traitor. Our guest will be Andrew Pearce, Chief Political Advisor to Senate Majority Leader Harold Melana."

Chapter 13

"Nurse, could I please have a look at Mr. Hasting's chart?" asked the somewhat short and thick-spectacled man wearing a lab coat over a plain blue shirt and solid maroon necktie.

"And who are you?" Orthopedic Ward Charge Nurse Amanda Conway asked.

"Oh, I'm sorry," the mildly frazzeled-appearing, middle-aged man said while reaching into his labcoat pocket for an innocuous-looking badge that sported his name and Southern Nevada Orthopedics. "I'm Matt Specter, Dr. Snider's new PA. He asked me to stop by and check on Mr. Hastings and get familiar with his case."

"Kind of late, isn't it?"

"We have had a very busy day. Non-stop and barely enough time to eat," William Wallace Frick replied, feigning perfect exasperation.

"Here you go, Matt," handing the chart to him. "You'll find him to be uh... hmmmm... a very pleasant man." She said with tone that suggested the exact opposite. Two other nurses nearby started to chuckle.

"So... You're telling me he's an asshole."

The nurses started to laugh as loud as they dared. "You are going to fit in here real nice, Matt!"

"Thank you!" Frick said with a completely fake smile. Having easily negotiated his first potential obstacle, the second would be even easier as the Vegas Police officer guarding Louis Hastings' door was hand-picked for the assignment. With barely a nod, William Wallace Frick entered the room holding his prey.

"Hello, Mr. Hastings. I'm Matt Specter, Dr. Snider's PA. He wanted me to check on you this evening. See if you needed anything."

"Yeah, I need something! The fucking nurses won't give me anything for pain until midnight! They come in here and ask me how bad I'm hurting, then tell me it's too early to get more! I've got two fucking rods in my legs, cuts and bruises everywhere… The only thing that doesn't hurt is my damn hair! None of the nurses or doctors around here give a shit! None of them!"

"OK, I understand your frustration, Mr. Hastings. Dr. Snider said I could increase the rate on your pain pump and I'll give you an extra dose of morphine. I have it right here in my pocket."

"Well, what the hell are you waiting for?"

"Certainly, Mr. Hastings."

Frick retrieved two syringes from his lab coat pocket, a 5cc syringe full of a clear liquid mislabeled with a blue 'morphine' sticker. The actual medication was succinylcholine chloride, an extremely fast-acting paralyzing agent in a concentration ten times greater than normally used in the operating room. The second was a 10cc syringe, also filled with a clear liquid and mislabeled with a 'Saline' sticker. It actually contained pancuronium bromide, a relatively long-acting paralyzing agent. Frick exposed the intravenous port nearest to Hastings right hand, wiped it with an alcohol pad and quickly injected the 'morphine.'

"This might burn a little bit as it goes in."

Before Hastings could protest the mild burning in his right hand due to the rapid speed of injection, his heart pumped enough succinylcholine to the muscles to begin a massive wave of hard and chaotic muscle contractions affecting every skeletal muscle in his body. Hasting's pain was instantaneously excruciating. More muscle contractions swept over his surgical sites on both legs, his deep body bruises, his muscle strains, his cuts and abrasions… All were flooding his brain with vicious, searing pain. Frick waited for the fasciculations to subside, then injected the pancuronium bromide, the coup de grâce that insured Louis Hastings would never take another breath.

Through the unbearable pain, there was something else Hastings started to notice. He began to feel as if he were holding his breath, yet he didn't seem to

have the ability to stop doing it! Panic quickly replaced pain in the forefront of his mind. As hard as he tried, he couldn't take a breath, nor could he open his eyes. He tried desperately to scream, but nothing came out... Not a damn muscle in his body was working!

Then, someone opened his eyes for him. Even with the double vision caused by the paralyzing agents, he could tell that it was the PA opening them. But, he wasn't really a PA, was he? He was an assassin, but why wasn't he leaving the room? Hastings panic was now full force. He was begging his body to take a breath while his killer continued to stare at him. As the carbon dioxide levels in Hastings blood increased, his ability to fight the coming darkness diminished.

The last thing he saw before unconsciousness and death were the creepy, piercing eyes of William Wallace Frick.

* * *

Frick was somewhat disappointed with his latest kill. The paralyzing agents caused a disconjugate gaze of Hasting's eyes and made it harder to see the look he craved for. Still, while not perfect, he saw enough to be satisfied. Frick positioned Hastings' body to face away from the door then turned the lights out so that a casual peek inside the room would reveal nothing out of place.

Frick monitored Hastings carotid pulse until it ceased to exist, then casually left the guarded room and handed Hastings' chart back to Nurse Conway.

"Did you enjoy your little chat with Mr. Hastings?"

"Why, yes! He's very charming and polite," he replied with a wink. "I've got a brother-in-law just like him."

"I'll pray for your sister!"

"Thanks!" Frick replied with a faux chuckle. He was now ready to add polish to an already successful assassination. "Oh, by the way, Mr. Hastings was, uh... complaining about being awakened. I believe he said, 'all fucking night' for vital signs. I got the impression that people coming in and out of his room is what bothers him the most. If he doesn't call you for pain meds, I'd just as soon not poke the bear and leave him alone. He's got a decent background rate on his PCA and I'm OK with changing his vital signs to Q12. Let's make the next one at 5 AM. Hopefully, that will make things a bit more pleasant for everybody."

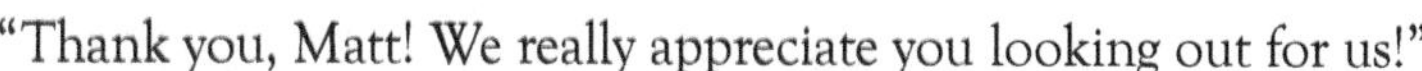

"Thank you, Matt! We really appreciate you looking out for us!"

"It's the least I can do. I'll see you again tomorrow morning around seven AM or so."

Ten minutes later, William Wallace Frick was on the road and $100,000 richer. He would sleep very well in his tower suite at the Bellagio. Very well, indeed.

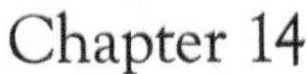

Chapter 14

At 8:30 AM EST, CNN was the first to break the news that Louis Hastings was dead.

"It has now been confirmed that the former project director of the controversial, top secret Cocheta installation in Canada, Louis Hastings, has died from injuries sustained during a high speed car crash south of Las Vegas. Hastings was indicted earlier this week on 15 counts of first degree murder in the deaths of former Project Cocheta scientists."

"According to University Medical Center spokeswoman, Marissa Whitney, Louis Hastings was found unconscious and unresponsive in his hospital bed at 5 AM local time. Attempts to resuscitate him were unsuccessful and he was pronounced dead at 5:25 AM. A massive blood clot to his lungs is considered to be the most likely cause of his death."

"In a related story out of Miami, Oklahoma, funeral services will be held today for Dr. Benjamin Hanson, Project Cocheta scientist and estranged husband of embattled Oklahoma Senator Teresa Hanson. The service will take place at 4:30 PM, Eastern Standard Time. CNN will have live coverage of the Hanson Funeral starting at 4:00 PM. We will also be covering the live Senate Hearings on the controversial Project Cocheta beginning on Friday Morning."

Chapter 15

"I had a hunch you might be here," Donna Hanson quietly announced as she sat down next to her mother on the ages-old park bench that was her parents' favorite place to hold hands.

"My disguise must be pretty weak," she replied with a grin that didn't quite cover her profound melancholy.

"No, it's pretty good, Mom. You ditched your security people, didn't you?"

"I'm not that clever, sweetheart. It's hard to spot them, but they're here."

"I guess you already heard the news about Louis Hastings."

"Yes... I did."

"How do you feel about it?"

"I'm not sure how to feel about it, sweetie," she replied without emotion. "He tortured your dad, he tortured us, he killed innocent people... part of me hopes he is languishing in hell, part of me feels ashamed for thinking that way."

"All those years lost, Mom. We'll never get them back."

"I know..." Teresa replied, lowering her head. "I know."

Donna was not sure how to comfort her mother. How do you comfort someone that has lost so much? How do you comfort someone when you desperately need comfort for yourself? How do you give comfort without sounding shallow or

cliché? The only thing Donna could come up with was distraction.

"By the way, how did you manage to avoid the press and all the crazies? Northeast Oklahoma is crawling with them!"

"I put on these old blue jeans and cowboy hat, caked on the makeup, practically crawled all the way to Edna's house and stole her car," she said without a hint of remorse. "High school friends for forty years and she still hides her keys in the same place."

Donna giggled a bit at the thought of her mom, a United States Senator, boosting a car for some much needed 'me' time.

"Do they throw Senators in jail for that?"

"Not if you're a member of Club Washington, Dr. Hanson," she said with detectable disdain.

Donna shook her head and decided a pleasant memory was in order. "I really love this place, Mom," she said, moving closer to her. "I remember that every time we came to visit Mimi and Pa Hanson and Nammie and Grandad Chandler, you and dad would take us here. We would climb up and down inside that old playground rocket ship while you and dad would sit on this bench and cuddle like teenagers."

Teresa allowed herself another grin. "Your daddy and I always felt like lovesick teenagers when we were together. He was always affectionate and attentive. Very gentle with me and you kids. I did notice some changes in your dad's mood when Captain Brogan retired and Louis Hastings took over, but he never let it affect our home life," she paused for a moment to compose herself for the next sentence. "Your dad meant the world to me, Donna. I was the luckiest woman on earth to have you kids and your daddy in my life."

"How much did you know of dad's work?"

"Almost nothing until Dr. Alexander came to visit."

"That must have been quite a shock, Mom."

"You have no idea, Punkin," she said with a long sigh. "It was the first I heard from your dad in almost 20 years. All I ever really knew about his career was that he worked on defense projects for the government. When your brother and I were forced to leave Las Vegas without any explanation, told to file for divorce and take back my maiden name… I knew your dad was in serious trouble and believed we would be in grave danger if we tried to stay. Now we know how ruthless Hastings really was. Your dad loved us so much he sacrificed his ability to be a part of our lives… and I'm certain we're alive today because of his selflessness."

Donna wiped tears from her cheeks as memories of her father poured forth. She never really understood the mysterious and traumatic breakup of her family so long ago, and even though she was 22 at the time and working on her masters degree at Ann Arbor, the news had a profound effect on her. As far as Donna Hanson knew, mom and dad had a solid marriage. They seemed happy, and to young Donna's frequent embarrassment, they were almost constantly affectionate at home and only slightly less so in public. It was a phone call from her distraught mother one frigid day in 1992 that taught her even the most sound of marriages could be burned to the ground overnight. What chilled her to the bone was her mother's plea for her to never speak of her father outside of immediate family and then, only in private. It was a devastating psychological blow for Donna Hanson. One that would leave her with doubts about her father and her future relationships with men.

If Ben Hanson had a favorite child, nobody knew which one it was. He was a dedicated father and spent countless hours playing with all three of his little ones. The one child most like him, however, was Donna. Teresa often commented that Donna was a female Ben Hanson with her mother's spunk. Most would say it was a fairly accurate assessment. Even from a very early age, it was clear Donna Hanson would possess an intellect as powerful as her father had. By the time she was in high school, with supplemental tutoring to keep her challenged, she was solving ultra complex problems faster than her dad. That pleased Ben Hanson to no end! It was during her junior year of high school that she announced her desire to pursue a doctorate in aerospace engineering. Reliable, eyewitness accounts reported by his colleagues at Project Cocheta had Ben Hanson smiling non-stop for well over a month.

Like her father before her, Donna Hanson became a much sought after talent coveted by most every aerospace company on the planet. In the end, she chose her father's dream job: Lockheed-Martin's Skunk Works, Plant 42 in Palmdale, California. Her contributions in airfoil design, stealth technology integration and compartmentalized assembly techniques were hot topics in places where such things could only be discussed in secret. Within 10 years, Donna Hanson became Chief

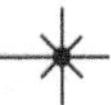

Engineer of the Skunk Works and a highly-respected pioneer in her field.

"Mom."

"Yes, sweetie."

"Now that I know what dad really did for a living... I mean, I know it's silly, but... did he pull strings to get me into the Skunk Works?"

"My sweet Dr. Hanson, I really couldn't tell you for sure, one way or the other. I do know that daddy was your biggest fan and he loved you more than you can ever know. He believed in you and your talents so completely that I seriously doubt he ever felt the need to pull strings. We always let you kids succeed and fail on your own so you could learn from mistakes and build upon successes," she replied, wrapping an arm around her not-so-little and middle-aged daughters' shoulder for a much needed, reassuring hug. Even brilliant, accomplished professionals can have moments of insecurity.

"I'm sorry, Mom," she said sheepishly. "It really was a silly question."

"It's OK, sweetheart," she said softly. "You're so much like your daddy."

Teresa Hanson pulled her daughter even closer as a powerful wave of sorrow swept over her. The road ahead was going to be, at the very best, treacherous. At the behest of their handlers, the press and the left spectrum of the blogosphere, along with a surprising number of those on the right, were already shredding her for divulging national security secrets, even though it was a routine practice for self-serving politicians and bureaucrats to do precisely that. Senator Melana publicly expressed his condolences to the Hanson family within an hour of their loss, then immediately began calling for a Senate investigation into Project Cocheta and the manner in which a 65 year-old state secret was revealed by its most respected scientist and his ex-wife, a very popular United States Senator.

The writing was already on the wall. The coming hearings would be yet another grand Washington circus, complete with sideshows and political blustering to a degree never before seen in a town where bloviating is a skillfully practiced art form. It would be about assigning blame and gaining political advantage in an election year, not the extraordinary revelation that extraterrestrial beings were visiting earth and what that may mean to the entire human race. It was almost as if the aliens were an insignificant oddity only loosely attached to the main event. Not surprising to those exposed to Washington culture for more than ten minutes.

The players inside the Beltway only saw the world through glasses that filtered out everything but politics. Angles, spin, power plays… it was a very grand and lucrative sport.

Senator Hanson was certain she could handle the poison-tipped spears thrown at her, but what about her family? What about the memory of her beloved Ben's legacy of life-robbing sacrifices for family and country? What about her only daughter? If the rumors about her were true, Donna would be tossed into the fire storm as well. Tears welled up in her eyes and flowed down her cheeks. All she could see was pain and suffering for everyone dear to her, and felt completely powerless to stop it.

"Mom, are you going to be OK?" Donna asked at the sight of her mother's profound change in countenance.

"Yes, sweetie. I have no choice," she replied with a steadily increasing waiver to her voice. "I need to put your daddy to rest… oh, God… I miss him so much!"

Teresa Hanson crumpled onto her daughter's shoulder and sobbed. Her grief was unrelenting and overpowering. In a few short hours, she would endure her soul mates' funeral, then her Only-est, the love of her life, would lie alone in a cold, dark grave.

It was a bleak and heartless reality she knew would haunt her the rest of her life.

After several minutes of heart wrenching tears flooding the faces of both women, Teresa Hanson found enough composure to speak to her daughter again.

"Donna… Sweetheart."

"Yes, Mom?" she replied while desperately trying to reign in her torrent of emotions.

"I wasn't sure about when I should give this to you," she said with noticeable hesitancy in her voice, "but I feel like you need to see it now. I don't want you blind-sided before you get a chance to read it. It's…" She paused momentarily to regroup her faltering composure, "a letter to you from your dad."

Donna froze, speechless and uncertain how to react to what her mother just said. Teresa saw the powerful change in her daughter's countenance and quickly pressed on.

"Dr. Alexander gave it to me to pass along to you," she said, new tears streaming down her cheeks. "I think I know what it is about, and if I'm right, you need to be prepared to make some very important decisions. It is for your eyes only, sweetheart. Whatever you decide to do, I will support you 100 percent. I'm going to head back to the house now and finish getting ready for daddy's funeral."

Senator Hanson reached into her small handbag and retrieved a plain white envelope with her daughter's name written by hand on the front and gently handed it to her daughter. Donna instantly recognized her father's handwriting from long ago. She stared at the envelope in her hands for what seemed to be hours. She was holding a message from her beloved father, whom she had not seen in twenty years, and not three days earlier, witnessed his final moments on earth. She wondered if the flow of tears would ever stop.

"Mom?" Donna asked with a wavering and barely audible voice. "I can't open it without you here."

"I understand, sweetheart. I'll stay here for as long as you need me to."

Donna mustered a feeble smile in return and carefully, as if holding a newborn kitten, opened the envelope and unfolded the message inside.

"*My Sweet Donna,*

Since you are reading this, I am either incarcerated and dying from lung cancer or at peace in the Lords' arms. It had always been my dream to live a long and happy life with your mother, my beautiful children and grandchildren, but I made a terrible mistake by underestimating an evil man in my midst and it cost me the only things I truly treasured in life: my family. For the safety of your mother and little brother, for all of you, I had to distance myself from you. It was the most agonizingly painful thing I have ever endured, but knowing you would not be harmed was worth every moment of separation. I am truly sorry for the way things turned out. Please forgive me!

Dr. Donna Michelle Hanson, I could not be more proud of you! Not only have you become a fine young woman, your genius, hard work and dedication have made you one of the most accomplished and respected engineers in the world. Lockheed-Martin was very wise and fortunate to snatch you up when your training was complete! I have followed your work very closely, read every peer-reviewed article you wrote and have quite a collection of your presentations and lectures on YouTube. You taught your old man a great many new things that helped me become a much better scientist and engineer. Thank you!

Sweetheart, the bulk of the aerospace community looks up to you with great respect, and with that degree of respect, it is only natural to attract people who have very special needs. By now, you already know what I really did for the government. I had the pleasure of working with some of the most brilliant minds on earth, each dedicated to unraveling the mysteries of extraterrestrial technology to both advance scientific knowledge and prepare a defense should the aliens prove to have hostile intent. Because the alien technology is so far ahead of our own, perhaps many thousands of years ahead, the reverse engineering is extraordinarily tedious, yielding very little for the effort and money spent. This critical research has been ongoing for 65 years and it must be continued as it might be the only hope our planet has of survival.

I cannot be certain of this, but I believe those who oversee Project Cocheta will relieve the current Project Director, Louis Hastings, and offer the position to you. I believe this because you are the natural choice. You have the perfect combination of brilliant scientific intellect with superb, CEO-level managerial skills. I seriously doubt there is another soul in the country, perhaps the planet, that can stand toe-to-toe with you. I expect the emissary will approach you much sooner than later.

I cannot, and will not, ask you to take this position. This must be your decision and only your decision. You already have a spectacular career at the Skunk Works and contributed much to your country's safety. Nobody would fault you for staying in Palmdale. If you do decide to take the Project Director position, insist that you run the show completely and pick your staff as you see fit. Dr. Steven McLachlan is a valuable resource and a dear friend of mine. He will take you under his wing and treat you like his own daughter. Lastly, recruit Dr. Alexander. He is a wonderful man, honest, brave and exceedingly intelligent. He would make a superb addition to the research staff as Deputy Director!

Donna, I can't possibly tell you how much I love and miss you. No man should ever be pried and separated from his children and their mother. There is no greater pain that a man, a father, can endure. Eventually, we will all be together, my sweet angel, and never again will we have to part from each other. Until then, take care of your mother and your brothers. They will need you in the coming weeks.

With all my love,

Daddy

Donna folded the letter as gently as she opened it. There were no more tears to cry. Her beloved father had just spoken to her from the grave. She felt as if she were a beaten puppy, waiting... resigned to the absolute certainty that more assaults lay ahead. She rested her head on her mother's shoulder. Both said nothing for what seemed like hours.

"Mom... what am I going to do?"

"What you have always done, sweetheart... excel."

Chapter 16

Ottawa County's child genius would be laid to eternal rest in a cemetery across the street from the church where he and a future United States Senator were married over 40 years earlier. It was a warm Thursday in early April, with billowing thunderstorm clouds gathering to the northwest and west. In the spring, severe weather was all too common in this part of the United States and Senator Hanson prayed feverishly for the threatening weather to stay away long enough for her and her family to bury her one and Only-est.

Sadly, another storm was brewing that would add a circus-like quality to a profoundly painful day.

Overnight, Ottawa County Oklahoma became the temporary focus of world attention, but it wasn't the kind of attention that most people in the rural county were interested in. A day after the news of Dr. Hanson's death and the nature of his work with the government released, his private funeral arrangements were leaked to the press by an unidentified local 'insider.' Within hours, the area was inundated with reporters, politicians and throngs of the simply curious. There were scores of the very odd and eccentric, attracted to the burgeoning circus like moths to a bright street lamp. Anything 'Hanson' was equivalent to a metaphysical gold mine. In short order, Ben and Teresa's sleepy little hometown of Commerce Oklahoma became an instant, if only temporary, Mecca for every imaginable variety of kook and attention seeker.

Only a small minority of the weirdo fringe were flamboyant enough to get any real attention from the steadily growing contingent of press. There was the predictable presence of every rank from Starfleet Academy, from freshman Plebes to

Senior Cadets, Ensigns to Admirals. There were people dressed as Wookies, Jedi's, Terminators and, of course, green aliens with bulbous heads and large black eyes. One of the strangest, and possibly the most delusional character, was a bearded gentleman walking through downtown Miami, dressed in a replica of first century Judaic tunic and mantle, telling the random passersby that they had the "eyes of Jesus." The fairground parking lot soon became ground zero for the fringe groups, including professional protesters there to humiliate the Senator and an infamous cult known for their brutal callousness at solemn occasions. Fortunately, policeman, firefighters, paramedics and other service minded individuals from around northeast Oklahoma, southeast Kansas and southwest Missouri were volunteering to help keep the peace and give the Hanson family and their friends a chance at a proper, solemn funeral without drama and disruptive sideshows.

The local police departments wanted to establish a 100 yard minimum buffer zone between curious onlookers, the local and national media, and those who were there to genuinely pay last respects to Benjamin Harris Hanson. A Walmart adjacent to the south fence of the church property made it difficult to establish a full 100 yards, but after a discussion between the Miami Police Department and Walmart management, the southern buffer would be allowed to extend into the northern third of the parking lot for the duration of the service. Predictably, the press and the fringe groups were outraged at the restrictions and a multitude of cell phone calls were made to lawyers, political allies and the national press. To a man and woman, the local police and volunteers vowed that the line would not be breached. Ben and Teresa Hanson were family and they felt obligated to ensure that Ben's funeral would not become tragedy heaped upon tragedy.

By 2:30 PM, the Sacred Heart Catholic Church was secure. Volunteer vehicles, police cars and semi trucks were lining vulnerable sections of the perimeter and the Welch State Bank had graciously agreed to close their doors for the duration of the funeral and become part of the buffer zone. When 26th Avenue Northwest was barricaded at 2:35, family members, friends, schoolmates, coworkers and supportive politicians were allowed to take seats in the relatively small church. Teresa, her children, grandchildren, their closest friends, Dr. Tim Alexander, Kevin Loeffler, and Hannah Simpson arrived at 2:45 and took reserved seats in the front.

The security perimeter held fast with few real incidents before the 3:00 PM Mass. The majority of onlookers were from Ottawa and adjacent Oklahoma, Kansas and Missouri counties. The fringe elements were vastly outnumbered by local citizens and sightseers, which provided the hoped for effect of protecting the mourners from taunts, slurs and riotous behavior. The only significant incident involved the small, heartless cult bent on disturbing the blasphemous Hanson funeral. Five local veterans took it upon themselves to "give those freaks a lesson in manners." Each were tossed in jail for the various bruises, fractures and dental injuries leveled on the dozen or so cult members. Each stated they would gladly spend whatever time in the Ottawa County jail they were sentenced to. However, it didn't seem likely that any of them would spend real time in jail because dozens of witnesses were absolutely certain that each cult member threw the first punches.

* * *

"Once again, greetings to all on this very somber occasion." Monsignor Robert Collier announced as he began the funeral homily. "Benjamin Harris Hanson... a loving son, a loving husband, a loving father and grandfather. Tireless seeker of knowlege that might serve and protect his fellow man. Patriot... that is how the world should remember the gentle soul we celebrate today.

I grew up with Ben and Teresa right here in Commerce. We went to the same school, we were in the same grade... well, we were in the same grade for a little while. Ben had this habit of jumping grades every few years and making the rest of us look dumb." He paused for a moment for the chuckles to subside.

"We also attended this very church together. I genuinely admired Ben because, in spite of his incredible genius, he was humble and thoughtful. I truthfully cannot remember ever seeing or hearing of Ben Hanson doing something mean or selfish. I really can't. Even with the tragic loss of his brother Paul, he focused on taking care of his parents rather than exercising his right to be angry. I believe Ben rarely, if ever, thought selfishly. Service to his family, service to his country... If we examine Ben Hanson's life, we could easily find valuable lessons in service, humility and patience. We would also learn the true meaning of the word 'sacrifice.'

I've been blessed to be the Parish Priest here for almost 25 years, and I clearly remember the terrible day Teresa and Arthur returned to Ottawa County. They were devastated by a sudden separation and pending divorce that we would only recently learn was forced upon them. For very important reasons, none of us were made aware of the circumstances that led to their separation. All we could do was give of ourselves to Teresa and her family... and pray for Ben. There were many amongst us who thought ill of Ben Hanson, given what little we knew of their situation. But, as many of you are aware, I could never bring myself to believe that Ben Hanson was anything less than an honest, decent and faithful man. Deep down, I

knew there had to be a sound reason why they split apart.

Our Teresa picked up the pieces of her life, got young Arthur through high school then turned to serving her community in a meaningful way. First, as Miami School Board President, then District 7 Representative to the State House, Congresswoman for District 2 in U.S. House of Representatives and is currently serving as our Senator in the United States Senate. Her accomplishments are far too numerous to list. Through it all, she stayed true to her principles and to her God. She never remarried, but I believe in my heart that she was waiting for her Ben to come home to her… and in the very last moments of his life, he did.

Against all hope, in spite of devastating illness, in spite of expert medical opinions proclaiming Ben was far more dead than alive… Ben was not listening to them. He was listening to the voices of his family and the loving touch of his soulmate's hand. He managed to fight off death long enough to emerge from a coma and be with his family one… last… time. And when Ben regained consciousness, his first feeble communication was to ask if everyone was safe. Even an inch from death's doorstep, Ben was thinking of someone other than himself."

A tear could be seen on the pastor's cheek as he paused to compose himself.

We know now that our Ben Hanson was a tortured soul, forced to distance himself from his family or face the unthinkable; their murder at the hands of an evil man. Unable to retire from his position, he continued his work for two decades without once seeing the family he loved so much. Can any of you imagine enduring such torment?" he said forcefully, letting his words sink in.

"Sacrifice. Sacrifice for family, for coworkers, for our nation. In my heart, I cannot be certain I could have endured what our Ben Hanson did. The enormity of his sacrifice is simply unimaginable."

Sacred Heart's Priest looked down at the closed coffin before him. "Ben, my friend, I will never… all of us will never forget you. You have shown us not as what we are, but what we could be. You made it look effortless because you lived it every day. The wise amongst us will take your values, your courage, your loyalty, your gentle spirit and make them their own."

"Teresa Rose, you are no stranger to suffering and sacrifice. When your world crumbled around you, robbed of your husband's love and companionship, you turned to selflessly serving your neighbors. For two decades you focused not on grief and personal tragedy, but on how to make Ottawa County, Oklahoma and

America, strong and prosperous. But, I truly believe that you will be best known as the brave woman who was willing to sacrifice everything to help her dying husband enlighten our world. It is that kind of devotion that touches peoples souls, that inspires hope that true love really does exist in these times when love is considered nothing more than a cheap, gilded trinket to toss in the trash when the luster fades. Our community and state has thrived under your leadership, Senator Hanson, and I know your husband is very, very proud of you.

Teresa, I am certain you will face many tribulations in the coming days, weeks and months. You will be taunted and attacked from every angle. Soulless people will question your faith, others will question your patriotism, some will even criticize the special relationship you had with Ben. Lies and slander will attempt to overshadow truth. Rest assured, Senator, Ben will be walking next to you in the conflagration. His hand will be stroking yours and his loving kisses will be upon your forehead. You will never, ever be alone!"

By then, many in the church were wiping tears from their faces, a few were openly crying. Perhaps the most poignant sight was that of a stoic mother and her daughter slowly and surely losing their fight against profound loss and desolation.

"In closing, let us all take a part of Ben Hanson with us when we leave God's house this afternoon. Let his life be our template for selfless service. Let his life be our template for devotion to God and family. Let his life be our template for everlasting love."

* * *

After the conclusion of Requiem Mass, most of the attendees gathered behind the church, awaiting the transfer of Ben Hanson's coffin to his eternal resting place in the cemetery immediately north of the church. It, too, was well cordoned off to insure Ben's interment would be as solemn as his funeral. The storm clouds that were on the horizon before the service were much closer now, blanketing much of the sky from north to southwest. By the time Ben's coffin was positioned over his prepared grave and mourners allowed to assemble, the winds had gathered strength and scattered drops of rain were starting to fall. Faint thunder could be heard in the distance, adding an urgency to press on with the grave side service.

There were dozens of mourners attending the grave side service, paying their last respects to Ben. Most were afforded shelter under three medium-sized canvas tents, but not all could fit. As the service began, so did the rain. To the Hanson family, it seemed as if the heartless twins of insult and injury were conspiring to

make the Hanson family more miserable than they already were. If there was any hint of a silver lining, it was the increased privacy created by the approaching thunderstorm. Onlookers were unable to see the grave side service through the trees and steadily increasing rainfall. Only the hardiest held their positions through the downpour mixed with pea-sized hail. Mercifully, the main storm cell passed north of Miami, sparing the Hanson family and their grave side mourners from the golf ball-sized hail that pounded the Oklahoma-Kansas-Missouri line.

At the conclusion of the service, Teresa Hanson stood up and with somewhat wobbly legs, approached her husband's casket and laid her chest and head upon it.

"Ben," she whispered, "I love you so much! Keep a light on for me. I'll be home before you know it..." she paused as tears began streaming down her cheeks, "...and we'll never, ever be apart again!"

A profound wave of grief swept over Teresa, causing her legs to buckle. Donna Hanson managed to catch her mother before she fell onto the muddy tarp. Hannah Simpson quickly moved to the grave side to assist Donna in escorting Teresa to the nearby black limousines that would take her family home for a change clothes, then to a potluck gathering at the American Legion Post 147 in Miami at 6 PM.

There were no shortages of volunteers to help the grieving family to their vehicles.

Chapter 17

About a hundred or so friends and relatives came to the potluck dinner and fellowship for the Hanson Family. A few welcomed dignitaries were present, including the Mayors of Miami, Commerce, Pitcher, Quapaw and Baxter Springs, along with Teresa's closest political ally, United States Senator Shelton 'Tightwad' Howell, MD from Ada. The location and time of the gathering was, once again, leaked to the press earlier in the day. Security was tight, with many of the same volunteers present that assisted with security during the funeral. Though the entire block was cordoned off, the Hanson Family was still treated to chants of "Traitor! Traitor!" and "Impeach Chandler NOW!" It was obvious to most that the chanters had not received the memo on the Senator's name change.

After an hour of hugs and tears, Teresa was completely exhausted. Politely, she excused herself from the gathering. Senator Melana insisted that the Cocheta Hearings would begin on Friday and that Senator Hanson would be there to "explain her questionable actions." Her supporters protested that it was cruel to make a grieving widow testify before a Senate Hearing the day after her husband's funeral, but anxious to start dismembering his political enemy, Melana was unmoved by the argument. Since there were no flights from Tulsa or Joplin that would arrive in DC before 7 AM, Teresa had to charter an executive jet and leave from Miami very early in the morning to get to the hearings on time.

Donna Hanson and Tim Alexander were sitting by themselves at a small table near the back of the building, half-eaten plates of food in front of them. Unless you were completely blind, it was obvious that the two had chemistry.

"Dr. Hanson," an elderly gentleman said as he approached their table, "I have something I would like to return to you."

He held out his hand and in it was a poorly painted, red clay figurine of a man and a little girl. Donna's eyes widened in surprise.

"Where did you get that?"

"It belonged to your father. He treasured it immensely and kept it on his desk since the day you gave it to him."

"You must be Dr. McLachlan."

"Yes, and you must know why I'm here."

"Teresa, do I need to step out for a while?"

"No... Tim, this may affect you, too."

Tim Alexander was stunned by Donna's words. "Affect me?"

"Tim, Dr. McLachlan is here to offer me the Project Director's position at the facility my dad worked in. I want to hear what he has to say and I want you to hear it, too."

"Uh... sure," he replied, still not quite sure why he was going to be included in the conversation.

"Dr. Alexander, it is a great honor to finally meet you," he said, extending his hand for a shake. "My kids and grand kids love your show and I'm fairly certain my youngest granddaughter has a crush on you."

Tim smiled at the reference to his granddaughter and shook his hand. "The honor is mine, Doctor."

"I have secured the small office behind us so that we can talk in private."

Three of the most incredible minds on earth settled into a small, almost cramped office in Miami, Oklahoma to discuss the future of the most important research project in human history.

"Dr. Hanson, your father and I were very close friends. We worked together all the way back into the early eighties. Back then, under Captain Brogan, Ben was a genuinely happy man. He loved his work and he loved to be with his family during the two week off periods. When Louis Hastings took the job your father was supposed to inherit, the whole facility changed. Overnight, the positive atmosphere simply disappeared. Hastings was despicable and ruthless and he proved it when he forced your mother and father to split up. It was a very frightening time for everyone. We all had families." McLachlan paused, remembering the darkest days at the Project. "We all felt vulnerable."

"Now that Hastings is no longer fouling the project, we have the opportunity to restore the vision that General Marston, Captain Brogan and your father had. We need to focus on the research, not flying back and forth to Washington. We need a hands-on, completely involved Project director that isn't afraid to get dirty. Dr. Hanson, you are the most qualified candidate on the planet. We need you."

Donna Hanson took a long look at Dr. McLachland's face and judged him to be sincere enough. But, as the well overused colloquialism says: the devil is in the details.

"This project has already killed my dad and wrecked my family. How do I know this won't happen again? Or to someone else?"

"The only 100 percent guarantee is that there are no 100 percent guarantees," McLachland replied honestly. "You will have complete control over the facility and may run it as you see fit. We all know of your impressive record at the Skunk Works, Dr. Hanson. I can only imagine how much more progress we could make with your scientific, engineering and managerial skills."

"I see," Donna paused. "Recruiting talent?"

"All yours."

"Equipment?"

"Anything you need. Our black-project budget is larger than several states and quite a few countries."

"Loeffler, he stays on... and Simpson."

"Loeffler is not a problem, but the FBI might want to hold on to Special Agent Simpson."

"Make it happen. I want the best, and from what I've heard, they are."

"I'll do what I can."

"Fair enough."

'Not many downsides as presented,' Donna thought to herself. 'The work would certainly be more challenging than any terrestrial aerospace career I could possibly conceive of...'

"Dr. McLachland, if you can convince Dr. Alexander to take the Deputy Project Director's position, I'll agree to run this project on a trial basis. Any interference from bureaucrats, or other worthless dead weights, and I'm outta there."

McLachland and Alexander looked at each other in surprise. Donna Hanson's reputation as a hard core businesswoman and engineer would remain intact tonight, yet just a few minutes earlier, she was asking Tim which rock band was his favorite.

"Dr. Alexander?" McLachland asked.

"Well, since I'm probably unemployed anyway... Of course I'll take the position! It is a scientist's dream come true!" He said enthusiastically.

"Then it is settled?" McLachland asked.

Both Tim and Donna nodded their heads.

"Dr. McLachland, what will our salaries be?" Dr. Hanson asked.

McLachland was surprised by the question. It seemed... well, out of character for her and really quite crass. "Both of you will receive $500,000 per year, tax free."

"Perfect!" she replied with a big smile. "Take 75 percent of it and start a 501-C to benefit the widows and families that Hastings destroyed. The project will also match my donation every year. It's about time this Cocheta place starts to clean up after itself."

"What a wonderful idea! Count me in, too!" Alexander chimed in.

Up until now, Tim Alexander had only seen the kind, soft, somewhat vulnerable side of Donna Hanson. That was more than enough to grab his attention. It didn't hurt that she was impossibly beautiful, too. But, the hard core side of her was every bit as intriguing as the soft side. He had a gut feeling that his life was going to get extraordinarily interesting.

"Would you like to tour the facility now?" McLachland asked. "I've got a brand new G650 waiting at the Miami Airport. We just picked it up in Savannah 2 days ago."

"You have a Gulfstream 650? Here?" Dr. Hanson asked, surprised that the Project owned a corporate jet of that magnitude. "I didn't know that they were already delivering them to their clients."

"We have one of the very first available. Hastings pulled some, uh... strings. I think he persuaded a few Georgia politicians to add some pork to a DoD bill and make sure that we moved to the top of the list for a 650," McLachland admitted. "Legally, it's registered to the Air Force as a C-37D based at Nellis. It is actually based at the JANET Terminal at McCarran."

"What did it cost?"

"Seventy million and some change. Would you like to fly it?"

"Of course I would, Dr. McLachland, but don't you think it is more than a little extravagant for our needs?"

"We all thought that, Dr. Hanson. Hastings didn't care how much it cost or what we could have done with the money. He was all about himself."

Donna shook her head. "We will do things differently, I assure you!" she said.

"I know. Your reputation precedes you Dr. Hanson!" McLachland said with a toothy smile. "So... are you and Tim ready to inspect your new home away from home?"

"Tim?" Donna asked, knowing already that he was ready to start this intriguing new chapter in his life.

"Count me in!" he replied enthusiastically.

"I just need to stop by my mom's place to let her know what I'm going to be up to," Donna said, then looked at Dr. McLachland with a smile. "Were you serious about letting me fly the 650?"

"The co-pilot seat is all yours. We'll get you rated in no time."

Donna's smile widened, "We'll meet you at the airport in an hour."

Chapter 18

"Mom, I already decided to take the position before Dr. McLachlan offered it to me," Donna explained to her mother. "I know why dad accepted his position at Cocheta. It is the same reason why I'm taking it. To be involved in deciphering technology from another world... it is an utterly unique opportunity in all of human history!"

"I understand, sweetheart, and I have no doubts that you will pick up where your father left off and accomplish wonderful things," she said, her exhaustion clearly evident. "You know how much family pain is tied to that project. Having my little girl step right back into it is... well, it's terribly frightening to me!"

"Please don't worry about me, Mom," Donna pleaded. "You know I can handle myself. I've made it clear that I will run the project my way and that my continuing presence there is completely dependent on keeping the bureaucrats and troublemakers out of our business."

"Who oversees your project, Punkin?"

"It's ultra black, mom. Funding is off-budget."

"That may be so, but somebody still has oversight. Somebody still has to get the money and equipment to you."

Dr. Hanson took a moment to consider her mother's question. Black projects were traditionally funded by off-budget cash showing up in a contractor's bank account. Oversight was through Congressional Armed Services sub-committees. It seemed logical to assume Project Cocheta was handled the same way.

"Doesn't it come through the DoD and CIA subcommittees?" Donna replied with some uncertainty. "That's how it comes to the Skunk Works."

"I have a dear friend on the House Armed Services Committee, sweetheart. Because of his seniority, He's one of the few senior House leaders that oversee the CIA and DoD black budgets and their highly classified projects. Until Monday, he had never heard of Project Cocheta," Teresa said. "Your oversight and funding comes from somewhere else. Considering the way out nature of Cocheta, it probably comes from sources far different from the government norm. Maybe it's a corporation heavily vested into high-tech military hardware or logistics. The money still comes from the taxpayers, but it is probably laundered through one or more of the 1300 plus Federal bureaucracies and agencies, and it's extremely well hidden."

Donna took it in all at once. 'Oversight completely outside of Congress?' she thought to herself. 'Nice way to hide an Ultra-Black project, but...'

She pondered the slippery slope before her. Cocheta was vulnerable, no doubt about it. The concept was to provide a research facility heavily shielded from disjointed noses. With the project exposed to the world, all manner of vermin with a forum will be oozing out of cracks and crawl spaces to exploit the project to their own ends. Senator Melana was such a lowly, political creature. One that, single-handedly, had enough clout to threaten Cocheta's very existence.

"I see your point, Mom," Donna conceded. "I'll keep my eyes open. They already know my terms and conditions and they know my reputation."

"I know they do, Donna. Just be careful. You're going to be under a very powerful microscope"

"I will, Mom," Donna said as she turned for the front door. "Good luck with the hearings! You're a strong and principled woman, Senator. You have nothing to worry about!"

"Thank you, sweetheart. Have a safe trip and give my regards to Tim!"

No sooner than the door closed, Teresa began to weep. Nothing good will come out of that cursed mountain. Nothing. If she had her wish, Cocheta Mountain would simply disappear from the face of the earth.

Chapter 19

Project Cocheta's G650 was an absolute dream to fly, and extraordinarily fast. Compared to the last ageing Lear Jet used by Cocheta, the 0.9 Mach of the Gulfstream was able to shave almost an hour off the transit time from McCarran to northern British Columbia. With a range of over 8000 miles, refueling at Cocheta for a return trip was completely optional. At a price tag of nearly $70 million dollars, the G650 was certainly the biggest Cocheta purchase Louis Hastings ever finagled out of the powers that be. If the late Project Director left a legacy, it would be his uncanny ability to milk the treasury. Of course, he acquired the G650 for his own personal comfort, loading the business jet with every creature comfort and option. Since Hastings assumed room temperature early Thursday morning, it appeared that Drs. Hanson and Alexander would likely be the ones benefiting the most, but only for important, time-sensitive travel. The JANET shuttle was a perfectly fine way to commute back and forth from Vegas to British Columbia.

Donna Hanson was truly in her element. Not rated for the G650, she was allowed to fly it from the copilot's seat under the supervision of Captain Olen Lloyd. To Donna, the G650 cockpit was a masterpiece of visual flight and systems data. Heads-up display, four 14 inch LCD monitors, synthetic vision, 3-D scanning radar... it practically flew itself! Now down to 10,000 feet and almost into the approach pattern, Donna turned control over to Captain Lloyd.

"Dr. Hanson, we're not far from our destination and I see we have company to our left and slightly behind."

"Is it a fighter escort?"

"No... I'm going to take a guess that Dr. McLachland hasn't yet told you about our rather interesting airspace."

Dr. McLachland stood from his seat and motioned for Donna to exit the cockpit and follow him to the left rear of the jet. Tim Alexander had long since fallen asleep in the incredibly comfortable seat on the right rear of the aircraft.

"Dr. Hanson, take a look out the last port window."

Donna obliged and leaned over the last seat on the left side of the aircraft.

"Oh... my... God..."

Donna Hanson could not believe what she was seeing! No more than 200 feet from the G650 was a glowing blueish purple disc flying in tandem with them, perfectly maintaining the same speed and decent of the business jet.

"Is that for real? I mean, is that an extraterrestrial aircraft?"

"Yes it is," McLachland replied. "Sometimes they follow us in, most of the time they don't. You got real lucky tonight!"

Donna turned to Tim Alexander and started shaking him. "Tim, wake up! Wake up!"

Tim stirred from his sleep and ever so slightly cracked open his eyes, "You are so beautiful." he said as his eyelids closed again.

"Tim!" Donna said louder and with more vigorous shaking. "That is awfully sweet of you, but I need you to wake up, NOW!"

Dr. Alexander suddenly bolted to an upright position. "What? What's going on? Everything OK?"

"Tim, come look out this window!"

"Sure...," he said as he tried to shake the drowsiness. With some unsteadiness, he stood up to lean over to the very large, oval-shaped port window.

The sight of what he saw out the port window vaporized any remnant of sleepiness. "Oh, crap!!! Is that what I think it is?"

"Yes it is, Tim!"

"Holy Mother of God..."

"Tell me what you see, Tim!" Donna asked.

Now, fully awake and heart pounding, Dr. Alexander began to closely observe the extraterrestrial craft through the large, oval window.

"Well, it's discoid... slightly more mass above the rim... maybe 10 to 20 percent more... various shades of blues and purple... looks like air and nitrogen plasma... definitely plasma, but it is obviously contained... windows around the rim edge... scratch that, too small for windows... must be something else... rock-steady in flight... plasma seems to have a pattern... waves starting at the leading edge, slowly propagating rearwards in subtle pulses... wait a minute, it could be a strobe-like effect... extremely rapid pulses might give the illusion that waves are moving very slow... left engine obscures length of plasma trailing the craft, if any... no visible antennas or other protruding structures... " Dr. Alexander's thought process was interrupted by the sound of the G650's flaps being lowered.

"Time to buckle up, folks." Captain Lloyd announced. "We'll be on the ground in 3 minutes."

"Here, Donna, why don't you sit next to the window and tell me what you see. I'll sit next to you."

Dr. Hanson continued the observation of the alien aircraft outside her port window.

"Can't see any control surfaces... no discernible thrusting... discs are really terrible airfoils... must use some kind of wild pixie dust to make it fly so perfectly."

Tim laughed. "Pixie dust? Is that how you got all those crazy-looking stealth fighters to fly?"

"That... and duct tape. Maybe a little Elmer's Glue. Baling wire..."

"You are a funny, funny lady!"

"I have my moments," she said with a sly grin.

Tim leaned closer to the window, his cheek nearly touching Donna's. "All my professional life I tried to instill a sense of open-mindedness into my students and my audience, yet I never really believed that interstellar travel was even remotely possible. This alien aircraft I'm looking at... It's really putting me in my place as a phenomenal fraud."

"Don't be so hard on yourself, Tim," Donna replied in a comforting tone. "You're not a fraud. All of us fell into the trap of getting too comfortable with our current scientific beliefs."

"Well, at least my students were taught right, even if their Professor was not as open-minded as he pretended to be."

"Tim, this place... this Cocheta Project... this alien aircraft tailing us. If all this is even half of what we think it is, you just might be the physicist that intoduces an entirely new perspective of the physical laws governing our universe."

Tim looked at Donna with a warm smile. "Redemption?" Tim asked.

"Only if you earn it, Dr. Alexander." She replied, returning the smile.

Chapter 20

The two hour flight from Miami Oklahoma to Washington Reagan was nowhere near smooth enough for Senator Hanson to sleep through. The same massive spring storm system that made her husband's interment a near disaster was moving swiftly eastward across the Mississippi basin states, spawning multiple tornados and huge hail. Only the last 20 minutes of the flight were comfortable enough for the cat nap that, in spite of her exhaustion, continued to elude her. Senator Hanson's security detail was accompanying her on the flight, and to her mild ire and jealously, they had no trouble sleeping at all.

"Senator Hanson," the flight attendant whispered, "we've been cleared to land. We'll be at the Signature terminal in about 10 minutes. Your cars and security are awaiting your arrival."

"Thank you," Teresa replied, "and could I get a cup of strong, black coffee?"

"Yes ma'am, but you'll have to drink it quick."

Since Teresa was already exhausted, Coffee was surely going to be one of her life lines. Going toe-to-toe with the likes of Senator Melana was always a challenge. The last thing you wanted to do was grapple him with a fuzzy mind.

Teresa pondered the coming hours and days as she sipped the first of what would be many cups of coffee that day. Melana did not have her in the cross hairs because she divulged state secrets. It was the fact that she garnered a lot of enthusiastic attention from her political party the last several months. So much so that she was at, or nearly at the top of Vice-Presidential prospects for this year's election.

Melana's goal was to knock her out of contention for the Vice-Presidency. Ideally, it was to run her out of Washington altogether. After the week she just endured, her career was at the very bottom of her priorities.

She closed her eyes and thought of Ben and her family. So much had already been asked of the Hansons and she instinctively knew that even more sacrifices were to come. All Teresa wanted to accomplish in the days and weeks ahead was to protect her family as best she could and defend her husband's legacy. That she would do with the ferocity of a wounded grizzly bear. Melana might just get what he wishes most, but she vowed that it will come at a price.

The coffee was beginning to take hold.

'If Melana wants a fight,' she thought to herself as a mild grin appeared on her face, 'by God I'll give him a fight!'

Chapter 21

Donna Hanson and Tim Alexander exited the G650 in front of a huge hangar door recessed into the side of a mountain. The tarmac was unlit, yet there were dozens of armed men with night vision goggles running into fortified positions in the fields around the tarmac. Donna instantly recognized three HUMRAAMs equipped with racks carrying five AIM-120C AMRAAM radar-guided missiles. One HUMRAAM was near the hardened positions, the other two were barely visible at each end of the taxiway. Only a handful of HUMRAAMs were ever built and her guess was that these three were built and delivered off the books. She also began to notice that some kind of military action or exercise was taking place.

"Dr. McLachland, what is going on?" Alexander asked.

"It's a code green. When an alien aircraft enters our area, we mobilize military assets into a shield, of sorts, covering the front of the mountain and the entire airfield. It's kind of a holdover from the cold war years when we worried about the aliens and the Soviets. Since the aliens have never made aggressive moves against us and terrestrial enemies know better than to violate Canadian airspace, it all becomes just a readiness exercise. The Marines piss and moan about getting out in the cold or the mosquitoes, but that's just a ruse. They love every minute of it! In fact, they compare deployment times amongst the squads. They call the slow pokes 'shitbirds' and the fastest ones 'pullers,' named after the Marine General Chesty Puller. In all these many decades, not a single shot has been fired by either side." He paused for a moment to look around for the offending alien aircraft. "I'll wager it is the same aircraft that followed us in that has the Marines all riled up. Let's walk to where the civilians are gathered. It looks like they might have a good view."

Donna and Tim looked at each other with faces that clearly suggested the classic 'what have we gotten ourselves into' look. A few moments later, they were staring at what seemed to be the same alien craft that followed them to the outer perimeter of the airfield. The alien craft was now on the far side of the valley some three miles away, motionless except for faint, almost imperceptible swirls of decaying plasma underneath.

"Dr. Hanson, we had been getting visits like this every second to fourth night for decades. Over the last six months, these visits have become much farther apart, averaging maybe one or two a month. We are not sure if there is any significance to this. I know it bothered your dad a lot, but he never said why."

"My dad was a born worrier, but he usually had a good reason," Donna replied. "Maybe the drastic change in frequency spooked him."

"Whoa!!!" Alexander yelled in conjunction with the gasps and screams from the assembled audience that was beginning a hurried, chaotic retreat to the perceived safety of the concrete and steel building behind them. Tim lost his balance and fell to the ground, taking Teresa with him. McLachland instinctively reached out to catch the couple, but lost his balance as well.

"Sweet Jesus!" Tim yelled, shielding his eyes from the sudden brightness of the alien craft that had just closed a three mile distance in three-quarters of a second, stopping abruptly 30 yards from, and 100 feet above their heads. "Donna, are you OK?"

"Yeah, I think so," she replied through a fading daze. "Dr. McLachland?"

"I'm OK."

"Dr. McLachland, what is it doing?" Teresa asked, her senses quickly returning to normal

"My guess is that it is looking you two over," he replied without detectable stress in his voice. "This approach has easily broken the old record! Dr. Hanson, Dr. Alexander, this is as close as anybody has ever been! Analyze what you see! Tell me what you see and feel!"

"Pulsed plasma! I can see the strobe effect very clearly now! I can feel and see the distortion of heated air and plasma being pushed downward... like a jet exhaust."

"Like an old Harrier or the F-35," Donna added. "Thrust vectoring, only this thing can vector thrust in any direction it wishes! Tim, what kind of energy would be needed to duplicate what this craft is doing."

"Almost more than I can imagine!" he replied with a smile. "A reactor small enough to put in that thing and make it do these wild tricks... it must be using some very exotic energy. Anti-matter... dark matter... nano-black holes... premium unleaded... I really have no idea!"

Before anyone could reply, the craft quickly descended another 50 feet. "Oh my God! It's going to land!" Teresa exclaimed, noticeably sans the usual sureness in her voice.

"I think it is about time we make our way to the building," McLachland said coolly. "If it makes an aggressive move, which I seriously doubt it will, all hell is going to break loose!"

The trio made a hurried retreat towards the nearest entrance to the massive facility they had not the time to really appreciate upon their arrival. Before they reached halfway, the alien aircraft shot to 500 feet directly above the three scientists, paused for a few seconds, then sped away at blinding speed to the southeast at an 80 degree angle. A few seconds later, a second craft, previously unseen, arrived from the north, stopped in the exact same spot 500 feet above the trio, then precisely followed the path of the first craft.

The three brilliant scientists looked at each other for what seemed to be an eternity. Dr. Hanson finally managed to break the silence.

"Dr. McLachland," she started quietly with an uncharacteristic waver in her voice, "when was the previous record for the closest alien approach to this facility?"

"1968."

She closed her eyes tightly. "Who was there?"

"Your Father... Welcome to Project Cocheta, Dr. Hanson."

Chapter 22

"Greetings to all. For those in the audience who do not know who I am," Senator Melana announced with a smile, pausing a moment for a healthy dose of chuckling to subside, "I am Senator Harold Melana, Majority Leader of the Senate and Chairman of the Armed Services Committee. I hereby convene this investigative hearing into the extraordinary events surrounding the release of heretofore highly classified information concerning a quasi-military research initiative now known as Project Cocheta. It will be the goal of this hearing to establish the particular details that led to the rather astonishing way one of our nation's most critical secrets were disclosed in a highly public and worldwide forum. We will call professional witnesses from many scientific and sociological disciplines to assist us in assessing the impact of these revelations on individuals, our government and the planet. Lastly we will investigate the possibility that federal laws may have been broken during the release of this information and, if need be, recommend punishments to the Senate that are befitting of the infractions. These hearings will last as long as necessary and will be broadcast live by CSPAN and all major news networks.

The format today will be as follows, I will present my opening remarks, then Senate Minority Leader, Senator Darrell Wilcox from the great state of Wyoming will present his. There will be a short break, then we will ask our first witness, Senator Teresa 'Hanson,' I believe her name is now, to take the stand and present her opening statement. If time permits, we will begin questioning the Senator from Oklahoma. Otherwise, we will begin questioning after lunch."

Melana began tidying a few notes on his section of the desk. Not that he

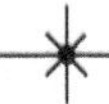

needed them, but more so out of habit. He knew precisely what he was going to say and how he was going to slip a verbal noose around Hanson's neck.

'Easy targets!' he almost laughed aloud. 'Rural hayseeds!' Melana had no love for flyover country, as did most in the inner circles of Washington. Even their own representatives rarely gave a real rat's ass about them. They were merely useful tools at election time. Votes... and access to the great wealth that winning elections created, was all that mattered to Harold Melana.

Melana was aware that Senator Hanson could be a potential scrapper, but not this time. She just buried her husband and was being investigated by her peers. He was certain that she would take the stand with no more bark than a freshly beaten puppy.

"We, the citizens of the United States and the world, have just finished a remarkable and historic week," Melana continued. A mere six days ago, the people of our planet did not universally believe that citizens of another world were visiting earth. In a rather spectacular fashion, the notion that we are alone in the universe was forever dispelled by a member of this legislative branch of American Government. Senator Teresa Chandler made a guest appearance, of sorts, on Dr. Tim Alexander's cable television show, Science for the Rest of Us. We will always remember that very moment and what we were doing when we learned we were not alone in the universe. We will also remember the poignant moment of desperate tears shed by a devoted spouse about to lose her husband. I am certain that this surprise moment in media history will be considered one of the most memorable ever witnessed.

While we can all appreciate this historic moment on a personal level, we must also be aware of the cost to our country, in unintended consequences, by releasing such startling, life changing news without bracing the world for it ahead of time. This revelation created a diplomatic fire storm around the world. Our allies were not prepared for it and other nations chose to use it against us. Several countries, including the Russian Federation, China, North Korea, Saudi Arabia, Iran, Iraq, Egypt and a long list of others, condemned the way we released the information. Many of our staunchest friends around the world were dismayed by it, including Canada, which is our partner in the joint project. Perhaps the single most damaging aspect is the project facility itself. Many nations feel threatened by it, in spite of assurances that it is engaged in peaceful research. The State Department and our diplomats are working night and day to calm nerves on all sides. In short, we have a real mess on our hands.

In the last several days, there has been a growing number of voices demanding the Cocheta Project be scrapped. Admittedly, I was one of them, until fully briefed on their mission and capabilities. It is a pure research facility designed to analyze and replicate exotic alloys and technology. I have been told that a few of these discoveries are already being put to use in our technology."

The last paragraph was mostly a lie, largely due to a disturbing call Melana answered in the wee hours of Tuesday morning, followed up by a personal visit to his Washington office on Wednesday. Both contacts featured high-end name-dropping and were menacing enough in nature to persuade Melana into becoming a reluctant supporter of the project. It had been a long time since he felt as if he were perched upon a lower level branch of the food chain. Melana didn't like it. Not one bit.

"In the American system of government," Melana continued, "we discuss policy before we vote on it and enact it only when it becomes law. That was not the case here. One person, acting alone and without the consent of America's governing bodies, released classified information to friend and foe alike. It will be our job, our duty, to analyze the societal, cultural, fiscal and criminal ramifications of this event. To sweep it under the carpet would be gross dereliction of our duties as United States Senators."

Melana spent another thirty minutes speaking of lofty, senatorial duties and mandates required of them in circumstances such as this. In essence, Melana was building the political pole to which Teresa Hanson would be tied to when he and his colleagues lit the fatwood and logs under her feet. More than half of the Republicans would reluctantly join the Democrats because she did, after all, release highly classified state secrets. In private, Melana bragged that he would preside over the first expulsion of a U.S. Senator since 1797, that is, if you didn't count the 14 Senators that sided with the Confederacy and all the other busted Senators that resigned before they could be expelled. By expulsion or resignation, it was going to be a grand sport relieving Chandler... Hanson... whatever the hell name she was going by... of her seat in the Senate.

Chapter 23

As tired as she was, Project Director Donna Hanson could not fall asleep. The close approach of the alien aircraft was a huge part of her insomnia, but she had a feeling that sleeping in her father's former apartment, tastefully tweaked for a female, was just as large a part of her inability to rest. She took a hot shower around 5 AM to see if that would help her relax, but two hours later she was still, very much awake. Now it was almost 9 AM, five and a half hours since the alien encounter, and Dr. McLachland would be arriving any minute to take her and Dr. Alexander to breakfast. Afterwards, they would begin their tour of the massive facility carved out of a mountain.

A peek at her reflection in the bathroom mirror seemed to confirm that she looked like hell, but nothing could be further from the truth. In fact, Donna Hanson rarely used makeup because she simply didn't need to. It was a blessing she shared with her mother. She washed her face and pulled her hair back into a pony tail, finishing just in time to answer the knocking on her apartment door.

"Good morning, Dr. Hanson," Dr. McLachland said cheerily. "I trust you slept reasonably well last night?"

"Not really, Dr. McLachland. It's kind of difficult to sleep after having an alien aircraft almost sit on your lap. Where is Tim..., I mean, Dr. Alexander?"

Dr. McLachland grinned at the newly appointed Project Director. The attraction between her and Dr. Alexander was more than obvious. Normally, he would be very wary of workplace romance because it almost invariably ended in a disaster for one or both. Drs. Hanson and Alexander were mature, stable and reliable. If a romance developed between them, he had no doubt that they would be both discreet and professional.

"Tim had a little shaving accident and didn't want to startle you with a gaping gash on his neck!" he answered with a smile. "We'll stop by his apartment on the way to breakfast. He seems very conscientious when he is around you."

"He's a very accomplished and decent man, Dr. McLachland. He will make a fine addition to your staff."

"Your staff, Dr. Hanson," McLachland reminded her. "We work for you, now. To a man and woman, our personnel are very excited about you and Dr. Alexander managing our little hole-in-a-mountain. After years of abuse, we are finally starting to look forward to our shifts here!"

"I will need to know what kind of working conditions our people have had to endure and for how long," Donna replied, her countenance darkening. "My team at Lockheed is the best there is. Period. I'll pit them against any similar group of engineers on this planet and easily walk away with all the marbles. I didn't make them that good, I provided them an environment that helped them better themselves. Pride, achievement and satisfaction motivates talented men and women, not money.

I will work them hard, Dr. McLachland, but I will always be right there next to them. They'll know, without a doubt, who is on their side."

"I've heard that about you, and I'm pretty sure everyone else has, too," Dr. McLachland paused for a moment as a bit of sadness touched his soul. "The people here really loved your dad, so don't be surprised if they want to share their memories of him. His death was a huge blow to all of us."

"I understand. He was a great father and a very good man," She paused, wiping a tear from her lower eyelid. "I look forward to hearing their stories. I've got quite a few of my own."

Dr. McLachland smiled. He could almost feel the transition from labor camp to family workplace taking shape before his eyes.

"You are going to fit in very nice here, Dr. Hanson. We have some of the finest minds on earth in this frozen little slice of heaven and we have plenty of opportunities to engage in heated and highly technical discussions. You might also be interested to know that most of these high octane scientists have become accomplished

Texas Hold'em poker players. Well, maybe ruthless is a better description. Project Director or not, they will gleefully take all your money if you show the slightest bit of weakness at the table."

"Sounds a little like the old west, Dr. McLachland."

"In many ways it is. The facility is located in wilderness and must endure harsh conditions that, sometimes, keep us from coming or going as we please. We have a potential adversary that appears to be keeping tabs on our activities. Our supplies must come from sources hundreds, perhaps even thousands of miles away, but contingency plans also allow us the flexibility to harvest fish, birds and ungulates, like deer, moose and elk if need be. In fact, we have our traditional Hawaiian Luau every spring when it warms up a little. The Marines harvest a large moose, or perhaps a couple of elk, then we prepare them in the ground 'Imu' style, just like they do in Hawaii. I believe the next one is a week or two from today.

Now, let's see if Tim has managed to bleed to death or get himself ready for breakfast!"

Donna laughed out loud as she started to close the door behind her and walk with McLachland. "He is such an brilliant man, yet so... well... approachable and warm."

"That he is, young lady. I have three grown kids of my own. Widowed now. Would have been nice to have at least one kid that wanted to follow in my footsteps, but mine became happy and successful in other endeavours and that's plenty fine for me. Your dad was very fortunate. Some of his happiest moments were talking about your footsteps following his." He paused for a moment to reflect on the past two decades, "What Hastings did to him... and to your family... He never talked about it. All those years he suffered alone, without a family to come home to. We did our best to keep his spirits up. The torment he endured left scars on all of us."

Donna smiled at McLachland, "I'm glad my dad had good friends here. I can't imagine what he would have endured without them. I'll do my best to lighten this place up, Dr. McLachland. I don't want the past intruding into our present and future."

"You will do just fine," he said with a cheerful smile. "We had better get a move on, though. I'm sure Dr. Alexander has the bleeding under control by now. I assure you, our cafeteria serves the best food south of the Arctic circle! I didn't get this pot belly of mine by eating at McDonalds."

* * *

"Wow, how does a government-run facility like this make such awesome food?" Tim Alexander exclaimed while leaning back in his cafeteria chair.

"The story goes back years ago when our first director, General Marston, was in charge," McLachland said. "The project facility was about to be opened when the General tasted his first breakfast there. Well, it was so bad he blew his top and demanded that good cooks replace the bad ones or he would demolish the whole facility and start from scratch."

"That must have been one really bad meal!" Donna said, wrinkling her forehead.

"I can only imagine! We have a metallurgist here who dates back to the Marston era," McLachland said, holding his full belly and leaning back in his chair. "Brilliant man with a photographic memory. Dr. Floyd Wolfe, he can tell you all about Marston and your Dad's exploits. Bet you didn't know your father was a honest-to-God hero. He actually saved General Marston's life!"

"My Dad saved a Project Director's life?"

"Yes he did." McLachland said with a smile. "They were on what we call a 'field trip' to Mexico to recover an unmanned alien aircraft that crashed in the desert near Coyame. Because there was a strong possibility of xenobiologic contamination, the team had to sterilize the area by conflagration. General Marston suffered a heart attack and collapsed near the area to be sterilized. Your dad noticed that Marston hadn't followed the rigid egress plan, so he jumped out of the helicopter and went looking for him just as the huge fire was ignited. Your dad managed to find him in the smoke and drag him to safety."

"My dad… did that?"

"Yes he did, and it earned him the admiration of everybody here. We have the alien aircraft he recovered in this facility. You can see it and touch it on this morning's tour."

Donna looked at Tim and saw the surprise on his face that must have reflected her own.

"When you're ready, we'll begin your tour," McLachland said with a big smile. "I assure you, this will be the most astonishing morning of your life."

Chapter 24

"Thank you, Senator Melana," replied Wyoming Senator Darrell Wilcox, minority Chairman of the Senate Armed Services Committee, as he began his opening statement, "and to the rest of the members of the Senate Armed Services Committee, Senator Hanson and those in the audience, here and at home.

Senator Melana and I share many of the same concerns about the startling way a highly secret research facility was disclosed to the world, both to our allies and potential adversaries at the same time. Since Senator Hanson's surprise announcement, there has been quite a bit of diplomatic finger-pointing going on and disingenuous bloviating from the usual suspects. On the other hand, we now have a much clearer view of the universe and, perhaps, what our newly disclosed place is within it. I'm not saying that the positive aspects from this disclosure outweigh the potential impact on national security, but I do believe we should keep an open mind to the possibility that this new reality that we find ourselves in is not going to be appreciably different than the one before last Sunday evening.

It seems that our visitors have been around for quite some time. Those who are versed in the phenomenon claim the modern era of alien visitation started in the mid 1940s. Many others believe that we have been visited periodically over the last four millennia. Well, I'm just a country Senator from Wyoming, so I'll stick with the present and let archeologists deal with the ancient. Apparently, no weapon has ever been fired from an alien ship since 1947. Not one. There have been a few mishaps, but none that could be blamed on the aliens. So, I think it is safe to say, for the moment, that our visitors are non-aggressive and do not seem to be interested in anything other than sightseeing.

All that being said, doesn't it seem to be a bit silly to engage in political witch hunts and spend trillions of dollars we don't have on utopian nonsense that was cooked up by, originally, the United Nations? Yes, we should address Senator Hanson's actions and levy an appropriate punishment, but remember this: leaking classified information in this town is as common as cherry blossoms in April. Members of this very committee have done it, so I don't believe a witch..."

"That is outrageous!" the Senator from California, Royce McBride stood up and yelled. "Mr. Chairman???"

"With all due respect, Senator McBride, this is my opening statement. Please take your seat and be quiet. You'll get your turn."

"Senator Wilcox," Melana said sternly, "You will refrain from making accusations against your fellow Senators. They are not under investigation by this committee, Senator Hanson is."

"Very well, Mr. Chairman, but I genuinely believe this hearing has more to do about politics in an election year than ascertaining the damage done to our national security, if any."

"You are free to believe what you wish, Senator Wilcox."

"Why all the negative spin against Senator Hanson, much of it coming from your own staff, Senator Melana? Why the vicious talking points. Why the lightning-fast Senate Hearings? Why are we putting this grieving woman in front of this committee when she buried her ex-husband not 24 hours ago?"

"Senator Wilcox, are you finished with your opening statement?"

"The majority of Americans support what Senator Hanson did."

"Polls are not our concern. We are here to police the actions of one of our own. Again, Senator Wilcox, are you finished with your opening statement?"

"We, the minority members of this committee are not going to stand idly by while the majority members railroad Senator Hanson!"

"Please take your seat, Senator Wilcox! Your opening statement is concluded!"

Chapter 25

The first stop in Donna and Tim's tour of Project Cocheta was the immense aircraft hanger. The G650 was neatly parked inside, near a massive hanger door capable of allowing any aircraft on earth to park inside. Having been serviced overnight, the business jet was poised to be towed on to the tarmac in short order. It was the first time that Dr. Hanson saw the aircraft in full lighting.

"I have got to get rated in that beast."

"We'll get that taken care of, Dr. Hanson," McLachland said. "We only plan to park it at McCarran and Groom Lake, but you can fly it to and from Plant 42 if you like. I'm sure your Skunk Works buddies will be glad to see you. We'll get you rated in no time."

Donna grinned from ear to ear. The perks seemed almost endless.

"Where are we headed now?" Tim asked.

"Well, I'm trying to retrace the steps of Donna's father when he took his first tour," he replied with a touch of uncertainty in his voice. "There have been a lot of changes made over the years, so we may have to wing it a bit."

The trio worked their way to the first building within a cave at the very back of the enormous hangar. At one time, two armed Marines guarded the entrance to this unique structure. With the invention of magnetic card keys, the Marines were replaced by automated technology and no longer necessary. After opening the overly heavy door and closing it behind them, the card key was again used to open the second door. Before them was the very same, totally intact alien aircraft that

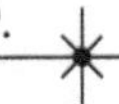

Dr. Ben Hanson first examined in 1968.

Donna's examination of the alien craft and preliminary conclusions were strikingly similar to her dad's, except for the hesitation her father had about entering the craft. Donna walked straight into it with a wide-eyed, somewhat reluctant Tim Alexander right behind her.

"Tim, this is the most fantastic thing I have ever seen! We're standing inside a craft constructed by beings from another star system!"

Tim didn't answer. He was still trying to process what he had seen and felt over the previous ten minutes. The improbability of it all was clashing head-on with his well-ordered view of the universe. Everything he believed about the impossibility of faster-than-light travel was swept away at that very moment. It wasn't the aircraft he was standing in that had the most impact on him because it was obvious that the craft was not built for space travel. No, it was the reality that something much larger must have ferried the craft to earth. The energy required to travel faster than light for a huge, interstellar aircraft carrier? Absolutely mind boggling, yet the proof of it lay right before his eyes.

"Tim, are you OK?"

"No, I'm not, Donna," he replied ominously. "They had better be friendly or we are in very serious trouble. It's the math, Donna. This species has harnessed almost unlimited energy. We wouldn't last ten minutes in a fight against them."

"Then... I guess we'll need to double or triple the effort," she said calmly. "I've never backed down from a challenge in my entire career. I'm not about to start now."

"I'm right there with you, Donna. I just hope there is some terrestrial technology we can build upon and use effectively."

"Then we had better get busy weaponizing whatever we can."

"Dr. Hanson, Dr. Alexander..." Dr. McLachland said as entered through the rear bulkhead of the craft. "I might have something for you along those lines at our next stop. Something you can sink your teeth into. For now, it is probably best we don't discuss that sort of thing in here."

"Why is that, Dr. McLachland?' Donna asked, her ear detecting a glaring non sequitur. "I cannot think of a safer, more secure area on earth than this fortified room inside of a mountain!"

"You have to understand that this aircraft was recovered in pristine condition over 40 years ago. It was abandoned in Canadian wilderness, intact with the interior lights on. Which, by the way, we now believe to be somehow incorporated into the outermost metallic layer of the inner hull. It's this alloy that emits a steady, even light without heat or radiation like tritium. Remarkably, the illumination has not varied more than one-tenth of a lumen since we started monitoring it in 1977." McLachland paused for a moment, sensing he was getting off topic. "Sorry, I have a habit of babbling when I talk about all the things we've discovered here. All these many years and I still get a little giddy when I step into this thing!"

"Believe me, I'm not sure if I'm giddy or shaking scared!" Tim replied. "Please tell us more."

"Well, the reason we don't talk about base operations or the success or failures of research initiatives while we are in this building is that there is a possibility the aliens may be trying to monitor us from the craft. That's why we heavily shield this particular building."

Tim and Donna looked at each other in astonishment. "You mean, the aliens might be listening to us? Right now?" Tim asked.

"Maybe… We have monitored every conceivable frequency, from ULF on up. Nothing. Still, they could be using something so exotic we are unable to detect it."

"That is very unnerving, Dr. McLachland," Donna replied. "Is it possible they can conduct more than just passive surveillance of this facility?"

"Maybe, but who can know for sure. The more I think about how incredibly advanced they are, the more magical their technology becomes. I make it a habit not to underestimate anything around here, no matter how ridiculously improbable it seems to be."

"I am not well-versed on aerospace engineering as my new and esteemed boss is," he paused for a second to smile at Donna, "but I get the feeling this craft cannot operate in space, or at least not very long in space. I see no thrusters of any sort."

"I wholeheartedly agree with my astute and brilliant Deputy Director." Donna said, returning the smile. "If magnetohydrodynamics is the most likely propulsion system, they need something to ionize. Water, especially seawater, contains ready-

made ions and air can be heated enough to strip electrons off oxygen and nitrogen atoms to make plasma, They would need to carry fuel to do something like that in space. Given the size of these aircraft, they couldn't carry enough fuel to reach escape velocity, unless..," she pause for a moment to solidify her idea, "...unless they could substantially exceed escape velocity before exiting the atmosphere! Depending on their speed and destination, they could coast in orbit or head into interplanetary space to their rendezvous."

"Mother ship," Tim said darkly, "There has to be some sort of larger support vessel to retrieve them. That, or they have bases on earth or the moon."

"We have no knowledge of alien facilities on earth, Dr. Alexander," McLachland said. "If they do, they would likely be deep underwater and well concealed. Perfect environment for magnetohydrodynamics. The moon? Maybe. Over the years, we've managed to scour every square foot of the lunar surface using the highest resolution photographs available and found nothing. That, however, doesn't mean it isn't there. Just using some of our most recent advances in active camouflaging, they could have a Walmart Supercenter in the middle of the Sea of Tranquility and we might never see it."

The thought of a lunar Walmart made the three laugh out loud.

"Doctors, there is much more to see before lunch, and we don't want to miss that," McLachland said. "The cafeteria is serving up crispy apricot-glazed flounder today. It is a real treat! Must be somebody's birthday to get it for lunch."

The next stop in the tour was the newly remodeled Exobiology Department. While it still had a 1950's feel, the equipment was state-of-the-art. Even the alien corpses were warehoused in more efficient and modern facility. The so-called 'reference specimen' with its highly unusual dissection was in as good a shape as it was 40 years earlier. Both scientists examined the alien body for quite some time, drawing some basic conclusions from their limited knowledge of human anatomy. Both were impressed by the highly intricate folding of the cerebral cortex and lack of clear delineation between left and right hemispheres. If they were sure of one thing, it was that the complex infolding clearly suggested a more powerful brain.

After a brief stop at Ben Hanson's office and file room, adjacent to the Necropsy Room and Microbiology Lab, they proceeded to the newest addition to the complex.

"What we have here is actually a part of the Metallurgy Department," Dr.

McLachland began. "Our original mission was to analyze and replicate alien technology for defensive and offensive purposes, which, I understand, our President has decided to reduce to defensive applications only. We needed a way to find out how much damage we could inflict on their aircraft using our most lethal weapons. In the old days, we tested everything from pistols to 155mm Howitzers at an outdoor range, then assessed the damage caused by the bullets or warheads. Now, thanks to a substantially beefed-up nuclear reactor on site, we can use a 7000 meter-per-second rail gun with a 700gram tungsten carbide projectile to test the strength of these exotic alloys. The good news is that these projectiles can punch through the alien metal with ease. The bad news is the unknown. What kind of countermeasures might the aliens possess? Can they can track and intercept a hyper-velocity tungsten projectile with an equally powerful countermeasure? Well, if so, using our most state-of-the-art technology would be useless against them. The only way we can know for sure is to test their countermeasures by shooting at one."

"That could be suicide!" Alexander said excitedly.

"And precisely the reason why we haven't done it. That, and the fact that rail guns, especially this one, are not exactly mobile."

"There might be another good reason not to punch a hole in one." Donna pondered aloud. "Tim, if a hyper-velocity round passed through their hull and breached a reactor..."

"...it might vaporize a huge area of Canadian real estate!" Tim finished the sentence, shaking his head. "One pound of anti-matter is roughly equivalent in explosive power to 20 million tons of TNT. Even worse, they might have ultra-powerful reactors that use an energy source we haven't even dreamed of."

"Treacherous waters, indeed," McLachland added, "Project Cocheta faces a serious conundrum: We are tasked to unravel the mysteries of alien technology and develop countermeasures for their weapons, while paralyzed by our own justifiable fears of creating a cataclysmic accident if we touch the wrong control panel or probe into their reactors. Then there are the politicians that will go to great lengths to politicize this research facility as a means to gain advantage over their opponents. Even our President is tying our hands by banning the development of offensive weaponry."

"Dr. McLachland, the difference between an offensive and defensive weapon can be very, very subtle," Dr. Hanson replied. "This rail gun, for instance, could easily be both offensive and defensive. We, however, will give it a description that

suggests it is purely defensive, like a Patriot missile, yet it will still have the capability to engage and destroy air and ground targets using the same tungsten projectile."

"You are quite the scammer, Dr. Hanson!" Tim said with a smile and a laugh.

"Not a scammer, Tim, just that little girl at Lockheed that knows how to get her way by convincing bureaucrats and other meddlers that it was their idea."

Both men laughed and shook their heads. "Dr. Hanson," McLachland said, still grinning, "I'm going to retract the warning I gave you earlier. I have a feeling our proud band of poker players are the ones in serious trouble!"

Chapter 26

It was mid-afternoon by the time Senator Hanson and her small entourage of assistants took their seats before the Armed Services Committee. Though dressed smartly, it was evident to most that she was very tired, perhaps even close to exhaustion.

"Senator Hanson," Melana began, "you may begin your opening statement."

"Senator Melana, Senator Wilcox, members of the Armed Services Committee, Americans and the wonderful citizens of the great State of Oklahoma. Thank you for this opportunity to explain my actions and motives for my appearance last Sunday on Dr. Tim Alexander's cable television show. Let me make something clear right at the very start: The Science and Technology Channel and the production team at Science for the Rest of Us, were completely unaware that a special satellite feed was arranged to briefly preempt their programming. I humbly apologize for any inconvenience I may have caused to the good people working for Future-Span Communications LLC, the parent company of the Science and Technology Channel. I take complete responsibility for my actions.

Last Sunday evening, I announced to America and the World that we were being visited by an extraterrestrial culture. In doing so, I apparently ended 70 years of official and steadfast government denial that aliens were visiting our planet. My late husband, Dr. Benjamin Hanson, the chief scientist and engineer at the facility you now know as Project Cocheta, asked me to make the public announcement on behalf of him and his colleagues, many of whom have devoted their entire adult lives to uncovering the mysteries of a highly advanced alien civilization. My husband strongly believed that it was very important to discover as much information

as we could about the extraterrestrials and their technology.

It was a passionate dream of his to collaborate with scientists from around the world to solve the mysteries of their technology, culture and intentions regarding our planet. In January of 1992, the Cold War ended with the collapse of the old Soviet Union. My husband was convinced that a window of opportunity had opened for his vision to become reality. Instead of embracing the opportunity, Project Director Louis Hastings became furious and soundly rejected the idea. My husband, Dr. Hanson, gave his verbal resignation and made it clear he intended to bring his proposal directly to Washington. What happened after that profoundly changed the lives of our entire family... and as I learned later, put us under constant threat of being murdered.

It was not known at that time that the accidents, which eventually claimed the lives of 15 retired scientists, were actually murders, orchestrated by Louis Hastings, to ensure that they would never leak information to the public. Louis Hastings made it very clear that if my husband did not back down, his family would suffer the consequences. As a result, my husband, fearing for the safety of his family, sent us back to Oklahoma and broke all ties to the family he loved so much."

Tears began to well up in her eyes as she mustered more will to press on. "We divorced without any explanation other than it was for our safety. My family and I suffered immensely. For over 20 years we were deprived of father, grandfather and husband. I thank God he defied death long enough to see and touch the grandchildren he always wanted.

When I finally heard from my husband again..," she paused again, wiping tears, "he asked only two things of me. The first was to make the announcement on Dr. Alexander's program. The other, to give an important letter to my daughter, Dr. Donna Hanson. I have fulfilled those requests.

If the members of this committee care to know why I did what I did, I can sum it up in one word: trust. I trusted my husband's motives. I trusted his judgment. I trusted his love for me, his children and of America. My husband was not a rogue. He was gentle, thoughtful, loving, hard working, selfless and most assuredly, a patriot. He opened all of our eyes to the real nature of the universe and participated in a great effort to make us safer.

In closing, we have two roads to chose from. The first is the usual Washington nonsense: creating alternate realities, witch-hunting and grandstanding. The second is to embrace my husband's vision to unite scientists of all disciplines, from around the world, to better help us understand the alien technology and culture. Unlike the President, I believe we should also be prepared to defend ourselves should the need arise.

Lastly, a warning: My daughter, Dr. Donna Hanson, has accepted the Project Director's position at the Cocheta facility. Leave… her… alone! Leave her facility alone! She is one of the most brilliant aerospace engineers on earth and was a superb executive at Lockheed-Martin. She does not need your help and she does not tolerate meddling."

"Thank you, committee members, for allowing me the time to make my statement," she said, closing her eyes with a tightness that betrayed her pain and anger if anyone were looking closely.

The circus was about to begin.

Chapter 27

"That was quite a tour, Dr. McLachland!" Tim said as the trio sat down to enjoy a well deserved lunch. "Overwhelming... I almost feel like I should be waking up by now."

"I feel the same way, Tim," Donna replied in hearty agreement. "So much to digest. So many obstacles."

"Ms. Foreman, you'll get accustomed to all this in a hurry," McLachland said with a smile.

"I'm sorry, did you refer to me as Foreman?" Donna asked.

"Why, yes. Yes I did," McLachland replied while savoring the tantalizing aroma of expertly prepared fresh flounder. "It is a pet name, of sorts. General Marston was the first real Project Director at Cocheta. Tough as nails and brilliant. You might remember him. The staff admired him so much they gave him the title. When Captain Brogan took the reigns, he too was given the title. Hastings? He assumed the title himself, but few of the staff and none of the Marines ever referred to him as Foreman. If you don't mind, the staff and the Marines would like to call you that."

"I don't know what to say?" Donna replied, truly taken back by the honor. "Thank you! Of course I will! I hope I can live up to the honor!"

"The off-shift support staff here learned that you would be offered the position a day or so before my flight to Miami," McLachland said. "This place lit up! Everyone was smiling and crossing their fingers that you would take the position. It was only this early morning that they learned both you and Dr. Alexander were actually joining the team. I assure you, by this evening, you two will have shook quite a few hands!"

"It must have been very rough working here," Tim said with a frown. "I can't imagine working in a place run by a complete jerk. A murderous one at that."

"It was bad, Tim. Very bad, but good times are upon us now," McLachlan said with genuine optimism. "By the way, you better get started on your lunch. This glazed flounder is a rare treat... and it's going to get cold!"

Lunch was every bit as good as Dr. McLachland said it would be, and then some. Like all the other scientists and support crew before them, Donna and Tim wondered how they were going to fit into their clothes eating like this every day. Tim was admiring the smile on Donna's face. There was no hint of shallowness to it at all. Without a doubt, she was every bit as honest and caring as her father. He could feel the attraction to her getting stronger as his awareness of that around him diminished.

"Why are you looking at me that way, Tim?"

Mildly startled at the question because he hadn't realized Donna was starting to look back at him. "I was just noticing how much your eyes look like your dad's," he replied with a hint of some embarrassment in his voice.

"My mom tells me that all the time, and thanks for noticing," she said with a growing smile. "The two of you are going to give me a really big head!"

Tim laughed at the remark, then noticed that Dr. McLachland was staring at something. He looked in the same direction and saw a plasma screen monitor turned to C-SPAN, with Donna's mother testifying before the Senate Armed Services Committee!

"Donna, you need to see this!" Tim said with urgency in his voice. 'Your mom is on C-SPAN!"

Donna turned and stood up. Not 30 feet away was the image of her mother testifying in Congress and front of the entire world. All three hurried to the monitor and turned up the volume.

"She looks completely exhausted," Donna said with great concern.

"I can't believe they made your mother do this right after Ben's funeral," McLachland said in disgust. "Washington bastards! Like a bunch of mindless piranhas with blood in the water."

A growing number curious staff members began to gather around the monitor. The Cocheta hearings were very important to everyone involved in the project and the President's remarks earlier in the week made them nervous. Political and bureaucratic chicanery could easily cripple the Cocheta mission, perhaps even eliminate it.

"... Lastly, a warning: My daughter, Dr. Donna Hanson, has accepted the Project Director's position at the Cocheta facility. Leave... Her... Alone! Leave her facility alone! She is one of the most brilliant aerospace engineers on earth and was a superb executive at Lockheed Martin. She does not need your help and she does not tolerate meddling."

A cheer erupted from the 20 or so staff. It was an obvious affirmation that the Project staff was enthusiastic about their new management after years of misery under a treacherous bureaucrat.

"Your mom is tough as nails, Dr. Hanson," McLachland said. "They hate that in a woman. I'm sure they will do everything they can to beat her down."

"And they'll spit out their own teeth," Donna replied with a sly grin.

Dr. McLachland looked at Donna with a wink. "You know, I don't doubt that one bit. You two are peas in a pod."

"Yes we are. I'm very proud of her!"

"Where to now, Dr. McLachland?" Tim asked enthusiastically.

"I'd prefer an afternoon nap, but... briefings on project history, organization, security, compartmentalization, military interface and command structure, financing, equipment requests, recruitment, field trips, boring administrative stuff like payroll, benefit packages... You'll be ready for a nap after we get through with you!"

"I guess there is no escaping red tape, even in a facility that didn't exist before last Sunday," Tim said, remembering the strong human penchant for making things much more difficult than they needed to be. "You mentioned field trips. I'm assuming they are not excursions on yellow busses."

"No, Tim," McLachland chuckled, "they are investigations of alien mishaps or other incidents of significance that require thorough investigations. When a qualifying IoS occurs, the Project Director assembles a team to investigate it. These used to be very secret agent-ish sorts of affairs with us wearing dark suits and equally dark sunglasses when we interfaced with the public. Pretty intimidating. The whole men in black myth wasn't a myth at all, it was our people investigating an important IoS."

"What about women in black?" Donna asked whimsically. "I don't think I'm tall enough to intimidate anybody, though."

"Actually, we have had a few women in black over the years, Donna, but I'm afraid that with Project Cocheta and our mission out in the open, I really don't see the need for us to do anything but pure investigation."

"Well, that kinda sucks!" Donna said with a smile. "I think I'd look pretty hot in a black business suit!"

The three laughed as Dr. McLachland waved the two project directors to the exit. "Your next stop is a sea of paperwork and briefing, my friends. There are plenty of pens and hot coffee. When you're finished, we'll have a nice chat about one Wilhelm F. Heischler, PhD."

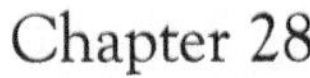

Chapter 28

"Senator Hanson," Melana said in a moderately menacing tone, beginning the individual cross examination phase of the inquiry, "what gave you the right to break Federal law and divulge highly classified information?"

"My oath of office demands that I protect and defend the Constitution, my moral oath is to protect the citizens of Oklahoma and the United States from harm. I only divulged information pertaining to the existence of extraterrestrial beings on earth and our efforts to study them. That is information everyone has the right to know."

"You, Senator Hanson, divulged the existence of Project Cocheta, an ultra-top secret project conducted by the United States government."

"I did no such thing, Senator Melana."

"Yes, you did, Senator Hanson! You implied that there was a secret facility by stating your husband worked at one."

"I have the transcript right here, Senator Melana. I said no such thing. I said facility, not top secret facility, or secret facility, or classified facility. Just facility. I did not mention its location. I did, however, say highly classified project."

"You are mincing words Senator Hanson!" Melana said with growing anger. "I will not play these games with you. Did you, or did you not divulge the status of the project?"

"First of all, Senator Melana, I'm not playing games. Appearing before a Senate investigative committee is hardly playing games. You seem to be having trouble reading the transcript of what I said, so I'm merely helping you out. Yes, I did say that little has been learned about alien technology and culture, but that is hardly divulging detailed or useful information."

Melana was furious. 'How dare this redneck bitch speak down to me!' He thought to himself. 'Make a fool out of me... I'll see her fry first!'

"Can you sit there, and tell me honestly, that you did not divulge state secrets, Senator Hanson?"

"I am most certainly guilty of breaching protocol, Senator Melana, and I have already apologized to the President for that. Prior to my announcement, 80 percent of Americans already believed the government was keeping information about UFOs a secret from the public. Turns out they were 100 percent right! Nearly 80 percent believed that aliens left evidence of their existence on earth. More than a third of Americans believed that aliens had already visited earth. Today, nearly 100 percent do! How could my announcement have any significant impact on national security? Look at the polls, Senator Melana! There was no mass hysteria because a significant portion of the population already believed in extraterrestrials!"

"Polls do not interest me, Senator Hanson..."

"That would be a first," Senator Hanson interrupted with a perfectly straight face as subdued laughter broke out.

"Quiet, all of you!" Melana bellowed. He was clearly close to blowing his top. "I will not allow this hearing turn into a circus! Senator Hanson, you will refrain from trying to disrupt my session of questioning! Do you honestly believe that no federal laws were broken when you made your speech last Sunday evening?"

"Yes, that is correct. I only told the American people what they already knew instinctively, so it will have little, if any, long lasting effect on Americans and our society."

"Do you deny that your speech created a diplomatic nightmare for the State Department?"

"If you call the obligatory Russian posturing and Chinese hypocrisy a nightmare. Why, yes. I suppose I did."

"Senator Hanson, this is not the time nor place for flippancy. Please answer

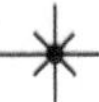

my questions with proper respect!"

It was Teresa Hanson's turn to blow her lid.

"Respect? Are you kidding me Harold Melana, you unprincipled ass? You and the rest of your pathetic ilk are not worthy of respect! You talk high and mighty in public while making lucrative insider deals when nobody is looking. These are not hallowed halls of righteous American government to you, halls bought and paid for by the blood of patriots. They are a marketplace for power, cash and..."

"Senator Hanson, you WILL sit down immediately or I will have you removed!"

"... sex!" The Oklahoma Senator continued. "What intern are you breaking in this week, Harold? Wife know about her?"

"Sit down Senator Hanson! Right now!"

"You know what the really pathetic thing is?" Hanson said in a slightly more subdued voice. "This whole week, you and your attack dogs have been so caught up in the politics that not even once have you mentioned the aliens! The greatest revelation since the birth of Christ and you completely ignore it! If that is not illustrative of the dysfunction in this place, nothing is!"

Senator Hanson stood up slowly, brushed a few wrinkles from her skirt and began to walk towards the chamber exit. Photographers were holding their shutter releases down creating an intense barrage of flashes flooding the committee chamber.

"Senator Hanson, you have not been excused! Please take your seat!"

"I'm excusing myself," she said in an almost imperceptible voice. The chaotic camera flashes were now closer and the roar around her was starting to become disorienting. An odd, powerful feeling was starting to well up in her stomach.

"Senator Hanson, we WILL find you in contempt of Congress!"

"You are contempt..." An overwhelming wave of nausea swept over Teresa as her vision quickly faded from tunnel vision to black. She fell forward and landed very hard onto the floor, losing consciousness in the process.

Chapter 29

"Vitya, my young nephew," President Korolyvov yelled, "come quickly and watch this video feed from CSPAN! The American Senate is trying to punish the Hanson woman, perhaps to oust her from office!"

"Dear uncle, what silliness!" Viktor laughed as he put down his Sovetsky Sport newspaper. "You said yourself that this American political trial is a charade to gain more power for the party that opposes her. Besides, this woman you admire is much too skinny for you."

"I make exception for this one, nephew. She has fire in her belly! She must be part Russian!"

Viktor stood up to catch a glimpse of the American his uncle seemed so preoccupied with. "She is very handsome, uncle."

"That she is, and much more so for her age. At this very moment, she is very angry! What is that expression the American cowboys say? Smack down? Yes! That is it! She is putting the smack down on this corrupt fool Melana!"

"That is very entertaining, Alyosha, but it is getting late. May I retire?"

"This is unheard of Viktor!" Korolyvov almost gasped. "She is leaving the hearing without permission!"

Sitnikov stood up again to look over his uncle's shoulder. "From what I know of these American political proceedings, they are very much structured. What might she be doing?"

"She has lost patience with the insolent politician, Vitya! Much good for her!"

Sitnikov laughed again at his uncle. "I believe this to be an entertainment, Aloysha, much like dramatic cinema. Is this not common in American politics?"

"Viktor! Did you see that? The Hanson Senator has collapsed! This is very bad!"

"Yes, uncle! I saw it! It appeared that she fell right on her face without putting her hands up. Perhaps I misjudged this politician."

"If she goes to the hospital, make sure we send flowers and draft a public statement wishing her a quick healing. Do this before you retire, young one."

"Aloysha, with respect, do you not think that this is grand foolishness?"

"Absolutely not, Viktor! Our country sends many messages of sympathy upon the deaths of dignitaries and wishes of well being to those with illnesses or injury! Sometimes we do this even when the dignitary speaks of us unkindly. Diplomacy is an important part of running our great country."

"But, do you not have a sexual attraction to her?"

"Vitya! Such a terrible assumption! My soul is not so shallow! Can I not admire a woman's beauty and fire without being thought of as a man with questionable intent?"

"I meant no disrespect, Aloysha. I know you are lonely."

"Not so lonely when my favorite nephew helps me govern Mother Russia!" Korolyvov said to lighten the conversation.

Sitnikov smiled. "The Hanson Senator appears to be moving, uncle. The orderlies are tending to her now."

"That is good news, Viktor." Korolyvov replied while noticing his cup of tea had run dry. "You must tend to business and I must find more hot tea."

Chapter 30

"Do I need to come to Washington, Mom?" Donna asked of her mother. "I can be there in a few hours."

"No, sweetheart. I'm fine," Teresa replied with a heavy nasal tone due to the placement of nasal packing to treat a serious nose bleed and nasal fracture. "Dr. Keller said I passed out from increased vagal tone, stress and fatigue. I broke my nose, too and I have a black eye that seems to be getting worse by the hour. I haven't seen a mirror, yet. I don't think I want to."

"Mom, the people here are phenomenal! If you need me there, I'm sure..."

"The nice folks here at Bethesda are taking very good care of me. They have already splinted my nose and Dr. Keller said he wanted to watch me for two or three days to make sure I get some rest. You have important work to do and I'm OK. Really!"

Donna wiped a tear from her eye. "You sure?"

"Yes, sweetie! I've got a nice room, good doctors and nurses... and the room is already filling up with cards and flowers. I even got a beautiful bouquet and card from the Russian President!"

"That's funny, Mom!" Donna Hanson replied, wiping a tear rolling down her left cheek. "I watched the exchange between you and Senator Melana. You have a lot of devoted friends here at the project that are pulling for you!"

Teresa laughed the best she could manage. "That's good because I don't seem to have a lot of them anymore. It's good to know your staff is picking up the slack. Sweetie, the pain medicine is starting to take effect. Please call me tomorrow. I'm sure I'll be more awake then."

"Sure mom, You take care of yourself! Promise me?"

"I promise!"

Senator Hanson hung up the phone and almost immediately fell asleep. It would be her first, truly restful sleep in well over five days.

Chapter 31

"How is your Mom, Donna?" Tim asked with genuine concern in his voice.

"She's exhausted, beat up, hurting and under the influence of drugs," she replied. "I'm really concerned about her, Tim."

"She's a real scrapper. I'm sure she will be OK."

"I don't know... I remember reading a statistic that surviving widowers have a much higher risk of death within a year of their loss."

"It's been a terrible week, for sure, but your mother is far healthier than the vast majority of women her age. I don't think you have anything to worry about."

"Still... I wish I could be there for her."

"I know, but if there is a silver lining to this, she should be able to get plenty of rest before she beats up on poor little Harold again."

Donna smiled. "Even completely exhausted, Mom took him to the woodshed, didn't she! He's going to wish he'd never started this ludicrous witch hunt."

"Maybe I'm not a very nice man, sweetheart, but I swear I'm going to thoroughly enjoy watching Melana pop all the arteries in his head!"

Tim instantly realized what he said and froze, wondering if Donna had picked up on it. Both looked at each other and said nothing for what seemed to be an eternity.

"I'm..," Tim began to appologize when Donna gently put a finger to his lips and looked at his eyes... then smiled.

Without saying another spoken word, a flood of emotions were exchanged in in an instant. Their attraction to each other was growing stronger and both hoped what they were feeling was going to last.

"I don't mind you calling me that, Tim, if you don't mind me doing the same."

"I'm certain I can live with those terms, Dr. Hanson," Tim said with a slightly nervous smile, relieved that he hadn't shot himself in the foot.

"It's about time to get back to the briefing, Tim. There will be more opportunities."

"For what?"

"One of the sharpest minds on earth and all you can say to me is 'For what?'!"

Tim smiled. "I have no earthly idea what you are talking about."

"Good Lord, do I have to do everything around here?" she said with faux frustration as she stepped close to Tim and gave him a warm, passionate kiss.

When their lips parted, Tim stroked her hair gently. "Was that all you wanted?"

Donna smiled and pushed at his chest. "And all this time I thought you were a mild-mannered physics nerd!"

"I still am! Wanna see my Sigma Pi Sigma pin?"

This time Tim pulled Donna close for a lingering kiss that neither wanted to end.

"We had better get back, Tim, before they send out a search party."

"I'm with ya." Tim replied, his mind somewhat dazed from their first encounter as a couple.

"Donna," Tim asked as they approached the briefing room, "would you join me on a date tonight? I have never seen the Aurora Borealis and the viewing conditions are supposed to be phenomenal."

"Will we need a chaperone?"

"I don't think so."

"Then count me in!"

Chapter 32

"I want her back on the stand as soon as possible!" Senator Melana bellowed. "I don't care how beat up she is!"

"Harold, don't push this!" begged Andrew Pearce, Senator Melana's chief advisor. "I've seen injuries like her's before. They don't look all that bad the first day, but give them a few days and they look far worse. Give it at least a week."

"A week?" Melana bellowed again. "Have you forgotten we an election coming up?"

"I'm going to be frank with you, Harold... Hanson owned you for the short time she was on the stand. You lost your temper with a woman and that never plays well. Even worse if she's a recent widower. I know you want to get even and you'll get your chance, I promise you, but we have to play this smart."

"Well, when do we get her back on the stand?"

"Lets call some early witnesses and experts. Maybe tee up Hanson on Thursday."

"Thursday?" Melana bellowed again. "That is an eternity in politics!"

"Do you want her to show up with a black and blue face and a nose splint?"

"Damn! You don't suppose she set this up, do you?" Melana asked, searching for some way to make her look like she was feigning a loss of consciousness.

"I saw her fall, Harold. Fairly close up. She was out cold before her face hit the floor."

"Maybe you're right, Andrew. Maybe we should play it cool this weekend," Melana said, resigned to the fact that perfectly good weekend would yield no gains against the opposition. "I don't like this at all, and I still think she staged this somehow..." He paused to shake his head. "No hardballs on the Sunday shows. Keep it civil. We'll catch up next week."

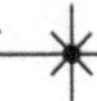

Chapter 33

"Dr. McLachland, this food is outrageous!" Tim said, wiping his mouth with a napkin after his last bite of the most wonderful Prime Rib he had ever tasted. "Do you have a chef here?"

"Well, sort of." McLachland replied with a grin. "Ol' Frogman Willie and his hand-picked staff keep us fed and spoiled. He's been here for almost as long as I have. Very colorful character, too. Sometimes you can hear him cuss all the way to the bowling center. I'm not talking about a bad word here and there. Frogman can make a pirate blush! He's former Navy UDT, the guys that predate the modern Navy Seals."

"Is he mean?" Donna asked quietly.

"The Marines think so. They have their own mess in the Company Barracks and Frogman runs that, too. He takes great pleasure in taunting the Marines at the serving line, most often by questioning their gender and sexual preferences. He does have a weak spot, though."

"What would that be?"

"Patty."

"His girlfriend?"

"No, his dog. A mixed breed mutt. Kinda ugly. No, I take that back. The dog is seriously ugly, but Frogman loves that dog more than his own life."

"He has a dog? Here?"

"Yep! He feeds us so well we bend the rules for him. Even Hastings signed-off on the dog without bitching about it!" McLachland said with a toothy grin. "It's a great arrangement for most of us."

"But, not for the Marines."

"No, they eat very well, too. For them, the downside is his constant harassment and.." McLachland stopped to control his snickering, "well, three times a day, Frogman takes Patty out to the Marines' physical fitness training area and lets her deposit presents for them!"

All three laughed heartily.

"So, this is the only five star restaurant in northern British Columbia, and it's run by a cursing Frogman with an ugly dog!" Donna said with a grin.

"That it is it in a nutshell. It can only be weirder in the Yukon!" McLachland said, then allowed his countenance to become noticeably darker.

"You've both read the Heischler Report. What did you think of it?"

"Very plausible and frightening," Tim said. "His arguments are impossible to completely dismiss."

"I agree with Tim. Heischler makes a very compelling case for an aggressive pre-disposition," Donna added. "Only, we have no reported acts of aggression from them."

"That is what continues to perplex us," McLachland lamented. "Heischler was either wrong, or we are missing something."

"OK," Donna began, heralding a new session of brainstorming, "We have two basic types of alien aircraft: one that carries aliens, the other, unmanned drones. My first question would be: 'If they possess highly sophisticated drones, why are the aliens risking confrontation on a highly militarized planet?'"

"I suppose they might be arrogant enough to fly wherever they want because their aircraft outperforms our absolute best by a huge margin," Tim offered.

"Maybe, but arrogance can be a very dangerous lifestyle," McLachland countered. "The illusion of invincibility."

"So, let's say our visitors have learned their lessons about being cocky, no mat-

ter how inferior they believe us to be. Could that be the reason they don't appear aggressive?"

"Waiting," Tim suggested. "They are loitering... waiting for something."

"That's good, Tim!" Donna said with a smile. "Very good. Assuming this is correct, what have they been waiting for over the last 70 years?"

"Maybe nothing," McLachland said. "Maybe earth is just some sort of outpost for them. A truck stop, maybe."

"If they are just passing through, what's with the fully intact aircraft they handed to us? That might also be spying on our progress." Tim asked.

"I've never been comfortable with it, Tim," McLachland admitted. "It appears to be functional, at least in the interior lighting aspect, and it hasn't shown any hint of losing power, even after more than 40 years. Then there is the damnable fear we all have about messing with its innards, not knowing how much serious tinkering it will take before we screw something up enough to detonate it."

"The fact that the aliens intentionally gave it to us might actually speak volumes about their intentions," Donna postulated. "Think about it this way: if they are very careful and meticulous, they would want to know what our most advanced technology is. Our cars and aircraft are fairly primitive compared to the technology we use to try and understand the alien technology we have right here. Maybe this alien aircraft is something entirely different. Maybe it is just a shell and its primary purpose is surveillance far beyond recording our conversations within the craft itself. They could be using nanotechnology or other exotic technologies to tap into every information system we have!"

"Oh my God! We never considered that possibility!" McLachland said, his blood running cold. "Our information systems are linked to the Department of Defense and dozens of other defense and security related agencies!"

"I'm not a computer expert by any stretch of the imagination," Tim said with deep concern evident in his voice, "but if they are capable of interstellar flight, they must surely be able to hack a network and imbed incredibly stealthy code that could potentially monitor every internet-linked computer on Earth!"

There was, what seemed to be, a long pause in the conversation as each scientist pondered the horror they might have stumbled onto. It was Donna that broke the silence.

"It makes sense," She started with a chill running down her spine. "The aliens knew of my father back in 1968. They did the same thing to me and Tim last night. Somehow, they knew we were on the 650!"

"We've been compromised for decades!" McLachland said, the horror taking full effect. "My God almighty..."

Chapter 34

"Triple C, Master Sergeant Grimes speaking."

"This is Dr. McLachland, I need a secure line and patch me to CINC USNORTHCOM immediately."

"Affirmative, Sir. Right away!" Grimes replied smartly. The Cocheta Command Center was staffed 24 hours a day by a senior enlisted Marine and a field grade watch officer. Together, they handled outside communications, air traffic control and facility-wide public announcements. "Major Alleyne, I'm connecting Dr. McLachland to CINC USNORTHCOM. Must be pretty important!"

"Must be," she replied while walking in from an adjoining office. "Wonder if it has something to do with the Code Green last night."

"I don't know... that was several hours ago. Maybe our new project director is reporting back to NORTHCOM." Grimes speculated while patching McLachland's urgent call to the Commander-in-Chief of US Northern Command.

"Northern Command, Colonel Miles speaking."

"Colonel Miles, this is ANR-CRF. I'm going to patch you to Dr. McLachland. He would like to speak with CinC USNORTHCOM. Please hold."

Peterson Air Force Base, near Colorado Springs, was the home of NORAD, the North American Aerospace Command and USNORTHCOM, which was the primary military interface for ANR-CRF. Technically, the Cocheta Research Facility was actually located within the Canadian NORAD Region (CANR), but for a more streamlined chain of command, CRF was bundled into the Alaska NORAD Region (ANR). Acronyms are the bread and butter of military speak, as if pronouncing the entire name might measurably shorten the number of words that can be spoken in one's lifetime.

"Dr. McLachland, it has been a while since we last heard from our chilly little mountain," Major General Clifton Huber said. "I'm very sorry for your loss. Ben Hanson was a brilliant and decent man. I don't agree with the way he made damn sure CRF wasn't going to be much of a secret anymore, but I genuinely admired his convictions and his courage. He will be missed."

"Thank you, General Huber," McLachland said, "I have Dr. Donna Hanson here and she needs to speak with you."

"General Huber?"

"Donna Hanson, how are you? It's been... what? Three, four years ago at Plant 42?"

"I think so, Cliff. It has been a while."

"Sorry about your Dad, Donna. I know I speak for everyone in the chain of command when I say the we all loved and admired Ben. We will really miss him at the quarterly briefings at Peterson," the General said with genuine sadness in his voice.

"Thank you, Cliff. I miss him, too."

"Donna, I can't tell you how glad as hell I am that you're running CRF now! That Hastings character was a shithead! Good riddance!"

"Cliff, we might have a real serious problem."

"What kind?"

"Cyber security."

"Who's hacking you, Donna?"

"The aliens."

"Sweet Jesus! Are you sure?"

"I can't prove it right now, Cliff, but we think the intact alien aircraft we've

 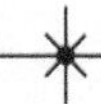

had on ice for forty years has surveillance capabilities far greater than we ever imagined! I am almost certain they have hacked our computers."

"Please tell me you are kidding! What kind of evidence do you have?"

"The aliens knew Dr. Alexander and I were coming to Cocheta! Nobody but us and the Command Center knew! Cliff, after we landed, one of them flew to within 50 feet of us! The only way they could have known about our whereabouts was by tapping into our Command Center computers!"

"Your computers are linked to ours and ours to..."

"The DoD, CIA, FBI, FEMA, DHS... and probably a lot more," Donna interrupted. "We must assume every computer, perhaps the entire internet, has been corrupted with unbelievably sophisticated code that we might not be able to detect!"

"If this is true, we are in serious trouble!" General Huber said, hoping this new nightmare was just a bad joke. "I'll contact J-6 at the Joint Chiefs of Staff and fill her in."

"Thank you, and please keep us informed, General. We'll do what we can here, probably start by dumping this thing in a hole and encasing it in concrete."

"That might be a good start, Donna. We will keep you up to speed and, by the way, congrats on your new job! I can't think of anyone better qualified for the position than you!"

"Thank you, General. We'll keep you informed, as well."

Chapter 35

"Seriously, what did you just say?" asked Jason Hull, Network Security Specialist at the DoD Cyber Crime Center (DC3).

"You heard me," replied Doug 'The Hackinator' Ellerman, senior cyber crime analyst. "USNORTHCOM has reason to believe that DoD computers and servers have been compromised by the aliens. They also believe that the problem may go back as far as 40 years!"

"Aliens?" he asked incredulously. "You mean the creatures that Senator Hanson was going to testify about?"

"The very same. Look, all I know is that J-6 got a call from General Huber regarding a potential cyber infiltration of the DoD network and she wants us to look into it... like, yesterday."

"OK, I'll bite. As of about 10 minutes ago, all DoD servers, networks, and websites, along with every other Government network and website seem to be running just dandy. So, where do you suggest we start?"

"Alien malware or not, we start the same way we always do, Jason: The obvious to the impossible. Check for user complaints, then start with our servers. Look for odd or invisible files. Apps that don't belong."

"Waste of time."

"What? Why do you say that?"

"Well, we are, arguably, one of the finest teams in the Cyber Crime world,"

Hull said, "yet we have absolutely no chance of solving this problem."

"That is a helluva defeatist attitude, Jason!" Ellerman replied with real ire in his voice. "We can figure this out if we put enough firepower on it!"

"Not a chance!" Hull said with a dark laugh. "These aliens come from another star system, for cryin' out loud! If they have been hacking our networks for decades, the odds that we would be able to find evidence of it is about the same as finding a needle in a haystack the size of the moon!"

"You can't pick and choose your assignments, Jason," Ellerman said. "The Boss Lady wants us to verify that we've been compromised. It's important!"

"I don't think you quite understand the enormity of the problem. The things they are capable doing would look like frickin' magic to us! Bottom line is: we're screwed! The only way to get them out of our system is to shut it all down. Wipe every drive, every server, every network, every home computer, every iPhone... and even then, that might not be enough. They could have stand-alone microbots that are small enough to infiltrate practically anything and record everything they see and hear!"

"So, you think we should just give up?"

"No, we should not expect much, if anything, in return for our efforts."

"Then let's get the team together and come up with a strategy to tackle this problem," Ellerman suggested. "We don't know how time-sensitive this is, so we should assume the worst."

"Sounds like a plan," Hull replied. "Just remember, if an alien pops in, I'm outta here!"

Chapter 36

The most advanced technology on the target planet was many hundreds of thousands of local stellar orbits behind the Centralians. Even so, they would not give in to arrogance and the carelessness that comes with it. Their own history was replete with great cultures falling to supposed 'inferior forces,' almost entirely due to failures in maintaining the social and technologic infrastructures that made them great in the first place, or simply underestimating the resolve and cunning of their adversaries. The extreme social trauma associated with the Great Interstellar War that nearly led to their extinction put an end to arrogance on Centralia. No opponent was to be taken lightly and well-proven military tactics, handed down through thousands of Centralian generations, would be followed to the letter, no matter how militarily inferior the target species appeared to be.

The Great Interstellar War led to a completely different survival stratagem for the Centralians. The spread of colonies beyond half of their sphere of influence came to an abrupt halt, opting instead to preemptively sterilize planets with potentially dangerous intelligent life. Colonization of the third planet, like its murdered sibling before it, was never an option for the Centralians. The planetary system was located just past the outermost edge of their comfortable sphere of influence. The outer half of the sphere was a buffer zone, of sorts, should an equal or superior species attempt an attack on the colonized Centralian inner sphere. This buffer zone was approximately 1.37 million Centralian solar distances wide, 25 "light-years" in the terminology of the dominant species on 'Earth.' This distance was considered sufficient to allow time to prepare an adequate defense against an aggressor.

For nearly 70 local solar orbits, Centralian scout vehicles gathered vast

amounts of data on the target planet. Most of these ultra-performance aircraft were unarmed and unmanned, relying on raw speed and maneuverability to evade potential fire during dozens upon dozens of encounters with military aerial vehicles and surface launched weapons from the many different cultural subdivisions on the target planet.

Most... but not all.

Passive reconnaissance of the target planet was the first phase in the military action leading to planetary sterilization. The next step, initiated when the Centralian military armada was within 0.5 local stellar orbits from the target, required the use of armed airships. These 'Aggressor' vehicles were a third larger than the scouts, the added volume necessary to house a second dark matter reactor completely dedicated to the three weapon systems on board. Lacking the ability to maneuver in space, the Aggressors would be launched from the largest Centralian military ship via hyper velocity cannon. Once in the planet's atmosphere, magnetohydrodynamic propulsion becomes available. Egress from the planet involved a high performance technique using a high altitude maneuver at speeds greater than five times the planet's escape velocity, sending it on a ballistic path to the appropriate recovery craft.

The mission of the first Aggressors, and the few armed drones already present on the planet, would be to evaluate and tune their weapons with data gathered during select attacks on military and non-military targets. Direct confrontation with the planet's military forces en masse was not the objective. If a military response resulted from a probing action, it would merely be evaded, then evaluated for the tactics the adversary used.

After over two Centralian years of space travel, the waiting was almost over. Parked in a 'blind spot, four local lunar distances from the target planet, the largest of the two military ships launched a pair of Aggressors with orders to seek, select and engage targets under varying atmospheric and hydrological conditions.

The second phase in the sterilization of Earth was about to begin.

Chapter 37

"Tim, you were right. The Aurora is absolutely breathtaking!"

"This is the first time I've seen them, Donna," Tim said in an almost whisper. "They're beautiful!"

"Thanks for suggesting this, Tim." She said softly. "I have a bad habit of getting so wrapped up in work I forget to enjoy myself every once in a while. Seasoned workaholic, I suppose."

Tim smiled at her. "We all fall into that trap, but out here... My God! We can really experience the Aurora and the sounds of the night without our minds analyzing it all."

The British Columbia air was crisp and chilly, with a light breeze wafting through an open area greenbelt that was, up until recently, a cold war minefield between the taxiway and the Marines' fortified positions. A handful of concrete picnic tables and charcoal grills were scattered about the five-plus acres devoted to what amounted to be a community park of sorts. Tim and Donna chose the table closest to the taxiway, affording them the most privacy. A soft light created by billions of stars in the cloudless, crystalline black sky, and the shimmering green sheets of the Aurora, were the only source of night time illumination. Deep neon blue patches of the last remaining snow were faintly visible where daytime shadows allowed the remnants of the last snowfall to melt more slowly.

"What have we gotten ourselves into, Tim?" Donna asked earnestly.

"The greatest adventure two scientists could ever dream of," Tim replied while

reaching for her hand.

"Up until this afternoon, I genuinely felt that way. Now, with the possibility that our entire national defense network has been compromised? That genuinely frightens me," she said, letting down her usual titanium veneer. "My Dad was right, Tim. These creatures are aggressive. They're waiting for something. The right time, I suppose."

"Donna, you may be right. You probably are right..." Tim paused to visually take in an extraordinary sheet of ionized atmosphere overhead. "All we can do now is dedicate ourselves to finding an effective strategy to defeat them. But not tonight, sweetheart. We have God's brush beautifully painting the night sky in real time and I'm really enjoying the company of a sweet, gentle woman. I have no idea what's going to happen, Donna. I only know that, somehow, we'll find a way to get through it."

Donna looked at the remarkable man in front of her. She knew of his wife's death from ovarian cancer and that he led a life totally dedicated to his students and his cable TV show. Within the span of a week, he became her trusted colleague, helping her unlock the technologies that posed a threat to the human species. His students, his show... all that he cared for was replaced by a vow that he would stand by her and her project... even to the very end.

She reached her hand to his face and stroked his cheek. All of their communication at that moment were without spoken words. Looks, gentle caresses of each other's hands... it was the moment when a kindling ember of attraction threatens to erupt into something more meaningful. There was no way to stop it. It was inevitable as the next glorious sunrise.

After a half hour of small talk and holding hands, the outside PA speakers crackled to life.

"Code Green, Southeast Sector, range: two point one miles. Code Green, Northeast Sector, range: one point four miles."

Jolted from their intimate moment, Tim and Donna instinctively jumped from the picnic table and began to search the sky for the alien intruders.

"Tim, I see the one to the northeast! It's coming this way!"

"Donna, I can't see the other one clearly because of trees, but I can see the glow. It seems to be coming this way, too! Let's get out of here!"

Tim rounded the concrete table, grabbed Donna firmly by the hand and began running tandem as fast as they could towards the Cocheta complex, slightly more than 300 yards away. The Marines were already pouring out of the doors on the north side barracks and running towards their assigned positions.

"Donna, the one on our left is coming in behind us! What's the other one doing?"

"The one to our right is doing the same! We need to split up, Tim!" she yelled with a cough induced by cold air and running.

"No way, Donna! No way!"

The two alien aircraft assumed positions directly behind the running couple 150 yards away... and began to steadily close the distance. Tim and Donna were running as fast as they could, but it began to appear the alien vehicles would easily overtake them before reaching the perceived safety of the nearest fortified positions. Several Marines saw the running couple and chose to run past their emplacements to intercept them. By the time they were 100 yards from the tarmac, fatigue and coughing in the thin, cold air were rapidly draining the couple of their remaining stamina. Both craft continued to close the distance until they were 70 yards behind. That was when Donna tripped on an unseen indentation in the turf, falling hard on her outstretched left arm, taking Tim down with her.

"Donna!" Tim turned and called to her in near panic. "Are you OK?"

"I think... I broke or sprained my... ankle, Tim. Hurts really bad... I can't... run anymore and... I can't catch... my breath!" she replied in a labored voice. "Please... go, Tim!"

Tim said nothing. The two alien vehicles were now 50 yards away and slowly descending. Tim crawled to Donna's side and covered her with his body and thick, oversized jacket.

"Please Tim... please go!" she pleaded.

Again, he said nothing as he pulled her closer to him. The aliens were now 30 yards away at an altitude of 50 feet. Tim could feel the heat from the powerful downdrafts of the approaching vehicles and hear the crackling of heated vegetation. He could also hear voices... voices that were screaming obscenities at the approaching threat! Tim looked up to see Marines, at least a dozen of them, running towards their position. Most were carrying M4 carbines, one had a M249

Squad Automatic Weapon (SAW) and another was brandishing an M9 pistol. All were pointing their weapons at the alien ships. Even though he was certain the aliens could easily annihilate every human in front of them, Tim was relieved the Marines were almost there. If anyone could get them out of the fix they were in, it would be them.

The aliens halted their advance when the first small band of angry Marines arrived. While highly intimidating, the aliens showed no outward signs of aggression towards the growing band of Jarheads. Tim noted that the alien vehicles appeared noticeably different than the specimen inside Cocheta. The ones before his eyes were larger, maybe by 20 to 30 percent... and both had a single, small, knob-like protrusion on its rim. 'A weapon? Antenna?' he thought to himself, hoping it was only an antenna and not a directed energy weapon of some sort.

"Donna... please! Do not move! Are you OK?"

"I'll be... OK," she said as quietly as her breathlessness would allow. "Ankle is messed up... Still trying to catch... my breath."

"The Marines are here and a lot more are coming."

"Please, Tim. Let me up. I want to see what is going on!" She pleaded.

"Donna, I need you stay still right now!"

"Are we going to die, Tim?"

"No!" he said with questionable conviction. "They are just trying to intimidate or test us!"

Within minutes of the initial standoff, the bulk of the Marine contingent at Cocheta formed a wide arc in front of the potential battlefield and were aiming weapons nearly point blank at the two alien vehicles hovering a mere 50 feet above the grassy greenbelt. Two Marine squad leaders armed with M249 SAWs and two Navy corpsmen assigned to the Marine contingent were crouching next to the project directors to provide armed cover and medical attention to Dr. Hanson's injured leg. Amongst the late arrivals were two Marines with Man-Portable Air Defense System FIM-92 Stinger missiles. All were ready to defend their new project directors... and they would defend them to the death. The cacophony of taunts, threats and disparaging remarks about alien women made by dozens of armed Marines was, to make a gross understatement, surreal.

After the longest 10 minutes anyone could ever remember, the alien vehicles slowly egressed to the east and disappeared over the mountain ridge on the opposite side of the valley.

"It's over, Donna." Tim whispered in her ear. "They're gone."

"You covered me," Donna said, trying to contain the torrential flood of emotions pouring through her soul. "You put your body between me and the aliens. You thought they were going to kill me!"

"I wouldn't let that happen to you, Donna," Tim said. "You are our best hope for a defense against these creatures. Besides, I kinda like being your sidekick."

Donna smiled. "You are a wonderful, brave man, Tim Alexander!"

The Marines began surrounding the exhausted couple, shaking their hands and welcoming them to Cocheta while the Corpsmen were splinting Dr. Hanson's ankle and preparing her for a short HUMVEE ride to the Marine infirmary. The garrison commander, LTC Fred Jeffries, made his way through the throng of celebrating Jarheads to speak with the new project directors.

"Dr. Hanson, Dr. Alexander, are you OK?" Jefferies asked.

"Colonel, I'm OK but Dr. Hanson has a pretty busted up ankle." Tim replied.

"We've got the best Corpsmen around, Dr. Alexander. I'm sure they'll have her running laps within a week. And, by the way, welcome to the Cocheta Research Facility! Helluva welcome, wouldn't you say?" Jeffries asked with a smile.

"Colonel, if it is all the same to you, I'm OK with nothing more than a minor excitement here and there!" Donna replied with a grimmace as the Corpsmen were putting the final touches on her lower leg splint.

"I can't guarantee that, Dr. Hanson. Our little green friends pop in and out at odd hours." Jeffries replied with a grin, then turning his attention to Tim. "That was a very brave thing you did out there, Dr. Alexander." Jeffries said. "Not the kind of thing I would have expected from a TV Star."

"Honestly, I was scared to death, Colonel!"

"Son, I'd be real worried about you if you weren't. I assure you, as brave as my Marines are, all will be checking their underwear when the get back to their dorms. Heroes come in all different shapes and sizes, Dr. Alexander. It's what's in their

heart, not a uniform, that compells them to rise above timidity and fear."

"Those are very kind words, Colonel Jeffries." Tim replied.

"Marines!" Colonel Jeffries unexpectedly yelled.

"Sir, yes Sir!!!" the Marines yelled loudly in return.

"Because you all are a misguided bunch of ugly shit birds who somehow managed to scare the piss out of the Martians, I'm declaring tomorrow a training holiday!"

"Oo-Rah!!!" the Marine Company yelled, followed with thunderous cheers.

The Marines were in a celebrating mood and their cheers deafening. They stood their ground against an alien encroachment that appeared to be threatening key elements of Project Cocheta's command. No military unit in human history ever stood toe-to-toe against an adversary such as this. It was unprecedented and everyone seemed to know and savor it.

A half hour later, Donna and Tim were sitting in an examination room in the Marine infirmary. An x-ray of her left ankle was digitally transferred to the Radiology Department at Madigan Army Medical Center in Tacoma Washington for an expert reading. Hospital Corpsman First Class Fred Horten didn't believe that any bones were broken in her left foot or lower leg, but it was always best to get a definitive answer from a physician.

"Tim," Donna started to ask when they were finally alone, "is it possible we overreacted?"

"Maybe, but the aliens seem to be getting more aggressive since you and I arrived here."

"Aggression or curiosity?"

"Sweetheart, I was in fear for both of our lives! I've never been more frightened in my entire life! Most of all, I was worried about your safety."

"You are such a sweet man... I was feeling the same thing, Tim. I really believe their actions were meant to intimidate us."

"It worked, Donna! I felt appropriately intimidated!"

"Why now?" she pondered aloud. "Why would they consider you and I a greater threat to them than my Dad?"

"Maybe it is your association with the Skunk Works that intimidates them."

"I suppose... Our state-of-the-art hardware is still well behind theirs. Maybe by hundreds or thousands of years. They clearly have the upper hand as far as I can tell."

"They could be testing us. Poking the bear to see how we react."

"We sure gave them a reaction tonight!" she replied with a half grin, half grimace.

"One other thing, Donna. These two vehicles are different than the one in the hangar. They're bigger, and both had an interesting protrusion on the rim. Small, but both were pointing towards us."

"A weapon?"

"Maybe. Could be communications related. The fact that they seemed to be pointing right at us is unnerving."

"I'm sorry, Tim, the pain medicine is really kicking in. I'm getting sleepy."

"I'll help you to your apartment and keep an eye on you, Donna."

"I'd appreciate that Tim, but it would be inappropriate right now. I'll manage."

"I completely understand." Tim replied with a hint of disappointment. He was genuinely concerned about her nasty spill and wanted to take care of her, but decorum necessitated that they sleep in separate quarters.

"You know I'll be there in a flash if you need something."

"I know," she replied through the narcotic fog. "I know."

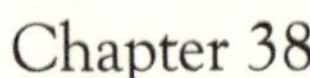

Chapter 38

Sergeant Travis Lowry looked out over the moonless desert to the southeast of his vantage point on one of Kirtland Air Force Base's lonely access roads. If it were not for the high-pitched whine of a Fed-Ex jet taxiing into position on runway eight 3.5 miles behind him, the only sounds he would likely hear on a wind-free night at 2:30 AM would be nocturnal insects, coyotes and perhaps a distant tractor-trailer rig on I-40, 5 miles to the north-northeast. Having just completed his second graveyard shift patrol of the world's largest nuclear weapon storage facility, SGT Lowry decided it was time for a welcome break. He sat on the warm hood of his HUMVEE, pulled a pack of cigarettes and a throw-down lighter from his cammie jacket and lit up.

Even though he was properly dressed for the chilly desert night, the heat from the HUMVEE engine compartment warmed his bottom side quite nicely. While he smoked, his eyes fixated on the lights coming from a collection of buildings 450 yards to his southeast and a large subterranean tunnel entrance 300 yards to his south. It was home to the underground workshop of the 898th Munitions Squadron... and 2000 nuclear bombs and warheads owned by the United States Air Force and Navy. The massive storage complex was over 300,000 square feet total, and as a member of the 377th Security Forces Squadron, his job was to protect it.

'Lowry, Son, guarding nuclear weapons is the most important job in the whole goddamn Air Force!' Chief Master Sergeant Bonilla told him when he reported for duty. 'Well, it might be every bit important as Chief said it was,' he thought to himself, 'but there is absolutely nothing more boring than night patrol at Kirtland!' He shook his head at the thought. At least he wasn't patrolling the perimeter of a desert Air Force Base in the friggin' Middle East! A slight grin formed on his face as he took another long drag. 'Yeah, it could be a lot worse than this!' he almost said aloud.

The roar of the Fed-Ex jet taking off behind him barely registered on his brain as he continued to stare at the lights that marked the location of enough nuclear firepower to thoroughly flatten his home state of Texas. He imagined himself swimming in the cool, spring-fed waters of Threadgill Creek near his home in Mason County. Carefree summers... That's what he missed most right now. The hot summers in west central Texas he spent goofing off with his high school buddies were long gone. He had a bona fide career now, ready to sign-on for another tour with good ol' Uncle Sam, who was essentially funding his new Shelby GT-500 and a girlfriend's lust for tokens of affection.

He was deep in thought when he finally noticed he was starting to throw a shadow on the pavement in front of him. No doubt it was the HUMVEE lights of his patrol teammate SGT Al Harding, or 'Weird Al' as he was nicknamed for his all too frequent gags and displays of gut-turning consumption of every insect imaginable. Bug eating was a disgusting penchant, to be sure, one Harding learned during Air Force survival school at Fairchild Air Force Base in Washington State. It was also a source of considerable income. Weird Al made all kinds of cash winning bets by eating cockroaches at the Albuquerque area taverns.

"Travis!" his radio squawked with an unusually high amount of static. "Travis! Where the hell are you?"

He keyed the hand-held microphone attached to the two-way radio on his belt. "Right in front of you, Al," he replied annoyingly without turning around. He was not in the mood for one of Hardings' practical jokes.

"Holy... Do... ...ing thing... it... Damn! ...dispatch!" The interference was too intense to make out any more words, then the transmission abruptly stopped as his radio went dead. Lowry turned his attention to the malfunctioning radio, repeatedly depressing the transmit button and turning it on and off to no avail. He looked up from his belt to the roadway in front of him and noticed the shadow of his HUMVEE was getting becoming more pronounced... and shorter, with much of the desert around him now illuminated in a soft, blue-white light. 'That's weird,' he thought to himself as he began to turn around, expecting to see Harding's HUMVEE with his high beams and spotlight on.

His reaction was purely instinctual, diving off the front of his vehicle as he

fumbled to unholster his M-9 Beretta 9mm sidearm. He hit the ground hard with his left shoulder, but paid no attention to the pain caused by the impact. His heart rate was soaring and the rapid influx of adrenalin into his bloodstream was making his movements feel clumsy. It took him no more than four seconds to chamber his weapon, but to him, it seemed as though an eternity passed. He assumed a sitting position in front of the HUMVEE and pressed his back into the front of the vehicle as hard as he could, holding the Beretta with both hands in front of him.

The shadow was getting shorter and shorter.

He dared not look up. 'This is not happening to me!' he yelled internally as he watched the desert become increasingly illuminated... and the light eating away at the HUMVEE's shadow on his body. A wind was beginning to pick up, swaying the desert flora at the sides of the road and sending wisps of dust into the air.

'It should be making sound! Why doesn't it make any sound?' he thought, shear terror welling up from the depths of his mind where his very worst nightmares were stowed.

The light was moving up his pistol.

SGT Lowry's boots and battle dress uniform pants were in the light, and he could feel the heat rapidly building on his skin underneath. He forced himself to begin looking up just as the light reached his hands.

"Shit!" Lowry yelled aloud at the sudden discomfort in his hands. The pain was like immersing a cold extremity into hot water, causing him to withdraw his sidearm to beside his right ear and immediately turn his head away from the encroaching light. He quickly fell from sitting to prone and rolled under the HUMVEE, keeping a death-grip on his sidearm. He repositioned himself under the vehicle so he could watch the... whatever the damn thing was... pass overhead without getting burned. He could smell the hot pavement and see the effects of the heat on the desert brush as it passed overhead. There was something else in the air around him, something that looked like swirls of glowing smoke that appeared and disappeared like mischievous spirits.

After what seemed like an eternity, the source of the light and heat had moved far enough down the road to clearly see what it was from his vantage point under the HUMVEE. Lowry couldn't believe what he was seeing! It was an aircraft of some sort, but not like any he had ever seen. It was large, maybe 40 or 50 feet in diameter, disc-shaped, and it glowed bluish-white hot with even whiter spots along its edge. The object was hard for him to focus his eyes on, like looking at a shiny piece of metal through fogged glasses. It was if there were no defining edges or features. Then it dawned on him. "It's a friggin' alien spaceship! Just like the ones they've been showing on TV since that Senator lady caused all that trouble!"

Then another dreadful thought entered his mind: it was now turning right and heading south... straight towards the nuclear weapons!

Lowry's brain began to swim. 'What if the bastards were there to detonate the weapons? Holy shit!' he thought to himself. His training was beginning to surface, converting his fear into action. Approaching the stockpile without authorization was, by definition, a hostile act and he was authorized to use deadly force to repel such an aggressive move. He simply couldn't allow them to get close to the nukes or he would be seriously derelict in his duty!

Lowry quickly crawled out onto the still hot pavement, stood in a crouch and opened the passenger side door. He retrieved his M-4 automatic rifle and a satchel containing several 30 round clips of ammunition. He pushed the weapon and ammo underneath the HUMVEE then assumed the same position he was in a few short moments earlier, only now he was facing south towards the facilities' north-west entrance. After attaching a clip underneath the weapon and using the charge handle to place a cartridge into the chamber, Lowry took careful aim. The disc was no more than a hundred feet away and maybe 15 feet above the desert terrain it was now passing over. 'A child could hit it from this range!' he thought to himself.

Lowry was vaguely aware of the pain in his hands, but was not injured enough to prohibit him from accomplishing his new mission. It crossed his mind that engaging this 'flying saucer' with small arms fire might be his last mortal act, but what choice did he have? If they managed to trigger the nukes, he and a shit-load of people in Albuquerque would be waking up dead that morning. He had to do something! Lowry turned the selector switch from safe to auto, steadied the rifle, aligned the open sight on the object's center of mass... then squeezed the trigger.

The desert silence erupted into the 13.3 rounds-per-second staccato of automatic rifle fire. The roar under the HUMVEE was deafening, and at the same time invigorating to SGT Lowry. Spent 5.56mm cartridge casings were striking the undercarriage of the HUMVEE above his right shoulder, with some of the hot casings occasionally deflecting forward to painfully pelt his bare neck and hands. Knowing he could empty a fully-loaded clip in three seconds, Lowry fired in pulses, only taking his eye off the sight to gauge the effect of his assault on the alien aircraft.

Round after round of high velocity, 62 grain bullets struck the craft, or at least Lowry assumed they did. He was so close, how could he miss? Even so, he never saw as much as a spark or heard the unmistakable sound of puncturing metal or ricochet. Seemingly undisturbed by Lowry's assault, the alien craft leisurely passed underneath high tension power lines on a steady course towards the underground storage facility.

SGT Lowry ran out of rifle ammunition when the disc was a little over 150 yards away. Angry that he had not deterred the trespassers in the least, yet relieved that an alien laser hadn't burned a hole in his skull, he crawled out from underneath the HUMVEE with his Beretta. It was difficult to hit much of anything with a pistol at 150 yards, but he was sure as hell going to try. After exhausting every 9mm clip he had on his belt and achieving no better results, Lowry jumped into the driver's seat of the HUMVEE to begin pursuit... only the vehicle was completely dead. Unarmed and without means of communication, SGT Lowry could only sit and watch as the disc, now 200 yards away, entered the pentagonal-shaped fenced area he was sworn to protect.

Lowry noted the presence of the craft caused a power outage that affected the bulk of Kirtland Air Force Base and parts of southeast Albuquerque. As he watched the aliens boldly trespass over one of the most restricted pieces of real estate on Earth, he wondered if it could actually set off the nuclear stockpile. He decided that since detonating a few thousand nukes at one time would probably blow the aliens to hell and back, it was not likely to be one of their first choices. He reassured himself, if somewhat nervously, that their intent was probably to reconnoiter the area. The assessment made him feel better, but only marginally so.

Lowry never took his eyes off of it. The damn thing was now very close to the Northwest entrance and almost 400 yards away. 'After it's finished doing whatever it's doing, it might come back after me, couldn't it?' he asked himself, the surging adrenalin already hammering his heart relentlessly. He was completely unarmed if the aliens wanted to tidy up loose ends.

As he watched the alien craft pass over the critical entrance to the nuclear stockpile, he caught a glimpse of a faint spark or something falling from the disc. Shortly afterward he noticed that the object began picking up speed and heading southeast. A few seconds later, the disc became noticeably brighter, angled hard to the southwest, streaking into the cloudless night sky at an absolutely unbelievable speed.

Power returned to the area a few moments after the craft's spectacular departure, and with it, several alarms began sounding from locations around the entire facility. Lowry's radio crackled to life and within a few seconds, Weird Al was frantically calling him.

"Travis! Travis, buddy... You OK?"

Lowry retrieved the dangling microphone to his hand. "I'm OK, Al. I mean, I think I'm OK," he replied, hands shaking.

"Were you in a fire fight?" Harding asked excitedly. "It sounded like all hell was breaking loose out there!"

"I couldn't stop it, Al! I kept shooting it... It passed right over me... I mean, I couldn't have missed it... and the fucking thing just kept heading for the nukes!"

"Both of you shut up! This is an unsecured frequency!" an angry third voice barked. It was Master Sergeant Palmer and he was quite obviously pissed. "What's your position, Lowry?"

"Just northwest of the storage facility."

"Harding?" Palmer growled.

"About a mile northwest of Lowry, en route. I should be there in a few moments."

"Fine. Hold your position when you reach Lowry. I'll be there in five. No more chatter!"

"Roger that!" Lowry hung the microphone on his jacket and scanned the area around him. He could see the lights and emergency beacons of several vehicles off to the west and northwest of his position. Immediately around him were the unmistakable signs of combat. Spent cartridge casings littered the street, along with M-4 and M-9 magazines. He unholstered his flashlight and began inspecting the HUMVEE for damage. The sheet metal on the top of the vehicle was still hot to the touch, but otherwise unscathed. As Harding was parking his HUMVEE next to his, Lowry began inspecting the desert brush adjacent to the roadway. The plants were clearly scorched, and while not burning, there were small plumes of light smoke rising from each.

"Dude! You OK?" Harding asked as he rounded the front of Lowry's HUM-

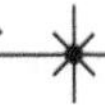

VEE.

SGT Lowry inspected his left hand with the flashlight, noting that a several small blisters were already forming. “My hands got a little burned, and I had some hot brass land on my neck, but I’m OK.”

“Man, I cannot believe you actually shot at that thing!”

“I hit it, too!” Lowry replied angrily. “I know I hit it! Shit, it was so close I could have peed on it!”

“Dude, I saw it fly in from the west! It was moving way faster than anything I’ve ever seen! Then, it freakin’ stopped on a dime somewhere behind you!”

“Al, it didn’t make any sound at all! Did you here anything?”

“I was taking a leak at the side of the road and all I could hear was piss hitting pavement! I knew you were in the area where it stopped, and I tried to reach you on the radio, but there was too much static. Dude, I thought you were totally hosed!”

“I thought I was hosed, too! It flew right over me, twenty feet up, tops!”

“What do you think it was?”

“It’s not anything we’re messing around with here!” Lowry said, shaking his head. “I think it was one of those UFOs people have been talkin’ about lately.”

“Holy shit, Travis! You think so?” Harding said excitedly. “When all this UFO stuff started showing up on TV this week, I heard a couple of officers talk about the flying saucers that have come around here in the past. I thought they were full of crap, but maybe they weren’t!”

Kirtland Air Force Base, in fact, had been the location several reported sightings of strange aerial phenomenon, the most notable, and the only one to receive any degree of public attention, occurred in the late evening hours of November 4th, 1957. Two Air Traffic Controllers from the Civil Aeronautics Authority, now known as the Federal Aviation Administration, sighted a dark, egg-shaped object with a light underneath approach the airfield at a high rate of speed. It loitered about the area for several minutes, in clear view of the witnesses who were viewing it through binoculars, then egressed into the overcast sky as fast as it had arrived.

The Air Force’s scientifically untrained Project Blue Book staff superficially examined the incident, but the University of Colorado's purportedly unbiased Condon Committee Investigation into the phenomenon explained away the sighting as a lost civilian aircraft that flew into the wrong airfield. These official investigations and explanations were for public consumption. The Eisenhower administration, however, was every bit as alarmed about UFO encroachment on sensitive military installations as was the Truman administration before it.

"Yeah... maybe," Lowry replied, his voice trailing off as he gazed into the night sky where the strange craft had made its hasty departure. He instinctively knew that this little 'incident' was going to become a major pain in the ass for him and Weird Al.

And he was right...

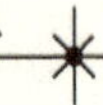

Chapter 39

"Mr. President?"

"Yes, Larry... I guess this must important enough to wake me up an hour early."

"We've had two incidents in the last few hours that you need to know about."

"Go on."

"Both involve aliens, Greg."

"What the hell is it this time?"

"The Cocheta Research Facility had an incident that the Marine Garrison Commander described as an 'aggressive act of intimidation.' Dr. Hanson was injured trying to escape from an extremely close approach."

"The Marines were involved?"

"That's correct, Greg."

"What part of my speech did these people not understand?" he almost shouted. "I do not want the aliens intimidated in ANY way by our military!"

"Mr. President, according to Colonel Jeffries, the Marines assumed a defensive posture only."

"Were they armed?" he asked gruffly.

"Yes, they were."

"Then we were the provocative party! It's a damn miracle they didn't touch off a skirmish or a full-fledged war!"

"Greg, this other incident may add a little more perspective," Osborn offered. "An alien ship incapacitated Kirtland Air Force Base early this morning and flew at very low altitude over our largest nuclear weapon storage facility. An Air Force Sergeant opened fire on it when it approached the nukes. There was no return fire from the alien vehicle. USNORTHCOM is in the process of alerting CRF to send an investigative team."

"We FIRED upon an alien ship?" Bertram yelled into the phone. "Good God Almighty, does anybody pay attention to what I say? A sergeant took it upon himself to shoot at an alien vehicle? Did he get permission from his command?"

"I'm sure they have standing orders to engage anything threatening the nuclear stockpile. I also understand that base communications were completely knocked out."

Bertram was furious. "I'm trying to create a pleasant atmosphere for a dialog with the aliens and I've got enlisted cowboys with itchy trigger fingers screwing things up!" The President paused to gather momentum for his next outburst. "Should I assume that Senator Hanson's daughter will be heading up the Kirtland investigation?"

"If her injuries permit it."

"I tell you, Larry, these damn Hansons are driving me insane!" he said with unmistakable exasperation. "One was a traitor that blew the lid off of an important black project, the other is a traitor AND making Melana apoplectic, and the third... before it is all over, I'm sure that bitch will screw me around somehow!"

"Greg, you need to calm down," Osborn said in a subdued tone. "The first Hanson is dead, the second one is busted up and won't be embarrassing Melana for a few days... the third one? You already know about the special arrangement that made her Cocheta's Project Director."

"Yeah yeah..."

"She is the most qualified, Greg... by a longshot."

“She’s a Hanson, and in my book, that spells trouble.”

“I doubt she will give you any. At least not for a week or two.”

“Was that supposed to make me feel better? You’re a real jerk, Larry!”

“Well, you didn’t hire me for my looks. I’ll keep you informed.”

Chapter 40

Dr. Hanson's telephone began ringing at 2:32 AM.

"Hello?" she answered, barely half asleep and still under the lingering effects of narcotics.

"Dr. Hanson, this is the Cocheta Command Center, MAJ Alleyne speaking. We have a CAT 2 IOS, Kirtland Air Force Base, New Mexico. Wheels up in 60 minutes."

"I'm sorry, a what?"

"You and your team members will be flown to Kirtland Air Force Base to conduct a thorough investigation of an Incident of Significance. Departure time is in 60 minutes. The G650 has been fueled and serviced."

"I'm kind of busted up, I'll..."

"Ma'am, we already have a wheelchair outside of your door. We also have 'Go Bags' and jump suits prepared and stowed in the cabin. Drs. McLachland and Alexander will be accompanying you on this mission. If you need assistance in getting ready, we can provide whatever you need. Dr. McLachland will thoroughly brief you en route."

"Wow, you folks don't miss a thing," she said, still trying to shake off the narcotics given to her earlier.

"That's our job, Ma'am."

"Thank you Major, for doing it well."

Donna retrieved the crutches from beside her bed and began the slower-than-usual process of showering and changing into fresh clothes. Cocheta provided jumps suits for everyday wear, which was fortunate for Tim and Donna because they had not yet made it back to their homes to retrieve more casual wear and other essentials. The CX, or Cocheta Exchange, was a handy little store that made available a nice selection of toiletries, comfort foods, cigarettes, over-the-counter medications, clothing items, wines and, oddly enough, Cuban Cigars, a leftover tradition from the General Marston years.

Dr. McLachland and Tim arrived at Donna's apartment 15 minutes before wheels up to provide any assistance she needed.

"Donna, you do not need to go on this field trip if your ankle is too sore to walk on." McLachland said with real concern. "That's a nasty sprain. Tim and I can handle it"

"I'll be fine. Besides, I wouldn't miss this for the world!" She said with a smile. "Now, where's my black suit and dark sunglasses?"

Dr. McLachland and Tim laughed at the Men-in-Black reference. "We could stop by the Exchange and get you a pair of dark sunglasses," McLachland said, "The suit and the 'neuralyzer' will be a lot harder to come by."

Donna laughed. "The jumpsuit is fine. I just hope I don't slow things down."

"We're bringing the wheelchair with us just in case," McLachland said. "My contact at Kirtland said the area in question should pose no problems for wheelchairs."

"What happened there?" Donna asked.

"What almost happened here a few hours ago," McLachland answered.

"You mean there was a fire fight?"

"It was rather one sided. An Air Force sergeant guarding the nuclear munitions warehouse fired about 300 rounds of ammunition at an alien craft, 240 rifle shots and about 60 pistol shots. Lucky for the Sergeant, the alien craft did not return fire."

"That is both extraordinary and frightening at the same time!" Tim exclaimed.

"Lots of physical evidence on this little field trip," McLachland said. "I think this will be a great opportunity for our Project Directors to get their feet wet. Better grab your jackets, it's 20 degrees outside and we have a jet waiting for us."

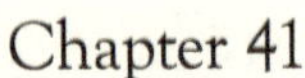

Chapter 41

After almost 1900 non-turbulent miles, the G650 made a long, leisurely right turn to line up with Runway 26 at Albuquerque International Airport. Given that all three passengers were exhausted from the night's ordeals, the flight crew let them sleep through final approach, waking them up just in time to fasten their lap belts for a gentle landing.

"It's still dark outside," Donna noted, rubbing her eyes then looking at her watch. "Almost 2000 miles in 2 1/2 hours! Not bad!"

"How's your ankle feeling?" Steve asked. "You up for some field investigating?"

Dr. Hanson tested her ankle movements with a grimace. "It still hurts quite a bit. I'm not sure I'll do very well without crutches."

"I'll help her along Steve," Tim offered. "Donna, how bad is the swelling?"

"Significant, but I'll be OK."

"I really think we should use the wheelchair," Tim said with enough conviction to let everyone know that the wheelchair was going to be the only option.

After a few minutes of taxiing and passing several four-engined C-130 transports, the G650 came to a stop next to a large white hangar with an Air Force C-37A Gulfstream, the military version of the smaller GV bizjet, parked nearby. A plain white van with a wheelchair lift and a military police HUMVEE were parked near the hanger. Since the coming investigation seemed to be rather straight forward, go bags and personal items were left in the G650.

Upon opening the door, cold air made its way into the cabin. It wasn't the frigid 20° they left behind at Cocheta, but a desert dry 35°. By noon it would be close to 75° with a near cloudless sky and a light breeze from the northwest.

"No need to use your wheelchair," a young Airman said as he stepped towards the open cabin door. "We have one right here."

An Air Force officer, COL Ernest Marshall, joined the airman at the cabin door as Dr. Hanson was given assistance to the waiting wheelchair.

"Dr. Hanson, what a great pleasure it is to see you again! Every time I see a Raptor, I think of your team at the Skunk Works. Sorry to hear about your injury. We'll try to keep you as comfortable as possible."

"Thank you, Colonel. I appreciate your help."

"The Flight Kitchen is providing breakfast for you and your flight crew. We will meet with Sergeant Lowry afterwards and your team can interview him for as long as you wish. We'll proceed to the location of the incident afterwards."

"The area, has it been cordoned off?" Donna asked.

"Absolutely, Dr. Hanson. We've blocked all roads leading to the nuclear munitions facility. Every shell casing has been left where it landed and we've checked the area and the vehicles for radiation. Thank God this happened on a weekend! All the traffic to Sandia and the other ongoing projects... What a mess that would have been!"

With help from Tim and the airman, they gently lowered her onto the wheelchair and made their way to the waiting van.

"Does everybody in the Air Force know who you are?" Tim laughed as the motorized lift whined to life.

"No... there is an airman at Ramstein that doesn't know me."

Tim shook his head and laughed again. She was putting on a good show, but he could see hints of grimacing with each bump that caused her right ankle to move. 'Once this was over,' he thought to himself, 'light duties for her!'

Chapter 42

"Sergeant Lowry, we've read your incident report. Please tell us what you saw when you turned around to see what was behind you," Dr. Alexander asked the somewhat nervous witness.

"Your show is really cool, Dr. Alexander!" Lowry started. "I never cared much for science until I started watching it. I didn't know you helped with Air Force investigations."

"Thank you, Sergeant. Please continue."

"Well, I thought I was going to see Weird Al pulling up in his HUMVEE, but it was a UFO or something. Scared the shi... I'm sorry... It scared the crap out of me! It was coming in along the access road to the nukes. Movin' slow with steam or smoke or something coming from underneath."

"How low was it?"

"Twenty feet, maybe. Fifty yards behind me."

"Anything else unusual?"

"God! It was all unusual! I jumped off the front of my Hummer to hide from it!"

"What happened when it passed over you?"

"It burned my hands real quick! Doc says I have second degree burns!" he replied with residual terror in his eyes. "It got hot fast, but I did get my M4 and all my clips before it could burn me even more."

"Did you see any smoke when it passed over?"

"I did when it passed right over my Hummer. It was weird, though. It was like little dust devils that glowed. I could smell the pavement getting hot. Plants were burning, too."

"You shot at the object. Is that correct?" Donna asked.

"Yes Ma'am!" he replied nervously, half convinced he was going to buy a one-way ticket to prison. "I had no choice! It was heading right for the nukes!"

"Relax, Sergeant. You're not going to jail unless you have outstanding parking tickets."

"Thank you, Ma'am!"

"Did you hit it?"

"Yes Ma'am, I did."

"How many times?"

"I know I hit it with my M4 every time. I know I did! But I never heard a ricochet. It was so close there was no way I could miss! I don't know about the pistol. It was at least a hundred yards away when I used the Beretta."

"You're certain?"

"Yes Ma'am. I've shot rifles since I was five years old. I score 'Expert' on every qualification and I can shoot Texas crows in the head at 250 yards."

"Your vehicle. Did it suffer any damage?"

"The roof and hood were seriously hot. The HUMVEE wouldn't start and my radios quit working, but they came right back on after that thing flew away."

"Were there any other objects in the air?"

"I did hear a jet take off before all this happened. FedEx takes off around that time."

"Can you think of anything else that happened that might be important?"

"I don't know..." Lowry paused, "when it passed over the northwest entrance to the stockpile, I thought I saw something tiny fall off of it. Maybe something I damaged when I was shooting at it. I don't know... it was about 300 yards away."

"That was not on your written account of the incident," Donna said with a light measure of sternness.

"I'm sorry. I didn't think all that much about it at the time."

Donna looked at Tim and Steven. It could be exactly what the airman said it was, or something deliberately deposited near the entrance of a high-tech warehouse full of unimaginable destructive force. Donna's mind quickly catalogued the only few possibilities available and decided that a very close look at that area was in order. It was probably nothing more than an optical illusion or a reflection off debris stirred up by the alien propulsion system. Or... it could be a clever Trojan Horse bringing something terrible into the facility.

"Sergeant Lowry, please try to remember every detail of your encounter. Something that might seem insignificant could be incredibly important."

"I really can't think of anything else, ma'am. I mean, it flew outta here real fast after it buzzed the nukes."

"Did you see any color changes in the object?" Tim asked, leaning a little forward to hear his response.

"It was fuzzy, Dr. Alexander. Kinda like a mix of purple and blue. Swirly like. Well, until it sped away. Then it got really bright."

"Dr. Hanson, can you think of anything we haven't covered?" Tim asked.

"I believe we've gone as far as we can here," she replied, turning her head back to SGT Lowry. "It's time to look at the area where this encounter took place, Sergeant. If you will accompany us, we'll take our investigation to the scene and see if we can come up with something interesting."

* * *

The sun was well above the horizon when the caravan of military vehicles and a white van began the five mile trip to the spot where SGT Lowry engaged the alien aircraft. The last remaining chill of the desert night was rapidly giving way to the warmth of a new and cloudless morning. After a 10 minute drive that rounded the east end of runway 26 and down a paved, restricted access road that lead to the storage complex. A roadblock was established a half mile from the scene, manned by several of SGT Lowry's colleagues sporting fully automatic M4 rifles. Each of the four HUMVEEs were armed with a heavy machine gun mounted on the roof. Anyone crazy enough to run through the checkpoint would end up as coyote food. The entourage was waved through quickly and a few moments later, directed to park on the dirt shoulder about 150 yards from where Lowry's and Weird Al's HUMVEEs were left untouched.

"I'm sure glad this isn't summertime!" Donna said while her wheelchair was being lowered to the black top road. "We'd already be miserable! It's actually very pleasant this morning."

Donna was very fond of the desert, having lived and worked in the arid climate of Plant 42 between Palmdale and Lancaster California for nearly all of her career. The more level areas of terrain at Kirtland were very similar to Palmdale. Assorted desert plants of the very northernmost region of the Chihuahuan Desert made up the bulk of local foliage but lacked the Joshua Trees that defined the boundaries of the Mojave Desert region. Rain was scarce in both locations, but the abundant and diverse, water-conserving desert flora managed to survive quite well and provide suitable habitat for everything from lizards to mountain lions.

"The physical effects of the alien encounter start here," COL Marshall began, "about 150 yards or so from the two HUMVEEs. You can see small, singed plants beyond the shoulder of the road. You can also see that the road surface was subjected to enough heat to smooth it out a bit compared to the untouched road."

"Sergeant Lowry, how far back was the object when you first looked at it?" Donna asked.

"No more than 50 yards, ma'am."

"Could you smell the road surface getting hot?"

"No, ma'am, but there wasn't any wind last night. I could sure smell it when that flying saucer was right above me!"

"Sergeant, please lead the way and tell us again what you were seeing and hearing before you noticed the object coming up behind you."

Tim was pushing Donna's wheelchair as the small group of scientists and military personnel made their way to the two HUMVEEs parked on the black

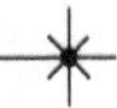

pavement in front of them. Lowry's account was essentially the same as his written report and interview.

"Colonel," Dr. McLachland began to ask while looking at the nuclear weapon storage and maintenance facility, "how many nukes do we have in there these days?"

"Less than 2000 now." He replied with a hint of ire. "Under President Bertrams' unilateral disarmament policies, we're sending a lot of weapons to Pantex for disassembly."

Pantex, located about 20 miles from Amarillo Texas, was America's only nuclear weapon assembly and disassembly facility. An old firm, Pantex originally started as a conventional weapons manufacturer during World War II and was closed shortly after VJ Day. Six years later, the Atomic Energy Commission and the military acquired the property and spent millions re-tooling the plant to make nuclear weapons. In more recent years, Pantex also took on the burden of storing America's extremely valuable and highly dangerous plutonium stockpile.

"You sound disappointed, Colonel," Tim said.

"Dr. Alexander, 'unilateral disarmament,' by military definition, is dropping your pants and hoping everyone else does the same. The only thing it really accomplishes is insuring that potential adversaries gain more advantages over you in addition to losing a lot of respect."

"How many nuclear weapons are enough?"

"Enough to keep your adversaries honest," Marshall replied. "We kept a nuclear Soviet Union at bay for decades just by having the ability to effectively use nukes against them. Back in the day, they called it 'Mutually Assured Destruction'... seemed to work pretty well and it likely saved many millions of lives. The fact that we haven't had a nuclear war since 1945 speaks volumes."

"Colonel, I absolutely love the physics of splitting and fusing atoms, I just can't bring myself to love the idea of weaponizing it!"

"If it makes you feel better, Dr. Alexander, I hate them, too," COL Marshall replied in all honesty. "I've got six wonderful grand kids and I'd like nothing better than to have a world void of nuclear weapons. But, so long as there are those who wish to destabilize the world with them, we must maintain a credible deterrent."

"Not to change the subject," Donna said, "but I've noticed that the pavement is noticeably free of dirt and dust, unlike the previous five miles."

"We had a front move through yesterday morning with quite a bit of wind associated with it. The roads get pretty dirty when that happens." Marshall replied.

"SGT Lowry, didn't you report that you felt hot air blowing down on you and your vehicle?"

"Yes ma'am, I did."

"That would explain the clean pavement, but... shouldn't there have been a lot more heat and down draft?" Donna pondered out loud. "Our encounter last night, and our brave young sergeant's this morning... All of us should have been plasma-roasted to keep objects of that size and weight in the air."

"Maybe the magnetohydrodynamics work in tandem with something else?" Tim speculated. "They could be manipulating gravity."

"Anything and everything seems to be possible these days." Donna replied while chewing on Tim's hypothesis. "Reverse-gravity for lift and magnetohydrodynamics for speed and directional control?"

"We still haven't nailed down the graviton exchange particle yet, but maybe the aliens not only understand it, but developed ways to harness it."

"Tim, those ships last night and the one here... they were practically right on top of us and we didn't become weightless. Could the anti-gravity affect be that local and that directional?"

"If it is, that might explain why we were still glued to the ground when they came close."

"OK, so... if we could somehow interfere with the gravitational lift component of their propulsion..."

"They would fall like a rock!" Tim finished her sentence with a smile. He could almost see the neurons in her head bumping up to overdrive. Donna was looking for a way to immobilize the alien vehicles without making a blatant offensive weapon. The hurdles, however, would likely be insurmountable. Anti-gravity research reached a peak in the 1950s, with interest gradually declining over the next 40 years. While there were plenty of gizmos purported to defy or manipulate

gravity, none were ever proven to work. A device invented by physicist Evgeny Podkletnov using superconductive ceramic rings was reported to create anti-gravity in a small scale, but no other physicist on Earth had been able to duplicate the experiment. In terms of hard core scientific research, the notion of anti-gravity had become nothing more than fanciful science fiction.

'Given a few hundred thousand years?' he thought to himself.

"Is there anything in your bag of physics that could help us design such a device?" Donna asked, even though she already knew the answer.

"No, I can't think of any. Most physicists believe that it is impossible. You might be able to detect it by directing lasers above an airborne craft and see if the gravitational distortion bends the beams. The problem is..." he paused, eyebrows furrowed, "...if they're getting more aggressive, they might shoot back."

"If you think using lasers to measure the degree of distortion would give us useful information, we could remote the lasers," Steve offered. "Maybe even use you for bait."

Tim laughed. "No. I think I've had enough 'Close Encounters' for one weekend."

"Here we are," Lowry announced. "My HUMVEE is the one on the right."

Evidence of the earlier, one-sided fire fight were clearly evident on the roadway and dirt shoulder. Littered about the black road surface on the passenger side were dozens of spent 5.56mm NATO brass cartridge casings. In front of the HUMVEE were 9mm automatic pistol casings.

"After it flew over my HUMVEE, I grabbed my M4 and some clips, then got under the HUMVEE. Since it started turning right and towards the northeast entrance to the nukes, I had to shift my position to get the best view. I hammered it, but they didn't even flinch. When I ran out of rifle ammo, I got out from under the HUMVEE and started shooting at it with my sidearm. It was a good 150 to 200 yards away by then, but I still tried."

Donna looked in the direction of the northwest entrance. There was a faint but traceable trail of singed desert flora right up to the pentagonal-shaped perimeter fence and patrol road. Fifty yards beyond that was the road leading into, and out of, the 300,000 square foot underground storage and maintenance facility. The roads were constructed on five foot high beds to ensure that monsoon season storms would not flood the roadway or the almost 20 foot deep entrance and exit ways.

"Tim, other than cartridge casings and slightly melted black top, there is not much here to see," Donna said. "The craft flying under the power lines is interesting. SGT Lowry, did the power go out before or after the craft passed under the power lines?"

"Ma'am, the power went out when that thing was coming in behind me. My radio went dead and my HUMVEE wouldn't start."

"So the power failure was a much larger phenomenon than a UFO passing under power lines. I think it is time to make our way to the northwest entrance. I really want to see the piece of debris that fell off that aircraft."

After loading Dr. Hanson back onto the van, the group made the short, 350 yard drive to the Kirtland Underground Munitions Storage Complex main gate where they were waved through by the security detail at the gate. Four, well-armed HUMVEEs were waiting at the 'Y' intersection. Two blocked the roadway while the other two followed Dr. Hanson's van. Seventy yards in front of them, the roadway widened for the next 200 yards, undoubtedly a staging area for tractor trailer rigs waiting for permission to enter the facility. After a 180 degree turn to the left, the open doors of the underground nuclear weapons storage facility could be seen.

"Stop! Stop right here!" Donna said as they approached the 75 yard entrance into the man-made cave. "I want to inspect every foot of this ramp."

The driver complied, stopping on the dirt roadway where it clearly showed that HUMVEEs made tracks on both sides of the paved road. After gently lowering Donna to the roadway, a careful inspection of the 75 yard ramp was in order.

"What are we looking for, Dr. Hanson?" Colonel Marshall asked.

"Anything that doesn't belong," she replied. "Anything out of place."

Forty yards later, McLachland noticed something on the roadway next to the south retaining wall that looked like a relatively large splash of bird excrement. The closer he got to it, the more it looked like the kind of radial streaked road blemish created by fireworks that contained magnesium.

"Donna, I think I see what you're looking for up ahead, next to the wall on the right and a few yards from the entrance."

The pace of the group picked up, closing the next 35 yards quickly. The 18 foot doors to the subterranean freight docks were open, exposing only the outermost workings of the KUMSC. To the right were familiar structures and machinery seen commonly on every dock with heavy lift capabilities. A large central receiving area and corridor were located about 140 yards into the massive, 280 yard tunnel brightly illuminated with mercury vapor flood lamps.

"That's what I'm looking for, and if it turns out to be what I think it is, this facility has been compromised," Donna said calmly.

"What?" COL Marshall almost yelled in surprise. "Compromised? How?"

"Colonel Marshall, we have good reason to believe that our facility in Canada has been corrupted by some sort of nanotechnology inserted into our systems, perhaps by a kind of microscopic trojan horse. We also believe many, if not all, DoD computers have been hacked by the aliens. I think this smudge on your roadway is where the nanotechnology was deposited. Thank God there is very little wind today. We'll need to protect this area from wind and get the pros out here to secure the evidence. They need to go over every suspicious grain with an electron microscope."

The Air Force Colonel looked as if he had seen a flying elephant. "You're telling me this entire base AND the DoD have been compromised?"

"Possibly... probably," Donna replied without a hint of stress in her voice. "Do you have any fused nuclear weapons?"

"Not that I know of."

"You'll need to monitor each and every nuke for tiny structural changes that might represent alien attempts to construct a makeshift fuse in an unfused weapon. Their technology is well beyond unbelievable."

"We have almost 2000 of them in here... what you're asking is impossible! We don't even know if they've actually compromised anything!"

"It only takes one, Colonel," Donna replied calmly, "and a huge portion of our remaining nuclear stockpile disappears, along with a significant number of Albuquerquians."

"I'll brief the General and get her up to speed... and I'll have a chat with the Sandia folks, too. We can probably get the alien sample professionally analyzed in-house."

"Thanks, Colonel. I know it is a lot to ask, but my gut feeling is that our President's extraterrestrial buddies are up to no good."

"Hearing you say that frightens me to the core, Dr. Hanson!"

* * *

After the road trip to the scene of his epic battle with aliens, SGT Lowry sat through another three exhausting debriefings with a gaggle of assorted Majors and Colonels... and some geek from Sandia Labs. It seemed that everyone with clout wanted to hear about the encounter first hand. Only the chief janitor hadn't interviewed him.

'That,' he thought to himself, 'would be the first debriefing tomorrow.'

Lowry had listened carefully to conversations between the pretty Hanson lady and Dr. Alexander. The seriousness of their collective voices were more than enough to convince even the notoriously mouthy Weird Al that he should forget that anything ever happened at all.

Lowry finally collapsed into bed around 20:30 hours and almost immediately fell into unconsciousness. His last thought before sleep overtook him was that he, at least, got the next two nights off for his suffering.

Chapter 43

The 655 mile, hour-long afternoon flight to Palmdale California, USAF Plant 42, was entirely too short to be restful. It seemed as if the G650 had no sooner taken off from Kirtland when they entered the approach pattern for runway 25 at the airfield home of the Skunk Works. Both Donna and Tim needed to retrieve essential personal items to take back to Cocheta, drop off house keys and arrange for the van lines to load and move their personal belongings to Las Vegas. As had always been the case for crutial CRF staff members, new homes in moderately affluent neighborhoods within a 20 minute drive to Nellis AFB were purchased for them. For Tim and Donna, it was nearly effortless to relocate. Both were given the option to keep or sell their old homes on the open market or have the government purchase them. Given the political climate, Donna and Tim elected to keep their homes in case the oftentimes bipolar powers that be decided that aliens just weren't all that interesting anymore. The only real snag in the relocation plans was what Tim had the additional burden of finding a friend or relative that might watch over and care for his beloved and loyal dog Quark. Fortunately, he had a reliable cousin in the Inglewood area that was more than happy to help out.

Since Donna's tasks were far less complicated than Tim's, primarily because she had no pets, lived less than 3 miles from the Skunks Works and was using crutches, she volunteered to keep him company for his drive into LA and back. As per usual, the Los Angeles area megaplex provided plenty of harrowing driving experiences and gnarled traffic for late afternoon entertainment. Once Quark was settled in, Tim treated Donna to 'the best Pizza in Westwood' followed by 'the best ice cream in Westwood.' Both were thoroughly enjoying the brief respite between errands and aliens.

"Tim?"

"Yes. What's on your mind, sweetie?"

"This has been a really wonderful evening. Thank you! I hardly noticed the pain in my ankle the entire time."

"And all along I thought it was the narcotics doing that," he said with grin.

"You underestimate your power over women!"

Tim laughed out loud. "Now I KNOW it's the narcotics talking!"

Donna returned the laugh, then took on a more serious tone. "Would you mind if we returned to Cocheta tonight? I know we originally decided to use this Sunday for me to recouperate, but I really need a lot of quiet time to make notes on what I'm going to say to the assembled staff at the Monday morning 'conclave.' I need access to records and maybe ask questions of the people who make Cocheta what it is. The skeleton crew and Marines have already convinced themselves that a bright new era has finally arrived. I hope they won't be disappointed. The full staff likely knows nothing of the monumental changes that occurred during their two week 'off' period. They have been thoroughly abused for years and they need to be reassured that it will never happen again. No doubt, there will be staff that need to be dismissed. Hastings was a political animal that placed loyalty far above competence. I've got to cull them quickly and replace them with the best talent available. Tim, of all the motivational speeches I've made in my career, this next one will be the most important one I'll ever make. I want to do it right, Tim."

"You really need the down time Donna, but you'll press on anyway, no matter what I say." Tim said with a smile. "You know I'll be there to help you."

"I'd give you a big kiss you if you weren't driving."

"I'd probably let you."

"Probably?"

Tim snickered, "Do I look like somebody that could resist you?"

"Smart man!

* * *

It was close to midnight by the time Donna and Tim boarded the G-650 for their two hour flight back to the British Columbian wilderness. Exhausted, they fell asleep in each other's arms and slept soundly in the lower oxygen tension of the pressurized cabin.

Fifty miles from the Cocheta airstrip, two alien aircraft assumed positions approximately 200 meters from the wing tips of the Gulfstream and maintained their position until the jet touched down. Given their passenger's state of unconsciousness, the flight crew saw no need to awake them until the jet came to a stop.

Chapter 44

"Captain Barsukov, please come to the sonar station immediately."

Ludomir Velimirovich Barusukov, Captain of the Russian ballistic missile submarine *Pavel Pereleshin*, groaned at the sound of the intercom interrupting his shower.

'Such a young crew,' he thought to himself while dressing. 'Inexperienced and tense. What nonsense will it be this time?'

He immediately chastised himself for whining about cutting short a very relaxing shower. While inexperienced in the combat sense, his crew was hard working, loyal and, in time, would become fine undersea warriors in a newly revitalized Russian Navy.

The fall of the old Soviet Union led to a dilapidated naval force with hundreds of fine warships left to rust in the harsh environment of the northern Russian coast. The new Russia was all but bankrupt and the Federation that evolved from it simply did not have the will nor money to continue maintenance of Cold War relics. Barusukov remembered well those lean and morose years when he was, most likely, considered a young, annoying and inexperienced submariner.

'Perchance... could it be that my young sailors are less annoying than I was?' he considered to himself with a grin. 'Da! Da! Da! I was most certainly annoying!'

The *Pavel Pereleshin* was a nuclear ballistic missile submarine of the latest generation Borei class. Built by Severnoye Mashinostroitelnoye Predpriyatie, Sevmash for short, at the White Sea port of Severodvinsk, the *Pereleshin* was an absolute mon-

ster. Only 43 feet short of two football fields in length, the 'boomer' could launch 16 ballistic missiles, each carrying 10, independently-targeted nuclear warheads. It could also launch six nuclear or conventional cruise missiles and travel submerged at over 26 knots. Plagued by delays due to funding and technical issues with the Bulava ballistic missile system, the *Pereleshin* began sea trials in June of 2012 and was commissioned two years later.

The submariner's world is not one of sight or touch, but of sound. At 1500 feet below the surface of the ocean, there is no light. They stalk their adversaries in stealthy, visionless beasts that rely upon sensitive electronic ears to paint a dynamic, three-dimensional picture of the sea around it. Hydrophones listen to, and pinpoint, every detectable sound, from lovesick whale songs to unique quirks in the sounds that emanate from conventional and nuclear powerplants. Blind as they may appear, the modern submarine can 'see' and 'hear' almost everything in surprising fidelity.

"Sonarman, why do you interrupt your Captain's fine shower?"

"Captain, Sir, I have three contacts behind us. One is the intermittent anomaly we believe to be a Virginia class American that may have followed us for days. Best estimate is a speed of one-zero knots at bearing one-seven-five, range 2000 meters. The other two came from bearing one-eight-seven at... well... uh..."

"Yes, Sonarman, what was their speed?"

"Uh... two-two-five knots, Captain. They are in our baffles now."

"What? You call me to the sonar station for mischief? A prank?" Barsukov yelled, red-faced with neck veins bulging. "Sonarman, do I appear amused?"

The young sonar operator froze, terrified of the awful punishment that was sure to follow. Fortunately, the watch officer helped the young submariner verify the outrageous speed of the two submerged craft when they approached.

"Captain, he speaks the truth!" watch officer Iosif Kamkin said. "We ran hardware and software diagnostics twice. The equipment works to specification and accurately tracked the two targets until they took up positions behind us."

"You are both imbeciles! Nothing moves through water at that speed!"

"I agree with you, Captain. Nothing should move that fast in water, yet they did. Perhaps it is a new American weapon?"

"Perhaps..," Barsukov turned to the Attack Center. "Helmsman, hard right rudder, increase speed to two-eight knots, maintain depth four-five-zero meters and set course zero-nine-zero degrees. We shall have a look at these intruders."

The gargantuan submarine obliged the orders of her captain. Within moments of starting the right turn, the sonar operator announced that the two unidentified craft were now visible to the hull-mounted sonar. Almost before he could finish the sentence, the two craft split from each other, one taking up a position 100 meters from starboard amid-ship, the other, 50 meters below and slightly in front of the massive single propeller.

"Captain, I have a fix on both objects," the Sonar Operator announced nervously. "I also have an approximate fix on their size. Sir, the object to starboard is 12 meters in diameter, the one below is only 10!"

"Impossible!" Barsukov bellowed. "Nobody has small submersibles that can do these fantastic things!"

"Sir, I am very uncomfortable with the positions they have assumed," watch officer Kamkin said with an ominous tone. "Perhaps we should assume battle posture."

"Agreed. These are infant toys in size compared to our great *Pereleshin*, but what they can do in the water is very unsettling! Announce battle posture ship wide and prepare for evasive moves and decoys!"

* * *

Commander Tim 'Shark Whisperer' Johnson was glued to the Spherical Sonar LED monitors of his Virginia Class fast-attack submarine USS *North Carolina*. Submerged 1500 feet below the Pacific and 1270 miles northwest of Pearl Harbor, Johnson slowed his ultra-quiet boat to 10 knots when the two unidentified craft entered the area at outrageous speed. The 360 degree, spherical sonar array housed inside the nose of the *North Carolina* displayed a detailed tactical picture of the situation 2200 yards in front of him.

"What speed did you say those two submersibles came in at?" Johnson asked his Sonar Technician, Chief Petty Officer Rick De Sousa.

"Sir, 225 knots. Roughly 250 miles per hour."

"Underwater... you absolutely sure of that?"

"Yes Sir," he replied, certain of his assessment. "The equipment is working fine. I don't know how on earth they are managing that kind of speed underwater!"

Commander Johnson continued to watch the bizarre situation on the monitor. The two submersibles were clearly interested in the *Pereleshin* and that concerned him immensely.

'How did they find the Russian boat that quickly?' he asked himself. It took the *North Carolina* better part of two frustrating weeks of listening to freighters, whale farts and holes in the water just to find their stealthy opponent and record enough data to make it easier to find the *Pereleshin* again. The two submersibles seemed to find it without any difficulty at all.

One possibility that occurred to Johnson was that the submersibles were Russian and rendezvousing with the *Pereleshin*. He quickly dismissed that thought because there was simply no technology he could think of that could propel an underwater object at 250 mph, big or small, hydrodynamic or not.

Commander Johnson, eyes still on the screens, sat down in a vacant chair and sipped on a lukewarm cup of coffee. The command center of the *North Carolina* was a significant and welcomed departure from previous fast attack submarine classes. It was more spacious and comfortable than those in the Los Angeles and Sea Wolf-class subs. Gone were the chief of the watch, helmsman, planesman and diving officer. They were replaced by two pilots, both steering the sub using joysticks that, superficially, seemed to be more appropriate in a high-performance aircraft than a naval vessel. In truth, submarines have similar external control surfaces that allow it to move through the water very much like an airplane flies through the air.

"It looks to me like these two contacts might be stalking the *Pereleshin*. Radio, prepare a flash message to COMSUBPAC Pearl. Tell them we have two small, ultra high-performance submersibles tailing the Russian Boomer. Include the speed these two contacts made when they entered the area and our magnetometer readings."

"Aye aye, Captain."

Johnson considered the situation. There were a number of options available, but none left him with the warm fuzzies. He could break away from the *Pereleshin*, head for high frequency radio depth and send his message to Pearl, but it might take hours to find the *Pereleshin* again. His orders were quite explicit: tail the *Pereleshin* and gather as much data possible on the newly-comissioned behemoth. That task was straight forward enough: Find it, shadow it and record it. Now… add this unknown third party that can make 225 knots underwater? His first inclination was to bid the *Pereleshin* 'sayonara' and be anywhere but here.

"Pilot, increase speed to match the *Pereleshin* and match his every move at this range."

"Aye aye, Captain." Replied Pilot McDaniel.

"Captain, the *Pereleshin* is making a hard right angles and dangles! Contacts one and two have repositioned themselves. They are now on course three-five-five at two-eight knots, bearing zero–eight–five, range 2000 yards. The smaller contact is below and in front of the propulsor, the larger, midship starboard. Both are now matching the *Pereleshin's* speed. Hold on… Aspect change on the contact underneath the *Pereleshin*!" Announced CPO DeSousa. "It has turned on its side!"

"OK, this is getting very, very strange in a hurry," Johnson said. "XO! I've got a gut feeling they are about to attack the *Pereleshin*… and we might be next! Sound general quarters!

* * *

The submersed, unmanned Aggressor underneath the *Pereleshin* positioned itself so that its primary weapon emitter port was aligned on the long axis of the great vessels' hull. The second 'manned' Aggressor would be monitoring weapon operation, efficiency and effectiveness.

The first calibration 'test' was about to begin.

* * *

"Captain! The craft underneath us has rotated on its side!"

"Flank speed and hard left rudder, 15 degrees up on the bow plane and brace for emergency ascent! Deploy decoys NOW NOW NOW!!!"

It was the last order Captain Barsukov would ever give.

* * *

The Aggressor's dark matter reactor and antimatter synthesizer instantly at-

tained maximum output when it began to project the thread-thin conditioning beam on the *Pereleshin's* hull. The seawater between the two vessels ionized as the pinpoint beam expanded to a two millimeter tube with a perfect vacuum inside. A microsecond later, a powerful stream of antimatter began bombarding the hull, annihilating every normal atom in its path and releasing blinding light and gamma rays in the process. The Aggressor raced underneath the hapless boomer along its long axis as if it were gutting an animal's underbelly for butchering. Bulkheads and decks were severed up to 30 feet into the hull, very nearly cutting the submarine into left and right halves. The massive influx of seawater under 700 pounds per square inch of ambient pressure, and the secondary explosion caused by the breached reactor core, ensured the death of over 150 Russian submainers would be swift.

Having gathered the necessary data from the primary weapon calibration test, both Aggressors leisurely egressed from the area at a relatively slow 100 knots.

* * *

"Oh my God! The *Pereleshin* just exploded!" Yelled De Sousa."

"Jesus! Hard to starboard and flank speed! Prepare for evasive maneuvers and countermeasures! Quick, what are the new contacts doing right now?"

"Both are moving away from us, Sir. Course zero-five-zero, bearing zero-eight-five at 100 knots and ascending. De Sousa announced with genuine terror in his voice.

"Thank God!" Commander Johnson said as he sat down hard and exhaled loudly. "Belay those last orders!

"Sir, the *Pereleshin*... there is a massive amount of air in the water... probable multiple hull breaches... a secondary explosion... sir, no turbine noise... he's... he's sinking fast, Sir."

Nobody said a word. Every submariner in the control room was quietly listening to the break-up of the Russian boomer. The hapless Russians were beginning their ethereal 'Endless Patrol,' roaming the seas and oceans for eternity as ghost sailors on a never ending mission.

"Pilot, turn to course zero-seven-five degrees, decrease to full speed and bring us to radio depth. Maintain general quarters until further notice."

'It could have just as easily been us.' Johnson thought to himself, hands trembling and sweat beginning to soak through his shirt.

It was sobering to think of him and his crew ending up like the Russians: sliding into the abyss in a billion dollar coffin... destined to settle onto a lightless, barren graveyard under three and a half miles of water. No real grave for the wife and kids to visit. Just a flag presented to his widow, a condolence letter from the President... and a lifetime of knowing that her husband, her children's daddy, was entombed somewhere below the surface of the North Pacific. A monstrous chill swept down his spine.

"What in God's name were those damn things?" De Sousa asked, clearly shaken and pale.

"I really don't know, De Sousa, I really don't... but I seriously doubt they came from this planet."

Chapter 45

"Mr. President, we have a situation," Larry Osborn whispered into President Bertrams' ear. "We'll need to return to Washington after you give your speech."

"Bad enough to cancel the rest on my campaign stops?"

"Greg, the Russians lost a Borei class ballistic missile submarine."

"So what? I'm not going to deviate from my schedule because they build leaky, billion dollar death traps!"

"It's more complicated than that, Greg."

"OK, like what, Larry?"

"Greg, you need to trust me on this one. There are too many people and reporters around here. Air Force One will be ready to go by the end of your speech. We can work on a cover story on the way back."

"That bad?"

"Give your speech and give 'em hell. I'll get you up to speed afterwards."

* * *

"Submarine Pacific Command received a flash message from the USS *North Carolina* stating that they witnessed 'two, very small and ultra-high performance submarines attack and destroy the *Pavel Pereleshin* about 1300 miles northwest of Oahu at 5:36AM local time. No survivors,' Osborn said, starting off the briefing in

Air Force One's Presidential office located right behind the cockpit door.

"What do they mean by 'very small and ultra-high performance?'"

"They reported both craft were under 40 feet in length and entered the area at 225 knots."

"In laymans' terms, how fast is 225 knots?"

"According to the information I received from the Pentagon, about 250 miles-per-hour. Our fastest submarines can do about 30 or so. These are armed, alien vessels Mr. President. I have been assured that nothing built on this planet can perform like that underwater."

President Bertram leaned back into his chair, eyebrows furrowed in thought.

"Larry, the only thing I can make of this is that the aliens must be on our side. Our sub was right there and wasn't attacked. I'd say that is pretty good news." Bertram said with a somewhat upbeat tone.

"I'm not sure that really makes a solid case for them being on our side, Greg."

"What if the attack was in retaliation for something the Russians did to them?"

"It's a possibility, I suppose... but as far as I know, we don't have intel that suggests anything like that has happened," Osborn replied, sensing that the President had already made up his mind about the aliens. "They did seem to be acting aggressive towards Hanson and the Marines at Cocheta."

"Hanson again!" Bertram scowled. "Jesus, Larry, if I was an alien, I'd be pissed off, too if I had a bunch of Marines aiming rifles at me for no good reason!"

By cherry-picking details of Friday night's alien encounter at CRF to fortify his narrative, Osborn now had no doubts that the President was going to solidly back the aliens as a means to advance his domestic agenda.

"Greg, this is potentially dangerous political water. If the aliens decide to attack one of our assets, you will look extremely weak and foolish, not to mention the panic that will ensue. The opposition will eat you alive."

"If they attack us... well, we're all screwed anyway," Bertram replied calmly. "The only stance that makes any sense right now is siding with the aliens."

Osborn felt a chill in his blood. His next logical question for the President was what he intended to do if the aliens did attack America or American interests, but was genuinely afraid of what Bertram might say.

Since World War II, the United States had not fought a focused, sustained global war with the unambiguous objective of crushing the enemy and occupying their homeland until they could be trusted to play nice. The strategy worked well in defeating Imperial Japan and the Third Reich. Once forcibly purged of their lust for territory, they returned to the ranks of civilized nations. Not so with Korea, Vietnam, Iraq, Afghanistan and the Global War on Terror… all were half-hearted efforts that ended in shaky truces, insurgencies and governments that were as bad or worse than before. Modern war paled in comparison to the desperation and destruction levied on Europe and the Pacific during World War II, and Larry Osborn wondered if President Bertram would fold if the aliens began attacking America or her allies.

"Greg, what would you do if they start attacking us?"

"You heard what Talbot and McNeill said last week and you just told me two small subs whacked a gigantic nuclear submarine. Given their technologic superiority over us, we'd be pissing into the wind to engage them."

"What would you do?"

President Bertram turned his overly comfortable executive chair to look out one of the starboard windows. Above was rich, deep blue skies completely void of clouds, below were the deep green forests of West Virginia. Burning it all up in a grossly one-sided interstellar war? Unthinkable! He was getting rid of America's nuclear arsenal, for cryin' out loud! It didn't make any sense to win a war if you left the face of the planet with a horrible case of nuclear acne.

"Make a deal. Surrender… anything but global nuclear war."

"I suggest you never utter those words again, Greg," Osborn replied sternly. "It's just you and me in here right now. If that is going to be your policy if we are attacked, then so be it. But, if this official policy were to get out? I assure you, all hell will break loose! I would actively dodge any question on this subject."

"You don't approve?"

"I'm your Chief of Staff. I give you the best advice I can. You're the President. You take it or you leave it. It doesn't matter if I approve or not."

"Dammit, Larry! I'm asking you as a friend! Do you not approve?"

"Half of the country won't give a damn what your policy is as long as they are being entertained and taken care of, 25 percent will approve and 25 percent will want to fight the aliens to the last man, woman and child. It's the latter that you will catch the most grief from."

"Again, do you not approve?"

"No, Greg. I don't approve of giving up without a fight. I'd rather die than be enslaved to a hostile alien culture."

"Thank you, Greg," Bertram replied. "I appreciate your candor. That's why you're my Chief of Staff and my friend. I can't, however, allow the planet to die by our own hands using nuclear weapons! It is a much larger issue than whether or not the human race is subject to alien rule or enslavement."

"What if most, or the rest of the world chooses to fight?"

"Then, they will do so without us."

"We have treaties, Greg!"

"None of them include a suicide pact."

"What about Cocheta? Their mission?"

"Just because they are 'protected' doesn't mean we just jump through hoops to deploy anything they come up with. Besides, they have nothing operational. Don't forget, Cocheta is responsible for the cyber-security screw up that may be allowing the aliens to hack every electronic device on earth. Larry," the President said with a more ominous tone, "the aliens may already have us by the balls!"

Larry Osborn had no more arguments left. "Do you think they'll contact us?"

"If they don't, we'll do our best to contact them."

"What do you want to do about the Russian sub?"

"We tell the Russians their sub suffered some sort of catastrophic failure and sank. No survivors. We're not going to mention the aliens."

"I'll get Arball on that immediately."

"We also need to convene the NSC."

"One step ahead of you. They're gathering in the Situation Room at this very moment."

"Good. We have a lot to talk about."

Chapter 46

"The *Pavel Pereleshin* was a nuclear-powered Borei-Class Ballistic Missile Submarine recently commissioned by the Russian Navy," began Admiral Hal Fletcher, Chief of Naval Operations. "He was a big one. Lethal too, with MIRV-ed ballistic missiles and a handful of nuclear cruise and anti-ship missiles. The Russians are going to be mighty pissed when they learn of its demise."

"If we didn't tell the Russians their sub is dead, how long before they find out on their own?" President Bertram asked.

"Depends."

"On what?"

"When the submarine is ordered to report their status via extremely low frequency radio," Admiral Fletcher replied. "In the open ocean, subs can receive messages deep underwater by this type of radio. Transmitting while submerged, however, is far more difficult. They move near the surface and transmit their message to fleet headquarters via direct transmission or satellite relay."

"So, it might be minutes or days from now before the Russians discover the *Pereleshin* is missing in action."

"That is correct, Mr. President."

"Is it possible the *Pereleshin* knew the *North Carolina* had been behind them for days?"

"The Virginia-Class subs are incredibly stealthy, but I wouldn't bet the farm

that the *North Carolina* remained completely undetected."

The President didn't need to weigh the options. If the Russians knew that the *North Carolina* was tracking their boat and he didn't immediately inform them of its sinking, all kinds of diplomatic hell would break loose. The last thing he needed was the Russians crawling up his backsides.

"Larry, me or Arball on the press conference?"

"You, Greg," Osborn replied. "There will be a lot fewer questions if you personally handle the announcement. We'll shoot for 8 PM."

"Agreed." The President slowly leaned forward in his chair. "Now, Admiral Fletcher, can you tell me how two tiny submarines can travel at 250 mph, underwater and scrap a huge, ballistic missile submarine in the open ocean?"

"Alien technology, Mr. President. There are no other explanations. Nothing made on this planet can even remotely duplicate what these alien submersibles can do."

"But why attack the Russians right in front of us?" CIA Director Brust asked. "Why didn't they attack *North Carolina*, too?"

"Maybe they were making a statement," Admiral Fletcher replied. "Or maybe they were just going after the biggest fish."

"Perhaps this represents a planned change in their strategy," Sarah Whiting offered. "The question is why, after 70 years of non-agressive behavior, are they now becoming aggressive enough to destroy a billion-dollar sub and kill 150 Russian submariners in the process?"

"Could this be nothing more than a beef between the Russians and the aliens?" Bertram asked, interjecting his favorite and most comfortable theory to draw attention from Whiting's question.

"Only the Russians could confirm that," Brust replied. "We have nothing in the way of intel suggesting anything like that has happened."

Whiting persisted. "This is a much larger threat than an isolated, one sided skirmish between the Russians and the aliens. I have preliminary reports on my desk from Kirtland Air Force Base and Sandia Labs suggesting that our largest nuclear stockpile may have been compromised by alien nanotechnology."

"Nanotechnology?" Bertram asked.

"Mr. President, imagine millions, perhaps billions of microscopic machines programmed to infiltrate and compromise our most sensitive facilities. They could create a communications relay that could send and receive information to and from the outside. They might be programmed to manufacture things from available resources and completely change how our own machines operate. Dr. Hanson is concerned that the aliens might be able to alter the nuclear weapons, make them inert or perhaps even fuse them."

"Dammit all to Hell! Is it possible to have one friggin' meeting... just one, without her name coming up?" Bertram nearly yelled.

"Whether you like it or not, Mr. President, Dr. Hanson is probably smarter than all of us combined and she has served her country well. I understand that you have a passionate dislike of the woman and her family, but ignoring her input would be a monumental mistake."

Bertram glared at Sarah, wishing he could get rid of her and Hanson at the same time. The logical side of the President, however, knew that would be extraordinarily stupid.

"Granted. So, what is Kirtland and Sandia doing about it?"

"They have started three shifts of technicians to inspect every nuclear weapon for subtle changes. They are seriously understaffed for the mission, Mr. President. I recommend sending staff from Pantex to Kirtland. Maybe even bring in retirees. I also recommend that all inbound weapon shipments to Kirtland be halted and that all outbound trucks exposed to the maintenance facility be parked in the adjacent desert. Nothing that goes into the facility should be allowed to leave the immediate area. Even personnel should be decontaminated for possible hitchhiking nanotechnology."

"Good God!" Exclaimed the CIA Director. "You've got to be kidding me!"

"No, Director Brust, I am not," Sarah Whiting replied. "A highly advanced technology could manufacture and program microscopic devices, perhaps powered by flecks of polonium or plutonium, to do a wide range of missions ranging from surveillance to sabotage. They must certainly have an artificial intelligence that can operate independently if separated from the rest, yet still be part of a much larger intelligence when in proximity to each other. Sort of like a RAID array of several

hard disc drives. Each carrying their share of data so that the artificial intelligence can continue to function should a 'nano-bot' machine become damaged or destroyed. It is also possible that they might even have flight capability."

"That is absolutely preposterous!" Brusk scoffed. "Something that tiny with those capabilities?"

"Might I refer you to the crew of the *Pereleshin*. They may have a much better perspective on what 'tiny' can do."

The Situation Room room fell quiet. The *Pavel Pereleshin* was destroyed in seconds by a submersible one-sixteenth its size and over eight times as fast. Not by a torpedo, but an unknown weapon capable of ripping through a highly reinforced hull and compromising several watertight compartments. As was always the case with Sarah Whiting, her analysis was to-the-point and delivered with emotionless candor. It earned her the nickname 'The Vulcan,' though nobody dared repeat it to her face.

"That is very sobering, Sarah," Bertram said grimly. "If the Russians did nothing to provoke the attack, why did they kill the *Pereleshin*?"

"There are not many possibilities, Mr. President," Whiting began. "It seems to me that such an aggressive act shows a clear inclination that they intend to engage in hostilities."

"I don't buy that, Sarah," Bertram replied hastily. "We have 70 years of sightings and a warehouse full of their junk. That's it. We've done nothing to provoke them."

"Mr. President, I think it might be a huge mistake for you to assume their thought processes and motives are similar to that of our own."

"Why not?"

"Because they evolved on another planet. Their evolutionary pressures may be similar to ours, but history is what shapes their minds."

"I still don't buy it, Sarah. Just all of a sudden they want to kick our ass? It makes no sense!"

"How far away is their planet?"

"How in Hell would I know that, Sarah?"

"It may be a crucial, Mr. President. They may have been waiting for their military to arrive."

"Wait a minute, you're saying that the aliens here on earth have been waiting 70 years for their military to arrive?"

"It is a possibility, Mr. President," Sarah replied blandly, almost as if the topic was boring her. "If we knew how far they must travel to get here, and the speed in which they can move through space, we might be able to determine when we can expect them."

"That might be an exercise in frivolity, Sarah," Brusk said with more than a hint of finality. "Judging by what they've done to the *Pereleshin*, their military may already be here."

"One lost sub does not equal an invasion!" Bertram protested. "What about all this 'taking forever to travel to our nearest star' I've heard all my life? That these science fiction shows are just that: fiction?"

"Mr. President," Admiral Fletcher said loudly enough to distract the NSC members from the current verbal dogfight, "I'm just a salty ol' sea dog a rock's throw from retirement," He paused briefly for the chuckles to subside. "I've put my time in Annapolis where I learned book warfare. In real military life, I've been through two wars where I learned real warfare and this other kind of warfare we call the ongoing Global War on Terrorism." He paused for a moment to take a sip of ice water and set up a heavy dose of reality. "Blowing up schools, roadside bombs and this bullshit idea of 'asymmetric warfare' is just that: bullshit. Thugs with guns. War, real war, is the art of crippling a country until it surrenders completely under your terms. It is a constant, unrelenting assault to deprive your enemy of the ability to take the offensive and fight back. You do that by first destroying his most dangerous weapons before he can use them on you. The next step is to soundly kick his ass into surrendering and secure his conquered property to prevent insurgencies. The Russians lost one of their deadliest weapons and are about to learn they are at war with the aliens. In short order, we are going to learn that, too."

"Again, why does this need to affect us?" Bertram said with far less confidence than before.

"Mr. President, do you believe that the aliens have traveled for 70 years just to engage the Russians?" Fletcher asked somberly.

Bertram leaned back in his chair and stared at the ceiling for a moment. "Until further notice, the policy I announced last week still stands. We are not going to make any provocative moves towards the aliens nor place our military on any kind of alert. I repeat... we will NOT make ANY threatening moves of any sort towards the aliens."

"What if they do engage us?" Brusk asked.

"We'll cross that bridge only if it happens."

"Are we going to inform Cocheta of this development, Mr. President?" Whiting asked.

"I see no compelling reason to do so."

Chapter 47

"Vitya, this is a most terrible day for our great nation!" President Korolyvov howled as he entered his office.

"Uncle, what has happened?"

"We have lost the submarine *Pereleshin*! Our mightiest weapon of war! This is a great tragedy for Russia, my young nephew!"

"How could this be, Alyosha? Our submarines are the envy of the world!"

"The American President called to inform me that his Navy heard sounds of an imploding submarine hull in the North Pacific! He claims they know nothing of the submarine's identity, but he shamefully lies! Their fast-attack submarines shadow our ballistic missile submarines, our Shchukas follow theirs. There are only two possibilities, Vitya. Our *Pavel Pereleshin* destroyed itself in front of the Americans, or the Americans destroyed the *Pereleshin*!"

"Uncle, why would the Americans make such a dangerous move against our Navy?"

"This puzzles me as well," Korolyvov admitted. "It makes little sense for them to do so, but the self-destruction of a newly-commissioned submarine is just as improbable!"

"What will you do, Alyosha?"

"I shall send the Americans an unmistakable message, nephew," the Russian President said darkly. "I will allow our Shchukas to... what is it the Americans say

when someone is annoyingly close? Ah, yes... 'Intrude into their space!'"

Chapter 48

"What's this all about, Larry?" Trey Klein of the *New York Times* asked as he and the rest of the White House Press Corps assembled. "Nobody has given us a hint."

"The President is going to give a brief announcement in a few minutes. He hasn't decided if he is going to take questions afterwards."

"You're killin' me Larry! Can you at least give us a category?"

"You'll survive, Klein," Arball replied. "It's military related. That's all I can tell you."

There was nothing of significance on the wires. No new military actions of any sort. Sunday evening? Klein was intrigued.

After he made a few fruitless inquiries of his press corps colleagues, he took his seat on the second row behind the Reuter's correspondent.

Right on schedule at 8 PM EDST, White House Press Secretary Larry Arball asked the correspondents to rise.

"Please be seated," President Bertram said in a neutral, business-like fashion. "At 5:36 AM local time, 1:36 PM Washington time, the nuclear submarine USS *North Carolina* was on routine maneuvers 1300 miles northwest of Hawaii when they detected a massive underwater explosion in their vicinity. According to the captain of the *North Carolina*, the sound of the explosion was consistent with submarine hull failure in deep water. Upon notification of this, I directed the

Secretary of State to contact the Russian ambassador and verify the loss of one of their submarines in the North Pacific. Approximately four hours later, the Russians would only confirm that they have been unable to contact one of their submarines.

I have spoken to Russian President Aleksei Korolyvov and offered our assistance. On my orders, the USS *North Carolina* is now conducting rescue operations in the area and will continue to do so until relieved by the Russian Navy or until it is determined there is no possibility of survivors.

Please join the First Lady and I in prayer for the Russian sailors and their families.

I will now take a few questions."

Several journalists began shouting "Mr. President" at the same time.

"Trina," the President said, choosing the Washington Post journalist sitting to the left of Trey Kline.

"Mr. President, do we know which Russian submarine was lost?"

'The Russians have not confirmed the name of the lost submarine. Brian."

"Mr. President, " Brian Byrne from the Associated Press began, "was the USS *North Carolina* assigned to follow the Russian submarine that's missing?"

"The USS *North Carolina* was on routine maneuvers. I must assume the Russian submarine was doing the same. I am told that it is not uncommon for submarines to hear loud noises from hundreds of miles away. Trey."

"Mr. President, the Russians finally commissioned the Ballistic Missile Submarine *Pavel Pereleshin* earlier this year. I read something a while back that it was going to the Pacific. Could that be the submarine we're looking for?"

"Again, the Russians have not released the name of the missing submarine. When they do, Larry will fill you in."

After answering a half-dozen similar questions, President Bertram exited the press briefing room for a short walk to the oval office study where a glass of 16 year-old Lagavulin scotch was already waiting for him. It had been a long day and the Scotch was a welcome comfort from the stress of non-stop campaign appearances and dealing with a furious Russian President who was not fully buying into the official account of the *Pereleshin's* disappearance. With any luck, he would get some real rest before his 5 AM departure from Andrews Air Force Base.

"What are odds?" he thought to himself as he sipped his favorite Scotch and closed his eyes. "What are the odds?..."

Chapter 49

"Well, that was a brief and interesting Press Conference," Donna Hanson said with half a mouthful of buttered popcorn. The CRF Project director had, not an hour earlier, finished the late Saturday and all-Sunday chore of writing her pending address to the battered staff of the most improbable research facility ever conceived. Knowing the critical importance of her speech, Tim kept mostly out of sight during Donna's self-imposed imprisonment, spending most of his free time on-line in his apartment handling finances, arranging longer-term care of his dog and sending a myriad of e-mails to his academic colleagues who might be wondering if he were languishing in prison.

"How so, sweetie?" Tim queried as he reached into the popcorn bag for his own handful, not having a clue that there was anything odd about the President's announcement.

"Well, usually, military mishaps of this type are kept quiet until most all the facts are known and can be manipulated for public consumption on both sides."

"What's there to manipulate?" Tim asked. "Seems cut and dry to me. The Russian sub had a catastrophic hull failure and our navy heard it as it happened."

"Not the 'navy,' only the USS *North Carolina* heard it. I guarantee you, they were right behind that Russian sub when it imploded!"

"Doing what?"

"Recording, measuring and cataloging every sound and maneuver the Russian sub makes so they can find it again in relatively short order. Just like the Skunk

Works aircraft, it's all about stealth, Tim. If you are a skilled captain in a stealthy sub, you can sneak up to your opponent, tailgate him and he'll never know you're there."

"You're serious!" Tim said incredulously. "Right behind a Russian sub?"

"Surprisingly close. So close you could almost put a thermometer in its rear end," Donna replied as she snuggled up closer to him on his almost comfortable government couch. "Our Virginia-class fast-attack subs routinely shadow Russian ballistic missile subs just like the Russian Akulas shadow our Ohio-class ballistic missile subs. If an all-out war was declared, our fast-attack submarines would likely be ordered to torpedo the enemy subs before they could launch any of their missiles. Some of our torpedoes even have nuclear warheads that could take out a number of ships at one time."

"Hey! How is it you know so much about submarines?" Tim asked playfully. "I thought you were a fighter jet kinda woman!"

"Silly man! Lockheed has their fingers in all kinds of pies!" she replied just as playfully. "I've helped on some other projects outside the Skunk Works, including sub-launched cruise missiles."

"Then... that must make you a very dangerous woman!"

"You have no idea, Timothy Alexander!"

Their eyes locked and both instinctively knew that their attraction for each other had finally reached a level of passion far beyond their collective ability to resist. The swell of emotions driving them together was as natural as their next breath. Their love-making would last long into the evening. Afterwords, both in each other's arms, quiet in the still of an improbable subterranian apartment, they became more than a couple, they were two souls fused into one.

A tragic family loss, under the most strange and difficult of circumstances, brought two lonely people close enough to ignite a tiny ember of attraction that would quickly blossom into an eternity of sharing everything together. It was the perfect moment... and both held on to it until they fell asleep.

Donna awakened a half hour before the night stand clock was set to wake them for their Monday morning preparations. She was sobbing in her pillow. After several seconds of disorientation, Tim awakened enough to know something was wrong.

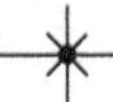

"Sweetheart, what's wrong? Are you OK?"

"It's my dad! I saw him!" she said while profusely weeping. "He was smiling at me and stroking my hair!"

Tim, still trying to come out of the fog of interrupted sleep, wasn't sure what to say.

"It felt so real! I could even smell the after shave he wore every day!"

Tim pulled her close to him. "Your dad was a very special man. His love for you didn't die with him," he whispered.

"I know," Donna said, wiping tears from her face with her palms. "He said, 'I love you, sugarplum!' That was a nickname Dad gave to me when I was born."

Tim didn't reply and began gently stroking her hair as she held him tight. In the dark, he could see the alarm clock was two minutes away from its annoying beeps.

'Back into the fray,' Tim thought to himself, wondering if there would ever be time for nurturing their new love while at CRF. If not, Tim was sure they would make up for it during the two week off-shift.

Chapter 50

"Distinguished scientists, engineers, Marines, contractors and Cocheta's invaluable support staff... for those who have not met me, I am Dr. Hanson's little girl!"

The assembled Cocheta staff laughed and cheered for what seemed like several minutes.

"I am humbled, truly humbled, to be standing before this amazing group of people as your new project director. I simply cannot adequately express how honored I am to be part of this important endeavor. One that spans over 60 years and has employed some of the most brilliant minds and hardest working patriots in history. Only the Manhattan Project rivals the scope and importance of the research being done here.

Up until last week, this facility... this incredible facility... the tireless, brilliant people who work here and the billions of dollars invested in this project, was only known to a privileged few in government. Right or wrong, my parents changed the paradigm by literally making this project known to the world overnight. My dad believed that the nations of the world should work together on a common defense against potential extraterrestrial aggression. I believe that too, but convincing countries to work together is a monumental challenge... and time may be running out."

The last sentence caused a stir throughout the auditorium. Dr. Hanson paused for a moment to let it subside.

"I know of the suffering this staff has endured over the last 20 years. I know of the harsh working environment created by the late Director Hastings. I know of

his improper appointments and murderous ways. To say he was vicious and cruel would be a gross understatement. He robbed my family of a father and my mother of a husband. He robbed you of fellowship with your retired colleagues and he robbed you of your dignity. It is tremendous testament to the resiliency of this staff that you stayed true to your commitment and made progress in spite of Director Hastings. I am truly in awe of the Cocheta Research Project staff. I assure you, the working conditions here will improve overnight."

"They already have!" Yelled an electronics technician at the back of the auditorium. Cheering and applause immediately erupted.

"Thank you... thank you, please... but it is your enthusiasm, hard work and the working environment YOU create that will turn this place around! Most, if not all of you, know that I am a product of the Skunk Works. When I was running it, everyone's input was important. I challenged them every day and I worked them hard. Not with a bullwhip, but with rewards of peer recognition and praise for their hard work and innovations. Money may be a great motivator in a short haul, but recognition of achievement stays in the soul long after the money is spent. We will have that kind of work environment here in every department."

Vigorous applause and cheers erupted again.

"This facility is not the Skunk Works, nor will it ever be. It would be a huge mistake for me to try and bend Cocheta into something that it isn't. There are hints all around this place that Cocheta is unique, not only in its proud history, but in its style. My personal favorite of Cocheta culture is the, must be, 50 plus year old plaque of Marvin the Martian in the main hanger. I'll venture a guess that you have your own rituals or rights of passage for newcomers and those about to retire that Director Hastings was never made aware of. Elite groups, like you and special military forces, almost always have a special camaraderie that makes them unique. Am I correct, Colonel Jeffries?"

"Damn straight, Dr. Hanson!"

Laughter and cheering once again broke out.

"I'm not about to change what works for you. What I want you to know is that everything can be improved upon and I challenge all of you to find those improvements that enhance our efforts. I assure you, we are going to need to be as efficient as possible to meet the research, funding and political challenges ahead."

"Sadly, there are a few here amongst us who don't belong. I would hope that you are self-aware enough to know this already," Dr. Hanson said solemnly. "Please come see me and we'll arrange a reasonably generous separation package. I only want team players here. People with vision. People who do not shrink away from a challenge. I have no patience for the politically oriented plying their hobby in my shop. It's my job to handle the politics.

I want everyone to enjoy their work here. Most of you sacrifice family time so that you might give to your country in an important, if unusual way. One of my first projects will be to examine our expenses. I suspect that the previous director felt that outrageous toys like that Gulfstream out front were more important than the things that make a work environment more pleasant. Don't get me wrong, I'm a pilot and I am crazy in love with that jet, but it really is way more than we need. The money could have been put towards more important things. Maybe spruce up the physical plant and make your apartments less... 50-ish."

Laughter and another healthy applause ensued.

Donna paused for a moment, knowing her next words would be difficult to speak without crying.

"I miss my dad," Donna said sadly. "Most of you miss him, too. Until last week, it had been more than 20 years since I last saw him. I remember the days before Louis Hastings tore our family apart. I remember how happy we were... how happy my dad was. The backyard pool was our favorite place to play, but we hardly ever used it when he was on a two week stretch. It just wasn't the same without him in the pool splashing with us. I remember the disappointment we felt when he was called to travel on his off weeks. When he was home, all was well with the world.

I was away at college when Louis Hastings robbed my family of their father. We were devastated by the news, but it was my little brother, a teenager still living at home, who bore the brunt of the separation. It made no sense to any of us and, to make matters worse, we were forbidden to talk about it to anyone.

Then there were the 'accidents' inflicted upon our retirees. Fifteen murdered. Fifteen!!! All were respected scientists and engineers, slaughtered because of Louis Hastings' obsession and paranoia with operational security.

I assure you, as long as I am the project director, Cocheta will never face horrors like this again. We are a professional, scientific research project of the highest

calibre... and we will keep it that way! My door will always be open to each and every one of you! Thank you!"

The cheers and applause were deafening in the relatively small auditorium. Within a few moments, everyone was on their feet, cheering and clapping.

"I have just a quick announcement before we break to convene this week's Conclave," Dr. McLachland said as the applause waned. "Dr. Hanson, Dr. Alexander and I need to go over a disturbing memo I received from Sandia this morning and see if it warrants rush presentation at the Conclave. Otherwise, get some breakfast and we'll convene again at zero nine-hundred."

Chapter 51

"Is this is about the samples Sandia they took at the nuclear weapons storage facility?" Dr. Alexander asked.

"Yes, Tim," Dr. McLachand replied with a genuinely concerned look on his face. "It appears that scrapings retrieved from the burned area at the nuclear weapons facility show evidence of non-functioning, intact and damaged microscopic devices in the residue and confirmed by electron microscope. There are also trace readings of plutonium."

"Oh my God, Donna! You were right on the money!" Tim exclaimed with both shock and admiration. "They are definitely infiltrating our nuclear stockpile!"

"Yes, Tim, they are... and we need to make a difficult decision."

"What kind of decision?" McLachand reluctantly asked.

"To stay the course. Triple our efforts to discover weapons that are being compromised by nanotechnology and still run the risk of losing Albuquerque..."

"Or..," McLachland cringed.

"Rendering all of our nuclear weapons inert by removing their fissile material. Stalemate. Two thousand plus nuclear weapons only fit to be museum pieces." Donna sighed.

"Losing Albuquerque or giving up our nukes," Tim pondered aloud. "Could we get enough technicians to inspect the weapons every day?"

"Not likely," McLachland said shaking his head. I seriously doubt there are enough up-to-speed nuclear weapons technicians in the United States to maintain local stockpiles and monitor all of Kirtland's nukes 24 hours a day."

"I'll contact the Pentagon and see if we can recruit military and civilian retirees, maybe borrow cross-trained, active duty technicians that were working on nukes before they retrained for another MOS. I'll also ask to borrow techs from the 341st Missile Wing at Malmstrom and the 90th from Warren," Donna said, referring to the two active ICBM Minuteman III sites in Montana and Wyoming. "In addition, I think we should have all facilities that warehouse nuclear warheads look for and sample any charred areas around buildings containing a nuke. I'll make the calls when we finish."

"Do you want to present this at Conclave, Dr. Hanson?" McLachland asked.

"Absolutely, and I want to propose that we make our static rail gun portable and capable of being remotely aimed."

"What?" Tim asked, not sure he heard what he thought he heard. "You want to weaponize the rail gun?"

"Of course not!" she replied with a sly grin and a wink. "We're just modifying a research tool into a test platform to see how fast an alien aircraft can dodge an ultra-sonic projectile."

"Do you intend to open fire on the aliens?" Tim asked, hesitantly.

"Only if they become overtly aggressive, Tim. Besides, having the rail gun has got to be better than being a fish in a bucket. We already know it can punch holes in their most durable metals, but what we don't know is how fast the aliens can react to the incoming round."

"We also need to consider the nagging question of what would happen if we penetrated their energy source. Over the last 60 years, that one issue has sparked many dozens of heated exchanges in this mountain," McLachland warned.

"It's a tough problem," Tim replied. "If they use antimatter, 25 grams is enough to flatten this lovely valley we're in. If they have 80 pounds of antimatter in their reactor and we punch a hole in it? Something like 1.5 gigatons of TNT going off at once."

"A fireball from ground to space in an instant," MacLachland added. "Unimaginable."

"It might just boil down to 'heads or tails,'" Donna speculated somberly. "I see only two options. One: we opt out because it is simply too dangerous. We may be in a fairly remote area, but a 1.5 gigaton detonation would surely cause extensive loss of life and horrible burn injuries for hundreds of miles. Two: we try it out on our little spy ship. Seems to me, the risks would be no different than the first option. The spy ship might have the very same reactor."

McLachland shook his head. "There is a third option: We send our spy ship to the Marshall Islands and use a military rail gun to punch holes in it. If it goes off, we can study the blast and maybe calculate a yield. Might get some valuable info."

"But only if it has the same reactor as the others," Donna said. "Seems like a logical approach to start with."

"Hold on a moment, the people that live down there have been thoroughly abused for decades," Tim protested. "Tourism has only recently returned to Bikini Atoll. I seriously doubt we could or should use it."

"I didn't know that Bikini had been re-opened," McLachland said. "I'm sure we can still find something remote and usable."

"When I call the Pentagon later this morning, I'll include a request that they look for a suitable rock to detonate our pesky spy ship on."

"I guess we still won't know if they can dodge a Mach 5 bullet." Tim said without mentioning that he'd feel a lot better if that unknown variable were hammered down.

"I'd really like to know that too, Tim," Donna said smiling at him. "Just can't take the risk of having my favorite TV personality turning into sub-atomic particles!"

The three laughed at the scientifically macabre statement.

"Donna, do you believe they are going to attack us?" McLachlan asked, almost as if he really didn't want to hear the answer.

Donna hesitated for a moment, trying to come up with just the right words with just the right caveats. She instinctively knew what was coming, what she couldn't know was when and how.

"Dr. McLachland," She started.

"Please, you can call me 'Steve."

"Steve... My gut feeling is that we will be at war with them within a few months. Perhaps sooner."

"If that happens, do we have any chance at defeating them?" Tim asked.

"The technology difference between us is stark," Donna began. "I think Professor Heischler summed it up pretty well. We really don't have much of a chance. The rail gun idea is a reach. We might buy some time with asymmetrical warfare. Nuclear booby traps, maybe electromagnetic pulse... I know I sound very pessimistic, and I don't mean to, I just don't see how we can possibly defend ourselves against them."

Dr. McLachland lowered and shook his head. "Then we had better pray they have a conscience."

Chapter 52

"Dr. Hanson, please come to Triple C as soon as possible," the overhead speaker in her apartment announced.

'Damn!' She thought to herself. 'Just returned to the apartment from the Conclave to wind down, prop the ankle up... and off I go again!'

Between addressing the staff and a productive Conclave where she was brought up to speed on a number of research initiatives, Donna Hanson couldn't help but be reminded of her hectic days in Palmdale. She doubted the pace would ever reach that of the Skunk Works, but who knows? One major breakthrough and CRF could turn into a very busy place overnight.

One thing Donna Hanson knew of for sure, was that CRF was really growing on her. The staff was so appreciative of her presence that she could hardly walk 10 yards without someone telling her so. She knew it was only a temporary infatuation driven by profound gratitude. In time, the workplace would evolve and it was her job to make sure it evolved properly. Having her crew happy and productive would keep distracting confrontations to a minimum.

Donna arrived at Cochetas' Command and Communications Center within a few minutes.

"You must be Dr. Hanson!" MAJ Alleyne said enthusiastically. "I've heard so much about you and Dr. Alexander!"

"Thank you, Major. It is a real honor to be here."

"This place has changed so much in the last few days!" Alleyne almost gushed. "Everyone is happy and smiling, morale has turned around... I'll be honest, I was about to put in for a transfer. Another week with Director Hastings and I woulda gone postal on him! I'm a Christian woman, but I gotta say that Hastings got exactly what he deserved!"

"Things are going to get better, Major," Donna said reassuringly while dodging the Hastings comment. "Bear with me and this facility will be both pleasant and productive. Now, what was it that you needed me for?"

"You have a message classified 'eyes only,'" MAJ Alleyne replied as she handed the envelope to Dr. Hanson.

"It's been a very long time since I received a message like this," Donna said to Alleyene. "Any protocol I need to adhere to?"

"The usual, ma'am. Shred it or lock it up."

"Thanks, Major."

A few minutes later, Dr. Hanson was sitting at the desk in her apartment. If someone had been in the room with her, they would have seen the blood drain from her face.

> *Dr. Hanson,*
>
> *The fast attack submarine, USS* North Carolina, *witnessed two, very small alien submersibles completely destroy the Russian Ballistic Missile Submarine* Pavel Pereleshin *in the North Pacific. It took less than 5 seconds. The news reports being generated are false.*
>
> *Thought you would like to know.*
>
> *No Signature*

Donna felt nauseated for a moment, then picked up her phone and called Tim, who thankfully answered on the second tone.

"Tim,"

"Hey, sweetheart!"

"Get over here!"

"Is something wrong?"

"Please, Tim. Get over here NOW!"

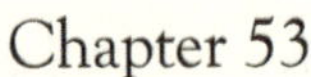

Chapter 53

"There is no doubt about it anymore, Tim. We seem to be at war, or the brink of war, only Washington isn't acting like we are!"

"I don't understand," Tim replied in disbelief. "Why would Washington pretend that the sinking of a Russian submarine by aliens somehow doesn't involve us?"

"Because they make up their own reality and to hell with concrete facts!" Donna ranted. "President Bertram made up his mind last week. He wants to be partners with the aliens. Sing folk songs and light up joints together. Maybe, just maybe, if you close your eyes and wish hard enough, the Bogeyman will go away! Tim, it's absolutely maddening! Here we are, on the brink of a lopsided interstellar war and I'll bet you good money that the White House and Congress are way too egocentric, too obsessed with politics and magical thinking, to see the flying saucers in their morning bowl of fruit loops!"

"We have at least one ally in the know."

"Yes, and I'll wager there are more. This little note must have come from someone inside the NSC. Joint Chiefs of Staff maybe. One of them is savvy enough to get this information through secure channels without getting caught."

"So, what do we do?"

"We get that rail gun mobile ASAP and map out the tunnels that lead to the other side of the mountain. If they hit us when the real hostility starts, we'll need to evacuate everyone out to the back side of the mountain. We'll need the mountain to shield us from any blasts there might be. We also need to alert the Marines."

Donna paused to organize her priorities. At the Skunk Works, she always had time to formulate precise and orderly directives. Early on in her career, there were plenty of people breathing down her neck about deadlines, but each rung of the ladder she ascended, fewer noses were attached to her neck. There was time to make critical decisions, because none of them were snap calls with life and death in the balance. Nothing in her career prepared her for this degree of responsibility. Every man and woman, every Marine, would be counting on her to help them get out alive. It was a profound and sobering thought. She may not get the chance to reverse engineer alien technology, but she'll do everything she can to protect her staff. 'This place really knows how to treat an out of town girl to a good time!' she said, laughing at herself.

"Tim, you and Dr. McLachland handle the rail gun, I'll coordinate evacuation plans with the Marines. We'll both work on the rail gun when I've finished taking care of our staff. It might be a good idea to send non-essential crew back to Vegas. Tim, we need to be very nimble if they decide to attack us."

Chapter 54

Kenshin Osada was peering out his window on the Boeing 777-200ER, wishing he could have obtained a window seat on the left hand side of the craft. Perhaps he might have caught a distant glimpse of the island of Kauai to the north, then watched the ancient mountain remnants of the long since extinct Waianae shield volcano on Oahu pass by as the jet descended on final approach to Honolulu International Airport. It was a sight he never grew tired of, in spite of the twenty or so identical trips he previously made to Honolulu as a mid-level executive for a Japanese corporation with extensive business assets in Hawaii. Unfortunately, the trip was last-minute, the flight booked solid and delayed two hours. Kenshin felt fortunate enough to get any window seat.

From his seat in the right rear of the aircraft, all he could see was the sparkling reflection of the mid-morning sun on the deep blue water of the Pacific Ocean and a smattering of tropical clouds the wide-bodied airliner was descending through. He also noticed an odd optical illusion that appeared to be pacing the plane on the surface of the ocean, below, to the right and slightly behind the aircraft. It was a pale and fuzzy iridescent blue discoid shape that Kenshin found difficult to focus his eyes on. The Japanese native was no stranger to the window view of an ocean from the vantage of an airliner and was certain he had never seen anything like it before. Still, it matched the speed and gentle turns of the aircraft precisely, much like the reflection of the sun and moon does when passing over water. Moreover, there were no discernible details on the phenomenon, further convincing the 33 year-old married father of three that it was merely light playing tricks on his eyes.

The whining mechanical noise of the massive flaps extending from the wing momentarily broke Kenshin's concentration on the phenomenon as he turned his head and eyes to watch the 777s' wings become strangely distorted in preparation for landing. When he looked back, the odd illusion had moved further away from the jet. What he thought was an illusion was actually an aircraft of some sort... but what? His heart started to pick up speed. Like many Japanese, Kenshin was a technophile, with a particular interest in aviation technology. What he was watching was certainly no conventional aircraft. There was a missile testing range on Kauai, wasn't there? Perhaps it was a test project or unmanned aerial vehicle. Kenshin was quickly mulling over the possibilities when he noticed the unmistakable color change in the water below, indicating reef structure and shallow water. He could see Barber's Point emerging into view from behind the extended right wing flap. The jet was a few seconds from being over land.

Kenshin watched the craft move farther away from the 777 in what appeared to be an obvious maneuver to stay over water. Looking at the southwestern shoreline of Oahu, he saw the familiar landmarks that welcomed him back to Hawaii. The Chevron and Tesoro oil refineries with their modest tank farms, the warehouse areas of Barber's Point and the Kalaeloa airfield that was once a proud Naval Air Station. When he turned his gaze back towards the ocean, his mind began to register an impression of movement, heat, and wind a fraction of a second before his brain and body were cleanly sliced into two pieces.

* * *

The unmanned Aggressor, its offensive weapon fully charged and operational, propelled itself at blinding speed towards the target. As it began to pass underneath, it abruptly turned on its side to align the discharge port towards the undercarriage of the large aircraft. An atmospheric conditioning beam less than one millimeter wide was projected onto the target, then expanded to a small hollow tube with a perfect vacuum inside to provide the optimal particle-free environment for channeling and focusing the main weapon. Less than a thousandth of a second later, a powerful and sharply defined stream of antimatter began cutting through the hapless airliner. The razor-sharp dissection of the Japan Airways 777 began between the right wing and horizontal stabilizer, cutting with ease, and quite neatly, through hull, luggage, cargo, and passengers. The cut had a distinct angle to it, exiting the fuselage nearly five seats forward on the left. As the tail section began to separate from the rest of the plane, the antimatter beam sliced through the left wing, exiting just to the left of the massive port engine. The effect of the antimatter beam on the remaining aviation fuel stored in the wing was catastrophic.

 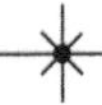

At an altitude of 2300 feet, the plane came apart and erupted into flames almost instantly. Unopposed lift from an intact right wing, along with loss of rear stabilization, caused the jet roll over to the left and begin a short corkscrew into the ground. Except for the fortunate few fatally sliced by the anti-neutron beam or hit with shrapnel from the left wing explosion, every other passenger and crew member on board JAL Flight 782 was alive when both sections of the severed fuselage impacted the ground.

The aggressor maintained its speed after the attack, but angled downward to pass just over the top of the western Koolau mountain range. It continued north by northeast over the Pacific at an altitude of 30 feet and a speed in excess of 8000 miles per hour. A few moments later, 115 miles offshore, the aggressor craft stopped and hovered, then began monitoring the electromagnetic spectrum for signs of a military response.

* * *

"American one-six-two-eight heavy turn right heading zero-seven-zero. Visual approach runway eight left. Note traffic ahead of you approaching EWABE. Japan Airways seven-eight-two..."

Weldon Duquesne blinked hard. It was there, right on course... boringly right on course approaching the EWABE middle marker for Runway 08 Left... now it was missing from his screen!

"JAL 782, what is your status?" he said, certain that the plane probably suffered from a transponder failure.

No answer.

"JAL 782, this is Honolulu approach. Do you copy? Repeat, do you copy?"

"Honolulu approach, this is American one-six-two-eight heavy," the excited pilot began, "I saw it go down! JAL 782 is down! Repeat JAL 782 is down somewhere around Kapolei! It just blew up in mid-air! Sweet Mother of God! Smoke is rolling into the sky! Requesting permission to abort approach and enter pattern for runway four right!"

Duquesne felt sick to his stomach and could feel the blood exit from his face. He had practiced similar training scenarios, but never believed anything like this would actually happen to him. He had to clear his head! The sky was full of planes and it was his responsibility to bring them in safely and orderly.

"Negative American one-six-two-eight heavy. Abort final as missed approach. Hold current heading and maintain altitude at 3000 until clear of airport, then turn right one-seven-one. Proceed to ALANA and hold. Stand by for further instructions."

"American one-six-two-eight heavy copy, clear airport then right one-seven-one to ALANA at three thousand. Thanks, approach!"

Duquesne clicked his microphone twice to acknowledge the pilot's appreciation.

"We've got a 777 down at Barber's point!" Duquesne yelled, "Somebody in the control tower confirm that visually... and get a supervisor in here, right NOW!"

The orderly, business-like atmosphere inside the control tower changed instantly as disengaged individuals bolted to western-facing window panels to have their worst fears realized: a heavy jetliner packed with tourists just crashed into a populated area. Black smoke was billowing into the sky six, maybe seven miles west of the airport. They were witnessing the unfolding of a transportation disaster far surpassing anything that previously occurred on United States soil, with a loss of life almost certain to exceed 300 souls.

"Honolulu approach, Hawaiian one-five-three. We saw it, too, from a mile to the south! It looked like... we... we thought we saw something hit it... something coming from the ocean offshore of Barber's Point. Approach... it might have been a SAM... repeat, it might have been a SAM! Request change to runway four right."

Duquesne almost froze. Hawaiian one-five-three was suggesting that JAL seven-eight-two was destroyed by a surface-to-air missile! In the span of a few seconds, a horrific aviation mishap turned into something far worse.

"Roger, Hawaiian one-five-three," Duquesne replied, holding his composure as if nothing happened, "negative on four right. Turn left zero-six-zero and climb to 3000. Delta two-seven-seven abort approach to eight left. Turn left two-zero-zero maintain 6000. Standby for further instructions. Hawaiian one-one-six, abort approach to four right. Turn left one-niner-zero. Proceed to ALANA at 3000 and hold."

Each pilot echoed Duquesne's instructions and obeyed. Duquesne knew these instructions were very, very temporary. If JAL 782 had been blown out of the sky by a SAM, he needed to clear the entire airspace and re-route airborne planes to the other Islands.

"Get Major Preston down here, NOW!" Duquesne yelled, requesting the presence of the military liaison officer for flight operations at Hickam Air Force Base. The radio frequency for Honolulu Approach, 118.3mHz, was monitored throughout the ATC facility and a mortified buzz was erupting everywhere. MAJ Al Preston heard the commotion from the break room and instinctively abandoned his coffee to race to the ATC room.

"Al, over here!" Duquesne yelled when MAJ Preston entered the ATC control room.

"What's wrong?"

"We have an inbound 777 down near Kapolei and a pilot who witnessed the explosion says it was hit by something coming from the ocean."

"You have got to be kidding me!"

"I wish I were!" Duquesne replied. "This was really bad to begin with, but now it appears JAL 782 may have been shot down! I've diverted the closest inbound traffic to holding."

"Lock down the airspace! Send everything to Maui, Kauai, and the Big Island. Stop all the early trans-Pacifics, too. I'll contact the watch officer at Hickam and work on getting some F-22s in the air. Maybe they will elect to involve Kaneohe and the Navy. I think the *Ronald Reagan* is still in the neighborhood from RIMPAC ops."

"What if there are other terrorists waiting to shoot down the diverted traffic?"

"Get plenty of law enforcement to all of the airfields in Hawaii. Have them look for any suspicious activity, big or small. Keep the air traffic on hold until fuel becomes an issue, then God help us... we can't send them anywhere else."

Both men immediately went to work. One shuffling aircraft, much the same way he did in the hours following September 11th, only this time, he could not allow any inbound planes to land at his facility, the other informing Hickham Flight Operations Command of the nature of the disaster. Within minutes, orders were given to dispatch all available Hawaii Air National Guard F-15s and Air Force F-22s from Hickam, as well as any F/A-18s, anti-submarine warfare aircraft and Sea Stallion helicopters from Marine Corps Base Hawaii. The Navy contributed to the response by catapulting FA/18s from the deck of the aircraft carrier USS *Ronald Reagan*, located 115 nautical miles to the southeast. Within thirty minutes, the skies over Oahu were roaring with armed military aircraft. Some assigned to combat air patrol, others were scouring the waters near Barbers Point, hoping to kill the culprit, a cowardly bastard for sure, hiding in a boat or submarine.

Chapter 55

Randal Fallon had just pulled into the parking lot of his Gardena California dentist when his cell phone began to vibrate. The chief field investigator for the Southwest Regional Office of the National Transportation Safety Board flipped open the phone without looking at the caller ID.

"Fallon here."

"Randy, where are you at?" queried Sherri Strickland, the most junior of the regional office's investigators.

"Actually, I just arrived at the dentist office for my three o'clock appointment," he replied, noting the stress in her voice. "What's going on?"

"We've got a bad one, Randy. Really bad."

"LAX?"

"No... HNL. Fully loaded JAL 777 exploded in mid-air and went down in a residential area."

"Jesus Christ!"

"It gets worse. A pilot in the pattern claims the 777 was hit by a SAM."

"Independent or radar verification?"

"Not as of yet, but the military is taking the report seriously. They are deploying assets and have ordered the airspace quarantined."

"I see...," he paused, assessing the situation in his mind, "O.K., Ms. Strickland, you know the drill. Notify Washington, make sure the FAA Regional Office has been contacted and assemble the team. I want to be off the ground within two hours."

"Consider it done."

"Oh, and see if you can get me a contact number for the military liaison officer at Hickam. Give them my Iridium number, too."

"Yes, sir," she replied, "I'm on it."

Fallon closed his phone and walked back to his car. He had investigated quite a few fatal aviation accidents in Hawaii, most involving tour helicopters and general aviation aircraft. Hawaii had never experienced a commercial aviation accident of this magnitude before. In fact, he could only recall three major accidents, all within 18 months of each other. The first was an April 28th, 1988 Aloha Airlines single fatality incident in which a significant portion of the forward cabin roof peeled away at 24,000 feet, sweeping a first class section flight attendant out of the plane during the explosive decompression. The second was a nine-fatality accident on February 24th, 1989 when an improperly latched cargo door on an outbound United 747 led to the shearing away of a part of the fuselage and explosive decompression. The third was a 20 fatality, October 28, 1989 Island Air crash of a commuter turboprop on the island of Molokai. The fatalities from this new accident would likely exceed the total from all commercial and general aviation accidents in the history of Hawaii.

Fallon began crunching the numbers in his head. A fully-loaded 777, as most coming from Japan were, carried up to 300 people. There were, in all likelihood, no survivors if the jet was actually hit by a SAM and exploded in mid-air. The second question was how many were killed on the ground. He looked at his watch. The accident occurred on a weekday around noon, so many would be at work or school. He considered the potential size of the debris field and surmised that perhaps as many as 50 or 60 people on the ground might be dead, maybe more if a school or shopping mall were involved. To add to the horror was the specter of terrorism. If the reporting pilot was correct, this incident would rank right behind 9/11 in the number of deaths caused by a single terrorist incident. After all the carnage he had seen in his 22 year career, there was little that could penetrate his tough emotional hide. Even so, the thought of what he was about to face made him shudder.

Terrorism... violence perpetrated against the innocent to force political, religious, or social change. In Fallon's mind, it was cowardice, pure and simple, regardless of how "noble" the perpetrator thought his goal was. Killing children was hardly a noble act. If this was an act of terrorism, he would be the one to prove it.

Fallon entered his dentist office and explained to the receptionist why he had to cancel today's office visit. Afterwards, he called his wife on the cell phone to inform her of his upcoming investigation, only to learn she had already seen the initial news reports on the crash and guessed he would be going there. After sharing a goodbye with his wife, Fallon made his way back to the NTSC Regional Office to help prepare for the trip. He would lead a total of six investigators, and all of them, with the exception of Strickland, were seasoned veterans. 'Strickland,' he thought to himself, 'would sure as hell earn her stripes on this one!'

Chapter 56

News of the Hawaiian disaster spread quickly through the Cocheta Research Facility and many were gathering in the large dining area to watch the unfolding horror. Much like 9/11, early reporting was a mix of conjecture on top of speculation, relying on a mix of cell phone calls coming from actual eyewitnesses and the inevitable calls from those passing along information from 'reliable' sources. The first video feed of the main impact location came within minutes of the crash. A local television station sent a crew to do a fluff piece on renovations to a popular water park that just happened to be across Interstate H1 from the pending disaster. The reporters were getting fresh video of the billowing black clouds blowing back to the southwest on the almost ever present trade winds. Early eyewitness reports had the Kamokila Boulevard shopping centers in Kapolei taking the overwhelming bulk of the falling wreckage and casualties, with a Tesoro filling station nearly at the epicenter of the primary disaster site contributing 10,000 gallons of gasoline to the conflagration.

Tim and Donna watched the disaster unfold on one of the four, 60 inch LED monitors hanging on the cafeteria walls. Within several minutes, a local traffic helicopter was reporting on the scope of the disaster, but had to return back to its helipad because all civilian air traffic was abruptly and mysteriously grounded by the FAA. Other strange reports were coming in with talk of increased military activity being spotted on the Island.

"Oh my God! It's a terrorist attack!" Donna gasped, having put all the clues together. "They're grounding civilian flights and military assets are ramping up! It's the only explanation!"

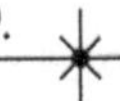

Noisy chatter began instantly amongst the 3 dozen or so staff members in the cafeteria. "Doctor Hanson, are you sure?" asked Staff Physiologist Dr. Linda Gillespie.

"I can't be absolutely certain, but the things I've just heard makes me about 99 percent sure. It's another 9/11... and it couldn't have come at a worse time!"

"Will we be able to begin the evacuations on time?" asked another concerned staff member.

"I don't see why not?" Donna replied. "We can pretty much go where we please, locked-down airspace or not. The first JANET arrives at 11 AM tomorrow."

Several different animated discussions ensued, each participant keeping an eye out for noteworthy developments on the monitors. Tim and Donna went to the serving line for a glass of iced tea, then sat at an empty table twelve feet from the nearest monitor. When the screen turned to a Special News Alert graphic, everyone instantly stopped what they were doing and glued their eyes to the monitors.

Chapter 57

Floyd Kahakelii, a local 68 year-old retired city worker saw the whole thing, and he wasn't shy about telling his story to the reporters swarming to the scene of the disaster.

"Brah, I was workin' in my garden, yah. When I look up at da plane and see dis ting come from da sout' real fass an hit it! Way bright light! Da tail, it fall off an da res' of da plane make lots of fire and smoke, yah. Well Brah, I ain't no fool, an I run cuz I ain't so sure dem parts and stuff gonna fall on my head or not! Lucky for me da stuff fall away from here, not here, yah."

"Mr. Kahakelii, are you saying the jet was shot down?" A local television reporter asked incredulously.

"Braddah, all I know is dat dis ting, it come from over dehr," he answered, pointing his finger towards Barbers Point, "an hit dat plane, yah. An it was movin' way fass!"

The genie was out of the bottle.

At about the same time Mr. Kahakelii was telling his story to reporters, word began to spread that the airspace over Oahu had been quarantined. The official explanation was that smoke from the crash was obscuring the approach to the airport. Most bought the story. Others who knew how major airports worked did not. You do not close Class B airspace because of a plane crash miles from the runway. Honolulu International had, at any given time, two departure runways, two arrival runways, and one seaplane landing and takeoff area. Inbound traffic could be re-routed to another runway, and in this particular instance, departing aircraft would take off from either of the available runways without going near the crash site or the smoke from it. Then there was the military aircraft beginning to taxi and take-off from Hickam and Kaneohe. Something was up, no doubt about it, and Mr. Kahakelii generously added the missing piece of the puzzle.

The national news media picked-up on the story immediately, breaking into scheduled broadcasts to announce that the crash in Hawaii they had reported on earlier might have been shot down by a surface-to-air missile and quite possibly a terrorist act. Within seconds, phone and cell phone circuits, fax machines, blogs and internet websites around the world were jammed with streams of concerned communication. Reporters began asking questions and demanding answers of public officials before anybody had a clear picture of what was going on.

From the perspective of those providing rescue services, the devastation could only have been worse if it occurred in downtown Honolulu. Because the unopposed lift of the right wing, the aircraft deviated enough to the north to send the bulk of flaming wreckage into a large shopping center in Kapolei. Every day, hundreds of people from nearby office buildings swarmed the strip shopping centers and eating establishments along Kamokila Road... and today was no exception. Dozens of people were killed instantly when the huge forward part of the fuselage and right wing impacted almost upside down in the parking lot. Dozens more died from the inferno that followed, many from asphyxiation as the massive fireball left adjacent buildings without oxygen. Many died from falling debris, including two souls near a hardware store where the left wing and engine impacted and dozens more when the severed tail section impacted in a residential neighborhood 1.5 miles west-southwest of the main debris field. For every one person killed on the ground, however, there were 20 or more injured, burned, or both.

Every available civilian and military rescue unit on Oahu was dispatched to the scene. Several engine companies battled the fires while ambulances were routed to a triage area in a parking lot east and upwind of the carnage. There, they would haul as many as four patients at a time to every hospital on the island. Per NTSB guidelines, the dead were left undisturbed, exactly as they were found. It took several hours to suppress the fire and evacuate the wounded. By sundown, the total number of fatalities approached 600. The passenger and crew manifest obtained from Japan Airlines listed 302 passengers and crew on board the 777. All were lost. There was a total of 297 confirmed fatalities on the ground between the two crash sites, some burned well beyond recognition. Many more were expected by the time the search for bodies was complete. Surpassed only by the 9/11 suicide attacks, the JAL 782 crash would be recorded as the second worst air disaster in aviation history.

Fallon and his NTSB team arrived on the scene around 9:15 PM, and although they were fatigued from the flight, they wasted no time getting to work. Fallon surveyed the illuminated scene before him, fully aware of the magnitude and historical significance of this tragedy. If a terrorist group had downed this aircraft with a surface-to-air missile, their organization would undoubtedly feel the terrible sting of American Military might. 'Perhaps Americans would finally understand what the Global War on Terrorism was really all about.' Fallon thought to himself. A moment later, he shook his head in disgust. 'No... they didn't really learn a thing from 9/11, judging by how soon afterwards they forgot, so there would likely be little in the way of permanent lessons to be learned from the horror around him.'

The first order of business was to make sure that the entire site was cordoned off properly so that valuable evidence could be examined where it came to rest, instead of ending up in a macabre collection purchased on line. Next, find the flight recorders, map the debris field while locating each body, or body part, then meticulously recording its position in relationship to the wreckage and to other bodies. The sooner this was done, the faster the lifeless bodies could be transported to the temporary morgue set up at Kapolei High School. While this gruesome task was performed, a second team of investigators would interview people who witnessed the accident. Of particular interest was one Floyd Kahakelii and the pilot of Hawaiian Flight 153. Others would also be interviewed, including air traffic control personnel, EMS and other rescue providers. A trip to Japan was also in order so that maintenance and personnel records could be scoured. With all that needed to be done to conduct a proper and thorough accident investigation, there was the single most important task that trumped most everything else: to quickly find out if this was a terrorist attack. The island was locked tight and millions of dollars of tourist income evaporated with every hour of closed airspace that passed. Fallon needed a bit of evidence he could make a snap call on, and if the plane had been shot down by a SAM, it should be fairly easy to find.

It didn't take long to get an answer.

"Randy!" Steve Voss almost yelled in his cell phone. "Drop whatever you're doing and get over here to the second debris field!"

"What did you find?" Fallon asked, wondering why his normally stone-faced investigator was so clearly agitated.

"Just get over here fast! I know why the heavy crashed... and you are not going to believe it!"

"Be there in five."

Fallon never heard Steven Voss, a seasoned veteran of dozens of gruesome crashes while on his team, sound so shaken. What could he have possibly seen at the impact site of the tail section that would get him so worked up? Maybe there was conclusive evidence that a SAM knocked JAL Flight 782 out of the sky. Perhaps... but that still didn't ring quite right. Voss was rock solid and all business... until now. As Fallon jogged to his rental car, a very uneasy feeling swept over him.

'Something very bizarre must have happened to Japan Airlines flight 782...' he thought with a grimace.

Chapter 58

Every phone line in the Department of Homeland Security was clogged with calls from the press, government officials, and concerned citizens seeking more information about the crash of JAL 782 and the possibility it was the target of a terrorist attack. Secretary of Homeland Security Kathryn Beckman was on a cell phone in her office trying reach federal authorities on the scene. She had already spoken to FEMA Director Roy Garrison and warned him of the possibility that JAL 782 may only be the first of a series of assaults on America. If this was a terror attack, she needed specifics so that she could recommend an appropriate level alert and course of action to the National Security Council meeting the President ordered to convene.

Secretary Beckman's gut feeling was that JAL 782 succumbed to mechanical failure and that this incident was just another TWA Fight 800. Conspiracy theories blossomed within hours of the July 17th, 1996 crash of a Boeing 747 into the waters off East Moriches New York that claimed 230 lives. Even though it was proven that an electrical failure caused the center fuel tank to explode on the immense plane, many people still subscribe to the notion that the plane was brought down with a surface-to-air missile. For that matter, there were thousands of people who believed the terror attacks on the World Trade Center towers were staged! Beckman could not stop a conspiracy in the making. At best, she could counter its spread and impact by repeatedly quoting the "there is no evidence/fill in the blanks" company line, whatever in the world that might end up being. The *Pereleshin* incident was easy to paint over because it wasn't an American vessel sliding into the abyss. An attack on American soil with hundreds dead and thousands of witnesses? As they learned during 9/11, that was far more difficult to manage.

'The NTSB had a crack team on the ground already,' she thought to herself. 'If it was hit by a missile, they should have a working hypothesis within a day or two.'

Chapter 59

After a brief drive from the devastation on Kamokila Boulevard, Randy Fallon arrived at the impact site of the tail section in an apartment complex on Manawai Street. The apartment fires had long since been extinguished and casualties evacuated. The 73 fatalities at that location were already tagged, even the ones in the tail section awaiting clearance for their short trip to the Kapolei High School morgue. Steve Voss was waiting for him.

"Randy, if had not seen this with my own eyes, I would have never believed it!"

"What is it, Steve?"

"Come look at this part of the tail," he said excitedly. "It is the most remarkable thing I have ever seen! It is a piece of the starboard fuselage with the passenger deck and a few seats. Remarkably intact. You are not going to believe what I found."

"Evidence of a missile strike?"

"No, something far more disturbing!"

Fallon fought off the urge to tell his investigator to get to the point. Steve Voss was one of the best in the business and the last thing he wanted to do was chew his ass over the drawn-out nature of his discovery.

As they approached the piece of wreckage, Fallon could already see what Voss was excited about.

"Look! See the clean, angular cut? Like someone sliced the fuselage with a gi-

ant razor blade!"

Propped up by wreckage of both apartment and aircraft debris, the relatively small piece of tail section was easy to view. As opposed to the ragged edges of the rear portion of the segment, the front edge was surgically clean with a cut along the deck that perfectly matched the cut on the remaining section of fuselage.

"This is impossible! Freakin' impossible!" Fallon said, shaking his head.

"There is more, Randy... and it's pretty gruesome."

Both investigators carefully moved through the debris to get a view of the inside portion of the segment of fuselage. What Fallon saw topped everything he had ever seen as an NTSB Field Investigator. There were two corpses in their undamaged seats, the third seat in the row was heavily damaged and blood stained. The corpse in the middle seat, a Japanese female, was mostly intact with multiple injuries, including a cut across her trachea and left side of her neck. The widow seat corpse, a Japanese male, was still attached to his seat by restraints. Much of the left half of his head was missing from the left jaw to the top right of his skull, cauterized so that the internal structure of the face and brain were easily visible. His right forearm was also severed, along with his left arm and shoulder as a unit. Much of his right leg was missing, cleanly cut and cauterized just above his knee, and his left lower leg was similarly severed mid-calf. It was clear to both investigators that the surgical cut through the fuselage and deck was consistent with the window seat corpse leaning forward and turning his head to the right, perhaps looking out the window.

Fallon was desperately trying to find an appropriate description for what he just saw. Certainly, no SAM was involved in this incident. He knew of no deployable laser or particle beam weapon that could instantly and cleanly sever the tail section of a plane. The smoothness and precision of the cut; its depth and the enormous power that must be needed to accomplish such a feat in the blink of an eye. It was simply too mind-jarring to comprehend.

Fallon looked around at the apartment complex turned debris field, then gazed at the lights to his north where hundreds perished in what? A vicious terrorist attack? But, by who? Who on Earth could possibly possess the technology to carve up a heavy jet in flight?

'Who on Earth...' Fallon reiterated to himself, already knowing the answer but not wanting to acknowledge it.

"Steve," he finally said, "we're in way over our heads. We need to get the military involved in this one."

"I agree, Boss," Voss replied soberly.

Randy Fallon, NTSB's 'Iron Man,' veteran of dozens of disturbing transportation mishaps, could feel his legs and hands trembling.

Chapter 60

"Mr. President," the familiar voice of Larry Osborn said, knocking on the door of the Luxurious San Francisco VIP suite, "I need to speak with you about the airline crash in Hawaii."

President Bertram opened the door and waved his Chief of Staff into the room. The President was getting dressed for a breakfast strategy session with influential local progressives. As much as he loved to bash his opponents, today he just felt like sleeping late and watching mindless television. In particular, he enjoyed the so-called "reality" shows that documented the inane and contrived antics of bumpkins and rednecks gladly selling out their Southern culture for a buck. It never ceased to amaze the President how low people would stoop for a buck and fleeting fame. He had to admit that it was far better entertainment than sitting on his butt, watching baseball and drinking beer while the wife was out shopping.

"What is the latest news on the crash? Do they already know what brought the plane down? I sure as Hell hope so! The Hawaiian Governor is already shitting his pants over the potential loss of revenue!"

"Greg, the NTSB team on the ground states that the big airliner was hit by... well, in their own words, 'highly exotic' technology."

"What in the hell does that mean?"

"Reading between the lines, I'd say he was trying to say 'alien' technology in a round about way."

"So, just like that, we're switching gears from a terrorist SAM strike to the use of alien weapons against helpless, unarmed civilian aircraft."

"Randy Fallon is one of the best, perhaps the best, NTSB investigator we've ever had. The Pentagon liaison in this incident said he was pretty shook."

"Who in God's name contacted the Pentagon?"

"Fallon did, directly."

"He bypassed his chain of command? That was a dumbass move! A real dumbass move!"

"Greg, if I may, does it really matter? If Fallon was convinced alien technology brought down the plane within our sovereign airspace, that would constitute an act of war. The Pentagon needs to know what they are up against. They already have every plane, boat, vehicle and bicycle patrolling the whole of Hawaii."

"Dammit, Larry! Orders trickle down from me, not from the middle outward! Do we know, with 100 percent certainty, that Fallon is right? Besides a spooked investigator and a few people saying they think they 'saw something,' what real proof do we really have? Things fall off of airplanes, Larry! That's plenty good enough for me. If we wrongly accuse the aliens, we will end up with a much larger problem!"

Osborn was, once again, treated to denial and magical thinking by the President that he, up until very recently, loyally served. His next question for the President was to suggest that America's worldwide military assets be placed on high alert, just in case, but he already knew where that suggestion was going to go. Bertram would counter with the alert status being 'confrontational' and 'counterproductive.' In the end, President Bertram would surrender to the aliens and America would die with the decree. Osborn felt his duty was to stick close to the President and constantly remind him of his responsibilities to the American people. Perhaps he could prevent a huge disaster in the making. In any case, he could always send encrypted messages to Dr. Hanson at the Cocheta Research Facility if Bertram started heading for deep water.

"Greg, I know you're not going to like this," Osborn said, "the Pentagon has just issued a IOS Class 2 and will alert Dr. Hanson and her crew shortly."

"Tell the Pentagon to stand them down," he replied coldly.

"Mr. President... Greg... We've been through this before," Osborn reminded the President. "The 'hands-off' terms pertaining to CRF are non-negotiable."

"As of now, I'm changing them," the President said. "I'm going to issue an executive order placing CRF under the Department of Defense."

"That is a bad move, Greg," Osborn said forcefully. "I'm telling you, that is a very bad move!"

"Larry, what have they really produced there?" he growled angrily. "Decades of squandering billions in taxpayer money and we've got jack shit to show for it! My personal opinion? We should scrap it altogether!"

"This is all about the Hanson's, isn't it?"

"Larry, that's a bullshit call and you know it!"

"Greg, I'm on your side, but... if you stick with this course of action, I assure you, you will not win re-election!"

"I'm already leading in all the polls! Who's going to stop me?"

"The people who have protected and funded CRF for several decades."

"Let them try! We're going let the military take care of this Cocheta crap from now on."

Chapter 61

"What's going on?" Donna Hanson asked MAJ Alleyne in the Cocheta Command Center. "I get a 'field trip' alert call and two minutes later, its cancelled!"

"Ma'am, I wish I knew."

"False alarm, I guess," Donna said to Major Alleyne and Tim. "Just as well... we've got a lot of work to do, anyway."

"I'm fully awake, Donna," Tim said with a smile. "Before we start, perhaps I might treat you lovely ladies to some cafeteria coffee?"

"I'm sorry, Dr. Alexander," MAJ Alleyne apologized, "I can't leave Triple C while I'm on duty."

"A rain check, then?"

"Absolutely! I would be delighted!"

"And you, Dr. Hanson?"

"Show me the way, Dr. Alexander!"

The couple made their way to what they thought would be an empty cafeteria. Instead, there were eight souls there. Some were watching the big screen TVs, a few working on laptops and an aviation technician, Donna guessed by the yellow band on his ID badge, sipping on coffee after, undoubtedly, being called to prep the G650 for a cancelled trip.

After picking a table, Tim retrieved two cups of hot coffee from the serving line and returned to sit as close to Donna has he could.

"Were you flirting with MAJ Alleyne, Dr. Alexander?"

"Was it that obvious?"

"Butt hole!" she replied with a smile. "Major Alleyne is very pretty. I wouldn't blame you."

"She is pretty, but... I'm just a wee physics geek. She's a Marine... and could turn me into a pretzel while yawning!"

"What makes you think I can't turn you into a pretzel?"

"Because... I'm your boy toy!" he replied with a hearty laugh.

"That you are!" she laughed while beginning to lean close to his ear and hold his hands under the table. "I love you, Tim."

"I love you, too."

Without another word spoken, they abandoned their coffee and made their way to Tim's apartment to start the new day with passion... and a strong, yet tender reaffirmation of their love for each other.

Chapter 62

"What the Hell is going on here?" yelled COMSUBLANT commander Vice Admiral Glen Thomas. "I've got the *Tennessee*, *Georgia*, *Wyoming* and *Alaska* on the surface bitching about Akulas getting aggressive!"

"Admiral, I just got off the phone with COMSUBPAC." Lieutenant Mack Foster announced." The *Ohio*, *Jackson*, *Nevada*, *Maine* and *Pennsylvania* are also being harassed by Akulas!"

"What is that? Nine? That's one short of all the Akulas the Russians have!"

"That's correct, Sir," Lieutenant Foster confirmed. "Do you have any idea why they're doing this?"

"My gut feeling is that they believe we had something to do with the loss of their newest boomer, the *Pereleshin*."

"Why would they think that? What could we possibly gain by sinking it?"

"Mack, the *North Carolina* was right on their ass when it imploded. That's reason enough to be highly suspicious. It's obvious that they didn't buy the President's official story."

"That is a very dangerous game their playing," Lieutenant Foster said ominously. "One miscalcuation..."

"...two subs headed for the bottom." the Admiral finished. "We had better link-up with COMSUBPAC and inform SECNAV of what our naughty Russians are up to. Maybe the President can smooth things out."

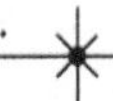

"Maybe..." Foster paused, not entirely certain he should open his mouth about a phone call he received from a good friend in California not an hour earlier. "Admiral, there is something I learned just recently that I'm almost certain you haven't been briefed on."

"What would that be?"

"Well, Sir, I have a good buddy in California that works for the NTSB office in Los Angeles. He told me the Japanese airliner that crashed in Hawaii yesterday..."

"The one they think was hit by a SAM?"

"Yes sir," he replied with some trepidation. "The Chief NTSB Investigator is convinced the aliens took it out, not a SAM. Something really bizarre he saw at the crash sight."

"Sweet Baby Jesus! The aliens whacked the *Pereleshin* AND a civilian airliner?"

"That's my take on it, Sir, but I heard it from a third party. He's a stand up guy and I trust him, but there is always the possibility it could be a certified crock of shit or mixed communications," Lieutenant Foster said. "Wouldn't the Pentagon advise you about such an incident, even if it didn't happen on your turf?"

"I sure as hell would hope so, but I haven't heard anything from them since the *Pereleshin*. Not a peep."

"Sir, something's not right. Why isn't the Pentagon briefing us? The aliens are obviously taking an aggressive posture, yet nothing from Washington?"

"I don't know, Lieutenant, but I'm about to find out!"

Chapter 63

"Another 'Eyes Only' message for me, MAJ Gordon?" Donna Hanson asked, wondering if would be from the same... what? Informant?

"Yes ma'am." The tall, muscular Marine officer replied. "Also, the JANET Flight is on schedule. Should arrive a little before 11 AM."

"Appreciate it, Major!"

"You're welcome, ma'am."

Donna began opening the envelope while walking down the now busy hallway full of the first group of evacuees that were, essentially, the ones that arrived the day before. The group was comprised of scientists, engineers and non-essential red shift maintenance support crew members. The remaining third of red shift staff would finish the remaining 13 days of their two week 'on' period. Plant operations would be substantially scaled down until the crisis was over. The Marines, however, would keep their current force level the same.

After entering her room and pouring a glass of orange juice, she opened the Top Secret, decoded message.

Dr. Hanson,

1) The Japanese airline that crashed in Hawaii was NOT hit by a surface-to-air missile. The Boeing 777 was destroyed by a directed energy weapon capable of cleanly severing the tail section from a very large airliner. Highly compelling evidence was discovered by the lead NTSB investigator and his team. Given the fate of the Pereleshin, *an alien aircraft with such a weapon is the only plausible culprit.*

2) A pending Presidential Executive Order will place Project Cocheta under the direction of the Pentagon. The President is convinced aliens do not pose a threat to the United States. If, however, hostilities do break out, the President has voiced his intent to surrender in order to save the world from destruction.

Again, thought you would like to know.

No Signature

Donna slowly placed the message on her desk. It was a lot to digest and deciding which revelation was the most disturbing made her mind spin. She wasn't at all concerned that Cocheta would be absorbed by the DoD. Through her comprehensive briefings on the inner workings of CRF, she now knew enough about the unusual way her project was funded that the President would run into a very thick, concrete wall if he tried to place Cocheta under the DoD. No... what concerned her most was the increasingly aggressive nature of the aliens and the fact that the POTUS had already decided to surrender should war ensue. She never cared much for President Bertram in the first place, but to surrender at the first sign of hostilities? Blatant cowardice? Was that the new 'American Way of handling a crisis?' Donna picked up her encrypted, in-house cell phone and called Tim.

"Hey, sweetheart!" Tim answered.

"I received another 'Eyes Only' message from our secretive friend."

"Bad news?"

"Unfortunately," she replied, shaking her head. "The Hawaii airliner crash?"

"Yes..."

"Our information source said the airliner was destroyed by the aliens, not a missile!"

"Are you serious?" he replied in horror.

"The chief NTSB investigator on location apparently saw something highly unusual in the wreckage that caused the crash."

"My God!"

"There's more. It seems that the President wants to put us under the Department of Defense and intends to accomplish it by Executive Order. That, I can tell you with almost 100 percent certainty, will not happen. Our benefactors are extremely well connected and loaded with cash. The President will learn there are practical limits to his power."

"I really don't pretend to understand the political nuances of all this, Sweetheart. I'm just a simple, country physicist and I trust you to take care of all those political odds and ends," Tim said with a smile to lighten the moment.

"Country physicist... that hangs around Westwood..." She rolled her eyes with a brief grin that quickly ended in a deeply troubled countenance. "Tim, if this source is a sound one, the President intends to surrender if we end up in a war against the aliens. Given their increased aggressiveness, hostilities could start at any time!"

Tim was clearly dumbfounded by Donna's words. 'Interstellar War' was a very disturbing concept, primarily because, in this case, only one side was capable of the 'interstellar' part. What chance did the human race really have? Movies almost always depicted humans as being clever enough to eventually find a way to outwit and defeat the technologically superior aliens... regardless of how vast the chasm between cat and mouse. Tim cringed at the hard reality soaking in. There could only be one outcome of a war between humans and aliens.

Tim looked down at one of the most advanced weapons developed by mankind, a railgun. Cocheta engineers and scientists only used it to test the strength of various exotic alien alloys hit by tungsten projectiles at hypersonic speeds. Tim was assisting engineers and mechanics in weaponizing it for possible use against the aliens should the need arise. The first task was to remove the railgun from the fixed position in the target tunnel and repositioning it in the hangar. The plan was to place the railgun barrel a foot behind the middle of the hangar door. From that vantage point, the railgun would have about a 150 degree field of fire. A fabricated base was fashioned that allowed the railgun assembly to move from level to 50 degrees. The HUMRAAM Thales-Raytheon MPQ-64 Sentinel radar system and Multi-Source Correlator Tracker would be used for automatic aiming of the railgun. The biggest hurdle would be adding roughly 200 feet of heavy electrical transmission wire to the large, million-plus amp power supply.

"We're in big trouble, aren't we," Tim finally asked.

"It looks that way, but we're not out of it yet," she said, trying to sound as

reasonably positive as she could. "How's the railgun coming?"

"Steady. The engineers believe they can finish installation by tomorrow evening, at the latest."

"Good! After the first JANET departs, let's catch some lunch. The second JANET doesn't arrive until 2 PM. After that, we'll be eating with the Marines in their Mess."

"That will be a hoot!" Tim said, hoping that 'a hoot' was going to be all the excitement he would have to handle in the coming days.

Deep inside, he knew he was likely facing the most difficult and dangerous time of his life.

Chapter 64

"Mom?"

"Hi, sweetie!" Senator Hanson answered cheerfully. "I was wondering when you would remember to call your mother!"

"Sorry, Mom. It's been crazy here. Are you out of the hospital?"

"It's OK, darling, you don't have to apologize, and yes, I'm at the apartment. They discharged me first thing this morning. I haven't been home much more than an hour or so."

"I'm really glad your OK..." Donna tapered off, not sure what to say next.

"What's wrong, Donna?"

"Mom, you need to catch the first flight to Oklahoma."

"I can't, Sweetie. Melana wants to resume the circus."

"Mom, listen to me, you need to get out of DC as soon as possible!"

"OK, Dr. Hanson, please tell your mother why she should skip out of town when she has been ordered to appear before a Senate Hearing?"

"Mom, somebody in the NSC, Joint Chiefs or the President's staff has been sending me encrypted 'eyes only' messages. Whoever it is, he or she informed me that the Russian sub that sank a couple of days ago was taken out by two alien submersibles!"

"Sweet Jesus..."

"That's not all! This morning, I received another message. This one said the Japanese airliner that crashed yesterday was actually shot down by an alien vehicle!"

"The NTSB has already stated that it wasn't a missile that brought the plane down. It was a structural failure in the tail section that caused the crash. They're re-opening all the Hawaiian airspace and grounding the 777s."

"If my source is correct, that is a huge cover up!"

"Why would anybody want to do such a thing?"

"Maybe this will help. President Bertram intends to place us under the DoD and surrender if the aliens start a war!"

"Sweetheart, you have always been my steady one... I know Bertram is way off on a great many things... most things, but I don't believe he would willingly turn us over to the aliens!"

"Mom, there are only two ways for me to get an 'eyes only' message here. The Base Commander at Peterson AFB and someone in the White House or NSC."

"You're certain of this?"

"Mom, you know me!"

"Yes, I do... and you should know me. Given what I know now, I must stay in Washington to do what I can to protect our country."

"Mom, please! I'm almost certain the aliens are going to start a war very very soon! You need to get out of there!" Donna pleaded.

"Donna, you, of all people, should know where the both of us needs to be. We may be in unique positions to help our country."

"I know, Mom," Donna said with sad and reluctant resignation. Both began to cry at the thought that they might never see each other again.

"Mom..."

"Yes, sweetheart."

"If it gets really bad, have the family meet up in Miami."

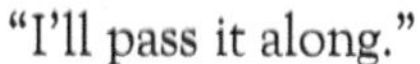

"I'll pass it along."

"Love you, Mom!"

"Love you, too, Pumpkin!"

Donna hung up the phone, tears streaming down her face and wondering if the madness would ever end.

Chapter 65

Oscar Rollins was pissed!

Stuck in bumper-to-bumper traffic on Savannah's Eugene Talmadge bridge because some lunatic, weaving in and out of the two northbound lanes while 'texting,' took herself and four others out of the ranks of the living. Twenty others were seriously hurt on the two southbound lanes, as well. Rescue trucks, ambulances, cops and firefighters were converging on the scene from both Savannah and Jasper County, South Carolina. Almost every inch of the two mile bridge was clogged with non-moving traffic, and Oscar was at the very top of it, 185 feet above the Savannah River.

Dozens of people, sensing that they had a long wait in front of them, got out of their vehicles either to help the injured or to enjoy the breathtaking view of springtime Savannah. Oscar was no friend to the sight of blood and elected to sit on the hood of his ancient Honda Civic and smoke a cigarette. It was a beautiful day with a pleasant cool breeze, a light smattering of clouds and no biting bugs to slap at. The spectacular view around Rollins was completely lost on him. He was a seasoned diesel mechanic, a 'nuts and bolts kinda guy' that took pride in his mechanical prowess. He could care less what Disney character might be found in a cloud formation and was about as distant to the Savannah culture class as one could possibly get.

As he was looking out over the Savannah International Trade and Convention Center, admiring one of the container ships that would soon pass under him, he caught a glimpse of something that was not there before he blinked his eye. He strained to see it better, but couldn't because of it's small size. As far as he could tell, it wasn't moving, either. Rollins continued to look back at the speck in the sky every few moments, noting it was pretty much in the same place each time. After about five minutes of looking, he noticed that there was now two of them, side by side and equal in size, neither seemed to be moving at all. He found it only mildly odd and barely worthy of his attention.

* * *

The two aggressor craft rendezvoused high above Calibogue Sound, just off the southern tip of Hilton Head Island, to perform the third weapons calibration test of the four test suite. The first two, performed by other aggressors and highly successful, were to test and calibrate antimatter beams against submerged vehicles and close quarters discharge on aircraft. The calibration test to be done during the third session was designed to analyze the performance of the antimatter beam at much longer distances, 16 miles in this case. It would also test targeting precision during rapid-fire discharge. The observation craft began recording the test the precise moment the first conditioning beam opened up and maintained a 16 mile vacuum for the first antimatter stream to follow. This would be repeated 71 times for the remaining fanned cable stays on the east side of the bridge and 12 heavier antimatter beams targeted for the concrete superstructure. The total calculated time needed for the attack was 11 seconds.

* * *

As Rollins was staring at the two tiny dots in the sky, the far peripheral vision of his left eye caught the first blinding flash, followed by a rapid sequence of more blinding flashes and deafening explosions coming from his left. The brilliant light blurred everything around him and the concussions of each antimatter strike drowned the screams of the hundreds stranded on the crumbling bridge. The roadway segments, freed from their stays, swung downward, dumping Oscar Rollins and many dozens of vehicles at a time into the Savannah River, River Street at the southwest superstructure and the marsh beyond the northeast superstructure. By the time the east-facing superstructures were engaged with a heavier antimatter beam, most everyone on the bridge was either dead in the water or dead on the ground.

Five minutes later, the heavily damaged superstructures failed, both collapsing onto the banks of the Savannah River, ensuring that it would be quite some time before port cargo could be shipped or delivered to deep water dock facilities beyond the bridge. In all, 358 cars and eight heavy trucks were dumped into the

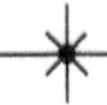

Savannah River. Another 322 cars and 11 heavy trucks toppled onto concrete or marsh. The death toll was nothing short of staggering.

Within 10 minutes, news wires were practically melting with traffic. Based on the very first eyewitness accounts of bright flashes and staccato explosions, the first and only assumption was a terrorist attack. The early speculation was that somebody wired the bridge with explosives and waited to detonate them when the bridge was packed with traffic. On cue, the polar ends of the political spectrum began to speculate, which usually ended up being the first barely-formed thought that entered their heads. The left immediately blamed right wing extremists and gun owners for the terror attack, the right blaming leftist anarchists and Muslim jihadists. Two major transportation accidents in two days would certainly keep the press and pundits running their mouths for weeks.

By the time late evening local news shows began, a vivid video surfaced that captured the entire attack in horrific clarity. Taken by a Savannah College of Art and Design student who was taping various Savannah landmarks for her semester project, the video showed the blinding flashes, explosions and the gut-wrenching view of people and vehicles tumbling into the water and land below. She kept the video running while she threw up several times during the ordeal. The video ended with the chilling collapse of the massive and heavily damaged superstructures on both sides of the Savannah River.

There were other videos. Videos not shown on broadcast television. Videos of bodies, many dozens of bodies, floating past the popular River Street wharfs on an outgoing tide. Many were reminded of the 2004 Indonesian Tsunami that carried corpses both inland and out to sea. Those gruesome videos would not be broadcast out of respect for the dead and the tender-hearted, but would be viewed millions of times on the largest of video archives on the web.

By midnight, the usual players were fully assembled, including the FBI, Homeland Security, FEMA and the Coast Guard, along with Georgia and South Carolina Departments of Public Safety. In the field, there was a unanimous concensus on what happened to the Eugene Talmadge Memorial bridge.

Inside a chilly, snow-capped mountain in Northern British Columbia, the consensus was far different.

Chapter 66

"Mr. President, please come with me," Secret Service agent Seth Chapman said quietly into President Bertram's right ear. "There has been an incident in Savannah, Georgia."

Agent Chapman backed away as the President excused himself from the strategy session with California politicos and followed Chapman to another conference room in the posh San Francisco hotel. Larry Osborn was waiting for him.

"What now, Larry?"

"A major bridge in Savannah was completely destroyed. It was packed full of cars and trucks waiting for a fatality accident to clear. Hundreds of people fell from the bridge. It's bad. Real bad. Seems to be a clear cut case of terrorism."

"We're not blaming the aliens this time?"

Osborn ignored the snide remark. "A Hunter Army Airfield Captain was an eyewitness at fairly close range. He said rapid-fire explosions started at the north end of the bridge and terminated at the south end. He counted 12 more vigorous explosions on the support structures."

"Somebody rigged that whole bridge for demolition! Good God almighty! How could somebody do that without getting caught?"

"They must of had a lot of outside help," Osborn paused. "We can't paint over this one like we did on the airliner. We need to call this what it is: 'Terrorism,' and make a forceful statement that we will track every one of these assholes down and bring them to justice."

"Agreed," the President said. "Get Air Force One ready for a quick departure. We're cutting this trip short. Every minute I stay here is ammunition for the nitwits on Capitol Hill I have to deal with."

"I'll take care of it, Greg." Osborn said, pausing a few moments to deliver his next bombshell. "There is one other issue I need to address with you."

"Sure thing, Larry."

"I'm submitting my letter of resignation, effective Friday."

"What???" the President almost yelled. "You can't do that! You're the best man for this job and we're right in the middle of a re-election campaign!"

"Greg, I'm tired, really tired... and Julie is getting restless. It's time for me to go. I've got a new grandson that the wife and I want to spoil rotten."

The President lowered his head and didn't say anything for what seemed to be an eternity. "Of course, Larry. I really hate to see you go. You have been a good friend and a trusted advisor. Hell, I couldn't have won the first election without you!"

"Greg, there is a lot of good talent out there. Sydney Barnes at State would make a great Chief of Staff. She's dependable and a quick thinker. Good instincts."

"She's good, but she's no Larry Osborn!" the President said with a smile.

"Thanks, Greg. Seriously, Sydney really is the best choice to replace me. Don't blow it off, dammit!" He paused to look at the tired face of a man with a noose tightening around his neck. Pangs of guilt made Osborn cringe. Both men were tightly bound to their shared political ideology, but held starkly opposed convictions on the subject of alien motives, making it all but impossible for each to stand on any sort of common ground.

"I guess I had better get busy hauling your ass back to DC." Larry said, his voice almost cracking.

"Thanks, pal!" President said warmly.

Osborn turned towards the door and grimaced again.

Chapter 67

"Look at that string of explosions!" Dr. Hanson said to Dr. Alexander and her newly arrived staff members. "Like a brilliant strobe light moving along the bridge!"

Chief of Security Kevin Loeffler and Deputy Chief of Security Hannah Simpson arrived on the last JANET flight to CRF for the foreseeable future. Upon their arrival, they were summoned to a small, Conclave satellite conference room to help analyze the SCAD student video on YouTube.

"Antimatter," Tim said gravely, "unless the bad guys are packing a lot of magnesium into the explosives. If it is antimatter, all those people on the bridge were getting big doses of gamma rays. Had they survived, they might have developed radiation sickness."

"Terrorists are not in the habit of spiking their explosives with fluff," Loeffler said, the intensity of his voice picking up. "What really bothers me is how orderly the detonations are all across the deck stays facing the camera, but not a single detonation on the far side. Now, look at the strikes on the bridge superstructure. Same thing! Detonations only on the side facing the video camera!"

"The attack came from one direction or the perpetrators only put explosives on that side of the bridge!" Tim said, feeling the wave of discovery taking place in conference room.

"The question I have is..." Simpson queried, "if this is a terrestrial terrorist attack, how did they manage to place that much explosive under a bridge without attracting attention?"

"People steal big items from department stores right in front of the salespeople," Tim said. "Many years ago, a friend of mine who worked at a large sporting goods store, helped a man carry out a canoe to his truck, then tied it down for the ride home. He later found out he inadvertently helped the man steal the boat right before his eyes! He never even considered the possibility that someone would steal something that big right in front of everyone in the store. The point is that some awfully bold actions can occur right under our noses."

"Good point," Donna said with an overly large grin. "It was you that helped the thief steal the canoe, wasn't it?"

"Please don't turn me in!" Tim said with feigned sheepishness

"Dr. Alexander, I'm sure the statute of limitations has expired on your crime," Loeffler said sternly, "but... now that I know about it, I'll be keeping an eye on you!"

"Don't worry, it'll be our little secret!" Donna snickered.

The small group of new colleagues took a short, welcomed break from analyzing the gruesome video to chuckle at the thought of their mild-mannered physicist being some sort of notorious shoplifter.

"Dr. Hanson, isn't demolishing a bridge that size a very complicated and precise undertaking? Like imploding an old building without damaging the building 20 feet away from it?" Hannah asked.

"Hannah, please, call me Donna. As far as I'm concerned, we are all family here. I'm really thrilled that you and Kevin showed up on the last JANET flight! Somehow, I didn't get the memo that the two of you would arrive today!" Donna said with genuine sincereness. "Hannah, to answer your question, I really don't know. That is way out of my field of expertise. Well..." she hesitated a little, "I have done work on warhead aerodynamics, but that hardly qualifies me as an expert on explosives."

"Do you know anybody in the DoD that can help?" Tim asked.

"Wait! Damn! I almost forgot!" she shook her head vigorously. "I worked at Lockheed up until a week ago!" she exclaimed, sheepishly. "Tim, I must be getting senile! I know exactly who to call, but first, I need to contact General Huber at

Peterson."

Dr. Hanson's countenance became visibly darker. "This is a big call and I trust your judgements. Are we all thinking this disaster is likely to be an aggressive alien strike on our infrastructure?"

"Donna, the brightness of the flashes... It looks way too powerful to be anything but matter/antimatter annihilation. The precision of the attack... I can't be 100 percent sure, though." Tim said. "Nobody saw an alien vehicle, or not that we know of. If I could just get there and examine a detonation point..."

"We're not going anywhere, Dr. Alexander!" Donna teased. "We barely have enough crew here to screw in a light bulb! But... I suppose if the trip were important enough, we could joyride on the 650."

"Dr. Hanson... Donna, I just can't wrap my brain around the idea that somebody secretly placed that much explosive on, what... 2000 feet of high profile bridge... and nobody noticed?" Simpson said firmly. "No, this had to be an alien attack on us."

"Hannah is right," Loeffler said, smiling at his new partner. "We have terrorist cells in this country who are dedicated to destroying American infrastructure, but none of them could reproduce the total destruction of that bridge short of using an suicide airliner attack."

"Dr. McLachland, you've been kind of quiet." Donna observed.

"Your father knew this day would come," he said sadly. "We talked about it for years. I was always the optimistic one, the one who believed that, in the end, our leaders would eventually take the threat seriously. Your dad knew otherwise." He paused for a somber moment. "I always thought his perception might have been tainted by the horrible tragedies he endured. The abuse he suffered. I should have known better. Your dad was the most intuitive man I have ever met. You, too, have that gift, Donna. I agree... as I believe your dad would have agreed... this attack must have been carried out by the aliens. It's the only option that makes sense."

Donna paused for a moment to take in what Dr. McLachland said. A tear formed as a fond memory of her dad bubbled to the surface. She had been so busy since her father's funeral, not a week before, that she had spent very little time in grieving for him.

"Then," she wiped the tear from her eye, "we are all in agreement?"

Everyone silently shook their head in the affirmative.

"I will call General Huber and break the news to him when we're finished.

"Donna, why did you evacuate the facility?" Hannah asked.

"After almost 70 years of passive behavior, the aliens are getting more and more aggressive," she said, pausing briefly. "They have harassed us a couple of times... and, there for a moment, I actually thought Tim and I were going to die during the most intimidating encounter! They also buzzed the Kirtland Nuclear Weapons facility and dropped-off nanotechnology. There have been high-profile and high death toll engagements around the globe. Now, it looks like they might have slaughtered hundreds stranded on a bridge... These actions clearly suggest, at least to me, that we may be at the threshold of war. To make matters worse, our President is in complete denial of this! Did you hear the Presidents' Press Secretary announce that Chief of Staff Larry Osborn put in his resignation today?"

"There was something about it on the TV monitor inside the JANET terminal, but I wasn't paying too much attention to it," Kevin replied.

"Well, I received three encrypted 'eyes only' messages from an anonymous government source. The first two informed us of alien involvement in the destruction of a Russian submarine in the Pacific and a Japanese airline crash in Hawaii. The source also informed us that President Bertram would surrender to the aliens if hostilities began."

"Oh my God!" Hannah gasped.

"I received the last encrypted message this afternoon. All it said was 'I resigned. Can't help you anymore. God be with you.' I'm 100 percent certain that Larry Osborn was sending us the messages."

"Inside information straight from the White House?" Hannah asked, wanting to believe that what she just heard was some sort of misinterpretation. "God, if this is really true, the ramifications are mind boggling! The President would actually just roll over and play dead? Can this possibly be true?"

"Osborn must have heard it with his own ears, Hannah," Kevin speculated. "I'm not a big fan of most of the politicians and bureaucrats that swim in the DC cesspool, but this fellow has certainly earned my respect!"

"What are we going to do about it?" Hannah asked. "We can't let him surrender to the aliens!"

"How would we stop him, Hannah?" Tim replied. "The people of America elected him. Sound judgment or not, we're stuck with him."

"All we can do is what we're chartered to do, and we'll do it well," Donna said. "We can't fight the dysfunctional ideologies of those who wish to oversee our project. We can, however, try to minimize the damage they do within the scope of our mission."

"And... perhaps, a phone call or two?" Tim asked, fully convinced that Donna was hiding something up her sleeve.

"Perhaps..."

"What about this: since we all have things we need to attend to, let's have a late dinner in the cafeteria after I get Hannah situated in her apartment?" McLachland said in an upbeat tone. "I have it on good authority that, at the very last minute, Frogman and Patty decided to stay! I was certain we'd be living on self-made sandwiches for the foreseeable future."

"Frogman Willie?" Hannah asked.

"Remember how good the food was when you ate here? Frogman Willie is our extraordinarily talented Chef," Loeffler replied with a grin. "Whatever you do, do not ask him about Patty unless you have an extra hour on hand to listen to him."

"Patty? His wife?"

"May as well be. Patty is his dog. Frogman will spend a half hour filling your ear full of reasons why he'll never marry again!"

All enjoyed the stress-relieving laugh and went about their assigned tasks. Dr. McLachland secured an apartment key from Major Alleyne and helped Hannah Simpson move her luggage. Loeffler and Alexander joined the railgun installation crew that was making tangible progress in completing a weapon everyone hoped and prayed would never be used. Lastly, Donna Hanson contacted General Huber to inform him, amongst other things, that aliens were likely responsible for the Talmadge Bridge disaster. She also placed another call to her mother.

The late dinner Frogman whipped up was nothing short of culinary genius. As an added surprise, Willie decided to join the five Cocheta staff members in

the almost empty cafeteria and entertain them with rants about Marines and bragging about how smart Patty was. His presence and off-color tall tales were a welcomed distraction. In all, the remaining CRF staff, excluding the Marines who always maintained a full garrison, consisted of a little over two dozen volunteers, 15 critical support personnel, Drs. McLachland, Alexander, Hanson, Loeffler and Simpson to keep Cocheta minimally operational. The most important of the physical plant staff were the NRTs, the Nuclear Reactor Technicians. The modified A1B Naval reactor was fairly low maintenance and could provide 600 continuous megawatts of power for the entire facility. More than enough non-stop energy to power everything in Cocheta for more than 30 years without refueling. Still, it had to be watched, maintained and tended to 24 hours a day by a pair of highly trained technicians.

After dinner, the CRF Command and Security Staff retired for the evening, each to their own apartments... four longing to be with their lovers, but not sure of how it might look in the eyes of their colleagues and staff. All were very tired and hoped for a quiet, uneventful night.

It was way too much to ask for...

Chapter 68

"I thought we decided that the Savannah Bridge was a real act of domestic terrorism. Now you tell me the Cocheta Crew thinks aliens were responsible for it?" Bertram scowled. "Why, of course it was the aliens! They're behind every corner! Their in our closets! Jesus Christ, Larry! Where does it end with those people?"

"As usual, Greg, I'm just the messenger," he replied with more than a hint of ire. "They analyzed the SCAD video and the consensus amongst the scientists, engineers and security personnel is that a, quote: 'alien directed energy weapon, likely using antimatter as an explosive, destroyed the bridge in Savannah.'"

"Antimatter?" Bertram echoed. "Bullshit!"

"Greg, it's ANTIMATTER for God's sake! We are obviously outgunned in every category! Their technology must make ours look like stone-age relics! We need to get the NSC fired up, put our heads together and come up with a solution other than denial and suicide!"

President Bertram glared at his Chief of Staff. "That was over the top... and you know it!"

"It is not 'over the top!' Can't you see? It was OK when the aliens sunk the Russian sub because you believed the aliens were, somehow, on our side. Next, they knock off a foreign airliner by cutting off of its tail section. Because it crashes on our soil, you countermand an NTSB expert, cover-up the details of the attack and reopen Hawaiian airspace for economic reasons while they are still picking up body parts! Now they are here, Greg, on this continent... and they've just killed

hundreds of innocent civilians during a brutal assault on a packed bridge! For God's sake, Greg! We're next! We're all next!" Osborn pleaded.

The President softened his glare, somewhat. "Larry, I'm not going to use weapons that will destroy our planet. THAT is non-negotiable!"

"What does the environment matter if THEY wipe us out or enslave us? WHO is going to give a shit?" Osborn asked forcefully. "Greg, they are going to strike again, and it will be worse... far worse!" Osborn said in a far more subdued voice. "We need to take a stand, even if they still kick our asses in the process!"

President Bertram said nothing. He turned his Air Force One Chair around and stared out into the darkness over West Virginia. From the start, he believed that advanced alien cultures MUST be peaceful and environmentally friendly. It HAD to be that way! If aliens had the capability of interstellar travel, they HAD to have environmentally friendly belief systems, didn't they?

As it happens, magical thinking has a way of introducing reality in cold and glaringly certain terms. All those years of political correctness and self delusion converged into a single moment on a single man, the 'leader' of the free world. The life and death of billions rested on the next sentence from his mouth. For President of the United States Gregory Bertram and the inhabitants of earth, it was the most pivotal moment in the history of mankind.

"Larry..."

"Greg..."

"If they make another aggressive move... I'll authorize a limited response to it, but only if it is over unpopulated areas."

Osborne winced at what he considered to be a completely spineless order, but knew the President well enough to know that it would be the only offer on the table.

It was then that Osborne truly felt the ugly chill of enevitability.

Chapter 69

"Two birds of prey prowled the chilly, moonless night. Their world was that of tactical, positional and performance information superimposed on an unearthly-looking landscape of incandescent green night-vision... rushing 200 feet underneath them at over 800 miles per hour. The two transonic craft had a familiar shape, yet altogether different look to them, with lean, almost sexy form accented by bold, angled lines that scattered radar pulses. With razor-sharp talons hidden from view, there were no external missiles or bombs to compromise stealth and raw sex appeal. They were a synergistic blend of Eagle and Nighthawk... far deadlier than the sum of both combined. To the unsophisticated, the single engine jet derived its name from a rather homely, carnivorous dinosaur made famous in a blockbuster movie. To the enlightened, they were deadly predatory birds; strong, sleek... and very, very fast.

They were Raptors.

"'Supercruise' they called it; supersonic flight without blowers. Helluva concept!" LTC Gus 'Mad Dog' Barker thought to himself as he went 'booming' the southern Nevada desert floor with massive sonic detonations. He allowed himself the luxury of a few brief moments to ponder how many desert rabbits were dying from little bunny heart attacks in the wake of his F-22A Raptor. Both him and his wingman, MAJ Buddy 'Buzzsaw' Johnson, went transonic shortly after their northward, low-altitude egress from Nellis Air Force Base, so fuzzy bunnies were not the only thing they were slaughtering on their way to the 'bandit.' They were breaking windows and cracking walls by the dozens... and Uncle Sam would pick up the tab for every single one of them.

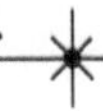

Barker began banking ever so slightly to the right to line-up with the short outcropping of mountains standing between him and his first real kill since patrolling Iraqi airspace so many years earlier. This was certainly not the usual Raptor tactic of blasting fighters out of the sky long before their adversaries could see them, or even conceivably pick them up on radar. Instead, their orders were to come in low and hot, using the southern Nevada terrain to hide their ingress. It was almost as if command thought the bogey might actually pick up their approach on radar, let alone survive their razor sharp talons. 'Not likely!' Barker thought to himself with a confident grin. For all intents and purposes, his Raptor was invisible and could easily sneak-up on the aviation equivalent of a hyper-vigilant deer on crystal meth... in broad daylight!

"Go secure," Barker said, announcing his switch to encrypted communications.

"Raptor one, Raptor two... You are cleared hot. Repeat, cleared hot," announced Nellis Command and Control, giving them permission to wage war on the poor bastard that was stupid enough to trespass all over their Nellis Test Range playground.

"Roger that, Home Plate." Barker replied

"Buzz, head east and parallel to Groom Range, low as you can. When you clear the mountains, ease right and engage. Keep your RCS low. I'll split right and stir-up dust from the northwest through Emigrant Valley. He'll be so busy dodging your missile he won't see me flying up his ass!"

"You got it, Dawg!"

Barker switched frequency. "Dreamland Tower this is Fastmover One, ETA two minutes. Bogey Dope?"

"Roger, Fastmover One. Bogey stationary, one-point-five miles east northeast of tower. Altitude one-two-zero feet. The field is clear."

"Roger that, Dreamland. Bogey stationary," he replied, then returned to aircraft-to-aircraft communications.

"Happy hunting, Buzz! Looks like we're hunting a helo! Breaking right in three, two, one... breaking right!"

The Raptor performed the high-G turn effortlessly, while her pilot grunted and strained to keep his blood from rushing down to his toes. In the long left, low RCS, or "radar cross-section" turn that followed the break from his wingman, LTC Barker cleared the northernmost foothills of the Groom mountain range and steadied his southeasterly course towards a dry, inhospitable piece of Nevada real estate known as 'Dreamland.'

Barker, Johnson and their pair of F-22A Raptors were assigned to the 57th Wing, 433rd Weapons Squadron at the Nellis Air Force Base Weapons School, developing combat tactics to best utilize the awesome capabilities of America's deadly air-superiority fighter. The work was hard, but immensely rewarding. The techniques they developed together were tested during Northern Edge exercises in Alaska, and locally during the Red Flag" exercises in Southern Nevada. These were joint service, multi-national war games played out in the skies of their respective areas. Red Flag involved everything from simulated surface-to-air missile launches and live bombing missions, to dogfighting with the Nellis-based Aggressor squadron, their F-16s painted like Russian Su-27s and 30s. To add even more realism to the exercise, the Aggressor squadron occasionally used real Russian aircraft procured from lemon lots around the world. It was great sport and excellent training for American and allied pilots. The F-22A had a flawless record in their early combat exercises, 'killing' over 140 F-15s, 16s and 18s without the loss of a single Raptor. The Skunk Works-designed air superiority fighter seemed destined to become one of the finest combat aircraft ever built.

The endless training gave LTC Barker and MAJ Johnson intimate knowledge of every nook and cranny in the Nellis Test Range. 'Home field advantage!' Barker thought to himself. This time, instead of inert "dummy" ordinance, each carried two live AIM-9M Sidewinder and six AIM-120C AMRAAM missiles. "No simulated kills tonight, my friend!" Barker told Johnson as they were running to their Raptors. "We're dispensing 100 percent death on a bad guy this time!"

The two pilots knew surprisingly little in the way of information concerning their mission. Thirty minutes before starting their engines, they were informed an unidentified, slow-moving aircraft violated the Tonopah Test Range and began to take a leisurely tour of some of the most restricted facilities and airspace in the continental United States. It eventually made its way southeast through the Nevada Test Site, then northeast to the ultra secretive facility originally known for its role in testing such aircraft as the U-2 and SR-71 Blackbird spy planes. It was located on a parcel of arid, high desert land surveyed and innocuously labeled 'Fifty-One' by the United States Government.

Other than that, the only other bit of information they had were orders to engage and destroy the wayward aircraft. No radio warnings. No "attention-getting" canon fire across its nose. No waiting months for a fuckin' UN resolution. Kill it, then Miller Time!

"Home Plate this is Fastmover Two. Have cleared the mountains... What thuh... Bogey in sight. Jesus! What is that thing? Wait a minute... it's a sure as shit flying saucer for cryin' out loud! Why didn't you tell me I was gunning for ET?"

"Fastmover Two, this is Home Plate. Bandit is hostile. Commit and engage NOW!"

'No humor at Nellis tonight!' he thought to himself. "Fastmover Two committed. Going hot... Getting intermittent lock... fox three, close!" Johnson yelled excitedly, announcing the launch of the AMRAAM and its unusually close range to the target.

The ordinance door underneath the belly of the Raptor opened and closed in just under one second, but long enough to quickly, and literally, shove an AIM 120C AMRAAM into the air stream below the jet. The missile's solid fuel rocket engine ignited on cue, sending it hurtling towards the target at four times the speed of sound.

"Pitbull!" Major Johnson announced, indicating that the AMRAAM had instantly locked onto the alien bandit. "Fastmover Two breaking left!"

"Roger that, Buzz. Closing on target. It's not moving at all."

"Disco on station," a highly-modified Boeing 707 AWACS jet chimed in, redirected from routine border patrol to follow the intruding craft and provide tactical support for the Raptors. "Positive link to AMRAAM. Impact in three, two, one... Lost link! Repeat, lost link!"

LTC Barker didn't need an explanation as to why the AWACS lost guidance and telemetry communications with the missile. He watched it detonate in a flash of bright light less than a half-mile from the hovering target.. It was so brief he could not make out the direction it came from... if there was one.

"Missile trashed short of target... possible interception! Switching to heat." Barker announced, electing to engage the strange craft with an infrared-seeking, AIM-9X Sidewinder missile. Only three miles from the target and streaking low over the Joshua Tree-studded desert 1.2 times faster than the speed of sound,

Barker listened to the electronic growl of the Sidewinders' infrared seeker. An instant later, a familiar and quite welcome tone superimposed on the growl. Like a venomous pit viper, the missile locked onto the heat radiating from its target.

"Going hot! Fox Two!" Barker announced as the port weapons bay ejected a single Sidewinder missile. Instead of breaking left to join his wingman, he decided to follow the missile for a few more seconds.

"Disco has positive link with Sidewinder. Four, three, two..."

There it was again! The bright flash of light, only this time he was much closer to it. As before, the missile detonated short of the object, but Barker could see where the light came from. Bad news... It seemed to originate from the missile itself!

'It's some kind of laser!' he thought, a sick feeling beginning to well up in his gut. While he had no idea of the weapons' true nature, he knew that the Sidewinder had not succumbed to anything he could see coming from the craft. The only option left in his terrestrial knowledge of possible weapons was an invisible, high-energy laser or directed-energy weapon. Many modern lasers are invisible to the unaided eye and laser-based range finding was very common on the battlefield. Armored vehicles and strike aircraft used them for targeting or directing precision-guided munitions. Some of these lasers were powerful enough to cause irreversible blindness if a soldier happened to be looking directly into the beam without protective eyewear. There were also many commercial and consumer applications for invisible lasers. Cops used multiple range-finding pulses to determine the speed of a vehicle, while hunters used a single pulse or average of pulses to determine the distance of game animals or objects. Surgical suites around the world used invisible lasers with enough power to char or vaporize living tissue. While most were invisible, the ones with significant destructive energy became indirectly visible at the point it struck a target. It could be smoke, flame, white-hot melting metal... or bright light!

"Breaking right and extending!" he yelled, translating the command to the joystick tightly gripped in his right hand. His Raptor enthusiastically obeyed, taking Barker over the Groom Lake airfield and complex in excess of mach one and at a startlingly low altitude, shattering many dozens of windows in the process. His upward trajectory took him over Papoose Mountain range behind the secretive facility, clearing it by a mere 75 feet.

"Directed-energy Weapon! Repeat, directed-energy weapon!" he announced,

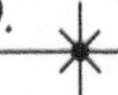

the absence of stress in his voice belying the building terror inside.

The game had suddenly changed.

He knew the tactics of all of his terrestrial adversaries and personally fine-tuned the slick moves all Raptor pilots would use to defeat them. This... this 'thing' was obviously not from any earthly enemy! Chaff, flares, twirling his bird of prey like an acrobatic ballerina... he could defeat a radar homing or infrared-guided missile with those tools. Why? Because of time! If you saw it coming, you could react. A laser moved at the speed of light. LTC 'Mad Dog' Barker and his beloved Raptor were quick, but nowhere near that quick.

"Disco, Fastmover One. No joy!!! Bogey status!" Barker announced to the AWACS that he did not have visual contact with the bandit, hoping it hadn't latched onto his six.

"Bogey stationary, Fastmover One."

"Buzz, meet me at TTR. We'll come in together from the southeast, low and fast. I'll ripple two AAMRAMs and you ripple your Sidewinders. Whatever it is, we know it can handle one missile at a time. Maybe it'll have trouble with four."

"Roger that, Dawg!"

Several minutes later, the two Raptors were once again racing over the desert floor at low altitude. This time they were on afterburners, or 'military power,' and quickly approaching 1.4 Mach. It was a very bad night for desert bunnies.

"Going hot... Missiles locked. On my mark..." Barker announced, "three, two, one... Fox Three, two!"

"Fox Two, two!" Johnson called.

"Buzz, break right and rollover to cover my six. I'm following up with guns in case they take out the missiles."

"Breaking right!" Barker's wingman replied. "Good hunting, Elmer!"

Barker didn't answer. He was focusing on four missiles converging on the target, barely listening to the AWACS countdown to impact. As he thought might happen, each missile disappeared in a bright flash of light. He immediately switched the AN/APG-77 radar to the mode he personally referred as 'Wild West.' His heads-up display began showing the unmistakable moving impact circle and waving tail of gun mode. As the plane changed direction, the impact circle adjusted accordingly to compensate. Essentially, the circle was where a computer calculated the impact point of next cannon round fired. Streaming from the circle was a waving string of dots connected by lines indicating where previously fired cannon rounds were traveling. Back in the early years of dogfighting, a pilot peered through a simple reticle and 'leading' the target was your best 'guestimate.' Now, it was a matter of maneuvering the aircraft to keep the computer-generated impact circle on the target, which could still be quite difficult if your opponent didn't want 20mm holes in himself or his aircraft. The Raptors' radar computer calculated Mad Dog's target was in cannon range, and with a few tweaks of the right joystick, the circle was dead on.

"Guns guns guns!" he yelled, depressing the trigger and unleashing a deafening roar of sizzling metal.

Guns on the F-22A Raptor were almost an afterthought. Many argued a stealthy, air superiority fighter laden with eight air-to-air missiles, capable of obliterating enemy planes from well beyond visual range, simply didn't need guns. In the end, it was a capability the Air Force wanted all of its fighters to retain, so guns it would have. Tucked away in the Raptor's right wing root was a six barrel, 20mm M61A2 Vulcan Gatling cannon and a paltry supply of 480 rounds of mach 3, high-explosive incendiary ammunition. This amounted to be about five seconds of sustained fire. Barker held the trigger down, feeling the 3000-plus pounds of jarring recoil pushing back on his Raptor until last round was expended on the target.

What he saw was weirdly beautiful, yet the significance of it instantly chilled his blood. Systematically, the mysterious craft vaporized each cannon round in a flash of brilliant light.

"Holy shit!" Barker said aloud as he instinctively banked hard left and skyward to avoid becoming the last flash of light in the chain. He applied maximum Military Power to boost speed, dramatically increasing the G-load on his body. Grunting, he desperately began looking behind him through the frame-less canopy to see if he was being followed, or fired at.

Suddenly, his cockpit filled with bright light as a deafening explosion shuddered the Raptor. He'd been hit! As the fighter began to tumble uncontrollably, the six, full color LCD screens before him began displaying a mounting list of system failures while 'bitching Betty' filled his helmet with audible warning alarms. The world was spinning, and his throttle and stick were useless to control it.

By design, the Raptor was completely fly-by-wire and so aerodynamically unstable that computers were required to keep it in the air. As a result, the same terrible outcome occurred if the computers were fried or the fighter lost its wings. His sexy killing machine was dead and it was time get out before he joined it in heaven. He grabbed the handles on the outer side of each leg and pulled them backwards. 'This is going to hurt!' he thought to himself as the canopy blasted free of the crumbling fuselage.

The counterbalance between momentum and increased drag of a tumbling aircraft slowed the airspeed to about 500 miles per hour by the time of Barker's ejection. A solid fuel rocket propelled the modified ACES II ejection seat clear of the dying Raptor, suddenly and dramatically increasing the gravity-induced load on Barker's spine. Low altitude, high-velocity Mode 2 drogue chute deployment and seat separation was automatically chosen and initiated by a computer in the ejection seat. In spite of the best ejection seat technology, tossing a human body into an air stream of that speed was a very violent act. Barker's head and chest felt as if hit by a freight train. The world was a jumbled mess of jarring sensations, a blur of deafening sounds, flashing lights... and pain. Lots of pain. Movies often depicted dashing pilots walking away from an ejection with little more than a few out-of-place hairs on a neatly groomed head. In reality, 10 percent of pilots died from injuries involving high-speed ejections, a fair portion of the remainder ended up in the hospital. Three seconds after ejection, Barker's main chute deployed automatically, slowing its motion to a gentle drift to the southeast.

Though seriously stunned by the egress from what remained of his mortally wounded Raptor, Barker was lucky. He cleanly cleared the disintegrating aircraft and his ejection seat and chutes performed exactly 'per manufacturer specifications.' He descended slowly towards the jet black desert below, desperately trying to shake the fog in his head. Through the daze, he could make out the flaming wreckage of what remained of his Raptor as it plummeted to earth. He couldn't be sure, but it looked as if the momentum of his last evasive maneuver allowed the remains of his $143 million fighter to impact onto the desert floor southeast of the Papoose mountain range. As his mind cleared, he began looking for his wingman. His ears finally beginning to function properly, he could make out the sound of a Raptor on military power. Twisting and turning to get a view behind him, he managed to slowly rotate the chute in the direction of the sound that was rapidly growing in intensity. Looking over his left shoulder, he could finally make out Buzz's Raptor by the stream of decoy flares... and its silhouette in front of the brightly glowing 'thing' on his six! To make matters worse, they were coming towards him at an astonishing speed!

"Dammit Buzz! Get the hell out! You can't outrun it!" Barker screamed at his wingman, paying little attention to the warning light in his mind trying to inform him that he was about to be passed, or struck by, two transonic aircraft.

Johnson was doing precisely that, using maximum afterburner power in a desperate attempt to extend from his adversary. Undeterred, the glowing discoid craft continued its close pursuit. Both aircraft missed Barker's position by a mere 200 feet to his west and 1000 feet above the ground. As he braced for the double shock waves of detonation and sonic booms, a brilliant light blazed before him. It had the same quality as the light heralding the demise of his Raptor, and LTC Barker instinctively knew his close friend and wingman was dead. A fraction of a second later, powerful sonic detonations mixed with the concussive force of the exploding Raptor jarred Barker's body with gut punching force. Before his brain could process rage and sadness over the loss of his trusted wingman, the heat from the explosion turned the cool, night air into an uncomfortably hot oven, if only for a moment. The burning wreckage of Johnson's raptor, tons of it, sailed through the desert night, propelled mostly by sheer momentum. It was a vision straight from the depths of hell! Thousands of shredded, flaming pieces of the most lethal fighter aircraft developed by humans rained down upon the desert floor in front of him... and what was left of Buzz was in there. Fury welled up inside of him as he began to search for the alien bastard that killed his partner. In spite of significant pain, he twisted and kicked out his legs to get his chute to rotate so he could keep his eye on the sonofabitch, but all he could see were two wide streaks of burning wreckage on the desert floor below and in front of him.

The light wind was carrying Barker towards a landing a few miles south of the Groom Lake facility. The normally dark and forbidding desert floor was alive with light. Burning wreckage created the illusion of hundreds of campfires and bonfires in the darkness below, and Barker could already see that some were coalescing, undoubtedly fueled by dry desert brush. In the seconds before his landing, he quickly assessed the situation. Normally, he would stay put and wait for the rescue teams from Groom Lake to pick him up. His ejection seat had a locator beacon on it, along with food, water and other survival essentials. With a northwest wind, Barker surmised his ejection seat would likely be a relatively short walk to the northwest. The problem was the fires... and they stood both upwind and between him and Groom Lake. Since there were fewer fires to the east, he would make his way northeast to get upwind of the fires as quickly as possible, then track west to

his ejection seat and wait. That is, if his ejection seat wasn't engulfed in fire.

With a excruciatingly painful roll onto the rocky desert floor, Barker found himself in the middle of a small patch of Joshua Trees no more than 25 yards from the nearest fire. Motivated by the fear of burning to death, the veteran pilot quickly unlatched his parachute harness, ditched his helmet and quickly made his way past the Joshua trees and into open desert. After a few hundred yards of painful hiking, he was well clear of the most threatening fires and began to head west to retrieve the sidearm, portable radio, GPS receiver, and survival kit from the ejection seat. It was only then did he realize his victorious opponent was watching him.

Barker noticed that the illumination of the desert floor changed from that of the flickering warm light created by the growing fires, to that of a much whiter and more even light. He turned around to see the alien craft hovering silently approximately 200 yards behind him. Staring at the craft that bested him and killed his wingman, rage and frustration began welling up inside.

"If you're going to finish me off, you bastard, then get on with it!" he yelled at the top of his voice. The object remained stationary as if unmoved by Barker's display of defiance. It was then he heard a helicopter. No... there were two of them! Sikorsky MH-60G Pave Hawks... and they were coming from Groom Lake. Before he could turn on his radio and warn the helicopters to stay away, COL Barker lost consciousness and crumpled to the desert floor.

Both Pave Hawks dispatched from Groom Lake crashed a few moments later, killing all on-board. The pilots, and every crew member inside, lost consciousness at the same time as COL Barker. Every soul at Groom Lake, awakened by the concussions of multiple sonic booms and shattering of windows, collapsed where they stood. To a person, every inhabitant of the sleepy, high desert town of Rachel was unconscious, as was every human within 40 miles of the alien craft.

The week-long suite of weapons calibration tests were now complete, the manned alien Aggressor slowly made its way over Emigrant Valley and Papoose Lake, monitoring the effectiveness of both the antimatter particle beam and the non-lethal, exogenous neuronal depolarization (END) wave. The craft eventually departed to the south at five times escape velocity speed. Within several seconds, the Aggressor was in space, hurtling towards the expedition force on the momentum of its escape from the target planet's gravitational field.

The only conscious witnesses to the alien departure were a small number of unscathed desert rabbits that dared to venture above ground.

Chapter 70

"Mr. President, the situation in Nevada has deteriorated. Both aircraft were destroyed and it appears that at least one pilot is dead. Probably both," General O'Neill announced with obvious reluctance in his voice. "We've also lost contact with Groom Lake and an AWACS is airborne, flying north but not responding."

"Oh my God! We sent our best technology... Has Groom Lake been attacked?" the President asked in a highly stressed voice.

"That is unclear at this time," the Air Force Chief of Staff replied, obviously shaken but maintaining his composure. "Several fighters were dispatched from Nellis and Cobra gunships from Twenty-Nine Palms. We are also mobilizing medical and rescue assets."

President Bertram sat back in his Situation Room chair, the gravity of the last several minutes pressing hard on his soul. No American president... no world leader in the history of the human race ever faced such a dire predicament. A highly advanced alien species, clearly guilty of pre-meditated mass homicide on an enormous scale, just provoked a limited military engagement from the most powerful country on the planet... and won!

'What next?' he thought to himself. No doubts lingered in his mind that the original assessments of both Dr. Hansons and three generations of Cocheta scientists were correct. Larry was right... the Cocheta staff was right. The aliens were aggressive and probably engaged in probing Earth's defenses in preparation for invasion. As much as he wanted to return to his magical thinking that the aliens were aligned with America, he simply couldn't ignore the obvious any longer.

"Larry, how long can we keep a cap on this?"

"If the base was destroyed, not long at all," he replied. "Hundreds of families will want to know what happened to their loved ones. If the base is off-line due to a systems failure, the increase in activity and the loss of two fighters could be explained away as a training exercise that went wrong."

The Oval Office phone began ringing before the President could ask how long before they would know something.

"President Bertram speaking."

"Mr. President," the familiar voice of his Secretary of Defense began, "another pair of Raptors just made a low pass over the Groom Lake facility. The lights are on and there doesn't seem to be any significant damage to the structures. There are numerous scattered fires to the south of Groom. That's the good news. The bad news is that they could make out a lot of bodies on the tarmac and two helicopters are burning."

"Holy Mother of God... what can we send to help them?"

"Mr. President, it might have been a chemical or biological attack. We'll need to send HAZMAT teams to Groom before anything else can land."

"How long will that take?"

"Once they land, they'll sample the air and examine the bodies. Hopefully, we will be able to enter the area within an hour of their arrival."

"Very well. Let's do it."

Bertram noticed that General Talbot was in a heated conversation on the phone. "What do you mean NTC and Mercury have been neutralized? They called in an hour ago, bitching about the intruder! Hold on, I'm putting you on speaker phone."

"Hello? Hello?" the obviously distressed voice said. "I had a helluva time getting through to you guys! I'm Gerry... Gerald Townsend, day watch officer at NTC. I came in real early to help the night watch officer catch an early flight out of McCarran, but everybody here is dead! Jesus! South Gate, guard shacks... security patrol cars off the road with engines running... everybody is dead! Tonopah Test Range is online, but Groom isn't. What the hell is going on?"

"Are you certain they are dead?" Talbot asked. "Did you check for pulses?"

"Look buddy, I'm no doctor, OK? They look dead to me and I'm not about to touch any of them. They might be contaminated!"

"I want you to stay put. We'll send help right away. It might take a while for them to get to you." Talbot said reasuringly. "I'm going to transfer you to the communications office. Tell them precisely where you are and what you need."

Bertram had been up the entire night in the situation room following the developing crisis... and sleep seemed so very, very far away. The day was promising to redefine the meaning of 'living hell.' What if there were hundreds of dead at Groom? How would he tell Congress and the American people without inciting a global panic? The human race had never faced such a threat. Could it be that the end-result was inevitable enslavement? Annihilation?

In the last week and a half, when the subject of conversation turned to aliens, the world seemed hopelessly split into three groups. Perhaps a third were frightened and suspicious of alien intentions. In stark contrast, another third were convinced their own race was always in the wrong, therefore the aliens had to be naturally and wonderfully beneficent... or at the very least, wiser, greener and more tolerant than humans. The remaining third were way too busy trying to scratch out a semblance of living to give a crap. What is one more looming disaster when you live on a dung heap and your life is less valuable than the fertilizer you're sitting on? The two-thirds of the world that have the luxury of worrying about aliens would polarize to an unprecedented degree. Those controlling the outlets of vital information and power, however, would dominate the narrative. That narrative had already been quickly defined as aliens being peaceful teachers that would gently counsel our unruly species to maturity.

Of all the challenges Bertram had faced in his lifetime, this one seemed absolutely insurmountable. Decades of political and cultural track records suggested that raw facts on alien aggression would be spun and distorted into whatever 'truth' seemed most palatable. Presumably, it would be the 'truth' that aliens were morally superior to humans and their acts of violence were in self defense against human aggression. In the end, homo sapiens would likely face a highly lethal adversary, armed only with rose-colored glasses. The ice cold splash of hard core reality in his face was the final cleansing that opened his eyes. Aggression was not isolated to a little blue planet on the outer rim of the milky way galaxy. Aggression was a universal constant.

There were never easy answers to impossible problems. Each pathway open to Bertram was littered with leg-shredding land mines. Considering the absolute technologic advantage the creatures possessed, would any decision he made in the next minutes, days, weeks or months make any difference at all in the final outcome?

"Damn you, Dr. Hanson!"

Chapter 71

LTC Barker wasn't sure what woke him up, the splitting headache or the multitude of ejection-induced aches and cramps all over his body. Perhaps it was the early morning desert sun beating down on his body, or the persistent and unpleasantly strong smell of... vinegar? There was a very strange taste in his mouth as well, and oddly, given the strong connection between taste and smell, completely unlike vinegar. It was more metallic, somewhat like the taste of blood, only repeated spitting showed no trace of old or active bleeding he could see. His vision was seriously out of focus and chaotic, mismatched signals in the balance pathways of his brain were causing the uncomfortable illusion of falling and the equally disconcerting illusion of the world spinning around him. The combination of pain, mild dehydration, dizziness and an illogical combination of what doctors call 'gustatory' and 'olfactory' hallucinations, caused Barker to become nauseated, and spend the first ten minutes of consciousness in dry heaves.

As his retching subsided, so did most of the causative factors. His vision, while still blurred, improved enough to get an idea where he was at. Fires were still burning to the south. To the north lay the smoldering remains of the two helicopters presumably sent to rescue him. In the distance, he could barely make out people scurrying about in vehicles and on foot. Some were around the debris field of the helicopters, others were searching for something a mile or so to his west, though he couldn't really make out any details beyond that. It was obvious they hadn't spotted him, so he began walking through the desert towards the burned-out helicopters. Within 30 minutes, LTC 'Mad Dog' Barker was spotted by friendly company and headed for an air-conditioned room at Groom Lake, assuming the previous night's multitude of low-altitude sonic booms left any windows intact.

As the HUMVEE bounced over the uneven terrain towards a sandy, unimproved road that promised a somewhat smoother ride, Barker relived the previous night's events and began analyzing the mistakes that lead to his friends' violent death. Two words quickly emerged from his mind: assumption and arrogance, the mother and father of all major fuck-ups. Against conventional aircraft, Raptors cruised high above the food chain, dispensing certain death with a yawn and a casual peek at the wristwatch. Barker 'assumed' his Raptors could use stealth and the most modern air-to-air missiles on Earth to defeat his opponents. Clearly, no such advantage existed in the engagement. His adversary was certainly no ordinary one. A more prudent assumption would have been to view the opponent as a potential superior until proven otherwise... and change tactics accordingly.

'If we had been fully briefed about the nature of the intruder, maybe Buzz would still be alive.' he angrily thought to himself. Both men honestly thought it was a surprise, live-fire exercise... until given orders to ingress at low altitude, supersonic flight. Even then, they thought the worst-case scenario would be nothing more than a helicopter piloted by an idiot with a death wish, perhaps loitering around the Tonopah Test Range and the Groom Lake airfield looking for the fabled UFO base. "Well, at least the 'UFO' part was right."

Private pilots occasionally strayed into the restricted airspace above the expansive Nellis Test Range. Most were mistakes, others pushing their luck. A pilot could easily lose their license over such a transgression. A 'defiant' pilot, ignoring radio warnings to return to unrestricted airspace, fell under the 'use of deadly force authorized' provision. 'Come on!' Barker growled to himself, 'if it was really a general aviation aircraft or helicopter, why send us? A fighter armed with anything fancier than a slingshot would have been overkill. Should've thought the helicopter thing through a bit more!' he chided himself.

A fact he hadn't considered suddenly surfaced into the forefront of his thoughts: Detachment Three had air defenses! If the trespasser was a retard in a helicopter, they could have easily dispatched it with one of their own helicopters! One by one, the pieces of the 'assumption' puzzle were falling into place, and each piece was a painful slap in the face.

Barker began wondering if it would have made any difference to know all the details. His orders from COL William 'Wild Bill' Hendricks were brief and unambiguous. "Y'all do whatever you need to do to toast that sumbitch!" he said in a genuine Texan drawl, loosely paraphrasing the order given by Northern Command. Hell, he could have gone unarmed and torn the rotor blades off a helicopter with one transonic pass! No missiles or cannon rounds... save the taxpayers a shitload of money! Thoroughly angered by the realization his chain-of-command likely knew from the very start the craft was exotic technology, LTC Barker promised himself a nice little chat with his wing commander.

A sudden change from unpaved to paved roadway jarred Barker from his concentration. The HUMVEE was now traveling northwest on an old runway marked "three-zero," heading towards the dozens of rather un-exotic buildings making up the fabled Area 51. Barker's vision was still blurred, but much improved from thirty minutes earlier. He could see there were a lot more aircraft at the facility than usual. Every JANET 737, Beech 1900 and King Air was there, along with a half dozen C-130s, several Marine Corps Cobra gunships, an AWACS and what looked like a big Gulfstream... a G650?!?

There was something else even more unusual for Air Force Flight Testing Center - Detachment Three: armed soldiers, and a lot of them! AFFTC-D3 was an Air Force base, or more precisely, a satellite facility of Edwards Air Force Base. As such, personnel in military uniforms were relatively common, but the vast majority of workers at Groom Lake were civilian contractors and government employees, busying themselves with testing the most technologically advanced military hardware on earth. To have the highly secretive research facility militarized to this extent was extraordinary! Barker instinctively knew something much larger than his botched dogfight was afoot. Or... maybe his botched dogfight started something much larger. The thought of touching off some kind of war with an alien culture possessing invincible military hardware sent chills down his spine.

'It had to be one of Senator Chandler's aliens, didn't it?' he asked himself. 'Surely they didn't send us on a suicide mission against something they were developing out here, would they?'

The only certain things he knew about Dreamland was that they were heavy into unmanned aerial vehicles and their more mundane duties of certifying new stealth aircraft by analyzing their radar cross sections. The thought was a conspiracy theorists' wet dream, but in reality, it was sheer madness to even contemplate such a notion. 'Why would they kill off two veteran Raptor Jockeys just to prove the deadliness of some new prototype?' With a shake of his head, Barker dismissed the thought entirely. Whatever it was, it seemed to know how to pick a fight and win it. What he experienced was certainly not the rosy picture of intergalactic harmony being touted by the whacko talking heads!

"Sergeant McGill, what's going on?" Barker finally asked the Air Force NCO in the HUMVEEs' front passenger seat.

"Sir, I am under orders not to discuss the current facility situation with anyone. Right now, we are taking you to Hangar 18 and have the medics tend to your injuries. I am told there are a number of people awaiting your arrival."

"Very well, Sergeant."

Barker would get his answers in due time. He sat silently in the back of the HUMVEE, periodically gulping a cold, lemon-lime flavored sports drink that smelled like vinegar and tasted like metal. As annoying as it was, his screwed-up senses were no match for the thirst brought on by a morning of sleeping late under a hot Nevada sun. As the HUMVEE neared the southern portion of the base complex, he could see Hanger 18 through the driver's side windshield. He noticed a large gathering of people milling about the open hangar, and two white commercial busses parked on the tarmac in front of the Plans and Engineering Building to the left of it. The bus was boarding passengers and all appeared to be... injured?

The HUMVEE turned west onto the very large and southernmost tarmac serving several hangars and support buildings. Barker had to shift to the opposite side of the HUMVEE to see the white busses out of the passenger side windshield. Closer now, he could see that nearly all boarding the bus were sporting bandaged heads and/or extremities, some were on crutches. Both military personnel and uninjured civilians were assisting with boarding the less able. Watching what he correctly assumed was a triage and medical transportation area, he heard the faint, but growing sound of an approaching helicopter. In the covered HUMVEE, he could not see it, but he recognized the sound instantly. It was UH-60 Blackhawk helicopter increasing the pitch on its blades in preparation for a slow, controlled landing. Undoubtedly, this was a MEDEVAC mission. One or more people must have sustained serious enough injuries to bypass the three-hour desert drive to Las Vegas. Barker's heart sank, wondering if he was responsible for the injuries.

The HUMVEE turned right at the Plans and Engineering building, then directed to proceed in front of the busses to a designated drop-off point in front of Hangar 18. An Air Force colonel in desert camouflage battle dress uniform was waiting.

LTC Barker unsteadily climbed out of the back of the HUMVEE without his gear and instantly greeted by Air Force Flight Test Center – Detachment 3 Base Commander, COL Quinton Barr.

"Colonel Barker, I'm Colonel Barr, the base commander here."

"Pleasure to meet you, sir."

"Welcome to Dreamland, Colonel Barker. Please, come with me. We need to have our medics look you over. Are you injured?"

"I have a few aches from the ejection, a nagging headache, and a bit of a sunburn. No big deal. What is bothering me most is the smell of vinegar and a strange taste in my mouth."

"Like metal?"

Yeah! How did you know?"

"Everyone here lost consciousness at the same time you did. When we woke up several hours later, all of us had headaches, blurred vision, a strange taste in our mouths most us describe as 'metallic,' and the persistent smell of vinegar."

Barker stopped in his tracks. "What? Everyone here?"

"Not just here, in Mercury, Alamo, Rachel, Crystal Springs, Ash Springs... everyone within 40 to 45 miles. If they were awake, they passed out. If they were already asleep, they woke up late. Even the AWACS crew was affected... and everyone has the same symptoms when they wake up."

"Jesus Christ!" Barker said trying to grasp the enormity of the situation.

"Over 5000 square miles were affected. The initial reports are that three are dead in motor vehicle accidents in Nye and Lincoln counties. Several civilians in the outlying communities woke up with fractured noses and extremities. Here? Everyone was watching your dogfight... heroic flying, Colonel Barker, heroic as hell... I'm sorry about your wingman. I heard you were close friends."

"We were, and thank you," he replied with genuine appreciation, "Please go on, Sir."

"When you flew over the facility the first time, some of my people standing by windows were injured by flying glass. None seriously... Oh, and don't worry about it, Colonel Barker, you did what you had to do to stay alive. The vast majority of the injuries you see here in Hangar 18 are from falls. We have quite a few broken arms and facial fractures, scrapes, bruises, second-degree sunburns, mild to moderate dehydration, minor concussions... There were a couple of unfortunate people

on stairs when they passed out. One has a severe concussion and may be bleeding inside of his head, the other a broken neck... legs are paralyzed and his arms are not working well." Barr stopped to shake his head. "The MEDEVAC is here to take them both to Vegas."

"That 'thing' caused all this?" he asked in utter disbelief.

"Probably, or something nearby we didn't see."

"Do we know what it is?"

"It's got to be extraterrestrial, but I can only speculate," Barr paused. "Colonel Barker, the scope of this incident has already gone well beyond the boundaries of the affected area. When Dreamland and the adjacent territory went dark, all manner of military assets were mobilized and rushed to the area. Nobody knew if we were alive or dead. Outside of the facility, unaffected people were driving into communities full of unconscious citizens they couldn't wake up. Rescue units from Vegas were dispatched and within a few minutes, the press was all over the incident. At this moment, the Pentagon is conjuring up a story to explain away the 'accident' as anything but extraterrestrial. My gut feeling is that this facility is going to take a direct hit. The only remotely plausible, terrestrial explanation for such widespread physical effects is chemical, an accidental release of toxic gas from Area 51. With any luck at all, the story will stick and the worst that will happen is a huge payout to settle the myriad of lawsuits that will follow. My guess is that the lawyers are beating the rescue units to the scene!"

Both men smiled at the dark humor that highlighted the sheer ludicrousness of a world where lawsuits are sometimes filed before the dead have had a chance to assume room temperature.

"Worse case scenario?" Barr continued. "Some politician looking for air time will demand a criminal investigation, congressional hearings, whatever. The inevitable outcome of that is a head on a platter. That would be mine."

Barker looked at COL Barr but didn't say anything. A disturbing trend developed in the military during the careers of both distinguished servicemen. When something high profile went wrong, accident or otherwise, a military career, or careers, went down in flames. Years before, a Los Angeles-class attack sub struck and sunk a Japanese research vessel while performing an emergency ascent for the junketing congressmen on board. It was the Captain who lost his career, not the Admirals or congressmen who concocted the ill-advised joyride in the first place.

Few officers in the Military believed for one moment that their chain of command, or the politicians above them, would admit any measurable degree of culpability in a high profile incident. Crap would simply roll downhill until it hit the most vulnerable and least connected serviceman or woman blameable.

Barr was right. In his worse-case scenario, every death, injury, and resulting lawsuit thereof, would be blamed on him, not to mention every birth defect, environmental quirk and case of cancer diagnosed within 1000 miles of Groom Lake... for the next 50 years. There might even be a new medical syndrome 'discovered' to punctuate Barr's crime. There would be no real science to back any of it up, of course. How could there be? The cover-up story was a farce to hide the fact that earth's alien visitors had a mean streak! Yet, facts and science would bend to create a believable modern myth etched in stone.

"Well, Colonel Barr, let's hope that never happens," Barker said reassuringly. "The work you do here is too valuable to lose."

"I appreciate the sentiment. In any case, there are a couple of people here to see you that probably know a helluva lot more about that 'thing' than I do."

"Who are they?"

"One is the new project director at the extraterrestrial research facility in Canada getting so much attention these days, Dr. Hanson. She is high speed, low drag and all business. She was at the top of the food chain at the Skunk Works before she took on the research project. The man with her is the deputy chief and scientific advisor of the project. I know you've seen him before. Dr. Tim Alexander?"

"The television scientist?"

"One and the same."

"Jesus, my kids love him! I swear, my sixteen year-old daughter has an impossible crush on him!"

"He's GS now, working for Uncle Sam. They have asked that every piece of Raptor wreckage be taken to a hanger for analysis. I'm clearing out Hangar 7. It's the least visible to our companions on Tikaboo Peak. After this incident, they will be up there in droves. If I could put a convenience store and a lodge up there, I would make a fortune!"

Tikaboo Peak, 23 miles to the east of Groom Lake, was the best location to view the facility outside of the restricted Nellis Range. It was not easy to get to the top of the mountain, yet the lure of viewing something you weren't supposed to see challenged many to make the arduous climb. It was human nature, after all. The more secret you made something, the harder people will work to see it. There were also professionals that frequented the mountain, dedicated to catching the first glimpses of emerging military technology. They monitored Groom Lake in every conceivable, non-restricted way.

Area 51 countered by only conducting critical flight testing of classified projects on moonless nights and using encrypted communications. As a result, a balance evolved between secrecy and the public right to know. The balance was decidedly in favor of secrecy, but one was allowed to view remarkable daytime satellite imagery and detailed photographs of the facility on the internet, you just couldn't see anything they were testing. Likewise, you were allowed to listen in on Area 51 air traffic control with a scanner, you just wouldn't hear any details about the black project aircraft being tested.

"Colonel Barr, I'm fine, really," Barker said to the Base Commander as they approached the area inside Hanger 18 where medics were assessing and processing the injured. "What I need right now is a little ibuprofen and some answers to a lot of questions."

"Very well, but I'm not sure how much Dr. Hanson and Dr. Alexander are allowed to tell you. From what I understand, they are here to debrief you, so they'll probably be the ones asking all the questions."

Barker frowned at the prospect of running into the 'you only need to know what we tell you to know' wall. 'Dammit!' he growled to himself, 'I lost a good friend this morning and had my Raptor blown out from under my ass! Don't I deserve some kind answer?'

In a world where a single national security secret could trump the personal needs of millions, Barker knew he was not likely to get much from the two scientists.

"Well, it'll be a start."

Chapter 72

"Colonel Barker," Donna Hanson started somberly, "Dr. Alexander and I are saddened by the loss of your wingman. I understand you two were like brothers."

"Thank you, Dr. Hanson, Dr. Alexander. Buddy Johnson was a good friend, a helluva wingman and a damn fine Raptor jockey. There is no way he can be replaced."

"I know, Colonel," Donna replied. "We won't take too much of your time."

Barker only nodded in reply.

"Colonel, could you describe what happened to the 6 missiles and 20mm cannon rounds you and Major Johnson fired at the bogey."

"Not much to say, Dr. Hanson. We fired Sidewinders, AAMRAMs and 20mm incindiaries... Poof! Just like that, they all disappeared in a flash."

"How bright a flash?" Alexander asked while leaning forward. "What color was the light?"

"Bright white. Like a camera flash or strobe light close up."

"Brief or prolonged?"

"Each flash was very brief. When I was trying to shoot the alien with cannon fire, it looked as if each round hit made a very brief and distinct flash... 480 of them."

“Matter-antimatter annihilation...” Tim said.

“It fits the pattern and explains a lot,” Donna concurred. “Colonel Barker, you witnessed the destruction of your wingman’s Raptor. Did you see a similar flash?”

“It all happened very fast, Dr. Hanson. I was dangling from a chute when I saw my wingman trying to extend. That alien asshole was on his six, maybe a quarter klick behind him. It looked like they were coming right at me. When they passed, I saw a bright flash and fireball when MAJ Johnson’s Raptor exploded.”

“Did you see any flashes of light from the alien vehicle?”

“No, none at all... and I had a front row seat.”

“Somehow, the antimatter is not interacting with nitrogen and oxygen atoms in the air. Otherwise, we would be seeing random annihilations in the beam they’re projecting,” Tim said.

“Would the random antimatter annihilations be frequent enough for the beam to be visible?” Donna asked.

“You would think so, given the density of air 1000 feet above the Nevada desert. Probably decreasing in intensity the higher the altitude.”

“Then, it would be invisible in space, right?”

“That’s it!” Tim excitedly exclaimed. “They must be creating a vacuum between their weapon and the target! It explains everything! Why we can’t see the beam. Why it works underwater. Why it can only target areas on a bridge that they can actually see!”

“Oh my God, that has to be it!” Donna nearly shouted. “I’m sorry for talking as if you weren’t here, Colonel Barker, but we think we’ve got a lead on how their beam weapon works. We know you have a lot to take care of today.”

“Don’t fret about manners, Dr. Hanson. I actually enjoyed how you pieced together the functioning of their main weapon. Please install one on my next Raptor so I can send them all to alien hell.”

“We’ll do what we can on that request!” Donna replied with a smile. “Just one more question: How fast are their reaction times?”

“Four hundred eighty rounds in five seconds, 96 rounds per second. I’d say they're pretty damn fast."

"Could they dodge a 7000 meter-per-second rail gun?"

"You've got one of those?"

"Picked it up at a garage sale."

Barker grinned. "Four-and-a-half miles per second, Dr. Hanson... It might be possible. I'd get your barrel as close to one of those bastards as you can. Quarter mile or less. You'll only get one shot."

"If we're forced to use it, one shot will be all we need," Donna said confidently.

"And Colonel..," Tim said, remembering the dangerous radiation dose the Raptor Pilot was subjected to.

"Yes, Dr. Alexander?"

"You've received a sizable amount of gamma radiation from the explosion on your Raptor. You're at a much greater risk of developing radiation sickness. You need to undergo treatment for it as soon as possible."

"Thanks Doctor Alexander, I'll let them know at the infirmary."

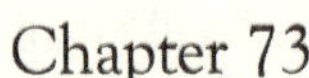

Chapter 73

"So, Hanson has scheduled a press conference for this evening," Senator Melana said. "About damn time she tells us when she's coming back to the Hearings."

"Don't you find it a little odd she's using a prime time press conference to announce her next move?" Melana's chief political adviser asked. "She might have something else up her sleeve. Also, don't forget, her numbers are still high."

"Then, we must be ready to counter everything she says. Andrew, we need our media stars to be prepared for just about anything. Keep the dumbasses off the air until tomorrow. I only want our biggest guns taking the first shots at Hanson... and really cherry pick the reporters. The dumbasses can go in for the leftovers after the third quarter... Monday afternoon, maybe. She'll be fucking toast by then!"

"You know, she's still going to look like hell," Pearce said. "Don't discount her battered looks."

"She wants to play with the big boys, we'll let her play with the big boys. Remember, she is the one who went on the offensive right off the bat."

"I don't know, Harry," Pearce said cautiously. "My take on Hanson is that she may be setting up a trap for us. The press conference is genuine overkill for something that amounts to be a return-to-work message. Her people could have handled that. Maybe I'm just overly cautious when it comes to situations like this, but over my career, I've seen a lot of politicians miscalculate public perceptions of themselves. The people love you until you beat up someone frail or hopelessly outgunned. People don't like bullies and one-sided gunfights. If she comes off soft, frail and busted up, you had better back off the pit bulls. If she comes out swinging and throwing accusations... Then, by all means, loose your dogs."

Melana truly trusted his friend and top political adviser, but the intoxicating scent of rival blood was in the air. Senator Hanson humiliated him in front of Congress and the world. For that, he would have his pound of flesh... and eat it raw.

After another hour of political scheming, Senator Melana excused himself from Andrew and his other aids working in the small conference room in the Senate Office Building. Tanya would be waiting for him in his private office, as would a 16 year-old 'friend' of hers. He was looking forward to an extraordinarily pleasant session with the girls before he topped off his evening viewing Senator Hansons' suicide speech.

Chapter 74

Donna Hanson had always enjoyed panoramic views of snow-capped mountains. There was something about them that made her heart leap. Perhaps it was the bold contrasts of pure white snow atop rugged terrain and deep green alpine forests. Maybe it was the whisper of peace and solitude that beckoned when the forest was still and the temperature crisp. She traveled a few times to alpine resorts, but had never seen anything as captivating as the numerous majestic peaks of northern British Columbia, 15 miles south-southeast of Sharktooth Mountain. She could almost picture her and Tim living in a quaint little cabin near the facility and walking to work every morning.

"Donna, your mother will be speaking in five minutes!" Tim said. "If we want to get a good seat in the cafeteria, we had better get moving"

Donna laughed. "Sweetie, there are four monitors in the cafeteria. That would be about four or five people for each monitor!"

"Yeah, but you KNOW I'll get a seat behind the lady with poofy hair and a screaming kid."

Donna shook her head with a smile. "And all this time I thought I was always the one who had to endure that kind of torture!"

"I guess we both have the curse, my sweet. Yet one more wonderful thing we have in common," he replied with a kiss on Donna's cheek. "Do you know what your Mother's going to say."

"I have a hunch..."

"That means I have to wait until she gives her press conference."

Donna winked at him. "You got it, sport! My dad was a superb master of tormenting my mom when it came to surprises. I guess I got the gene from him."

"I wish I could have spent more time with your dad. He was truly a brilliant and selfless man."

"I miss him a lot, but it is better that he doesn't suffer anymore..." she paused. "Tim, if what I think is about to happen in the very near future, we might not survive our escape."

"I know," Tim stopped and reached for her hands. Donna had never seen such a powerful, intense look on any man's face. It wasn't fierceness, it was more like hardened resolve.

"Donna, if we're going to die 10 minutes from now, or 10 years from now, I want to die with you in my arms! Not as two halves of a couple, but as two into one. Marry me, Donna Hanson! I want to spend all the remaining moments of my life with you as your husband. The garrison commander said he can do it for us right after your mom's press conference!"

Donna was clearly blindsided. She had hoped that Tim might have those feelings for her, but with the evacuations, railguns and field trips, there never seemed to be enough time to really cultivate their growing love for each other. She instinctively knew Tim was the right man and that made her response to him much easier to give.

"Of course, my sweet, sweet Tim! You have become such a wonderful blessing in my life. If we only have a short time left, I can't think of a more wonderful man to share it with!"

They both embraced each other with such boundless passion that neither wanted to part. Their tears mingled together on their cheeks and their kisses were the tender treasures of a timeless love finally fulfilled.

"Tim?"

"Yes, sweetheart?"

"Let's build a cozy little cabin here. Just for you and me... I want to wake up every morning seeing your face and the beautiful mountains all around us."

Tim smiled at her. “I’d like that,” he said warmly. “I’d like that a lot!”

Chapter 75

With the bulk of Cocheta staff tucked away in Vegas, there were plenty of good seats to view the Foreman's mother, the Senator from Oklahoma. The obligatory lead-ins were presented by the media with a not so surprising negative spin, most suggesting the press conference was yet another ploy to divert attention from her perceived failings as a public servant. Even with the media fix in, connected Washingtonians were wondering what kind of fireworks might Senator Hanson supply for the evening. The horrible accident in Hawaii, the act of terror that caused the destruction of a mighty suspension bridge and a baffling, large-scale military mishap in southern Nevada were weighing heavily on most Americans. And when Americans are paying attention, Washington gets extremely nervous.

At 9 PM EST, Senator Teresa Hanson, Junior Senator from Oklahoma, walked to the podium in a well lit conference room in the Russell Senate Building to begin her address. Most were shocked by the degree of her facial bruising, nose splint, contusions and lacerations. An attempt was made to cover the injuries with makeup, but were still very noticeable under the bright lights. She was wearing a smart power outfit that complemented her femininity flawlessly while helping to distract from her injuries.

"Good evening. First of all, I must apologize for my appearance. The floor and I had a minor disagreement concerning gravity. As you can see, the floor won."

Laughter erupted in the conference room, helping most in the audience with their natural uneasiness of seeing a bruised and injured woman.

"I'm sure most of you are wondering why I called for a news conference

tonight. I suspect that most in here are expecting me to announce when I will be able to return to the Senate hearings. I'm sure there are others that may want to hear my thoughts on the terrible assault on the people of Savannah Georgia or the mystery incident currently taking place near Las Vegas. Please bear with me, I do have answers to all your questions.

A little less than two weeks ago, I came before the American people to fulfill a promise I made to my dying husband, Dr. Ben Hanson. I believed in my husband and I believed in his selfless sacrifices for family and nation... In return, I was willing to sacrifice everything to ensure his vision might live on and, maybe, change the course of human history.

Since that historic Sunday night, much has transpired. Americans learned that the universe harbored intelligent life... and that beings from another world are visiting our planet on a regular basis. Overnight, the universe changed dramatically for us. Many proclaimed a 'new world order' was at hand, including our President. Bold, planet-wide initiatives were suggested, many of which would severely limit the freedoms Americans have always enjoyed. In the fervor, the disturbing lack of any alien contact with the governments of earth were missed or ignored.

My daughter, Dr. Donna Hanson and Dr. Timothy Alexander were chosen to shepherd and renovate the embattled Cocheta Research Facility in British Columbia. From the beginning of their tenure, ridiculous government edicts were created to hinder their primary mission: to analyze and duplicate as much alien technology as humanly possible, just in case our otherworldly visitors proved to be unfriendly. One such edict forbid Cocheta scientists from making an offensive weapon. Considering the aliens never disclosed their social or military intentions, I believe this restriction to be extremely foolhardy, at best.

What I am about to tell you, the citizens of the United States and the people of the world, is the absolute truth. A truth that must be quickly shared with all our brothers and sisters around the planet."

Donna paused until the swell of animated background chatter subsided.

"Early Monday morning, the Russian ballistic submarine *Pavel Pereleshin* was lost at sea with an estimated loss of life at 135-150 officers and sailors. The official explanation from Washington was a catastrophic 'hull failure' recorded by our Virginia-class submarine USS *North Carolina* that was, allegedly, patrolling the North Pacific many miles away."

Donna Hanson was heading straight into history as either the ultimate government whistle-blower, or vile traitor. She didn't care which. In her assessment, the President was so consistently dreamy-eyed when it came to the aliens that he completely refused to consider that there could be any threat posed by them. That made him not only naive, it made him a serious threat to the welfare of America. If her actions led to incarceration, she was prepared to endure it.

"The truth... The USS *North Carolina* was engaged in a routine mission of shadowing the Russian submarine *Pavel Pereleshin* when two, very small and extremely fast alien submarines destroyed the gigantic vessel, killing everyone on board. This was extensively documented by sonar recordings. Within several hours of the *Pereleshin's* destruction, Russian President Korolyvov ordered the bulk of his Akula attack submarines to harass our Ohio Class Subs, which continued unabated until this afternoon. I spoke directly and truthfully to President Korolyvov about the *Pereleshin* incident and he has wholeheartedly agreed to have his Akula-Class submarines discontinue the dangerous harassment of our submarine fleet.

The gasps and surprised roar instantly filled the Senate conference room and a massive wave of cell phones seemed to materialize instantaneously. Senator Hanson waited for the commotion to die down.

"The Russian president has also agreed to unilaterally share all their research into alien technology with Cocheta and assist in forming an international coalition to develop and deploy effective weapons to discourage, repel or terminate alien aggression. In return for his pledge and assistance, the Russian President only asked that I join him for dinner. I have, of course, accepted his invitation. Thank God my father's dream has been finally realized! The scientists of world can now openly function as a synergistic team to unlock the secrets of alien technology! Thank you, President Korolyvov!"

A second, larger wave of gasps and animated conversation erupted. A rogue American Senator intervening in foreign affairs... completely on her own! Preposterous and dangerous!

"There is more. Much more. We have irrefutable evidence that alien nanotechnology has been used to compromise Defense Department computer systems. Our nuclear stockpiles and missiles at Kirtland, Warren, Malmstrom and Minot Air Force Bases have also been infiltrated by the same technology. We must assume that most of our nuclear weapons are unusable, perhaps even unstable. Thankfully, there are enough viable weapons to maintain our deterrent capabilities.

As you already know, a large Japanese airliner crashed on the Hawaiian Island of Oahu on Tuesday. Early rumors suggested that a surface-to-air missile destroyed the aircraft. That, however, was not the case. The lead investigator for the National Transportation Safety Board found overwhelming evidence that an extremely exotic and powerful weapon cut the tail section off the Boeing 777. Since there are no weapons on this planet that can duplicate the type of damage inflicted on the airliner, the attack could only come from an extraterrestrial source. Within 24 hours, President Bertram ordered the NTSB to make a snap preliminary finding that the tail section broke free of the aircraft due to airframe fatigue. Within minutes of that announcement, the FAA lifted the airspace quarantine over Hawaii so that commerce could resume. No additional measures have been taken to increase security at any other airport in the United States."

The audience in the conference room maintained a steady rumble of background noise while Senator Hanson gave the most historic disclosure of government mismanagement in United States history.

"Yesterday, the Talmadge Bridge, spanning the Savannah River, was completely destroyed as a result of what was originally thought to be terrorist activity. So far, 284 people are confirmed dead, perhaps hundreds of others are missing and presumed dead. Cocheta scientists, including my daughter and Tim Alexander, carefully analyzed a high definition copy of the SCAD footage. These respected scientists were in complete agreement that the bridge was not destroyed by conventional explosives, but by a directed energy weapon of immense power. Yet again, we have been lied to.

The most disturbing incident occurred early this morning, an alien vehicle violated highly restricted airspace, threatening to disrupt vital operations in very sensitive areas of Nevada's Nellis Test Range. After consulting with the National Security Council, President Bertram authorized the destruction of the alien vehicle. Two F-22A Raptors from Nellis Air Force Base were dispatched to an area commonly known as Area 51. Both fighters were destroyed, one pilot survived. The aliens then discharged a non-lethal weapon that appears to temporarily render humans unconscious within a 40 mile radius of its use. Dozens of employees and contractors were injured, some severely.

Lastly, an inside source within the White House reports that our government is prepared to surrender immediately if the aliens wage war upon us."

The audience in the Senate conference room was, to a person, stunned and extremely disturbed by the multiple disclosures of Bertram Administration cover-ups of alien aggression against military and non-military targets. The torrential flood of cellular communications began to overwhelm the DC cellular system within seconds. What most thought would be a relatively benign press conference turned quickly into the most revealing and damaging disclosure of White House malfeasance and dereliction of duty in American history.

"Please, please settle down!" Teresa said forcefully enough to quiet the audience enough to proceed. "As of this moment, I am resigning my seat in the United States Senate. My continued presence in this legislative body will do nothing but add fuel to the already dysfunctional, malignant and politically correct partisan politics that prevent America from making sound decisions when it matters the most."

A second wave of animated voices swept through the conference room, but one loud and persistent voice, that of Washington Post reporter Jerry Daniels, seemed to cut through the wall of noisy chatter.

"Senator Hanson, Senator Hanson!" Daniels shouted forcefully enough to redirect attention to himself. "What does all this mean?"

The room fell deathly still as the former Senator from Oklahoma looked directly into the eyes of the reporter.

"It means that we are at war."

Chapter 76

"Why, Larry? Why this way?" President Bertram asked his now former Chief of Staff.

"You don't know? How could you not know!?" Osborn replied over the phone. "You put all your chips on the aliens from the very start and repeatedly ignored my warnings to you! The last straws for me were the JAL cover up and the notion that you would surrender to the aliens."

"I must do what is right for the planet, Larry. The only way to save earth is to..."

"What? Subject us all to alien rule and slavery? No thanks!" Osborn interrupted angrily. "They've slaughtered hundreds already! Did it ever occur to you that the people of earth might want to fight back?"

"It would be a waste of time, Larry. We need to negotiate with them."

"Greg, have I missed something?" Osborn almost growled. "They haven't contacted us yet! Doesn't that tell you everything we need to know?"

"Larry, you've been a good friend, and I'd like to keep it that way. I have to follow my convictions. Please respect that."

Something akin to panic was beginning to well up in Osborn's gut. "You have a full-blown crisis now that Hanson has blown the lid off everything that's happened since Monday. Are you going to hold a press conference?"

"Tomorrow morning."

“Good luck, Greg. Remember your oath for God’s sake!”

The President cradled the oval office phone, leaned back in his chair and closed his eyes. There was a heavy presence of what could only be called ‘doom’ in the air. Normally, an American President could command the use of over 5000 nuclear weapons to repel threats against the United States. Though Bertram’s ideology insured that nukes were never really an option under any circumstance, the aliens insured that they wouldn’t work even if they were deployed.

The National Security Council was going to meet soon. Bertram had no doubt that it would be a very contentious one.

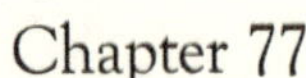

Chapter 77

"Take a look at these two radar images, Dr. Bradford," Dr. Lara Walter asked. "The one on the left that has only one object was taken four minutes ago. The one on the right is a refresh. There are now 31 objects... and they are very, very large!"

"What? That must be a glitch or artifact. How far out are they?"

"One-point-four lunar distances, about 345,000 miles," Dr. Walker replied. "I'm running a series right now. I'll see if I can tidy up one of the images."

The two Cal-Tech scientists were part of NASA's Jet Propulsion Laboratory team that scanned space for potential "NEOs" or "Near Earth Objects" using a powerful, 70 meter, deep space antenna located in the Mojave Desert at Goldstone, California. The Near-Earth Object Observations Program, or "Spaceguard," utilized ground and orbiting telescopes to identify potential hazards coming from deep space.

Over the next 90 minutes, Drs. Bradford and Walker watched each of the 20 astonishing images appear. All were completely stationary with an orderly, evenly spaced distance between each other... something that simply did not occur naturally.

The 21st image was the most startling of all. Instead of just 31 objects, there were now hundreds.

Chapter 78

“Your mother sure knows how to make a statement,” Tim said solemnly. “I really wasn’t expecting your mother to give up her seat in the Senate. We need more of her kind, not less.”

“She’s tired, Tim. I can’t blame her. She’s still grieving for my dad and had the better part of a week to decide what to do with her life. When I told her about our assessment of alien intentions, she said she would head back to Commerce after her resignation. Paul and Arthur’s family are already there.”

“Do you think it’s going to happen tonight?”

“Sweetheart, I have no idea,” she said, shrugging her shoulders. “Our local aliens have been kinda scarce the last few days. It may be many weeks or more before they attack us. When it does happen, and I’m convinced it will, I’m sure we’ll have little or no warning.”

“Well, my love,” Tim said with a big smile, “that is an amazingly depressing assessment! So... I think a change in the subject matter is in order!”

Tim wasn’t concealing his exuberance well. Donna knew precisely what was on his mind. It was on her’s, too.

I don’t have a tux or a ring, but I do have the most beautiful bride in all of recorded history! Do you still want to marry me?”

“I can’t imagine marrying anyone else!”

The couple made their way to the small, interfaith chapel within the Cocheta complex. When they arrived, Colonel Jefferies was standing outside the closed door.

"Dr. Hanson, Dr. Alexander... I'm afraid this Chapel is not available tonight," he said convincingly. "Please follow me."

Donna and Tim looked at each other in surprise, wondering what was coming next. They made their way through one of the two short corridors connecting CRF to the Marine barracks. A few moments later, they entered the Marine Mess Hall to yells of "Surprise!"

Tim and Donna froze. The Marine Mess was decorated, if somewhat sparsely, with ribbons, balloons and several impromptu signs of congratulations. Perhaps the most amazing decoration was a large and smartly decorated, tiered cake, compliments of the Frogman and Patty. All the Marines were in their Dress Blue uniforms.

"Oh my God, how did you all do this with such short notice?" Donna asked, the first tears starting to flow down her cheeks

"We're Marines, ma'am!" a young corporal yelled. "We can do anything in short notice!

"Oo-Rah!" the rest of the Marines thundered loudly.

"Marines," Colonel Jefferies yelled, "do we have an ordained minister here to marry this wonderful couple?"

"Sir! Yes sir!"

"Well, step forward Staff Sergeant Booth!"

"Oo-Rah!"

"Do we have a ring for this beautiful bride?"

Tim shook his head and bowed his head down a little.

"Sir! Yes sir!" the Marines thundered even louder.

Tim looked up to see Colonel Jefferies step towards him.

"Dr. Alexander, Tim... I'm an only child and married to the Corps. My mother gave me her wedding ring shortly before she passed away a few years ago. I would be honored if you would take this beautiful ring and place it on your bride's finger when the time comes."

Tim was stunned. "Colonel Jefferies, I can't take this from you."

"Marines! Was this a suggestion or an order?"

"Sir, an order, sir!"

Jefferies placed the ring in Tim's hand and briskly patted him on the back.

"How about a ring for the Groom?" Jeffries boomed.

"Colonel, the only thing I could find was this, sir," Lance Corporal Swenson said, stepping forward to hand him a cigar band.

Colonel Jeffries laughed heartily and held the band high. "Romeo y Julieta!!!"

The Marines began laughing and cheering.

"We have a beautiful bride, a good lookin' groom, a pair of rings and a preacher man!" Jeffries bellowed. "What the hell are we waiting for???"

"Oo-Rah!!!"

"Dearly beloved," Staff Sergeant Booth began as the mess hall fell silent, "we are gathered here in the sight of God, and in the presence of this company, to unite Tim Alexander and Donna Hanson in holy matrimony, which is instituted of God, regulated by His commandments, blessed by our Lord Jesus Christ and to be held in honor amongst all men. Let us therefore reverently remember that God has established and sanctified marriage for the welfare and happiness of all mankind. I charge and entreat you, therefore, in entering upon and sustaining this hallowed union, to seek the favor and blessing of Him whose favor is life, whose blessing maketh rich and addeth no sorrow. Let us now seek His blessing.

Our Heavenly Father, we beseech Thee to come by Thy grace to this marriage. Give to these who marry a due sense of the obligations they are now to assume, so that with true intent, and with utter unreserve of love, they may help each other while they journey through life. This we ask in Jesus' name. Amen.

If you are ready to assume these obligations and duties before God, please unite your hands and pledge your love and your lives to each other.

Tim, will you have Donna to be your wedded wife, to live together after God's ordinance in the holy estate of matrimony; will you love her, comfort her, honor, and keep her, in sickness and in health, and forsaking all others, keep yourself only unto her, so long as you both shall live?"

"I will!" he replied with warm smile.

"Donna, will you have Tim to be your wedded husband to live together after God's ordinance in the holy estate of matrimony; will you love, honor, and keep him, in sickness and in health, and, forsaking all others, keep yourself only unto him, so long as you both shall live?

"I will!" Donna replied, wiping tears from her already glistening cheeks.

"Tim," Booth began the ring vows, "what token do you give of the vows you have made?"

"This beautiful and wonderful wedding ring donated by the finest people I have ever known!"

A cheer erupted from the rowdy Marines.

"Bless this ring, O Lord, that he who gives it and she who wears it may abide in Thy peace, and continue in Thy favor, unto their life's end; through Jesus Christ our Lord, Amen. Tim, you may place the ring on your bride's finger."

Tim complied with a huge smile on his face.

"Donna, what token do you give of the vows you have made?"

"This cigar band from Cuba, given to me by the greatest, bravest bunch of crazy jarheads in the middle of freakin' Mooseland!"

The roar of laughing and cheering was deafening in a cafeteria with little in the way sound suppression.

Booth was having a terrible time trying to keep his composure. "Bless this ring, O Lord, that she who gives it and he who wears it may abide in your peace, and continue in your favor, until their life's end, through Jesus Christ our Lord. Amen. Donna, you may place the ring on your Groom's finger."

Donna complied, tears streaming down both cheeks.

"Forasmuch as Tim and Donna have consented together in holy wedlock, and have witnessed the same before God and this company, by the authority committed unto me as a minister of the Gospel of Jesus Christ, I declare that Tim and Donna are now Husband and Wife, according to the ordinance of God, in the name of the Father, and of the Son, and of the Holy Spirit. Amen."

"Tim, Donna, please join your right hands. Whom therefore God hath joined together, let no man put asunder. May the Lord bless you, and keep you. The Lord make His face to shine upon you, and be gracious unto you; the Lord lift up His countenance upon you, and give you peace: both now and in the life everlasting. Amen."

"Everyone, I present to you Timothy and Donna Alexander! Tim, you may kiss your bride!"

Another deafening cheer erupted as Tim and Donna kissed each other for the first time as a married couple. There was a new, unmistakable sound added to the mix of clapping, laughing and cheers... champagne corks going ballistic!

"Frogman!" someone yelled. "I didn't know you had champagne! Where do you keep it?"

"It ain't for you, retard!" he growled menacingly. "I keep some on hand for occasions like this."

"Like what? Weddings? How many weddings have we had here, Froggy?" another Marine chimed in, sensing he might get a chance to piss off Frogman."

"Keep it up, girly man! Patty knows where you sleep!"

"Froggy, if she comes into my dorm, I'm gonna make slippers outta her!"

"You do that Tinkerbell and the next wedding we'll have here will be you and a horny bull moose!"

The mess hall erupted again in loud laughter. Everybody enjoyed the banter and fellowship in spite of the underlying threat. The Marines at Cocheta led an ordered existence that consisted of daily physical fitness training, drills and marksmanship with a variety of weapons. Within the previous 48 hours, they added additional drills of evacuating to the western side of the mountain through one of two escape tunnels. Few knew the exact reasons why this was taking place, but all knew something dangerous was brewing.

After an hour of celebrating the impromptu marriage between CRF director and Deputy Director, the Marines began police the mess hall and wind the party down. A chilly morning of PT awaited them at 5:30 AM. Tim and Donna Alexander thanked everyone personally for a wedding that was more wonderful than they could have ever imagined. They made their way to Donna's apartment and quickly began to passionately consummate their fledgling marriage. Both fell asleep in each other's arms.

Thirty minutes later, a very unwelcome voice came through the overhead speaker system.

"Code Green. Northeast Sector. Range: 2.1 miles...

Code Green. East Sector. Range: 1.2 miles...

Code Green. East Sector. Range: 1.3 miles...

Code Green. Southeast Sector. Range: 4 miles..."

Epilogue

The first wave of unmanned Centralian Aggressors were assigned to obliterate the over 3000 operating and non-operating satellites orbiting the target planet. The remaining 5000 pieces of so-called orbiting "space junk" would also be targeted, but on a far lower priority level. Since these Aggressors carried fuel to operate in the vacuum of space, their range was limited. Once their mission was complete or their fuel cells nearing exhaustion, they were programmed to assume a standardized orbit for eventual retrieval and refueling.

If one were observing a clear, nighttime sky in the western hemisphere, the frequent flashes of matter/antimatter annihilations that marked the destruction of orbiting satellites was breathtaking. While most were nothing more than a bright flicker, other annihilations involving much larger satellites could actually cause shadows. The largest sustained flash of all was that of the doomed International Space Station, killing all 6 crew members aboard. It was so massive that it was seen in broad daylight.

Within three hours, all satellite connections were permanently lost. Any terrestrial receiver designed to capture radio signals from satellites in space were completely useless. The ramifications of these losses became very clear within moments after the first satellites were destroyed. These were the geostationary satellites that maintained a fixed position on the Earth's equator from 22,236 miles above. The bulk of these were telecommunication satellites and millions upon millions of people were losing their television, cable, internet and radio feeds by the minute. The most potentially dangerous of the satellite losses came when the entire Global Positioning System failed, forcing commercial and private pilots to switch to visual

means of navigation. Every moment that passed, years of communications infrastructure were lost.

As the news sporadically spread across the entire planet, waves of panic began to engulf the most vulnerable and least stable of human constructs: large cities. Riots, looting and vicious acts of violence began the instant it was clear that everyone was on their own. Outnumbered thousands to one, law enforcement simply collapsed as LEOs fended for themselves and their families. Even the most orderly and regimented of societies fell into the wave of panic as smart phones became increasingly less useful. It was Katrina all over again, but on an unimaginable global scale.

The second massive wave of unmanned Aggressors were launched towards earth at ultra-high speed from the largest ship of the Centralian armada. These Aggressors could only operate within an atmosphere, so they required a launching system similar in function to a terrestrial steam or electromagnetic catapult to aim them towards the target planet. Once the Aggressors reached earth's atmosphere, their extremely sophisticated artificial intelligence was tasked to suppress all sources of electromagnetic communications, from BlueTooth to Ultra Low Frequency submarine communications.

A small number of remaining atmospheric Aggressors were tasked to seek out and destroy submerged vessels. This was a more difficult task for the Aggressors, but only slightly so. Only the submarines already under the polar icecap would enjoy a somewhat longer lifespan.

As the thousands of atmospheric Aggressors arrived, tower and mobile-based communications began to fail in blinding flashes. A single, stationary Aggressor could hover over a large city and engage close to 100 radio frequency (RF) targets per second. It became incredibly dangerous to use ANY device that broadcast a radio wave. Millions would die from the harmless click of a button or a cell phone trying to link to a tower.

Within 12 hours of the initial attack, the number of man-made radio signals radiating from earth into space was decreased by 99.9993%.

For the first time since Nikola Tesla broadcast the first man-made radio transmission in 1892, the Earth was all but silent to the rest of the universe.

The Hanson Trilogy continues...

Book Three: The Hanson Prophesy

In only half a day, the initial alien assault on earth brutally returned the human race to the mid 19th Century. Millions were dead and millions more were dying by the hour. Cities burned while powerless and isolated governments could only watch in horror.

The sterilization of the planet had begun...

While evacuating the Cocheta Research Facility, Tim and Donna Alexander, along with a company of hard core Marines, make a desperate and likely suicidal attempt to disable or destroy an alien craft.

They will only have one chance to prove the aliens are not invincible...

...or that using the improvised weapon to defeat them is incredibly more dangerous than the aliens themselves.

The continuing existence of every living thing on earth hangs in the balance.

Biography

Vince Messbarger was born on July 30th, 1958 to Jack and Donna Messbarger of Kansas City, Kansas. After several nomadic moves from Kansas City, to Denver, to Atlanta and Washington DC, the Messbarger family eventually settled in Austin, Texas for good.

Vince graduated from Stephen F. Austin High School and went on to obtain degrees in Paramedic Technology from Austin Community College; Bachelor of Science degree in Basic Medical Sciences and Doctor of Medicine degrees at Texas A&M. Dr. Messbarger completed his residency in anesthesiology at Scott & White Hospital in Temple Texas.

After more than 9 years of military service as an Army Anesthesiologist in Georgia and Hawaii, Dr. Messbarger went into private practice in Oklahoma. After five years of a hospital-based practice, he accepted a clinic-based position in Savannah Georgia where he currently resides.

Vince has been happily married to Stacia for over 12 years and have 6 children between them: Christina, Jessica, Lowell, Patrick, "Little" Jessie, and Joseph. They also have 6 grandchildren: Celeste, Dawson, Amber, Leslie, Anthony and Levi. The Messbargers have two pets, a highly neurotic Toyger cat named "Kronos" and a yellow Labrador Retriever puppy, Gabby."

Dr. Messbarger began writing the Hanson Trilogy in 2005 and hopes to finish the last installment, The Hanson Prophesy, by late 2014.

www.ingramcontent.com/pod-product-compliance
Lightning Source LLC
Chambersburg PA
CBHW030819310726
48980CB00006B/556/J

* 9 7 8 0 9 8 1 4 9 8 4 5 4 *